LESSONS IN
CRIME

LESSONS IN CRIME

Academic Mysteries

edited by

MARTIN EDWARDS

This collection first published in 2024 by
The British Library
96 Euston Road
London NW1 2DB

Cataloguing in Publication Data
A catalogue record for this publication is available from the British Library

ISBN 978 0 7123 5545 2
e-ISBN 978 0 7123 6837 7

Original cover image © NRM / Pictorial Collection /
Science and Society Picture Library
Text design and typesetting by Tetragon, London
Printed in England by CPI Group (UK) Ltd, Croydon, CRO 4YY

MIX
Paper | Supporting
responsible forestry
FSC® C171272

CONTENTS

INTRODUCTION

An academic life, Dr. Johnson observed, puts one little in the way of extraordinary casualties. This was not the experience of the Fellows and scholars of St. Anthony's College when they awoke one raw November morning to find their President, Josiah Umpleby, murdered in the night.

So begins *Death at the President's Lodging* aka *Seven Suspects*, the first detective novel by Michael Innes, who proceeded over the course of the next half century to produce about fifty books in the crime field as well as pursuing an academic career of distinction under his real name, J. I. M. Stewart. He is one of many academics in Britain and elsewhere who have achieved success in the genre and his debut, a classic of "the Golden Age of Murder" between the wars, illustrates the appeal of crime fiction set in academe, which is the unifying theme of the stories in this book.

An extraordinary number of mysteries over the years have featured the world of education, to the extent that Roger Dalrymple and Andrew Green—themselves academics—have recently written a book on the subject, *The Idea of Education in Golden Age Detective Fiction*, which argues that "Golden Age detective fiction affords writers and readers a rich discursive and imaginative space for taking up and exploring educational ideas."

The world of education had featured in crime fiction in a variety of ways before the Golden Age; an especially enjoyable example is the Sherlock Holmes story "The Adventure of the Priory School", which is included in this book. There is, however, no doubt that the inter-war years saw the academic mystery flourish as never before, above all during the 1930s. Victor L. Whitechurch's last novel, *Murder at the College* aka *Murder at Exbridge*, appeared in 1932; "Exbridge" seems to resemble a thinly disguised Oxford rather than an amalgam of Oxford and Cambridge.

A year later, J. C. Masterman's *An Oxford Tragedy* was explicit in its choice of university background, although the college featured was fictional, probably to minimise any risk of accidental libel, given that colleges tend to be relatively small institutions. The success of this novel, which had an intriguing if slightly underwhelming successor in *The Case of Four Friends* almost a quarter of a century later, seems to have established Oxford, rather than Cambridge as the most popular scene of fictional crime. Masterman became Provost of Worcester College and later Vice-Chancellor of Oxford University.

Of all the many crime novels set in Oxford, the most famous is surely Dorothy L. Sayers' *Gaudy Night* (1935). Sayers was a graduate of Somerville College, and just as Harriet Vane, who agrees to marry Lord Peter Wimsey in this book, was based on Sayers herself, so Shrewsbury College stands in for Somerville. In those days, long before Oxford colleges became co-educational, the presentation of the all-female world of Shrewsbury made a great impression, especially on readers (such as the future crime novelist and critic Jessica Mann) who felt encouraged by Sayers to pursue academic excellence for themselves. Published in the same year as *Gaudy Night*, but forgotten until it was republished as a British Library Crime Classic, *Death on the Cherwell* was written by Mavis Doriel Hay, a graduate of St. Hilda's College, which was the model for her fictional Persephone College.

Michael Innes' writing was an influence on Bruce Montgomery, who wrote *The Case of the Gilded Fly* (1944), his first detective novel about Professor Gervase Fen, while still an undergraduate. Fen also appears in *The Moving Toyshop* (1946), one of the most entertaining novels to have been set in the city of dreaming spires.

After the Second World War, Oxford detective novels continued to enjoy popularity. Two good examples during the 1950s were *Landscape with Dead Dons* by Robert Robinson, later a well-known TV and radio personality, and the rather more obscure *When Scholars Fall*, the solitary novel by Timothy Robinson. In 1975, Colin Dexter launched his Inspector Morse series, which blended "town and gown" life very effectively. The Morse books were later televised with huge success, which was due not only to excellent acting and high-calibre scripts but also to Oxford's photogenic quality. The story settings—and in the TV spin-offs *Lewis* and *Endeavour*—were often, although by no means exclusively, academic.

There was no shortage of Cambridge-based academic mysteries, although they tended to attract less attention. Examples include Lois Austen-Leigh's *The Incredible Crime* (1931; a British Library Crime Classic), F. J. Whaley's *Trouble in College* (1936), and Douglas G. Browne's *The May-Week Murders* (1937), featuring one of his series sleuths, Major Maurice Hemyock. In 1945, the distinguished archaeologist Glyn Daniel published *The Cambridge Murder* under the pen-name Dilwyn Rees, but like Masterman, after making a good start he published only one further mystery novel in his lifetime, although he did make tantalising references to another book, which did not make it into print; the manuscript is now held in a Cambridge library.

Whaley, a Cambridge graduate who became a crime-writing vicar, began his career in the genre with the pleasingly titled *Reduction of Staff* (1936), set in a public school. Five years earlier, James Hilton had published *Was it Murder?* aka *Murder at School*, initially under the pen-name Glen Trevor. Hilton later earned fame and fortune with popular mainstream novels such as the non-criminous school story *Goodbye, Mr. Chips*.

Two excellent school mysteries appeared in 1932. *The Public School Murder* by R. C. Woodthorpe was set in a fictional version of Christ's Hospital, where Woodthorpe had taught before going into journalism and then embarking on a career as a novelist whose work was always interesting and sometimes witty, but had faded from view even before his school mystery was televised by the BBC in its excellent anthology series *Detective* in 1968.

The reputation of Sherborne-educated Anthony Berkeley as a gifted innovator in the genre has, however, endured. His venture into the public school mystery, *Murder at the Basement*, has been published as a British Library Crime Classic and is notable as the first example of the "whowasdunin" form of mystery.

Richard Webb, an Englishman who emigrated to the United States, was a talented mystery author who published two novels with backgrounds in the world of education. Set in Cambridge, *Murder at the 'Varsity*, appeared in 1933 under the pen-name Q. Patrick. Three years later, using the same pen-name but this time collaborating with fellow Englishman Hugh Wheeler, he produced *Death Goes to School*. In 1938, the pair were also responsible for *File on Fenton and Farr*, a "Crime Dossier" in the style of those popularised by Dennis Wheatley and J. G. Links a couple of years earlier, with the best-selling *Murder off Miami*. The dossier (which contains so much textual material it might perhaps originally have been conceived as a novel) involves the suspicious deaths of the eponymous couple, the principal of a school and his secretary. The scenario was almost certainly inspired by the famous real-life Halls-Mills case, but the storyline is very different. Webb and Wheeler enjoyed considerable success with their crime fiction, especially in later years, when writing under the name Patrick Quentin.

Nicholas Blake was one of the most talented authors to emerge during the Golden Age. His pen-name concealed the identity of Cecil Day-Lewis, who later became Poet Laureate. The first Blake novel, *A*

Question of Proof, was set in a public school and introduced the gentle-manly sleuth Nigel Strangeways, who enjoyed a long and successful career of crime-solving and enjoyed a new life as recently as 2021 when played by Billy Howle in a loose TV adaptation of *The Beast Must Die*.

As late as 1959, Agatha Christie published a mystery in the classic vein, *Cat among the Pigeons*, in which Hercule Poirot investigates rum goings-on at the upmarket girls' school Meadowbank. Christie had been educated mainly at home and never went to university, but she sent her daughter Rosalind to Benenden, and that famous school provided a model for Meadowbank.

By then, however, the times were changing. Just two years later, James Barlow, a talented mainstream author whose work sometimes veered into genre territory, published *Term of Trial*, a novel about crime and a trial rather than a detective story. The protagonist was an unhappy middle-aged teacher at Railway Street Secondary Modern School and the book was so successful that it was filmed in 1962 with a starry cast led by Laurence Olivier, Simone Signoret, Sarah Miles, and Terence Stamp. The only thing the novel has in common with *Death at the President's Lodging* is that one of the characters is called Umpleby. The story is a well-crafted example of kitchen sink realism, but is today as dated as the intricate mysteries of the Golden Age.

Why did Oxbridge and preparatory and boarding schools feature so heavily in vintage crime fiction, when redbrick universities and state schools were conspicuous by their absence? Was it a matter of snob-bery? I think there are two main reasons.

First, authors were writing about what they knew. A high propor-tion of Golden Age novelists were privately (and no doubt expensively) educated prior to going to Oxford or Cambridge. Indeed, the same is true of many of their detectives. Lord Peter Wimsey, for instance, was educated at Eton and Balliol. John Dickson Carr's Dr. Gideon Fell, R. C. Woodthorpe's Nicholas Slade, and Leo Bruce's Carolus Deene were also Balliol men. So was G. D. H. Cole, whose short story "A Lesson in Crime", co-authored with his wife Margaret, inspired the title of this anthology; the Coles were also responsible for *Disgrace to the College* (1937), a locked room mystery novella set in Oxford, which is one of their stronger stories.

Second, the closed communities within schools and colleges provide an ideal setting for a traditional whodunit; they are places where simmering tensions may erupt into murder, and where the number of credible suspects is finite.

Gladys Mitchell was a career teacher whose subjects were English, History, and games. Somehow she found the time to become an astonishingly prolific author of detective novels. *Death at the Opera* (1934), one of her earliest and best mysteries, centres on a school production of *The Mikado*, while *Laurels are Poison* (1942) is set at a women's training college. Josephine Tey, who studied and later taught at a women's physical training college, put her know-how to especially good use in *Miss Pym Disposes* (1946), an unusual but characteristically interesting and readable novel.

C. E. Vulliamy, who had published four interesting Golden Age novels (of which *Scarweather* and *Family Matters* have been published in the Crime Classic series) under the name Anthony Rolls resumed his crime writing career under his own name in 1952 with *Don Among the Dead Men*, in which Dr. Bowes-Ottery, a lecturer in chemistry, discovers a curious new poison which he soon puts to devastating use. This mildly eccentric story was filmed in 1964 as *A Jolly Bad Fellow* aka *They All Died Laughing*, but despite a cast including Leo McKern and Leonard Rossiter and a soundtrack by John Barry, the movie died at the box office.

Naturally, the British Library Crime Classics focus on British mysteries, but it's worth noting that, apart from the work of the expats Webb and Wheeler, crime writers from the United States also produced interesting work set in educational institutions. Timothy Fuller, the closest American equivalent to Edmund Crispin, had a short but lively hey-day; his novels featured Juniper Jones, whose first appearance was in *Harvard Has a Homicide* (1936).

Two gifted women writers who dabbled even more briefly in crime made notable contributions to the sub-genre of academic mysteries. Helen Eustis's *The Horizontal Man* (1946) was, in its day, a ground-breaking novel of psychological suspense set in a college evidently based on Smith College, where Eustis's first husband taught. The first of Marion Mainwaring's two mysteries, *Murder at Midyears* (1954), is an entertaining college story which deserves to be better known. In later years, Amanda Cross (the pen-name of the academic and feminist Carolyn Heilbrun) wrote fifteen highly literate if sometimes thinly plotted mysteries featuring Kate Fansler, whose cases include *Death in a Tenured Position* (1981).

Eustis's novel takes its title from a line in a poem by W. H. Auden, who said in his famous essay about traditional detective fiction, "The Guilty Vicarage": "It is a sound instinct that has made so many detective-story writers choose a college as a setting. The ruling passion of the ideal professor is the pursuit of knowledge for its own sake so that he is related to other human beings only indirectly through their common relation to the truth; and those passions, like lust and avarice and envy, which relate individuals directly and may lead to murder are, in his case, ideally excluded." Whether or not one agrees with his precise sentiments, there is no doubt that academic settings often make for a good mystery: hence this collection.

In putting this anthology together, I've benefited from suggestions made and information supplied by several friends and correspondents, including in particular Jamie Sturgeon, Nigel Moss, John Cooper, and Phil Stephensen-Payne; I'm also grateful to Andrew Green and Roger Dalrymple for giving me sight of a draft of their book. My thanks go to the publishing team at the British Library for all their work on this collection, and of course to readers whose enthusiasm for this series, with which I've now been involved for ten very enjoyable years, is so rewarding and motivating.

MARTIN EDWARDS
www.martinedwardsbooks.com

A NOTE FROM THE PUBLISHER

The original novels and short stories reprinted in the British Library Crime Classics series were written and published in a period ranging, for the most part, from the 1890s to the 1960s. There are many elements of these stories which continue to entertain modern readers; however, in some cases there are also uses of language, instances of stereotyping and some attitudes expressed by narrators or characters which may not be endorsed by the publishing standards of today. We acknowledge therefore that some elements in the works selected for reprinting may continue to make uncomfortable reading for some of our audience. With this series British Library Publishing aims to offer a new readership a chance to read some of the rare books of the British Library's collections in an affordable paperback format, to enjoy their merits and to look back into the world of the twentieth century as portrayed by its writers. It is not possible to separate these stories from the history of their writing and therefore the following stories are presented as they were originally published with the inclusion of minor edits made for consistency of style and sense. We welcome feedback from our readers, which can be sent to the following address:

British Library Publishing
The British Library
96 Euston Road
London, NW1 2DB
United Kingdom

THE GREEK PLAY

H. C. Bailey

Henry Christopher Bailey (1878–1961) was born in London and edu-cated at the City of London School prior to going up to Corpus Christi College, Oxford, to read Classics. He became a journalist and spent his career writing for the *Daily Telegraph*, notably as a theatre critic and leader writer before retiring with his family to Llanfairfechan. Bailey was a modest man, evidently popular with fellow members of the Detection Club—he was one of the very few living detective writers to be name-checked in an Agatha Christie novel, *The Body in the Library*—but so retiring that biographical information is limited. There's a darkness about most of his best stories, including "The Greek Play", but a wry sense of humour is apparent in some of his writing—as in "The Efficient Assassin", which contains the nice line: "In spite of Eton and Oxford, Geoffrey disturbed his father by showing signs of originality".

Bailey discussed the origins of Reggie Fortune in an essay writ-ten for *Meet the Detective* (1935), explaining that he was educated at Charterhouse and Oxford: "there were two formative influences in his young life: first the professor who amassed a larger amount of useless knowledge than any man in Oxford, secondly Sir Lawson Hunter, whose European reputation as a surgeon had been won by knowing his own mind." Reggie is on top form in "The Greek Play", which appeared in *The Windsor Magazine* in October 1931 and was included in *Case for Mr. Fortune* the following year. Such good form, in fact, that those stringent judges Jacques Barzun and Wendell Hertig Taylor described the story in *A Catalogue of Crime* as a "masterpiece".

M R. FORTUNE WAS CONCENTRATED ON AN INVESTIGATION. IN this state of mind, he is not aware of time or persons. He was in his garden. Some of the long experiments in producing his ideal sweet pea flowered about him in colours of the freshness of his own innocent complexion. He sniffed delicately, he sniffed profoundly. The sweet pea of his dreams was to give him the rich waved grace of the moderns with the deeper fragrance of the old. And his round face became wistful.

On this sorrow came the voice of a person of great personality. His black Persian, Darius, sat down on the lawn, gazed with large golden eyes, and announced that instant attention was required. Reggie awoke and came hastily. Darius lay on his back and stretched, exhibiting a stomach for homage. It was rubbed respectfully. Darius sang a small song, curled up on the hand and killed it, rose, walked away with his tail in the air. "Darlin'," Reggie murmured to his swaggering hinder end.

"My dear child!" he was rebuked. Mrs. Fortune came towards him.

"Oh, Peter!" Reggie blinked at her. She was dressed not for gardening, but for a garden party, in something filmy that revealed her adorably and shimmered apple-green and gold. He looked down at his crumpled grey flannel, and again at her and with alarm.

"You are, you really are," he murmured.

"Why aren't you dressed?" said Mrs. Fortune severely.

"I am. For this world. I didn't know we were going to heaven."

"You're not. You're going to Logate. Run away and make yourself respectable."

Reggie groaned. "Black coat?"

"Yes, dear. Full fig. Run. You've only half an hour for lunch and all."

But under pressure he can be very quick and neat. He sat down in the clothes of ceremony before she had finished her fish. He gave his whole mind to that, salmon trout in mayonnaise. He stopped and turned to the parlourmaid. "Tell Elise that chives in a fish salad are an error." He tasted the wine. "And you've got the Carbonnieux too cold."

"Don't be peevish, child," Mrs. Fortune smiled.

"I'm not. Only alert. The faculties have been aroused. And earnest." He proceeded swiftly by way of lamb in aspic to a soufflé. "Ah! Tell Elise that all is forgiven. And a few strawberries, please." He dealt with them; he was drinking his coffee while the soufflé still occupied Mrs. Fortune. "Why are we going to Logate, Joan?" he murmured.

"To see a Greek play, dear."

"My only aunt!" Reggie gazed at her. "What is Logate, Joan?"

"My dear child! Logate School. The girls' school. You know all about it."

"Do I?" Reggie said plaintively. "Fancy knowin' all about a girls' school! Well, well. Why did you marry that kind of man?"

Mrs. Fortune stood up. "You're not amusing." She looked down at him. "This is merely futile. It's no use being innocent to me, my child. You won't be let off. I told you ages ago we were going to the play at Logate."

"P'r'aps I wasn't listening, dear," Reggie sighed.

"Probably not. But you always hear," said she. "Come along, Reginald."

And he went. He did in fact know something about Logate. Everybody does. It is one of the more magnificent of those schools which were founded last century when the wild hope that girls might be educated first dazzled England. From the private adventure of a determined woman it grew into an established institution, with governors and endowments, and drew to its walls the daughters of people of importance. He knew also that his wife had acquaintance among those fortunate maidens, and he remembered with painful clearness that she had talked of an invitation to some festivity there. Her desire to take him into social crowds is the only tragic element in their married life.

He lay back in the car and contemplated her; an occupation always comforting. "Well, well," he murmured. "What is this play, Joan?"

"The Antigone."

"Oh, ah! When I was at Oxford a dear old don told me that nobody was educated who hadn't read the Antigone. So I did. In translation. And these young things are doing it in Greek! Well, well. The advance of women."

"They haven't done one in Greek before. That's the new classical mistress. Nan says she's a tiger."

Reggie's eyelids drooped. "Is that so?" he murmured. "Nan. Who is Nan?"

"You know. My young godchild, Nan Bundy. We're really going to see her."

"And very nice, too," Reggie murmured. "Nice legs. Is she Antigone?"

Mrs. Fortune laughed. "Heavens, no! How could she?"

"Nohow. Contrariwise. Would that matter?"

"It is a glorious part," Mrs. Fortune sighed. She was herself the Rosalind of men's dreams before she decided to be a wife.

"Yes. Yes. Resolute young woman. And we're going to see a school-girl play it."

"Nan says she's wonderfully good," said Mrs. Fortune. "It's a girl called Nora Brown," Reggie's eyes were nearly closed, but he continued to look at her. "Of course, she's not likely to get near it. But still Antigone ought to be a girl—it's like Juliet; you want a girl and a great actress too—and nobody is both at once. But sometimes a girl is wonderful." She began to talk about acting. This is most unusual. And

Reggie ceased to look at her. His mind played with a doubt whether it was the Greek play that he was being taken to see. But he did not say so. He has been married some time.

Logate School is established in a vast house in a park. Both were originally constructed for an eighteenth-century profiteer. The park keeps unspoilt its artificial lake, its delusive vistas, its sham ruins, its copied statues and temples.

The house has a huge portico to disguise the obvious fact that its front door is at the back. They went into what had been a good hall before its proportions were destroyed. Logate is much organised. The guests who enter there abandon freedom and walk in a straight and narrow path under continual orders from the staff.

"Oh, my hat!" Reggie muttered. "Joan! I want to go home." And they were passed into the presence of the head mistress and it was announced that they were Mr. and Mrs. Fortune.

He raised frightened eyes and saw a small, intense woman. Her set smile of welcome flickered. "Mr. Fortune?" she repeated. "How do you do?" It seemed that he caused her some surprise, some curiosity, if such a woman could be curious about a man.

"Do you know our chairman?" She passed him on to the Bishop of Lanchester. That plump and crimson prelate gurgled slightly and took pains to be affable. He made a mild joke about Mrs. Fortune being too young, oh, far too young, to have a daughter at Logate. He obviously desired to know who had sent Reggie an invitation. "Not a daughter, but a goddaughter," said Mrs. Fortune. "So we feel quite parental about Logate." The Bishop said it was very natural, the Bishop said he was delighted, and they were taken with ceremony to the terraced lawns which made a theatre for the play, they were set in the seats of the mighty. Reggie looked sideways at his wife. "Why do they love us so?" he murmured. "This is very alarmin', Joan."

"The penalty of fame, dear. Be a brave little man." She began to talk to the mistress presiding over that block of seats.

Reggie gazed about him. The lawns were cut like broad steps out of the slope on the top of which behind them the great house stood. Each lawn had its rows of chairs. At the foot of the slope on an open space between banks of rhododendrons a stage was built, with the front of a Greek palace for scenery. On either side and beyond, the park displayed its green vistas set with sham antiquities—here a ruined Gothic tower, there a classic temple.

Mrs. Fortune compelled him into her conversation with the mistress, who was delivering a lecture on the play. "Terribly sad, you see. Quite dreadful. Of course, it's very grand. Some people feel it's not nice for girls. The theme, you see—a girl defying the law and killing herself. You're meant to think she's a martyr to her own sense of right. An immortal protest, of course. But perhaps it is unsettling for girls."

"You think so?" Reggie murmured.

Mrs. Fortune was indignant. "It's a noble play! I can't imagine it could do anybody harm."

"Especially in Greek," Reggie murmured. "Do girls get Greek plays on their nerves? I was only a boy."

"Girls are so serious," said the mistress. "So earnest. One has to be very careful." She gave them copies of the play and fussed on to somebody else.

"Curious symptoms," Reggie mumbled.

"Why?" Mrs. Fortune turned to him. "What are you thinking of?"

"Vague suggestions of collective hysteria; or getting the general wind up. As you say—why?"

"I suppose it's first-night nervousness."

"Yes. I wonder. Yes. Well, well, what exactly did Antigone do?" He opened the book of the words. "Oh, ah! She was told not to bury her brother because he died fighting against her city, and she went and did it. So the king shut her up in a tomb and she said it was hard she couldn't have the life of other girls, but she'd done her duty and she hanged herself."

"Don't, Reggie. It's grand."

"I know. I'm not feelin' facetious, Joan." He looked about him and his round face was grave and plaintive, like an earnest child's.

Important parents and the governing body filled the seats about them. The head mistress and the Bishop, side by side, glanced at them and leaned over to say amiable nothings. And the play began.

Antigone was on the stage, a girl not more than common tall, slim as a boy in her Greek dress, not pretty beside the buxom fairness of her sister, Ismene. But she held the eye, she had dignity, she was desperately earnest, and the other only a girl in fancy dress. Her dark face was individual, a face to remember, proud, wistful, with a brow and a chin.

It is a quiet scene, to show Antigone as a girl who believes that she has a duty—to break the law. This Antigone was very quiet. But when she had gone, when the chorus were doing physical exercises in front of the stage and chanting a hymn to dawn, Reggie murmured: "Yes, she looks like somebody."

Mrs. Fortune was gravely interested. "She's feeling it, poor child. Did you notice the sister? Little pig!"

"Yes, missing a bit, wasn't she?"

"Missing! She was deliberately spoiling it. Playing as jealous as could be."

The bullying King Creon, a robust damsel, who wore her beard with a swagger and spoke in a shout, came on to hear that Antigone had buried her dead and defied him, and she was brought prisoner before him to declare she obeyed "unwritten laws, eternal in the heavens." Her voice rang clear, she had a good gesture.

"She is rather out of the way, what?" Reggie murmured. "Know her again, wouldn't you?"

"Very sincere and natural," Mrs. Fortune frowned a little. "Passionate, yes." Ismene returned to be companion of her sister's fate. She was very nice and pretty about it. She made a mess of Antigone's lovely dignity.

The chorus chanted the great ode to love as if it were a cheery hymn, and Antigone came to say her farewell to light and life. She looked desperate enough. Her voice throbbed. She was feeling the agony. "Unwept and unfriended"—she stopped, she held out her arms and let them fall, she looked up to the sky. And the raucous voice of the prompter rattled out the next line.

"Ah!" Mrs. Fortune flushed. "How ghastly!" But the prompter gave the words again and the chorus giggled. Antigone was shattered. She went on with her speech in a hurry. She had no more reality. She was a girl saying a lesson and caring for nothing but to get to the end. "Behold me, what things at the hands of what men I suffer." She was gone.

"Oh, that was a shame," Mrs. Fortune whispered, her hand on Reggie's. "She was being rather fine."

"Yes. Yes. As you say." Reggie looked at her with closing eyes.

The chorus, very brisk and lively, chanted that she came of a noble family, but Fate's everlasting hands availed to reach her, and a messenger came and described how in her tomb prison he "saw the maiden hanged, about her neck some shred of linen served her for a noose," and the chorus remarked that to be happy one must be wise, and marched off.

The audience began to chatter and move. Reggie was in no hurry. The head mistress and the Bishop stopped in passing. "A great play," said the Bishop.

"Oh, yes. Yes. And a very interestin' performance," Reggie murmured.

"I thought Antigone did wonderfully," said Mrs. Fortune.

"I am afraid she found it rather difficult." The head mistress lingered. "But she has ability."

"Yes. Strikin' child. Yes," Reggie murmured.

"Very hard for her." The head mistress looked at him keenly. "Do you know Miss Hopkins perhaps?"

"Is that the prompter?" said Mrs. Fortune with some ferocity.

"Oh, dear, no." The head mistress frowned. "That was Miss Evans, who has always produced our plays. Miss Hopkins has just taken charge of the classical side. She persuaded us to attempt a Greek tragedy. She has worked night and day for this performance."

"She found an Antigone," said Mrs. Fortune.

The head mistress slowly followed her bishop. But Reggie sat still, watching with dreamy eyes the rest of the governing body depart. "Well, well," he sighed, and turned to his wife with a smile. "And now, Joan—what was I brought here for?"

Her eyes met his large and solemn. "Nan Bundy asked us."

"Yes. You told me so. I also believe it. What exactly did she say?"

"Do you think there's something wrong here?"

"My dear girl! Oh, my dear girl, I've been thinkin' somebody thought so ever since we left home."

"And now?" she said eagerly.

"And now I think hysteria's catchin'. Don't you catch it, Joan. What did the sinful child say?"

"She said, 'Do bring the Cherub.'"

"Nobody respects me," Reggie sighed. "Is that all?"

"No. She said it again in a postscript, 'Do bring the Cherub. Things are being perfectly foul and I want to tell him.'"

"Oh, my aunt!" Reggie moaned. "More nerves."

"The letter did sound like nerves. But that isn't like Nan."

"No. No. She's more like an ice. Say strawberry Melba. Well, well, let's find the minx."

"She was in the chorus," said Mrs. Fortune.

They went down to the level turf about the stage where proud parents were waiting for their daughters to emerge from the dressing tent behind the rhododendrons. The pretty Ismene came out of it with a large woman who had been handsome in a florid way. The woman was in a hurry, but Ismene chattered fast. "Oh, Miss Evans, isn't she impossible?... But, Miss Evans..."

"Well, well. So that's the assertive prompter." Reggie watched her with dreamy curiosity.

"I should like to box her ears," said Mrs. Fortune.

Miss Evans had to be introduced to Ismene's mamma. She spared time to be gushing. Then she hurried away towards the house. Reggie continued to watch her. She passed into the crowd on the terrace. She was talking to some of the governors. She vanished.

"Oh, you lambs!" A buxom young person of vivid colour rushed upon them. "Bless you! Wasn't it the putrid limit? Poor old Nobs."

"Referrin' to Antigone, Miss Bundy?" Reggie inquired.

"Yes, Mr. Fortune," said she demurely. "Oh, Cherub, you are a darling to come. Angel face!"

"Thankin' you for these kind words—why am I brought to your maiden revels?"

"Well, I ask you! Wasn't it absolutely foul? Half of them rotting her and the Evanly one braying at her. Hoppy's furious. Poor old Nobs, she's wishing she was dead."

"Poor girl," Mrs. Fortune sighed. "I think she did wonderfully, Nan. Could I speak to her? I'd like to tell her so."

"You're a dear; she doesn't want to speak to anybody just now. She's in the tent still. Wants to get alone. She's like that when she's down."

"Yes. Yes. This show bein' a kind of climax. Now we'll begin at the beginning, Nan. Who is Antigone that Miss Evans and friends crab her?"

Nan stared at him. "Golly!" she said. "You're awfully clever. Yes, that is the beginning. I say, let's come out of the mob." She took them away to a stone seat in a hollow of the green slope, remote, and commanding wide spaces of loveliness from the lake to the temple above. "Shan't have anybody sneaking here."

"Oh! That's the state of society," Reggie murmured.

"We're a happy family, I don't think," said Miss Bundy. "Look here, you know the sort of shop this is. Absolutely it. Nobody wanted unless Father's somebody. That went all right. Things were very jolly when I came five years ago. Nothing mattered but the games, and they were top-hole. Then the old head went and we got this woman. She's a highbrow. Her strong suit is ideals. She's always blethering about the old noble purpose of Logate's, to raise the standard of woman's capacity. Well, of course, that sort of thing got people's backs up frightfully."

"Miss Bundy has no use for an intellectual head?"

"I don't mind, bless you. The woman's not bad, if she wouldn't preach. We wanted a change. The place was jolly slack. But naturally people hated it. Talked all sorts of rot. There was a yarn the mistresses were frightfully sick she got the job—thought one of themselves ought to have had it—the Evanly one was favourite. Somebody put it about the governors wouldn't back her up. But she carried on and went on stiffening things. And then she brought in scholarship girls. You know—entrance scholarships open to anybody. We'd never had that before. Six a year. She caught some rum fish. Clever kids from nowhere, looking like nothing on earth, didn't want to do anything but sap. That didn't make a happy home. Of course, they got treated like absolute outsiders, and some of the mistresses backed 'em and some gave 'em jip, specially the Evanly one. Then the Head brought in a new mistress or two of her own sort and Hoppy. Hoppy's a tiger. She's classics. That put the Evanly one's nose right out of joint. The

Evanly one had always run the idea that a little classics was classy, being her subject, so she got the smart set."

"Miss Evans likes the aristocracy?" Reggie murmured.

"She's a priceless snob," said Miss Bundy. "If a girl has a title somewhere or there's money about, the Evanly one's all over her. Well, in comes Hoppy and takes the top classics away from her. More trouble. The slackers have a rotten time and so there's the smart set against Hoppy and fawning round good Evans. Like that fatty Edith—you saw her—Ismene."

"Yes. Yes. Flaccid type," Reggie yawned. "Thyroid trouble perhaps. When were you coming to Antigone?"

"Poor old Nobs! She's a scholarship girl. Wouldn't think it, would you? I'm sorry—I'm a snob myself. But I mean she don't look the usual book grub."

"No. No. Not a grub. She might have a brain."

"She looks someone quite unusual," said Mrs. Fortune. "It's a fine face, Nan."

"Not one of the undistinguished proletariat. No," Reggie murmured. "By the way—to reach at last the beginning—who is she? What's her name, for instance?"

Nan said "Hush!" And her eyes directed his to Antigone. The girl had changed out of her Greek dress to the school uniform—grey serge tunic, white blouse and tie in the Logate white and grey colours—an austere garb which on that day of festival nobody else was wearing. Nan called out, "I say, Nobs, old thing!" The girl looked, frowned, and hurried on into the loneliness of the park. "Sorry," said Nan. "She's like that when she's upset. Can't bear anybody. And I'm by way of being a pal."

Reggie watched her. She seemed to have a determined purpose. "Often upset, is she?"

"She's had a rotten time. She's poor."

"Oh, yes. Hence the uniform—when the rest of you are in purple and fine linen."

"Of course, she's got other clothes—but nothing nice—just like her to wear the school rags on a show day. Sort of defiance. She's like that. You see, the other scholarship girls—well, they've got people of sorts, but Nobs came from a village school."

"Is that so?" Reggie murmured: he was still watching the determined march of Antigone. "From the village school straight to the exclusive and expensive Logate. Well, well!"

"Oh, she did. She's a wonder. There was a mistress who got keen on her and coached her and she took the first schol. She's not a bit like what you'd think, either. She's jolly good at games, and awfully decent. But she's had a beastly time. Just because she's specially poor and nobody. We are a lot of snobs. The Evanly one's had a particular down on her lately. Only Hoppy's kind of taken her up. Hoppy don't make favourites, but if you can do anything she shoves you along. Well, you saw what happened today—that was pretty ghastly, wasn't it? That's the way things are. Now you know why I wanted you to come, Cherub." She took Reggie's hand for a swift moment.

Antigone had vanished in the hollows of the park where the portico of the temple shimmered grey. Reggie turned and gazed at Miss Bundy. "My dear girl! Oh, my dear girl!" he sighed.

"I wrote about it to father and he said it was like a school story—"

"Yes. Yes. So it is, you know. The persecuted heroine has only got to save somebody's life and you'll all live happily ever after."

"You don't believe that," said Nan; and her frank eyes challenged him.

"You think not? Why wouldn't I?"

"You can see there's something wrong with the jolly old place."

"Oh, yes. Yes. That is indicated."

"Well, you can make people take notice. You can do things."

"My dear girl! Oh, my dear girl!" Reggie moaned again. "Not me, no. They never let me do anything till everything's happened. By the way—reachin' finally the beginning—what is her name?"

"Nora—Nora Brown. She hasn't got any people. An aunt or something brought her up. In a cottage."

A short sturdy young woman came out of the tent in the rhododendrons and stood looking all ways.

"That's Hoppy," said Nan. "Like to speak to her?"

Reggie said, "Help!" Behind her horn spectacles Miss Hopkins looked very brisk and strenuous.

She saw Nan and made for her and called her sharply, asking if Nora had been seen.

"She came out some time ago. I say, Miss Hopkins—I want to introduce you. This is Mr. Fortune—and Mrs. Fortune. My godmother, you know. They were awfully interested in the play."

"How do you do? I'm sorry it wasn't more successful," said Miss Hopkins. "Where did Nora go, Nan?"

"I think I can show you," said Reggie. "Allow me. This way." He walked on, and Miss Hopkins, having no choice, went with him. He stepped out.

Nan made a comical face at Mrs. Fortune. "Snubs to us." They followed some way behind.

Miss Hopkins was saying, "I've no doubt I can find her."

"I hope so," Reggie murmured, and went on with her.

Miss Hopkins looked at him keenly. "Are you the Mr. Fortune?"

"Yes. The one you mean. Yes. Any objection?"

"Not the least. Were you asked to come here?"

"By Nan Bundy. Not professionally. Any reason why I should be?"

"I don't know," said Miss Hopkins. "You seem rather interested in finding Nora Brown."

"And you," Reggie murmured.

"If you saw the play you can guess why. She was upset. I don't like her going off alone."

"No. No. That was my view. What do you know about her?"

"If you've been talking to Nan you know all that I know."

"But you thought I might have been called in professionally. What for?"

"I don't understand detective work, Mr. Fortune."

"Nobody does," Reggie murmured. "Nobody can. You never know what you're looking for, so you have to look for everything." He stopped. He looked about him. "I lost her somewhere here. Takin' one thing with another, I should say she went into that place." He pointed to the temple. "Let's see."

It was a small bad copy of a Doric temple in wood painted to look like stone. They stood under the portico. Lacking windows, the interior was dark. "Oh, Heaven!" Miss Hopkins gasped. Reggie ran in.

Nora's body hung swaying from a beam. Her school tie was knotted about her neck, knotted again to one of the hooks in the beam from which lamps had hung. Under her feet a bench was overturned.

He set that up again, he held her body in one arm and cut the tie and laid her on the ground...

"Is she dead?" Miss Hopkins whispered.

"Not yet. Not quite." He took off his coat, he began to work at the processes of artificial respiration. "There's a bad chance. Have you got a school hospital or anything? With doctor complete? Good. Run away and find her. Say Mr. Fortune's lookin' after a girl who's had an accident and wants her here quick. Don't tell anyone else. Then warn the hospital to have hot-water bottles and a mustard plaster ready. Hurry!" He laboured on with rhythmic movements and called, "Joan!"

She was already watching him, she and Nan.

"Go and bring the car."

"Oh, let me—I'll run," Nan cried.

"You stay here," said Reggie.

"Can't I do something? Can't I do anything? It's so dreadful."

"You can rub her legs," Reggie grunted, and worked on...

Miss Hopkins came back panting. "Dr. Headley, Mr. Fortune."

Reggie turned his sweating face and saw a gaunt businesslike woman. "Heard all about it?"

"Miss Hopkins told me how you found her." Dr. Headley knelt beside the girl. "She's far gone."

"Yes. Yes. I came late. My error. I didn't think of this."

Dr. Headley stared at him. "How could you? You didn't know her, did you?"

"Know nothing about her," Reggie grunted.

"She's a very clever girl. Very highly strung. I'm afraid she's not been happy here."

"You're not surprised, what?" Reggie glanced at her.

"Poor child," said Dr. Headley.

"Yes. Yes. That's better," Reggie murmured. "You carry on now." He wiped his face and watched... "Steady." He bent again over the girl... "Yes. Keep going. I think so. Yes. I think so. She's coming.".....

"Oh, Cherub!" Nan gasped. "Is it really—will she be all right?"

"It'll be a fight for her," Reggie said gently. "I'll fight, Nan."

Mrs. Fortune laid her hand on his shoulder. They looked at each other. "You—" she said with a sigh of content.

Reggie touched the hand. "Well, Doctor—my car's here. We'll get her to hospital. I think I'd better do a venesection." They wrapped the girl in a rug and laid her in the big car. "Oh, Miss Hopkins—you'll have to tell your head mistress—say Mr. Fortune has taken charge and considers it a grave case. Nan! Hop up by Joan and show her the best way to your hospital. Just a moment." He went again into the temple, looked round it with searching eyes, stood on the bench and cut down the remains of the tie. "All right." The car glided away with him...

⋆

Some time afterwards he came out of the hospital and Miss Hopkins and Nan met him eagerly. "She's doing as well as she could," he said.

Mrs. Fortune came and put her arm round Nan.

"You'll see the head mistress, Mr. Fortune?" Miss Hopkins asked.

"Oh, yes. Yes. I'm going to. You might tell her, would you?" He turned away, he contemplated with dreamy eyes the expanse of the park, and Miss Hopkins stared at him and departed. "I say, Nan," he murmured. "Take Joan and give her some tea." He wandered away, but not to the house. He had the air of a man strolling aimlessly; in time he reached the temple, and then, drifting still more casually, he went over the turf about it, in and out among trees and shrubs and so towards the house by a corkscrew route, and once he stopped for some time and was much interested in a clump of hawthorns.

The last of the visitors were departing. From their talk he learnt that they had been told Antigone had met with an accident. He went into the hall. A few of the staff were there, getting rid of the lingerers. Miss Hopkins met him. "Come to the head mistress's room, please."

"Oh, my hat!" Reggie smiled. "Sounds as if I were going to be swished."

Miss Hopkins did not approve of this frivolity. She marched ahead of him. The ample form of Miss Evans swept upon them. "Is that Mr. Fortune? Pray forgive me, how is poor Nora?"

Reggie spread out his hands. "Not a nice case," he murmured.

"Such a dreadful thing," said Miss Evans.

The head mistress had the Bishop in her room, and other pompous men. "Oh. Oh, I should like to speak to you alone," Reggie said plaintively.

"These gentlemen are members of the governing body," the head mistress explained.

"Well, well!" Reggie murmured, and contemplated them with benign curiosity.

The Bishop cleared his throat. "I am sure Mr. Fortune will understand that we are gravely concerned as a body—a terrible affair for the school."

"Yes. And for the girl," Reggie murmured.

"Quite. Quite. I feel that most deeply. We all feel it." He proceeded to introduce them—General Cutts, Lord Stourmouth, Sir Ingram Stow.

The head mistress interrupted. "How is Nora, Mr. Fortune?"

"I can promise you nothing," Reggie said slowly.

The head mistress put her hand to her brow and sighed. "Poor child, poor child."

"Dear me," said the Bishop. "Her condition is serious?"

"Oh, yes. Yes. Quite serious."

Sir Ingram Stow leaned forward. "You understand, Mr. Fortune, we're asking you for your opinion, an expert medical opinion: is the child likely to recover?"

Reggie looked at him with closing eyes. "I've given you my opinion. It's not a case in which I can promise anything."

"You're not very definite, sir," said the General.

"No. I'm not feeling definite," Reggie murmured.

"I suppose you can tell us if the girl will return to consciousness." The General glared.

"Oh, she has. And gone to sleep. Why did you want to know?"

"Naturally, we want to know," the General cried. "Are you being frank with us, sir? We want to know if the girl has given any reason for her attempt to commit suicide. We have a right to know."

"She hasn't. I didn't ask her. You won't be able to ask her. What happened and why it happened will be a matter for the police. Is that quite frank?"

"What, sir? You propose to inform the police? Then let me tell you, sir, I protest—in the strongest way I protest. It would be a most irresponsible and reckless abuse of your professional position. A scandalous interference which I should resent by every means in my power. We should all resent it."

"Would you really?" Reggie murmured. He surveyed them with curiosity. "You'd better not."

Lord Stourmouth, a little dry man, opened his mouth for the first time, and he said, "You're talking nonsense, Cutts."

The Bishop cleared his throat. "I am bound to say, I feel you are wrong, General."

"Pray allow me," Sir Ingram Stow stood up, a tall and handsome person making the most of himself. "Our first thought must be for the interests of the school. That is what influences the General."

"It's our duty, sir, our duty," the General gobbled.

"I feel that deeply. Now we must all see that to call in the police would be disastrous to the school. The publicity would be hideous. The school could never recover from such a scandal. We are also bound to consider the interests of this unhappy girl. Nothing could be more cruel than to make her or her memory the subject of a police investigation. I'm afraid, Stourmouth, you don't realise the suggestions, the insinuations about her which would be inevitable. It would be a cruel wrong to inflict—and without any reason. What happened is not in doubt. She was found by her own mistress hanging there in the temple."

"Did you really think you could hush it up?" Reggie murmured.

"I have made no such suggestion, Mr. Fortune. It is obvious that an inquest must follow her death. That cannot be avoided and none of us would wish to avoid it. There is nothing to conceal. But I protest in the strongest manner against calling in the police to turn it into a sensational case."

"So do I, begad! Making a scandal of it," the General cried. "Make the place a byword. Getting the school in all the papers. That's what comes of taking these scholarship girls. But I won't have it, sir. I'll see the Chief Constable myself."

"Don't worry. He knows all about it," said Reggie. "I telephoned from the hospital. Also to Scotland Yard."

The General glared at him. "Confounded impertinence!"

"You think so?" Reggie murmured. "Well, well." He turned to the head mistress. "I'll see Nora before I go," he said gently. "And Dr. Headley has my telephone number." He held out his hand. "I'm seeing this through."

"Thank you very much." Her eyes met his.

"Good-night, gentlemen." He looked them over. "Nora is not to be seen. There'll be a policeman at the hospital." He went out.

Stourmouth followed him. "Just a word, Mr. Fortune." He took Reggie into a little lobby where the hats of the governors hung. "You know you're right, of course. So do I. Cutts is an ass and Stow is a snob."

"Yes. Not quite a home of peace, Logate," Reggie murmured. He contemplated the hats with grave interest. And Stow and Cutts came in a hurry to seize theirs. Reggie stood aside and watched them depart. He gazed dreamily at Stourmouth. "Yes. That's one of the factors. Good night."...

When he came out of the hospital Nan was waiting with Mrs. Fortune in the car. She jumped down to meet him. "What, Nan?" he smiled. "You don't have to worry any more."

"Oh, Cherub—"

"Yes. My show now. You've done rather well. But you've done your bit. Go and sleep. You can."

The car carried him away. He lit a cigar and slid low in his corner, "Reggie, was that true?" said Mrs. Fortune.

"Oh, yes. Yes. The girl's comin' through. But I don't want it advertised just yet. She didn't hang herself."

"Ah, thank God!"

"Cause for satisfaction. Yes. They might have maddened her into suicide. Possibly that was in somebody's nice mind. Then it would have been a very difficult case."

Mrs. Fortune shuddered. "But what a devilish thing! Has she told you who did it?"

"She doesn't know. I don't know. That's one of the problems."

"One!" Mrs. Fortune cried.

Reggie looked at her with the large bewildered eyes of a child. "Only one, yes," he said plaintively. "By the way—two men comin' to dinner—the Chief Constable and Bell—I rang up Elise."

Mrs. Fortune laughed. "Martha!" she said and made a face at him. It is a term of abuse employed for his careful interest in domestic affairs. "Do I dine with you?"

"My only aunt! Please. I don't want to talk shop. I want my nice dinner. You're a necessary element, Joan."

"Pig," said she. "Essentially pig."

To the surprise of the Chief Constable of the county, an earnest, zealous official, they talked at dinner of roses and wine, of shoes and ships and sealing wax, of cabbages and kings. When Mrs. Fortune was gone and the cigars were lit, Reggie turned to the bewildered man. "Very nice of you to come over. Rather a complex case. Going to work out nasty. I thought you'd like to have it all before you at the start. This is what we've got." And he gave a sketch of his adventures at Logate.

The Chief Constable shook a sage head. "Shocking affair, however you take it. Quite right, Mr. Fortune, we can't overlook it. But you know in my experience adolescent girls do very queer things. And these clever ones are most uncertain. I should have said myself it looked like a plain case of attempted suicide. She thought everybody was persecuting her and the play put it into her head to hang herself. Just the way these tragedies do happen with young women."

"Yes. That's what you're meant to think. I daresay that's the way it was meant to happen. Quite an ingenious mind workin' at Logate."

"Looks a bit too natural to me," said Bell. "They put on a play in which a girl hangs herself, and the girl who takes the part goes and does it quick. I'd work the case over before I passed it for suicide."

"Certainly we shall have to investigate," said the Chief Constable. "But I've no doubt myself any jury would say it was attempted suicide."

"Oh, no. No. If it gets to a jury, I shall be givin' evidence. And I shall say it was attempted murder. The girl has two bruises on her head, one at the back, that's the larger—one on her brow. She couldn't have made them hanging herself. The inference is she was struck from behind and she fell. When she came to herself in hospital the only sensible thing she said was, 'Who hit me?' That is one of the problems."

"Murder? At Logate? It's one of the best girls' schools in the country." The Chief Constable was horrified. "You might say it's a girls' Eton."

"Yes. You might. That's an interesting factor. These things do happen in the best society. But not often."

"You say who did it is one of the problems, Mr. Fortune," Bell grinned. "It's the whole problem, isn't it?"

"For police purposes, yes. For the girl, no. And speakin' scientifically, it's a minor matter. The main problem bein'—why was it done?"

"Motive, eh?" said the Chief Constable. "Take it as suicide, you've got that plain enough. But taking it as murder, the motive's a puzzle. You make out there's been a lot of feeling at Logate against the scholarship girls concentrated on this one. Do you mean to say some of the other girls tried to murder her?"

"Oh, no. No. But thus two further problems are suggested. Who did start the trouble at Logate? And who is Nora Brown? Providin' us with lines of inquiry."

"About the school—" said the Chief Constable anxiously. "It isn't quite fair to talk about starting the trouble. There has been friction at Logate and it dates from the coming of this head mistress. Not her fault, I daresay. You know what big schools are. A new head comes. There are people who think somebody else ought to have had the job. The new head makes changes. More people get discontented and annoyed. And so on. It's very common."

Reggie blew smoke rings. "Yes. Quite. Yes. So some people wanted another woman head mistress. Who would they be?"

"Well, you know there was a strong feeling that one of the mistresses who'd been at Logate some time ought to have had the appointment."

"I see. Yes. Which one?"

"I couldn't give you a name." The Chief Constable was embarrassed. "You're not suggesting one of the mistresses would murder the girl? If you'll excuse my saying so, Mr. Fortune. I don't think you ought to have that kind of idea about Logate. All the mistresses are ladies."

Bell grunted. "Have you found that makes much difference, sir? I haven't."

The Chief Constable was shocked. "Well, I don't agree. But leaving out that—why on earth should one of the mistresses want to murder one of the girls? It's a mad idea."

"I daresay a mistress often wants to," Reggie smiled. "But it is unusual for her to try. Motive inadequate, as you say."

"I don't see anything like a motive myself," said Bell. "You can't always get to a reasonable motive. This is the kind of case I wouldn't expect one. The evidence is, there's a lot of bad blood in this girls' school—grievances and quarrelling and persecution. Given all that, you'll often find a woman run mad."

"Kind of hysteria, you mean?" the Chief Constable said. "Well, I suppose that's possible. You'll pardon me, Mr. Fortune, I can't help thinking it's not so certain we need look beyond the poor girl herself. An hysterical young woman meaning suicide often tries to make it look like murder."

"Sometimes. Yes. Ever tried to hit yourself hard behind the ear? Not easy, even in hysterics. I'm afraid you can't turn it into suicide. Do you know anyone on the governing body?"

The Chief Constable stared. "I know General Cutts."

"Yes. So he indicated. And Sir Ingram Stow?"

"I've met Stow. Why?"

"Well, they want to hush it up, you know."

"Mr. Fortune, you don't suggest that I—"

"Oh, no. No. You couldn't, anyway. But it wouldn't look well to play into their hands. What do you know about 'em?"

"General Cutts was my commanding officer, sir."

"You have my sympathy. And Stow?"

"I've merely met him. He's of a good old family, a rich man, a very pleasant fellow. Why do you ask all this?"

"Well, you know, it seemed to me that Cutts and Stow don't love the other governors. I suppose they were against this new head mistress, they were against the respectable and exclusive Logate takin' scholarship girls, and specially they're against this girl Nora Brown. That is, they've been backin' the trouble in the school."

"I can't let that pass, Mr. Fortune. Of course, it's well known General Cutts is opposed to the new policy at Logate and Sir Ingram Stow has supported him."

"Oh! You knew that," said Reggie sharply. "You didn't tell us. Rather a pity, isn't it?"

"I don't understand you, Mr. Fortune. There is no secret about their opinions. They're gentlemen of the highest reputation."

"Everybody always is in this kind of case," Bell grunted. "These are gentlemen and the mistresses are ladies. All the same, a girl nearly got murdered among 'em."

"But this is preposterous," the Chief Constable cried.

"Oh, no. No. Summary of facts by Superintendent Bell. Let's expand it. These two gentlemen have been behind the trouble in the school which produced the persecution of Nora Brown. Somebody attempts to murder her and they try to prevent inquiry into the case. And the attempt wasn't wholly feminine. What do you know about that?" He held out a specimen box containing a small piece of black fluff.

The Chief Constable gaped. "Came off a silk hat, what?" said Bell.

"Yes. It came off a silk hat. On to a hawthorn bough by the temple where I found it. With a man's footprints adjacent. Also the blow which knocked Nora out was beyond a woman's strength. Assistance of a man in the crime is strongly indicated."

"And a gentleman," Bell grinned.

"But it's bewildering," the Chief Constable gasped. "Surely, Mr. Fortune, you can't believe these gentlemen would murder a girl because of their opinions on school policy. The idea is crazy!"

"Oh, yes. Yes. Quite. To keep poor girls out of Logate by murderin' one who got in—that isn't a business proposition. But a man did try to murder her and these men are tryin' to hush it up. And when you kindly assisted in our first line of inquiry, who started the trouble at Logate leadin' to the persecution of Nora, you put us on to these same men. That was very helpful of you." He smiled at the scared Chief Constable. "Convergin' evidence, isn't it?"

"It's very strange," the Chief Constable stammered. "But the connection—what connection is there between the change of policy at Logate and this girl? She didn't come till lately."

"Till after the trouble began. Yes. The inference is, they started the trouble for other reasons, but when Nora Brown got into the school they found they had special reasons for turning it against her. Hence the persecution. Possibly with hopes of her suicide. In other words, Nora Brown is somebody who had to be murdered for her own sake."

The Chief Constable rubbed his brow. "I can't believe the General— I'd answer for him absolutely—."

"Yes. I should say he's merely an ass," Reggie murmured.

"You suspect Stow, then? But what possible reason?"

"I haven't the slightest idea," said Reggie.

The Chief Constable stared at him pathetically. "Of course, there must be an investigation, a thorough investigation. What would you like me to do?"

"Nothing. And do it carefully. Leave your man on guard over Nora. The woman doctor's all right. But a policeman is a good scarecrow for criminals. You might have some plain-clothes men watchin' to see if Stow comes to the school or has anybody go from the school to him. I'll attend to Miss Brown senior."

"Senior?" The Chief Constable gaped.

"Yes. The hypothetical aunt. Followin' the second line of inquiry, who is Nora Brown? Well, this being thus, that's all. You'll want to be goin'. Many thanks." He got rid of an unhappy man.

Bell filled a pipe and cocked an eyebrow. "Told him a lot, didn't you, sir? You talk about converging evidence. I'd say you haven't got any evidence to take to a jury."

"Not much. No." Reggie pulled out of his pocket the tie by which the girl was hanged. "What do you think of that?"

Bell turned it over. "Good knots, sailor's knots."

"Yes. Stow was in the navy. I looked him up."

Bell grunted. "Well, that's another pointer. But it's not much, is it? Looks like one of those cases where you feel sure but you can't put the man in the dock. Clever fellow."

"I wonder," Reggie murmured. "Very ingenious mind somewhere."

"If you hadn't been at this school today, the girl would have been cut down dead; nobody would have thought of anything but suicide. Stow would have had a nice quiet little inquest and been on velvet."

"Yes. That is so," Reggie smiled. "But I don't think he's feeling on velvet tonight."

"I don't know. I don't see where you're going to get your evidence, even now."

Reggie stood up. "The hypothetical aunt, my Bell."

"That's all very well. You may find some connection with Stow. You may find a motive for him killing the girl. But that don't make evidence he tried."

"My little ray of sunshine." Reggie contemplated him with affection. "Are we downhearted? No. We've saved the girl. Come to bed. We'll seek Aunt bright and early."

So early in the morning they drove away to the cottage of Miss Brown. It stood sixty miles from Logate and far from anywhere, in a flat and lonely country, a small cottage, at the end of a small village, looking from the outside homely and well kept. To their knocking at the door no answer came. Bell strode off to the nearest neighbours. He was told that they didn't know nothing but they thought Miss Brown was gone away. A motor car did come to her place the night afore and she went off in it and they never see her come back.

Superintendent Bell becomes annoyed when he meets attempts to frustrate his investigations. "Somebody's been very quick." He frowned at Reggie. "What's the game?"

"Somebody's got the wind up," Reggie smiled.

"Do you think Stow's made away with her?"

"It could be," Reggie murmured. "She knows something we mustn't know."

"That don't make sense to my mind. This woman's been living here with the girl; brought her up; let her go to Logate. And it's only when she gets there Stow meddles with her. Why did he wait?"

"Yes. Why did he? Interestin' question. You'd better ask Miss Brown."

"I'm going to have a job to find her."

"Oh, my dear chap! What about the advertised resources of our highly organised police force?"

"I'll set 'em to work," Bell frowned.

"Yes. Yes. You make 'em find out where she's gone," Reggie smiled. "I want to know where she came from." He left Bell working the telephone in the village post office. He went to call on the village school.

He found the mistress who had coached Nora for her scholarship, a worn and weary woman, but of a quick intelligence. She would tell him nothing till he told her what had happened to the girl. Then all she knew and all she thought was laid before him. She had always considered Nora a girl of uncommon ability and character; she had never heard of any relations, friends, enemies, anybody who took an interest in her. Miss Brown was an ordinary woman, rather dull, rather reserved, kind enough in a stolid way. She came to the village when Nora was a baby, a year old or less. Nobody knew where from. Miss Brown kept much to herself; having money enough to live on, considered herself above the village people. She had not wanted Nora to go to Logate, but gave way.

"I see. Yes." Reggie smiled. "You forced her hand."

"I'd have done anything to give the child her chance," the mistress said fiercely. "I told her so."

"Yes. Did she know anything about Logate?"

"She'd never heard of it. She only objected because she thought it was what she called a school for the gentry."

"I see. And what was Miss Brown? Not gentry?"

"Oh, dear, no. She'd been a hospital nurse, I believe. I heard her say once she'd been trained at Exeter."

"Is that so?" Over Reggie's face came a slow benign smile. "And her age?"

"I couldn't say. Forty—fifty. I have a photograph of her with Nora. You can form your own opinion. That was taken five years ago."

Reggie studied a photograph of a neat woman with fat and stolid face. "Splendid," he murmured. "Yes. Say forty plus now. At the Exeter hospital twenty plus years back. What's her colouring?"

"Oh, fair, florid, blue eyes and brown hair."

"Thanks very much. I may take the photograph?"

"You'll let me have it back? It's the only one I have of Nora at that age."

"Yes. Charmin' child. She is still. Yes. You shall have it safe. Thanks very much. Nora's had a good friend." He held out his hand.

"You're working for her, aren't you?" There were tears in the tired eyes.

"I'm for her," said Reggie gently. "Goodbye. I shall remember you."...

Some days afterwards the Chief of the Criminal Investigation Department saw in the personal column of the morning papers this advertisement:

DEWES: Any person having knowledge of Mrs. Veronica Dewes, who died at Beton, Devon, January 1915, is desired to inform the Criminal Investigation Department, Scotland Yard.

He was not pleased. He was making trouble about it in the Department when his telephone rang.

"Is that Lomas? Fortune speaking. From Beton, Devon. Good morning. Seen the papers?"

"Good Gad!" Lomas groaned. "I might have known it was you."

"You might. Yes. Didn't you? Dear, dear. Never at your brightest in the morning. Any news of the vanished Miss Brown?"

"Bell thinks she's sailed for Canada. He's wirelessing the ship. If it is the woman, we'll have her held on the other side."

"Good. And Stow?"

"Stow hasn't run. He's at his place in the country. We can't find any evidence he went to her cottage. He was out driving his own car that night. What's this new hare you've started?"

"Not new. No. Same old hare. Miss Brown. After training in the Exeter hospital Miss Brown became district nurse at this charmin' place. Mrs. Dewes was living here. Young wife of a man said to have been killed in the war. In 1914 she had a baby, christened Veronica. Miss Brown nursed her. In 1915 she died, Miss Brown still nursing her. Baby also died. Cause of death in the register pneumonia for both. Doctor who gave the certificate is dead. Shortly after these deaths, Miss Brown vanished from Beton."

"Queer story. So you want to find the relations of Mrs. Dewes? We'll look the man up in the casualty lists."

"Yes. I want to know who they were. I also want an exhumation order."

"What? Good Gad! For bodies buried fourteen years? You can't make out anything now, can you?"

"It depends what I find."

"You suspect foul play?"

"Oh, yes. Yes. Something wrong. Put it through."

"It's very unusual."

"My only aunt!" the telephone moaned. "Here am I livin' in a fisherman's pub, and you talk about what's usual. Get on with it."

But official objections might have delayed that order long if General Blaker had not called at Scotland Yard. It was some time before he interested Lomas. He had to explain why Jimmy Dewes was the best subaltern a man ever had and how he was killed at Le Cateau. But then he became relevant. Jimmy was the son of old Colonel Dewes and married without his father's consent and the old man wouldn't allow him a penny—didn't believe in early marriages for soldiers—poor old man, never thought there was a world war coming to kill all the lads off. Mrs. Dewes was a charming girl, dear creature, but the old man wouldn't look at her. So, naturally, when Jimmy was killed she was too proud to go to the old fellow—carried on as she could, till she died, poor thing, she and her baby, first winter of the war. Probably pined away when her man was gone—too many of 'em did. There was old Dewes left without a soul of his name. He didn't last long."

"What became of his money?" asked Lomas.

"Oh, he made no will—it went to the next of kin, a young cousin, a baronet. Stow the name is—Ingram Stow."...

Under a red Devon cliff Reggie lay watching the sea. The girl child who delivered the telegrams of Beton came to him. He read this message:

You win. Instructing county police. Arrange with them. Lomas.

He scrambled to his feet and made for the village telephone.

When the sun came over the cliff in the morning men began to dig into one of the nameless mounds in the little churchyard. They found the mother's coffin and the baby's lying side by side, and the tarnished plates. "All right. Carry on." He walked slowly away.

Some hours later he came out of the mortuary in Exeter and strolled to the railway station. The Cornish express roared through, the slip carriage from it slid to the platform and Lomas jumped out. "My dear old thing," Reggie beamed at him. "All ready for you. Come along."

"Has it gone all right?"

"Oh, yes. Yes. Very nice and neat."

Reggie put him into a taxi and said to the driver, "The mortuary."

"Good Gad!" Lomas gasped. "You don't want to show me—"

"Oh, yes. You'd better have a look."

"My dear fellow! I can't help you with this sort of thing."

"Not help, no. I've finished. There's nothing to be done with the mother. We can hope she died a natural death. But the baby—well, it's very interesting."

Lomas shuddered. "The baby didn't?"

"No. No. That is indicated."

They came to the mortuary and Reggie led him in. The woman's coffin was covered. In the baby's lay something wrapped in a shroud. Reggie beckoned to an attendant. "Unroll that again." It was lifted out and from the shroud came a pillow case. "There's the baby. A feather pillow with a few stones for makeweight. See? The baby didn't die. Miss Brown wasn't wholly inhuman. So we can hope the mother died by nature."

"Good Gad!" said Lomas. "I suppose that's what you had in your head all the time."

"Yes. Yes." Over Reggie's face came a slow benign smile. "That was the workin' hypothesis. Well, well. Now we can get on."

They went back to their cab. "Lunch is indicated. A grave but placid lunch. You'll want to wind up the case with the police down here. Then we'll go back and deal with Stow."

"It's not so easy to deal with Stow," Lomas frowned. "This doesn't make evidence that he tried to murder the girl at Logate. What have we got? It was his interest as the next heir to old Dewes to have this woman and her baby dead. The probability is he tried to arrange something with Miss Brown."

"Oh, yes. Yes. I should say she told him the baby was dead, hadn't the heart to kill it, but took the price for its death. She retired on that and brought the girl up. Thus making the best of both worlds. Then the child turned out clever and the village school mistress took her up and got her into Logate. Miss Brown not knowin' enough to object. Thus Stow found a girl looking like the Dewes family in Logate and called Brown. That must have hit him hard. If anybody came along who knew the Dewes, there'd be questions. She's a strikin' child. I suppose he looked up Miss Brown and decided he had to get rid of the girl. And he made a very good try."

"That's all very well. No doubt that's how it all happened. There's a very good chance of proving the girl heiress to the Dewes estate and showing Stow up. What do you think of the evidence for a criminal charge against him? If we can catch this Miss Brown and frighten her into telling the truth, we might make something of the fraud of the baby's death. But for the attempt to murder the girl at Logate, we're where we were. No case."

"Yes. As you say," Reggie murmured. "No case. But we might ask him about it. Very interestin'."

"Oh, I'll ask him," said Lomas. "But he's in touch with Logate. He must know we've got nothing more there. If you think he'll give himself away, you're hopeful."

"Yes. Perhaps you're right," Reggie sighed. "A sad world."

So they went to lunch and when Lomas had settled his business with the police took a train for Logate's county town. Reggie nearly missed it. He explained that he had been writing letters.

That evening they conferred with the Chief Constable, and having laid the case before that amazed man, arranged with him to drive over in the morning and interrogate Stow in his own house. When they were leaving, "By the way," said Reggie, "have you kept your men watching Stow?"

"Watched his house night and day, Mr. Fortune. And Logate. Made nothing of it. He's seen none of the school people. He's kept very quiet. Of course, he must know the girl's doing well and that would scare him. I have rather wondered he didn't try to bolt when he got that Miss Brown out of the country."

Reggie looked at him with dreamy eyes. "Yes. That's interestin', isn't it? Good-night."

The Chief Constable's car came to their hotel while they were still at an early breakfast. "Come on, Lomas." Reggie pushed back his chair. "All is best though oft we doubt—you're much better without that coffee. I wonder where they got it." And Lomas groaned and followed.

The Chief Constable was brisk. "'Morning. 'Morning. I thought we'd better lose no time. Seen the papers, Mr. Lomas?"

"I'm not awake yet," Lomas mumbled.

"They've got on to it. Look." And Lomas read:

In the little fishing village of Beton on the Devonshire coast an exhumation was made yesterday by order of the Home Office. Two coffins were removed to Exeter. It is understood that a sensational discovery was made. Further developments in a case in another part of the country are expected.

"That's as good as a straight tip to Sir Ingram Stow, isn't it?" said the Chief Constable. "If he's read that he'll be off."

"You think so?" Reggie murmured. "You've still got a man watching his house."

"I have, Mr. Fortune. And I sent off another on a motorbike as soon as I read this."

"Then that is that," Reggie sighed.

Lomas looked at him without affection, but his round face had a dreamy calm.

By Stow's gate a motorcyclist tinkering with his machine waved them on. They came to the house, a big new place built on to an old one. "Been using the Dewes money," Lomas frowned.

They were told by an aggrieved butler that Sir Ingram was still at breakfast. "He will see me at once," said Lomas. They were put into the library and he came.

He was visibly a weaker man than he had been at Logate. He had shrunken, he was pale. He greeted the Chief Constable with a show of joviality; he was shy of Reggie, anxiously civil to Lomas. "I must suppose you've come on business, sir. I'm quite at your orders. What can I do?"

"You'd better sit down," said Lomas. "I want to hear your account of your actions on the day Nora Brown was hanged at Logate."

"My actions?" Stow laughed. "I had no actions, so to speak. I went to Logate to see the play, saw it, went back to the school-house and was talking there till we heard the poor child had hanged herself."

"Oh, no. No," Reggie said. "That's not our information. The evidence is you went to the temple. You found the girl there. You struck her behind the ear and knocked her out. You took off her tie and hanged her. Then you went back to the school-house and talked."

"The evidence?" Stow gasped. "She's told you that?"

"She?" said Reggie, and he laughed. "Didn't you think she would?"

"It's a lie!" Stow cried.

"Oh! She is lying? Which she do you mean?" He leaned forward, watching the man's fear with smiling curiosity.

"The girl, of course." Stow licked his lips. "I don't understand."

"There's more evidence than the girl's," said Reggie. "You know that. Do you choose to tell your story?"

Stow looked at him white and shaking. "What do you mean, my story? I don't know what you've heard. I—"

But Reggie was not listening. There was the sound of a car outside. He made for the window. He watched a moment and turned quickly. "Here she is," he said with a chuckle and hurried out.

He came back grasping the arm of a large woman. She was red. She was protesting incoherently. She was Miss Evans.

"Oh, yes. Yes." Reggie's placid voice cut across hers. "Much obliged to you. We wanted you. He says it wasn't his idea at all."

Stow huddled in his chair. "I swear it wasn't," he muttered. "She thought of it like that. She said—"

"Ah, you hound!" the woman cried. She plucked at her bag, she pulled out a pistol and fired into his face. As she turned the pistol on herself, they flung themselves upon her...

"And that is that," Reggie sighed, watching the car drive her away to gaol. "One of my neater cases, Lomas, old thing." He lit a cigar. "We couldn't have hanged Stow. Now we've got 'em both. I daresay the late Stow told the truth in the end. I expect she put him up to the hanging. Feminine instinct about it."

"No doubt she did," Lomas agreed. "That's why she shot when the fellow rounded on her."

"It could be. Yes. I should say she was mad at losing what she played for. Always being frustrated."

"What do you mean?"

"That she wasn't going to be Lady Stow. When he wanted to get at the girl he had this disgruntled woman ready to be used. But she wouldn't do murder for nothing. Sort of woman who'd stood out for the top price. Marriage. I should say it was because she thought that was right off, she put a pistol in her bag when she came to call."

"But what brought her this morning?"

"My dear chap! Oh, my dear chap!" Reggie smiled. "She reads the papers."

"Good Gad! That cursed paragraph." Lomas stared at him. "That was you, of course."

"Yes. Yes. I thought it might draw her," Reggie murmured. "It did, didn't it? Quite a neat case."

THE ADVENTURE OF THE PRIORY SCHOOL

Arthur Conan Doyle

Arthur Conan Doyle (1859–1930) was a Scotsman whose family sent him to school in England. Through a relative, they knew Stonyhurst College in Preston, Lancashire, which flourishes to this day as "the UK's leading Catholic boarding and day school" and was founded by a Jesuit priest in 1593. The school's website proudly records that Doyle attended from 1868 to 1873. While at Stonyhurst, he developed a passion for cricket and became a capable player; the first names of Sherlock and Mycroft Holmes were probably inspired by Shacklock and Mycroft, two bowlers who played for Derbyshire in a match at Lord's against the MCC (of which Doyle became a member) in 1885, a couple of years before the publication of *A Study in Scarlet*. From 1876, Doyle studied medicine at Edinburgh University, which was where he encountered the surgeon and lecturer Dr. Joseph Bell, whose deductive reasoning was the inspiration for much of Sherlock's detective work.

By the time "The Adventure of the Priory School" was first published in the American magazine *Collier's Weekly* in January 1904, Sherlock had not only established himself as fiction's most iconic detective but somehow survived a close encounter with Professor Moriarty at the Reichenbach Falls. The Priory School is located near Mackleton in the north of England; the name is an amalgam of Macclesfield and Buxton. Doyle included the story in a list of his dozen favourite Sherlock Holmes cases.

WE HAVE HAD SOME DRAMATIC ENTRANCES AND EXITS UPON our small stage at Baker Street, but I cannot recollect anything more sudden and startling than the first appearance of Thorneycroft Huxtable, M.A., Ph.D., etc. His card, which seemed too small to carry the weight of his academic distinctions, preceded him by a few seconds, and then he entered himself—so large, so pompous, and so dignified that he was the very embodiment of self-possession and solidity. And yet his first action, when the door had closed behind him, was to stagger against the table, whence he slipped down upon the floor, and there was that majestic figure prostrate and insensible upon our bearskin hearthrug.

We had sprung to our feet, and for a few moments we stared in silent amazement at this ponderous piece of wreckage, which told of some sudden and fatal storm far out on the ocean of life. Then Holmes hurried with a cushion for his head, and I with brandy for his lips. The heavy, white face was seamed with lines of trouble, the hanging pouches under the closed eyes were leaden in colour, the loose mouth drooped dolorously at the corners, the rolling chins were unshaven. Collar and shirt bore the grime of a long journey, and the hair bristled unkempt from the well-shaped head. It was a sorely stricken man who lay before us.

"What is it, Watson?" asked Holmes.

"Absolute exhaustion—possibly mere hunger and fatigue," said I, with my finger on the thready pulse, where the stream of life trickled thin and small.

"Return ticket from Mackleton, in the north of England," said

Holmes, drawing it from the watch-pocket. "It is not twelve o'clock yet. He has certainly been an early starter."

The puckered eyelids had begun to quiver, and now a pair of vacant grey eyes looked up at us. An instant later the man had scrambled on to his feet, his face crimson with shame.

"Forgive this weakness, Mr. Holmes, I have been a little over-wrought. Thank you, if I might have a glass of milk and a biscuit, I have no doubt that I should be better. I came personally, Mr. Holmes, in order to insure that you would return with me. I feared that no telegram would convince you of the absolute urgency of the case."

"When you are quite restored—"

"I am quite well again. I cannot imagine how I came to be so weak. I wish you, Mr. Holmes, to come to Mackleton with me by the next train."

My friend shook his head.

"My colleague, Dr. Watson, could tell you that we are very busy at present. I am retained in this case of the Ferrers Documents, and the Abergavenny murder is coming up for trial. Only a very important issue could call me from London at present."

"Important!" Our visitor threw up his hands. "Have you heard nothing of the abduction of the only son of the Duke of Holdernesse?"

"What! the late Cabinet Minister?"

"Exactly. We had tried to keep it out of the papers, but there was some rumour in the *Globe* last night. I thought it might have reached your ears."

Holmes shot out his long, thin arm and picked out Volume "H" in his encyclopædia of reference.

"'Holdernesse, 6th Duke, K.G., P.C.'—half the alphabet! 'Baron Beverley, Earl of Carston'—dear me, what a list! 'Lord Lieutenant of Hallamshire since 1900. Married Edith, daughter of Sir Charles Appledore, 1888. Heir and only child, Lord Saltire. Owns about two hundred and fifty thousand acres. Minerals in Lancashire and Wales. Address: Carlton House Terrace; Holdernesse Hall, Hallamshire; Carston Castle, Bangor, Wales. Lord of the Admiralty, 1872; Chief Secretary of State for—' Well, well, this man is certainly one of the greatest subjects of the Crown!"

"The greatest and perhaps the wealthiest. I am aware, Mr. Holmes, that you take a very high line in professional matters, and that you are prepared to work for the work's sake. I may tell you, however, that his Grace has already intimated that a cheque for five thousand pounds will be handed over to the person who can tell him where his son is, and another thousand to him who can name the man or men who have taken him."

"It is a princely offer," said Holmes. "Watson, I think that we shall accompany Dr. Huxtable back to the north of England. And now, Dr. Huxtable, when you have consumed that milk, you will kindly tell me what has happened, when it happened, how it happened, and, finally, what Dr. Thorneycroft Huxtable, of the Priory School, near Mackleton, has to do with the matter, and why he comes three days after an event—the state of your chin gives the date—to ask for my humble services."

Our visitor had consumed his milk and biscuits. The light had come back to his eyes and the colour to his cheeks, as he set himself with great vigour and lucidity to explain the situation.

"I must inform you, gentlemen, that the Priory is a preparatory school, of which I am the founder and principal. *Huxtable's Sidelights on Horace* may possibly recall my name to your memories. The Priory is, without exception, the best and most select preparatory school in England. Lord Leverstoke, the Earl of Blackwater, Sir Cathcart Soames—they all have intrusted their sons to me. But I felt that my school had reached its zenith when, weeks ago, the Duke of Holdernesse sent Mr. James Wilder, his secretary, with intimation that young Lord Saltire, ten years old, his only son and heir, was about to be committed to my charge. Little did I think that this would be the prelude to the most crushing misfortune of my life.

"On May 1st the boy arrived, that being the beginning of the summer term. He was a charming youth, and he soon fell into our ways. I may tell you—I trust that I am not indiscreet, but half-confidences are absurd in such a case—that he was not entirely happy at home. It is an open secret that the Duke's married life had not been a peaceful one, and the matter had ended in a separation by mutual consent, the Duchess taking up her residence in the south of France. This had occurred very shortly before, and the boy's sympathies are known to have been strongly with his mother. He moped after her departure from Holdernesse Hall, and it was for this reason that the Duke desired to send him to my establishment. In a fortnight the boy was quite at home with us and was apparently absolutely happy.

"He was last seen on the night of May 13th—that is, the night of last Monday. His room was on the second floor and was approached through another larger room, in which two boys were sleeping. These boys saw and heard nothing, so that it is certain that young Saltire did not pass out that way. His window was open, and there is a stout ivy plant leading to the ground. We could trace no footmarks below, but it is sure that this is the only possible exit.

"His absence was discovered at seven o'clock on Tuesday morning. His bed had been slept in. He had dressed himself fully, before going off, in his usual school suit of black Eton jacket and dark grey trousers. There were no signs that anyone had entered the room, and it is quite certain that anything in the nature of cries or a struggle would have been heard, since Caunter, the elder boy in the inner room, is a very light sleeper.

"When Lord Saltire's disappearance was discovered, I at once called a roll of the whole establishment—boys, masters, and servants. It was then that we ascertained that Lord Saltire had not been alone in his flight. Heidegger, the German master, was missing. His room was on the second floor, at the farther end of the building, facing the same way as Lord Saltire's. His bed had also been slept in, but he had apparently gone away partly dressed, since his shirt and socks were lying on the floor. He had undoubtedly let himself down by the ivy, for we could see the marks of his feet where he had landed on the lawn. His bicycle was kept in a small shed beside this lawn, and it also was gone.

"He had been with me for two years, and came with the best references, but he was a silent, morose man, not very popular either with masters or boys. No trace could be found of the fugitives, and now, on Thursday morning, we are as ignorant as we were on Tuesday. Inquiry was, of course, made at once at Holdernesse Hall. It is only a few miles away, and we imagined that, in some sudden attack of homesickness, he had gone back to his father, but nothing had been heard of him. The Duke is greatly agitated, and, as to me, you have seen yourselves the state of nervous prostration to which the suspense and the responsibility have reduced me. Mr. Holmes, if ever you put forward your full powers, I implore you to do so now, for never in your life could you have a case which is more worthy of them."

Sherlock Holmes had listened with the utmost intentness to the statement of the unhappy schoolmaster. His drawn brows and the deep furrow between them showed that he needed no exhortation to concentrate all his attention upon a problem which, apart from the tremendous interests involved must appeal so directly to his love of the complex and the unusual. He now drew out his notebook and jotted down one or two memoranda.

"You have been very remiss in not coming to me sooner," said he, severely. "You start me on my investigation with a very serious handicap. It is inconceivable, for example, that this ivy and this lawn would have yielded nothing to an expert observer."

"I am not to blame, Mr. Holmes. His Grace was extremely desirous to avoid all public scandal. He was afraid of his family unhappiness being dragged before the world. He has a deep horror of anything of the kind."

"But there has been some official investigation?"

"Yes, sir, and it has proved most disappointing. An apparent clue was at once obtained, since a boy and a young man were reported to have been seen leaving a neighbouring station by an early train. Only last night we had news that the couple had been hunted down in Liverpool, and they prove to have no connection whatever with the matter in hand. Then it was that in my despair and disappointment, after a sleepless night, I came straight to you by the early train."

"I suppose the local investigation was relaxed while this false clue was being followed up?"

"It was entirely dropped."

"So that three days have been wasted. The affair has been most deplorably handled."

"I feel it and admit it."

"And yet the problem should be capable of ultimate solution. I shall be very happy to look into it. Have you been able to trace any connection between the missing boy and this German master?"

"None at all."

"Was he in the master's class?"

"No, he never exchanged a word with him, so far as I know."

"That is certainly very singular. Had the boy a bicycle?"

"No."

"Was any other bicycle missing?"

"No."

"Is that certain?"

"Quite."

"Well, now, you do not mean to seriously suggest that this German rode off upon a bicycle in the dead of the night, bearing the boy in his arms?"

"Certainly not."

"Then what is the theory in your mind?"

"The bicycle may have been a blind. It may have been hidden somewhere, and the pair gone off on foot."

"Quite so, but it seems rather an absurd blind, does it not? Were there other bicycles in this shed?"

"Several."

"Would he not have hidden *a couple*, had he desired to give the idea that they had gone off upon them?"

"I suppose he would."

"Of course he would. The blind theory won't do. But the incident is an admirable starting-point for an investigation. After all, a bicycle is not an easy thing to conceal or to destroy. One other question. Did anyone call to see the boy on the day before he disappeared?"

"No."

"Did he get any letters?"

"Yes, one letter."

"From whom?"

"From his father."

"Do you open the boys' letters?"

"No."

"How do you know it was from the father?"

"The coat of arms was on the envelope, and it was addressed in the Duke's peculiar stiff hand. Besides, the Duke remembers having written."

"When had he a letter before that?"

"Not for several days."

"Had he ever one from France?"

"No, never."

"You see the point of my questions, of course. Either the boy was carried off by force or he went of his own free will. In the latter case, you would expect that some prompting from outside would be needed to make so young a lad do such a thing. If he has had no visitors, that prompting must have come in letters; hence I try to find out who were his correspondents."

"I fear I cannot help you much. His only correspondent, so far as I know, was his own father."

"Who wrote to him on the very day of his disappearance. Were the relations between father and son very friendly?"

"His Grace is never very friendly with anyone. He is completely immersed in large public questions, and is rather inaccessible to all ordinary emotions. But he was always kind to the boy in his own way."

"But the sympathies of the latter were with the mother?"

"Yes."

"Did he say so?"

"No."

"The Duke, then?"

"Good Heavens, no!"

"Then how could you know?"

"I have had some confidential talks with Mr. James Wilder, his Grace's secretary. It was he who gave me the information about Lord Saltire's feelings."

"I see. By the way, that last letter of the Duke's—was it found in the boy's room after he was gone?"

"No, he had taken it with him. I think, Mr. Holmes, it is time that we were leaving for Euston."

"I will order a four-wheeler. In a quarter of an hour, we shall be at your service. If you are telegraphing home, Mr. Huxtable, it would be well to allow the people in your neighbourhood to imagine that the inquiry is still going on in Liverpool, or wherever else that red herring led your pack. In the meantime I will do a little quiet work at your own doors, and perhaps the scent is not so cold but that two old hounds like Watson and myself may get a sniff of it."

That evening found us in the cold, bracing atmosphere of the Peak country, in which Dr. Huxtable's famous school is situated. It was already dark when we reached it. A card was lying on the hall table, and the butler whispered something to his master, who turned to us with agitation in every heavy feature.

"The Duke is here," said he. "The Duke and Mr. Wilder are in the study. Come, gentlemen, and I will introduce you."

I was, of course, familiar with the pictures of the famous statesman, but the man himself was very different from his representation. He was a tall and stately person, scrupulously dressed, with a drawn, thin face, and a nose which was grotesquely curved and long. His complexion was of a dead pallor, which was more startling by contrast with a long, dwindling beard of vivid red, which flowed down over his white waistcoat with his watch-chain gleaming through its fringe. Such was the stately presence who looked stonily at us from the centre of Dr. Huxtable's hearthrug. Beside him stood a very young man, whom I understood to be Wilder, the private secretary. He was small, nervous, alert with intelligent light-blue eyes and mobile features. It was he who at once, in an incisive and positive tone, opened the conversation.

"I called this morning, Dr. Huxtable, too late to prevent you from starting for London. I learned that your object was to invite Mr. Sherlock Holmes to undertake the conduct of this case. His Grace is surprised, Dr. Huxtable, that you should have taken such a step without consulting him."

"When I learned that the police had failed—"

"His Grace is by no means convinced that the police have failed."

"But surely, Mr. Wilder—"

"You are well aware, Dr. Huxtable, that his Grace is particularly anxious to avoid all public scandal. He prefers to take as few people as possible into his confidence."

"The matter can be easily remedied," said the brow-beaten doctor; "Mr. Sherlock Holmes can return to London by the morning train."

"Hardly that, Doctor, hardly that," said Holmes, in his blandest voice. "This northern air is invigorating and pleasant, so I propose to spend a few days upon your moors, and to occupy my mind as best I may. Whether I have the shelter of your roof or of the village inn is, of course, for you to decide."

I could see that the unfortunate doctor was in the last stage of indecision, from which he was rescued by the deep, sonorous voice of the red-bearded Duke, which boomed out like a dinner-gong.

"I agree with Mr. Wilder, Dr. Huxtable, that you would have done wisely to consult me. But since Mr. Holmes has already been taken into your confidence, it would indeed be absurd that we should not avail ourselves of his services. Far from going to the inn, Mr. Holmes, I should be pleased if you would come and stay with me at Holdernesse Hall."

"I thank your Grace. For the purposes of my investigation, I think that it would be wiser for me to remain at the scene of the mystery."

"Just as you like, Mr. Holmes. Any information which Mr. Wilder or I can give you is, of course, at your disposal."

"It will probably be necessary for me to see you at the Hall," said Holmes. "I would only ask you now, sir, whether you have formed any explanation in your own mind as to the mysterious disappearance of your son?"

"No, sir, I have not."

"Excuse me if I allude to that which is painful to you, but I have no alternative. Do you think that the Duchess had anything to do with the matter?"

The great minister showed perceptible hesitation.

"I do not think so," he said, at last.

"The other most obvious explanation is that the child has been kidnapped for the purpose of levying ransom. You have not had any demand of the sort?"

"No, sir."

"One more question, your Grace. I understand that you wrote to your son upon the day when this incident occurred."

"No, I wrote upon the day before."

"Exactly. But he received it on that day?"

"Yes."

"Was there anything in your letter which might have unbalanced him or induced him to take such a step?"

"No, sir, certainly not."

"Did you post that letter yourself?"

The nobleman's reply was interrupted by his secretary, who broke in with some heat.

"His Grace is not in the habit of posting letters himself," said he. "This letter was laid with others upon the study table, and I myself put them in the post-bag."

"You are sure this one was among them?"

"Yes, I observed it."

"How many letters did your Grace write that day?"

"Twenty or thirty. I have a large correspondence. But surely this is somewhat irrelevant?"

"Not entirely," said Holmes.

"For my own part," the Duke continued, "I have advised the police to turn their attention to the south of France. I have already said that I do not believe that the Duchess would encourage so monstrous an action, but the lad had the most wrong-headed opinions, and it is possible that he may have fled to her, aided and abetted by this German. I think, Dr. Huxtable, that we will now return to the Hall."

I could see that there were other questions which Holmes would have wished to put, but the nobleman's abrupt manner showed that the interview was at an end. It was evident that to his intensely aristocratic nature this discussion of his intimate family affairs with a stranger was most abhorrent, and that he feared lest every fresh question would throw a fiercer light into the discreetly shadowed corners of his ducal history.

When the nobleman and his secretary had left, my friend flung himself at once with characteristic eagerness into the investigation.

The boy's chamber was carefully examined, and yielded nothing save the absolute conviction that it was only through the window that he could have escaped. The German master's room and effects gave no further clue. In his case a trailer of ivy had given way under his weight, and we saw by the light of a lantern the mark on the lawn where his heels had come down. That one dint in the short, green grass was the only material witness left of this inexplicable nocturnal flight.

Sherlock Holmes left the house alone, and only returned after eleven. He had obtained a large ordnance map of the neighbourhood, and this he brought into my room, where he laid it out on the bed, and, having balanced the lamp in the middle of it, he began to smoke over it, and occasionally to point out objects of interest with the reeking amber of his pipe.

"This case grows upon me, Watson," said he. "There are decidedly some points of interest in connection with it. In this early stage, I want you to realise those geographical features which may have a good deal to do with our investigation.

"Look at this map. This dark square is the Priory School. I'll put a pin in it. Now, this line is the main road. You see that it runs east and west past the school, and you see also that there is no side road for a mile either way. If these two folk passed away by road, it was *this* road."

"Exactly."

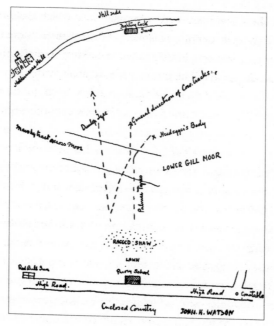

Holmes' map of the neighbourhood of the school.

"By a singular and happy chance, we are able to some extent to check what passed along this road during the night in question. At this point, where my pipe is now resting, a county constable was on duty from twelve to six. It is, as you perceive, the first cross-road on the east side. This man declares that he was not absent from his post for an instant, and he is positive that neither boy nor man could have gone that way unseen. I have spoken with this policeman tonight and he appears to me to be a perfectly reliable person. That blocks this end. We have now to deal with the other. There is an inn here, the Red Bull, the landlady of which was ill. She had sent to Mackleton for a doctor, but he did not arrive until morning, being absent at another case. The people at the inn were alert all night, awaiting his coming, and one or other of them seems to have continually had an eye upon the road. They declare that no one passed. If their evidence is good, then we are fortunate enough to be able to block the west, and also to be able to say that the fugitives did *not* use the road at all."

"But the bicycle?" I objected.

"Quite so. We will come to the bicycle presently. To continue our reasoning: if these people did not go by the road, they must have traversed the country to the north of the house or to the south of the house. That is certain. Let us weigh the one against the other. On the south of the house is, as you perceive, a large district of arable land, cut up into small fields, with stone walls between them. There, I admit that a bicycle is impossible. We can dismiss the idea. We turn to the country on the north. Here there lies a grove of trees, marked as the 'Ragged Shaw,' and on the farther side stretches a great rolling moor, Lower Gill Moor, extending for ten miles and sloping gradually upward. Here, at one side of this wilderness, is Holdernesse Hall, ten miles by road, but only six across the moor. It is a peculiarly desolate plain. A few moor farmers have small holdings, where they rear sheep and cattle. Except these, the plover and the curlew are the only inhabitants until you come to the Chesterfield high road. There is a church there, you see, a few cottages, and an inn. Beyond that the hills become precipitous. Surely it is here to the north that our quest must lie."

"But the bicycle?" I persisted.

"Well, well!" said Holmes, impatiently. "A good cyclist does not need a high road. The moor is intersected with paths, and the moon was at the full. Halloa! what is this?"

There was an agitated knock at the door, and an instant afterwards Dr. Huxtable was in the room. In his hand he held a blue cricket-cap with a white chevron on the peak.

"At last we have a clue!" he cried. "Thank heaven! at last we are on the dear boy's track! It is his cap."

"Where was it found?"

"In the van of the gipsies who camped on the moor. They left on Tuesday. Today the police traced them down and examined their caravan. This was found."

"How do they account for it?"

"They shuffled and lied—said that they found it on the moor on Tuesday morning. They know where he is, the rascals! Thank goodness, they are all safe under lock and key. Either the fear of the law or the Duke's purse will certainly get out of them all that they know."

"So far, so good," said Holmes, when the doctor had at last left the room. "It at least bears out the theory that it is on the side of the Lower Gill Moor that we must hope for results. The police have really done nothing locally, save the arrest of these gipsies. Look here, Watson! There is a watercourse across the moor. You see it marked here in the map. In some parts it widens into a morass. This is particularly so in the region between Holdernesse Hall and the school. It is vain to look elsewhere for tracks in this dry weather, but at *that* point there is certainly a chance of some record being left. I will call you early tomorrow morning, and you and I will try if we can throw some little light upon the mystery."

The day was just breaking when I woke to find the long, thin form of Holmes by my bedside. He was fully dressed, and had apparently already been out.

"I have done the lawn and the bicycle shed," said he. "I have also had a rumble through the Ragged Shaw. Now, Watson, there is cocoa ready in the next room. I must beg you to hurry, for we have a great day before us."

His eyes shone, and his cheek was flushed with the exhilaration of the master workman who sees his work lie ready before him. A very different Holmes, this active, alert man, from the introspective and pallid dreamer of Baker Street. I felt, as I looked upon that supple figure, alive with nervous energy, that it was indeed a strenuous day that awaited us.

And yet it opened in the blackest disappointment. With high hopes we struck across the peaty, russet moor, intersected with a thousand sheep paths, until we came to the broad, light-green belt which marked the morass between us and Holdernesse. Certainly, if the lad had gone homeward, he must have passed this, and he could not pass it without leaving his traces. But no sign of him or the German could be seen. With a darkening face my friend strode along the margin, eagerly observant of every muddy stain upon the mossy surface. Sheep-marks there were in profusion, and at one place, some miles down, cows had left their tracks. Nothing more.

"Check number one," said Holmes, looking gloomily over the rolling expanse of the moor. "There is another morass down yonder, and a narrow neck between. Halloa! halloa! halloa! what have we here?"

We had come on a small black ribbon of pathway. In the middle of it, clearly marked on the sodden soil, was the track of a bicycle.

"Hurrah!" I cried. "We have it."

But Holmes was shaking his head, and his face was puzzled and expectant rather than joyous.

"A bicycle, certainly, but not *the* bicycle," said he. "I am familiar with forty-two different impressions left by tyres. This, as you perceive, is a Dunlop, with a patch upon the outer cover. Heidegger's tyres were Palmer's, leaving longitudinal stripes. Aveling, the mathematical master, was sure upon the point. Therefore, it is not Heidegger's track."

"The boy's, then?"

"Possibly, if we could prove a bicycle to have been in his possession. But this we have utterly failed to do. This track, as you perceive, was made by a rider who was going from the direction of the school."

"Or towards it?"

"No, no, my dear Watson. The more deeply sunk impression is, of course, the hind wheel, upon which the weight rests. You perceive several places where it has passed across and obliterated the more shallow mark of the front one. It was undoubtedly heading away from the school. It may or may not be connected with our inquiry, but we will follow it backwards before we go any farther."

We did so, and at the end of a few hundred yards lost the tracks as we emerged from the boggy portion of the moor. Following the path backwards, we picked out another spot, where a spring trickled across it. Here, once again, was the mark of the bicycle, though nearly obliterated by the hoofs of cows. After that there was no sign, but the path ran right on into Ragged Shaw, the wood which backed on to the school. From this wood the cycle must have emerged. Holmes sat down on a boulder and rested his chin in his hands. I had smoked two cigarettes before he moved.

"Well, well," said he, at last. "It is, of course, possible that a cunning man might change the tyres of his bicycle in order to leave unfamiliar tracks. A criminal who was capable of such a thought is a man whom I should be proud to do business with. We will leave this question undecided and hark back to our morass again, for we have left a good deal unexplored."

We continued our systematic survey of the edge of the sodden portion of the moor, and soon our perseverance was gloriously rewarded. Right across the lower part of the bog lay a miry path. Holmes gave a cry of delight as he approached it. An impression like a fine bundle of telegraph wires ran down the centre of it. It was the Palmer tyres.

"Here is Herr Heidegger, sure enough!" cried Holmes, exultantly. "My reasoning seems to have been pretty sound, Watson."

"I congratulate you."

"But we have a long way still to go. Kindly walk clear of the path. Now let us follow the trail. I fear that it will not lead very far."

We found, however, as we advanced that this portion of the moor is intersected with soft patches, and, though we frequently lost sight of the track, we always succeeded in picking it up once more.

"Do you observe," said Holmes, "that the rider is now undoubtedly forcing the pace? There can be no doubt of it. Look at this impression, where you get both tyres clear. The one is as deep as the other. That can only mean that the rider is throwing his weight on to the handle-bar, as a man does when he is sprinting. By Jove! he has had a fall."

There was a broad, irregular smudge covering some yards of the track. Then there were a few footmarks, and the tyre reappeared once more.

"A side-slip," I suggested.

Holmes held up a crumpled branch of flowering gorse. To my horror I perceived that the yellow blossoms were all dabbled with crimson. On the path, too, and among the heather were dark stains of clotted blood.

"Bad!" said Holmes. "Bad! Stand clear, Watson! Not an unnecessary footstep! What do I read here? He fell wounded—he stood up—he remounted—he proceeded. But there is no other track. Cattle on this side path. He was surely not gored by a bull? Impossible! But I see no traces of anyone else. We must push on, Watson. Surely, with stains as well as the track to guide us, he cannot escape us now."

Our search was not a very long one. The tracks of the tyre began to curve fantastically upon the wet and shining path. Suddenly, as I looked ahead, the gleam of metal caught my eye from amid the thick gorse-bushes. Out of them we dragged a bicycle, Palmer-tyred, one pedal bent, and the whole front of it horribly smeared and slobbered with blood. On the other side of the bushes a shoe was projecting. We ran round, and there lay the unfortunate rider. He was a tall man, full-bearded, with spectacles, one glass of which had been knocked out. The cause of his death was a frightful blow upon the head, which had crushed in part of his skull. That he could have gone on after receiving such an injury said much for the vitality and courage of the man. He wore shoes, but no socks, and his open coat disclosed a nightshirt beneath it. It was undoubtedly the German master.

Holmes turned the body over reverently, and examined it with great attention. He then sat in deep thought for a time, and I could see by his ruffled brow that this grim discovery had not, in his opinion, advanced us much in our inquiry.

"It is a little difficult to know what to do, Watson," said he, at last. "My own inclinations are to push this inquiry on, for we have already lost so much time that we cannot afford to waste another hour. On the other hand, we are bound to inform the police of the discovery, and to see that this poor fellow's body is looked after."

"I could take a note back."

"But I need your company and assistance. Wait a bit! There is a fellow cutting peat up yonder. Bring him over here, and he will guide the police."

I brought the peasant across, and Holmes dispatched the frightened man with a note to Dr. Huxtable.

"Now, Watson," said he, "we have picked up two clues this morning. One is the bicycle with the Palmer tyre, and we see what that has led to. The other is the bicycle with the patched Dunlop. Before we start to investigate that, let us try to realise what we *do* know, so as to make the most of it, and to separate the essential from the accidental.

"First of all, I wish to impress upon you that the boy certainly left of his own free-will. He got down from his window and he went off, either alone or with someone. That is sure."

I assented.

"Well, now, let us turn to this unfortunate German master. The boy was fully dressed when he fled. Therefore, he foresaw what he would do. But the German went without his socks. He certainly acted on very short notice."

"Undoubtedly."

"Why did he go? Because, from his bedroom window, he saw the flight of the boy, because he wished to overtake him and bring him back. He seized his bicycle, pursued the lad, and in pursuing him met his death."

"So it would seem."

"Now I come to the critical part of my argument. The natural action of a man in pursuing a little boy would be to run after him. He would know that he could overtake him. But the German does not do so. He turns to his bicycle. I am told that he was an excellent cyclist. He would not do this, if he did not see that the boy had some swift means of escape."

"The other bicycle."

"Let us continue our reconstruction. He meets his death five miles from the school—not by a bullet, mark you, which even a lad might conceivably discharge, but by a savage blow dealt by a vigorous arm. The lad, then, *had* a companion in his flight. And the flight was a swift one, since it took five miles before an expert cyclist could overtake them. Yet we survey the ground round the scene of the tragedy. What do we find? A few cattle-tracks, nothing more. I took a wide sweep round, and there is no path within fifty yards. Another cyclist could have had nothing to do with the actual murder, nor were there any human footmarks."

"Holmes," I cried, "this is impossible."

"Admirable!" he said. "A most illuminating remark. It *is* impossible as I state it, and therefore I must in some respect have stated it wrong. Yet you saw for yourself. Can you suggest any fallacy?"

"He could not have fractured his skull in a fall?"

"In a morass, Watson?"

"I am at my wits' end."

"Tut, tut, we have solved some worse problems. At least we have plenty of material, if we can only use it. Come, then, and, having exhausted the Palmer, let us see what the Dunlop with the patched cover has to offer us."

We picked up the track and followed it onward for some distance, but soon the moor rose into a long, heather-tufted curve, and we left the watercourse behind us. No further help from tracks could be hoped for. At the spot where we saw the last of the Dunlop tyre it might equally have led to Holdernesse Hall, the stately towers of which rose some miles to our left, or to a low, grey village which lay in front of us and marked the position of the Chesterfield high road.

As we approached the forbidding and squalid inn, with the sign of a game-cock above the door, Holmes gave a sudden groan, and clutched me by the shoulder to save himself from falling. He had had one of those violent strains of the ankle which leave a man helpless. With difficulty he limped up to the door, where a squat, dark, elderly man was smoking a black clay pipe.

"How are you, Mr. Reuben Hayes?" said Holmes.

"Who are you, and how do you get my name so pat?" the country-man answered, with a suspicious flash of a pair of cunning eyes.

"Well, it's printed on the board above your head. It's easy to see a man who is master of his own house. I suppose you haven't such a thing as a carriage in your stables?"

"No, I have not."

"I can hardly put my foot to the ground."

"Don't put it to the ground."

"But I can't walk."

"Well, then hop."

Mr. Reuben Hayes's manner was far from gracious, but Holmes took it with admirable good-humour.

"Look here, my man," said he. "This is really rather an awkward fix for me. I don't mind how I get on."

"Neither do I," said the morose landlord.

"The matter is very important. I would offer you a sovereign for the use of a bicycle."

The landlord pricked up his ears.

"Where do you want to go?"

"To Holdernesse Hall."

"Pals of the Dook, I suppose?" said the landlord, surveying our mud-stained garments with ironical eyes.

Holmes laughed good-naturedly.

"He'll be glad to see us, anyhow."

"Why?"

"Because we bring him news of his lost son."

The landlord gave a very visible start.

"What, you're on his track?"

"He has been heard of in Liverpool. They expect to get him every hour."

Again a swift change passed over the heavy, unshaven face. His manner was suddenly genial.

"I've less reason to wish the Dook well than most men," said he, "for I was head coachman once, and cruel bad he treated me. It was him that sacked me without a character on the word of a lying corn-chandler. But I'm glad to hear that the young lord was heard of in Liverpool, and I'll help you to take the news to the Hall."

"Thank you," said Holmes. "We'll have some food first. Then you can bring round the bicycle."

"I haven't got a bicycle."

Holmes held up a sovereign.

"I tell you, man, that I haven't got one. I'll let you have two horses as far as the Hall."

"Well, well," said Holmes, "we'll talk about it when we've had something to eat."

When we were left alone in the stone-flagged kitchen, it was astonishing how rapidly that sprained ankle recovered. It was nearly nightfall, and we had eaten nothing since early morning, so that we spent some time over our meal. Holmes was lost in thought, and once or twice he walked over to the window and stared earnestly out. It opened on to a squalid courtyard. In the far corner was a smithy, where a grimy lad was at work. On the other side were the stables. Holmes had sat down again after one of these excursions, when he suddenly sprang out of his chair with a loud exclamation.

"By heaven, Watson, I believe that I've got it!" he cried. "Yes, yes, it must be so. Watson, do you remember seeing any cow-tracks today?"

"Yes, several."

"Where?"

"Well, everywhere. They were at the morass, and again on the path, and again near where poor Heidegger met his death."

"Exactly. Well, now, Watson, how many cows did you see on the moor?"

"I don't remember seeing any."

"Strange, Watson, that we should see tracks all along our line, but never a cow on the whole moor. Very strange, Watson, eh?"

"Yes, it is strange."

"Now, Watson, make an effort, throw your mind back. Can you see those tracks upon the path?"

"Yes, I can."

"Can you recall that the tracks were sometimes like that, Watson,"— he arranged a number of breadcrumbs in this fashion—: : : : :—"and sometimes like this"—: . : . : . : .—"and occasionally like this"—. ·. ·. ·. "Can you remember that?"

"No, I cannot."

"But I can. I could swear to it. However, we will go back at our leisure and verify it. What a blind beetle I have been, not to draw my conclusion."

"And what is your conclusion?"

"Only that it is a remarkable cow which walks, canters, and gallops. By George! Watson, it was no brain of a country publican that thought out such a blind as that. The coast seems to be clear, save for that lad in the smithy. Let us slip out and see what we can see."

There were two rough-haired, unkempt horses in the tumble-down stable. Holmes raised the hind leg of one of them and laughed aloud.

"Old shoes, but newly shod—old shoes, but new nails. This case deserves to be a classic. Let us go across to the smithy."

The lad continued his work without regarding us. I saw Holmes's eye darting to right and left among the litter of iron and wood which was scattered about the floor. Suddenly, however, we heard a step behind us, and there was the landlord, his heavy eyebrows drawn over his savage eyes, his swarthy features convulsed with passion. He held a short, metal-headed stick in his hand, and he advanced in so menacing a fashion that I was right glad to feel the revolver in my pocket.

"You infernal spies!" the man cried. "What are you doing there?"

"Why, Mr. Reuben Hayes," said Holmes, coolly, "one might think that you were afraid of our finding something out."

The man mastered himself with a violent effort, and his grim mouth loosened into a false laugh, which was more menacing than his frown.

"You're welcome to all you can find out in my smithy," said he. "But look here, mister, I don't care for folk poking about my place without my leave, so the sooner you pay your score and get out of this the better I shall be pleased."

"All right, Mr. Hayes, no harm meant," said Holmes. "We have been having a look at your horses, but I think I'll walk, after all. It's not far, I believe."

"Not more than two miles to the Hall gates. That's the road to the left." He watched us with sullen eyes until we had left his premises.

We did not go very far along the road, for Holmes stopped the instant that the curve hid us from the landlord's view.

"We were warm, as the children say, at that inn," said he. "I seem to grow colder every step that I take away from it. No, no, I can't possibly leave it."

"I am convinced," said I, "that this Reuben Hayes knows all about it. A more self-evident villain I never saw."

"Oh! he impressed you in that way, did he? There are the horses, there is the smithy. Yes, it is an interesting place, this Fighting Cock. I think we shall have another look at it in an unobtrusive way."

A long, sloping hillside, dotted with grey limestone boulders, stretched behind us. We had turned off the road, and were making our way up the hill, when, looking in the direction of Holdernesse Hall, I saw a cyclist coming swiftly along.

"Get down, Watson!" cried Holmes, with a heavy hand upon my shoulder. We had hardly sunk from view when the man flew past us on the road. Amid a rolling cloud of dust, I caught a glimpse of a pale, agitated face—a face with horror in every lineament, the mouth open, the eyes staring wildly in front. It was like some strange caricature of the dapper James Wilder whom we had seen the night before.

"The Duke's secretary!" cried Holmes. "Come, Watson, let us see what he does."

We scrambled from rock to rock, until in a few moments we had made our way to a point from which we could see the front door of the inn. Wilder's bicycle was leaning against the wall beside it. No one was moving about the house, nor could we catch a glimpse of any faces at the windows. Slowly the twilight crept down as the sun sank behind the high towers of Holdernesse Hall. Then, in the gloom, we saw the two side-lamps of a trap light up in the stable-yard of the inn, and shortly afterwards heard the rattle of hoofs, as it wheeled out into the road and tore off at a furious pace in the direction of Chesterfield.

"What do you make of that, Watson?" Holmes whispered.

"It looks like a flight."

"A single man in a dog-cart, so far as I could see. Well, it certainly was not Mr. James Wilder, for there he is at the door."

A red square of light had sprung out of the darkness. In the middle of it was the black figure of the secretary, his head advanced, peering out into the night. It was evident that he was expecting someone. Then at last there were steps in the road, a second figure was visible for an instant against the light, the door shut, and all was black once more. Five minutes later a lamp was lit in a room upon the first floor.

"It seems to be a curious class of custom that is done by the Fighting Cock," said Holmes.

"The bar is on the other side."

"Quite so. These are what one may call the private guests. Now, what in the world is Mr. James Wilder doing in that den at this hour of night, and who is the companion who comes to meet him there? Come, Watson, we must really take a risk and try to investigate this a little more closely."

Together we stole down to the road and crept across to the door of the inn. The bicycle still leaned against the wall. Holmes struck a match and held it to the back wheel, and I heard him chuckle as the light fell upon a patched Dunlop tyre. Up above us was the lighted window.

"I must have a peep through that, Watson. If you bend your back and support yourself upon the wall, I think that I can manage."

An instant later, his feet were on my shoulders, but he was hardly up before he was down again.

"Come, my friend," said he, "our day's work has been quite long enough. I think that we have gathered all that we can. It's a long walk to the school, and the sooner we get started the better."

He hardly opened his lips during that weary trudge across the moor, nor would he enter the school when he reached it, but went on to Mackleton Station, whence he could send some telegrams. Late at night I heard him consoling Dr. Huxtable, prostrated by the tragedy of his master's death, and later still he entered my room as alert and vigorous as he had been when he started in the morning. "All goes well, my friend," said he. "I promise that before tomorrow evening we shall have reached the solution of the mystery."

At eleven o'clock next morning my friend and I were walking up the famous yew avenue of Holdernesse Hall. We were ushered through the magnificent Elizabethan doorway and into his Grace's study. There we found Mr. James Wilder, demure and courtly, but with some trace of that wild terror of the night before still lurking in his furtive eyes and in his twitching features.

"You have come to see his Grace? I am sorry, but the fact is that the Duke is far from well. He has been very much upset by the tragic news. We received a telegram from Dr. Huxtable yesterday afternoon, which told us of your discovery."

"I must see the Duke, Mr. Wilder."

"But he is in his room."

"Then I must go to his room."

"I believe he is in his bed."

"I will see him there."

Holmes's cold and inexorable manner showed the secretary that it was useless to argue with him.

"Very good, Mr. Holmes, I will tell him that you are here."

After an hour's delay, the great nobleman appeared. His face was more cadaverous than ever, his shoulders had rounded, and he seemed to me to be an altogether older man than he had been the morning before. He greeted us with a stately courtesy and seated himself at his desk, his red beard streaming down on the table.

"Well, Mr. Holmes?" said he.

But my friend's eyes were fixed upon the secretary, who stood by his master's chair.

"I think, your Grace, that I could speak more freely in Mr. Wilder's absence."

The man turned a shade paler and cast a malignant glance at Holmes.

"If your Grace wishes—"

"Yes, yes, you had better go. Now, Mr. Holmes, what have you to say?"

My friend waited until the door had closed behind the retreating secretary.

"The fact is, your Grace," said he, "that my colleague, Dr. Watson, and myself had an assurance from Dr. Huxtable that a reward had been offered in this case. I should like to have this confirmed from your own lips."

"Certainly, Mr. Holmes."

"It amounted, if I am correctly informed, to five thousand pounds to anyone who will tell you where your son is?"

"Exactly."

"And another thousand to the man who will name the person or persons who keep him in custody?"

"Exactly."

"Under the latter heading is included, no doubt, not only those who may have taken him away, but also those who conspire to keep him in his present position?"

"Yes, yes," cried the Duke, impatiently. "If you do your work well, Mr. Sherlock Holmes, you will have no reason to complain of niggardly treatment."

My friend rubbed his thin hands together with an appearance of avidity which was a surprise to me, who knew his frugal tastes.

"I fancy that I see your Grace's cheque-book upon the table," said he. "I should be glad if you would make me out a cheque for six thousand pounds. It would be as well, perhaps, for you to cross it. The Capital and Counties Bank, Oxford Street branch are my agents."

His Grace sat very stern and upright in his chair and looked stonily at my friend.

"Is this a joke, Mr. Holmes? It is hardly a subject for pleasantry."

"Not at all, your Grace. I was never more earnest in my life."

"What do you mean, then?"

"I mean that I have earned the reward. I know where your son is, and I know some, at least, of those who are holding him."

The Duke's beard had turned more aggressively red than ever against his ghastly white face.

"Where is he?" he gasped.

"He is, or was last night, at the Fighting Cock Inn, about two miles from your park gate."

The Duke fell back in his chair.

"And whom do you accuse?"

Sherlock Holmes's answer was an astounding one. He stepped swiftly forward and touched the Duke upon the shoulder.

"I accuse *you*," said he. "And now, your Grace, I'll trouble you for that cheque."

Never shall I forget the Duke's appearance as he sprang up and clawed with his hands, like one who is sinking into an abyss. Then, with an extraordinary effort of aristocratic self-command, he sat down and sank his face in his hands. It was some minutes before he spoke.

"How much do you know?" he asked at last, without raising his head.

"I saw you together last night."

"Does anyone else beside your friend know?"

"I have spoken to no one."

The Duke took a pen in his quivering fingers and opened his cheque-book.

"I shall be as good as my word, Mr. Holmes. I am about to write your cheque, however unwelcome the information which you have gained may be to me. When the offer was first made, I little thought the turn which events might take. But you and your friend are men of discretion, Mr. Holmes?"

"I hardly understand your Grace."

"I must put it plainly, Mr. Holmes. If only you two know of this incident, there is no reason why it should go any farther. I think twelve thousand pounds is the sum that I owe you, is it not?"

But Holmes smiled and shook his head.

"I fear, your Grace, that matters can hardly be arranged so easily. There is the death of this schoolmaster to be accounted for."

"But James knew nothing of that. You cannot hold him responsible for that. It was the work of this brutal ruffian whom he had the misfortune to employ."

"I must take the view, your Grace, that when a man embarks upon a crime, he is morally guilty of any other crime which may spring from it."

"Morally, Mr. Holmes. No doubt you are right. But surely not in the eyes of the law. A man cannot be condemned for a murder at which he was not present, and which he loathes and abhors as much as you do. The instant that he heard of it he made a complete confession to me, so filled was he with horror and remorse. He lost not an hour in breaking entirely with the murderer. Oh, Mr. Holmes, you must save him—you must save him! I tell you that you must save him!" The Duke had dropped the last attempt at self-command, and was pacing the room with a convulsed face and with his clenched hands raving in the air. At last he mastered himself and sat down once more at his desk. "I appreciate your conduct in coming here before you spoke to anyone else," said he. "At least, we may take counsel how far we can minimise this hideous scandal."

"Exactly," said Holmes. "I think, your Grace, that this can only be done by absolute frankness between us. I am disposed to help your Grace to the best of my ability, but, in order to do so, I must understand to the last detail how the matter stands. I realise that your words applied to Mr. James Wilder, and that he is not the murderer."

"No, the murderer has escaped."

Sherlock Holmes smiled demurely.

"Your Grace can hardly have heard of any small reputation which I possess, or you would not imagine that it is so easy to escape me. Mr. Reuben Hayes was arrested at Chesterfield, on my information, at eleven o'clock last night. I had a telegram from the head of the local police before I left the school this morning."

The Duke leaned back in his chair and stared with amazement at my friend.

"You seem to have powers that are hardly human," said he. "So Reuben Hayes is taken? I am right glad to hear it, if it will not react upon the fate of James."

"Your secretary?"

"No, sir, my son."

It was Holmes's turn to look astonished.

"I confess that this is entirely new to me, your Grace. I must beg you to be more explicit."

"I will conceal nothing from you. I agree with you that complete frankness, however painful it may be to me, is the best policy in this desperate situation to which James's folly and jealousy have reduced us. When I was a very young man, Mr. Holmes, I loved with such a love as comes only once in a lifetime. I offered the lady marriage, but she refused it on the grounds that such a match might mar my career. Had she lived, I would certainly never have married anyone else. She died, and left this one child, whom for her sake I have cherished and cared for. I could not acknowledge the paternity to the world, but I gave him the best of educations, and since he came to manhood I have kept him near my person. He surmised my secret, and has presumed ever since upon the claim which he has upon me, and upon his power of provoking a scandal which would be abhorrent to me. His presence had something to do with the unhappy issue of my marriage. Above all, he hated my young legitimate heir from the first with a persistent hatred. You may well ask me why, under these circumstances, I still kept James under my roof. I answer that it was because I could see his mother's face in his, and that for her dear sake there was no end to my long-suffering. All her pretty ways too—there was not one of them which he could not suggest and bring back to my memory. I *could* not send him away. But I feared so much lest he should do Arthur—that is, Lord Saltire—a mischief, that I dispatched him for safety to Dr. Huxtable's school.

"James came into contact with this fellow Hayes, because the man was a tenant of mine, and James acted as agent. The fellow was a rascal from the beginning, but, in some extraordinary way, James became intimate with him. He had always a taste for low company. When James determined to kidnap Lord Saltire, it was of this man's service that he availed himself. You remember that I wrote to Arthur upon that last day. Well, James opened the letter and inserted a note asking Arthur to meet him in a little wood called the Ragged Shaw, which is near to the school. He used the Duchess's name, and in that way got the boy to come. That evening James bicycled over—I am telling you what he has himself confessed to me—and he told Arthur, whom he met in the wood, that his mother longed to see him, that she was awaiting him on the moor, and that if he would come back into the wood at midnight he would find a man with a horse, who would take him to her. Poor Arthur fell into the trap. He came to the appointment, and found this fellow Hayes with a led pony. Arthur mounted, and they set off together. It appears—though this James only heard yesterday—that they were pursued, that Hayes struck the pursuer with his stick, and that the man died of his injuries. Hayes brought Arthur to his public-house, the Fighting Cock, where he was confined in an upper room, under the care of Mrs. Hayes, who is a kindly woman, but entirely under the control of her brutal husband.

"Well, Mr. Holmes, that was the state of affairs when I first saw you two days ago. I had no more idea of the truth than you. You will ask me what was James's motive in doing such a deed. I answer that there was a great deal which was unreasoning and fanatical in the hatred which he bore my heir. In his view he should himself have been heir of all my estates, and he deeply resented those social laws which made it impossible. At the same time, he had a definite motive also. He was eager that I should break the entail, and he was of opinion that it lay in my power to do so. He intended to make a bargain with me—to restore Arthur if I would break the entail, and so make it possible for the estate to be left to him by will. He knew well that I should never willingly invoke the aid of the police against him. I say that he would have proposed such a bargain to me, but he did not actually do so, for events moved too quickly for him, and he had not time to put his plans into practice.

"What brought all his wicked scheme to wreck was your discovery of this man Heidegger's dead body. James was seized with horror at the news. It came to us yesterday, as we sat together in this study. Dr. Huxtable had sent a telegram. James was so overwhelmed with grief and agitation that my suspicions, which had never been entirely absent, rose instantly to a certainty, and I taxed him with the deed. He made a complete voluntary confession. Then he implored me to keep his secret for three days longer, so as to give his wretched accomplice a chance of saving his guilty life. I yielded—as I have always yielded—to his prayers, and instantly James hurried off to the Fighting Cock to warn Hayes and give him the means of flight. I could not go there by daylight without provoking comment, but as soon as night fell I hurried off to see my dear Arthur. I found him safe and well, but horrified beyond expression by the dreadful deed he had witnessed. In deference to my promise, and much against my will, I consented to leave him there for three days, under the charge of Mrs. Hayes, since it was evident that it was impossible to inform the police where he was without telling them also who was the murderer, and I could not see how that murderer could be punished without ruin to my unfortunate James. You asked for frankness, Mr. Holmes, and I have taken you at your word, for I have now told you everything without an attempt at circumlocution or concealment. Do you in turn be as frank with me."

"I will," said Holmes. "In the first place, your Grace, I am bound to tell you that you have placed yourself in a most serious position in the eyes of the law. You have condoned a felony, and you have aided the escape of a murderer, for I cannot doubt that any money which was taken by James Wilder to aid his accomplice in his flight came from your Grace's purse."

The Duke bowed his assent.

"This is, indeed, a most serious matter. Even more culpable in my opinion, your Grace, is your attitude towards your younger son. You leave him in this den for three days."

"Under solemn promises—"

"What are promises to such people as these? You have no guarantee that he will not be spirited away again. To humour your guilty elder son, you have exposed your innocent younger son to imminent and unnecessary danger. It was a most unjustifiable action."

The proud lord of Holdernesse was not accustomed to be so rated in his own ducal hall. The blood flushed into his high forehead, but his conscience held him dumb.

"I will help you, but on one condition only. It is that you ring for the footman and let me give such orders as I like."

Without a word, the Duke pressed the electric bell. A servant entered.

"You will be glad to hear," said Holmes, "that your young master is found. It is the Duke's desire that the carriage shall go at once to the Fighting Cock Inn to bring Lord Saltire home.

"Now," said Holmes, when the rejoicing lackey had disappeared, "having secured the future, we can afford to be more lenient with the past. I am not in an official position, and there is no reason, so long as the ends of justice are served, why I should disclose all that I know. As to Hayes, I say nothing. The gallows awaits him, and I would do nothing to save him from it. What he will divulge I cannot tell, but I have no doubt that your Grace could make him understand that it is to his interest to be silent. From the police point of view he will have kidnapped the boy for the purpose of ransom. If they do not themselves find it out, I see no reason why I should prompt them to take a broader point of view. I would warn your Grace, however, that the continued presence of Mr. James Wilder in your household can only lead to misfortune."

"I understand that, Mr. Holmes, and it is already settled that he shall leave me forever, and go to seek his fortune in Australia."

"In that case, your Grace, since you have yourself stated that any unhappiness in your married life was caused by his presence I would suggest that you make such amends as you can to the Duchess, and that you try to resume those relations which have been so unhappily interrupted."

"That also I have arranged, Mr. Holmes. I wrote to the Duchess this morning."

"In that case," said Holmes, rising, "I think that my friend and I can congratulate ourselves upon several most happy results from our little visit to the North. There is one other small point upon which I desire some light. This fellow Hayes had shod his horses with shoes which counterfeited the tracks of cows. Was it from Mr. Wilder that he learned so extraordinary a device?"

The Duke stood in thought for a moment, with a look of intense surprise on his face. Then he opened a door and showed us into a large room furnished as a museum. He led the way to a glass case in a corner, and pointed to the inscription.

"'These shoes,'" it ran, "were dug up in the moat of Holdernesse Hall. They are for the use of horses, but they are shaped below with a cloven foot of iron, so as to throw pursuers off the track. They are supposed to have belonged to some of the marauding Barons of Holdernesse in the Middle Ages."

Holmes opened the case, and moistening his finger he passed it along the shoe. A thin film of recent mud was left upon his skin.

"Thank you," said he, as he replaced the glass. "It is the second most interesting object that I have seen in the North."

"And the first?"

Holmes folded up his cheque and placed it carefully in his notebook. "I am a poor man," said he, as he patted it affectionately, and thrust it into the depths of his inner pocket.

THE MISSING UNDERGRADUATE

Henry Wade

Henry Wade was the writing name of one of the most interesting and accomplished detective novelists of the Golden Age; in his other life, he was Major Sir Henry Lancelot Aubrey-Fletcher, sixth baronet, KStJ, CVO, DSO (1887–1969). He was a pupil at Eton College (as was his great-grandson Harry, a contemporary and close friend of the present Prince of Wales) and studied at New College, Oxford prior to joining the Grenadier Guards, with whom he fought during both world wars. As a member of the landed gentry, when he wrote a country house mystery—as in novels such as *The Hanging Captain* (1932), he did so with an insider's authority and understanding.

Wade's impressive first novel, *The Verdict of You All* (1926) launched his career as a novelist. Because he did not need to write for money, he didn't fall into the trap of over-productivity; nor did he make the mistake of writing formulaic series books. His principal detective character, Detective Inspector Poole, is a talented puzzle-solver, but he is no maverick or genius and occasionally he makes mistakes. Wade's humanity and compassion are recurrent features of his writing, most notably in the stunning police novel *Lonely Magdalen* (1940). He published two collections of short stories; this one, which features Poole, appeared in *Policeman's Lot* (1933).

A s THE EXPRESS NEARED OXFORD AND BEGAN TO SLOW DOWN, Detective-Inspector John Poole gazed eagerly out of the right-hand window in search of the familiar landmarks. He had not been back to Oxford since he "came down" in 1921; a year later he had joined the Metropolitan Police, and hard work, combined with settled policy, had cut him off from nearly all his old associations.

Now he was coming down on duty. A message had reached Scotland Yard that morning, asking for a detective to be sent down to investigate the disappearance of an undergraduate of St. Peter's College, and Superintendent Wylde, aware of Poole's early training, had thought that his local knowledge might prove useful.

Poole knew nothing more of the case than he had seen in the papers, which had treated as a young man's escapade the disappearance of Gerald Catling four days previously, but now, apparently, the college authorities were beginning to take an alarmist view of the occurrence, and, presumably doubting the capacity of the city police had applied for help from headquarters.

Ah, there they were, the "dreaming spires" Magdalen's tower on the right—its modest counterpart, Merton, farther to the left—St. Mary's—in the foreground the old castle from which Queen Matilda had fled across the snow in 1141—behind it "Old Tom," the magnificent gate-tower of Christ Church, a handsome king lording it among his court of lovely princesses.

The train slowed down abruptly. Poole swung his small suitcase from the rack and within five minutes was presenting himself to the porter of St. Peter's and asking for the warden. The dignified official looked suspiciously at his card, and with obvious reluctance, after directing him to place his bag out of the way of the young gentlemen's bicycles, led the way into Bacchus Quad.

"The warden is indisposed," he threw over his shoulder. "Mr. Luddingham will see you."

Poole gasped. The warden of St. Peter's he had known vaguely by sight, and in his turn had been unknown. But Luddingham, the dean, had been his own lecturer in Constitutional Law. With the Oxford tradition of long memory, there was not the faintest chance of the dean failing to recognise him. With mingled feelings of shyness and pride, Poole followed his guide up the centre staircase of the quad to a doorway on the first floor, over which was written, in white letters on a small black tablet: "Mr. Luddingham." Leaving the detective on the landing, the porter went in with his card, returning at once with an invitation to enter.

The dean was standing with his back to a large open fireplace, in which a huge log of fir spluttered blue flames up the vast chimney. Not a sign of surprise or recognition was visible upon his pale, clean-shaven face. He waived to a chair.

"Good-morning, inspector," he said. "Good of you to come so quickly. Have they told you anything about this business?"

"Nothing, sir. I've seen the papers—that's all."

"And that's all wrong, needless to say. I'll give you the facts as I know them; then you can ask questions. Smoke if you want to."

His hands clasped behind his back, his grey eyes fixed upon the angle of ceiling and wall opposite him, and raising himself from time to time on to his toes, the dean gave forth his information in exactly the same dry, succinct manner as he employed in the delivery of a lecture upon the work of Bagehot or Stubbs.

"Gerald Trefusis Catling came up to this college from Harrow in the Michaelmas term of last year, 1928. He is the only son of Sir John Trefusis Catling, of Gardham Manor, Wakestone, Yorkshire, and his age is nineteen years and ten months. He has passed Moderations and is now reading for his Final School.

"On Friday last he did not return to college before twelve; his absence was reported to me in the ordinary course by the head porter. He did not attend roll call the following morning, and after making some inquiries from his tutor and some of his friends, I telephoned to his father at the House of Commons—where he represents the Wakestone division in the Conservative interest. His father replied that he knew nothing of his son's movements and that in all probability his absence was some form of practical joke. I should say that the boy has a leaning towards that form of humour and has on more than one occasion in his year and a half of residence been at issue with both the college and University authorities in consequence thereof.

"When Saturday night passed and he still did not return, I asked Sir John to come down here. He did so and was still inclined to treat the matter lightly, refusing any suggestion of reference to the police. On Monday evening, however, I received a letter from Lady Catling, written from Wakestone, saying that she was seriously alarmed, that, though her son was certainly fond of practical jokes, she was quite sure that he would not go to the length of frightening her in the way that his prolonged and unexplained absence from college must inevitably do, and asking me to take more active steps to find him.

"I again telephoned to Sir John, late last night, asking for his concurrence to my calling in the help of the city police; he replied that if the thing was to be done at all, it had better be done thoroughly, and asked me to communicate direct with Scotland Yard. He explained that he had to go over to France by the early boat train, and would not, therefore, be able to take any action in the matter himself. He gave me full authority to act as I thought fit, and an address in Paris to which to write. I telephoned to Scotland Yard first thing this morning, with the result that you know."

Poole had jotted down some notes as Mr. Luddingham's lecture proceeded; after finishing them, he thought for a moment, and then asked:

"Was Mr. Catling known to be in any trouble, serious or slight?"

The dean shook his head.

"The last word I should apply to him—he didn't know the meaning of it, I should say."

"Not in debt?"

"Not more than fifty per cent, of the members of this college are—a few tailors' and photographers' bills, perhaps!"

"No enemies?"

"Not serious. Of course, he was a nuisance at times, with his practical jokes." Poole gathered the impression that the missing undergraduate had been rather a thorn in the flesh of his dean.

"When was he last seen?"

Before Mr. Luddingham could answer, there was a knock at the door, and in response to his reply, a tall, gaunt man of about sixty, with drooping, tawny moustache, and wearing a gown and mortarboard, came in.

"Oh, Luddingham," he said, "I just called in on my way back from my lecture, to ask if you'd got any news of Catling."

"None, I'm afraid, Cayzer," replied the dean. "No doubt he'll be back today, though." He did not attempt to introduce his two visitors to one another. The tall don looked nervously from one to the other, fidgeting with his gown.

"So strange," he said, "so sad—a charming, high-spirited boy!" He paused, sighed heavily, and, turning abruptly, strode out of the room.

Poole looked inquiringly at the dean.

"Professor Cayzer," said the latter, evidently loath to bring in any matter that he considered unessential. "Chair of Egyptology. A member of this college. You asked when Catling was last seen; his scout took lunch to his rooms at the usual time—one-thirty; he was there then, and nobody seems to have seen him after that. He was not seen to leave college, but it is perfectly possible for him to have done so unnoticed, if the porter was engaged—telephoning or making an entry in his book."

"Had he a car?"

"Yes, at the City Motor Company's garage, in Gloucester Street, but he didn't use it that day—or subsequently."

"Nothing was seen of him at the station?"

"I haven't inquired; that is more in the line of the police."

After obtaining from Mr. Luddingham an approximate estimate of Catling's debts and a few further details about his habits and characteristics, Poole rose to his feet.

"If I may have a recent photograph, sir, and see one or two of Mr. Catling's friends?"

The dean thought for a minute.

"Yes," he said; "I'll send for Monash—he'll be back from his logic lecture by now. He'll put you on to others, and get a photograph. You'd better have my third room—I don't want more commotion about this business than is absolutely necessary. Perhaps you would ask anyone you interview to keep quiet about it—though I don't suppose they will!"

Ten minutes later, Poole, in the tiny "thirder," which the dean had fitted up as a supernumerary study, was interviewing Crispin Monash, young Catling's contemporary, and particular friend. Monash was a rowing man—a robust, unimaginative person, who was able to give Poole just the bare, unadorned facts that he required.

From his account, it appeared that Catling was not quite the featherbrained young man that Poole had pictured from the dean's description. He certainly was fond of ragging people, and rather fancied himself as an impersonator—he was already a prominent member of the O.U.D.S.—but he was also quite serious in his determination to take a good degree, and to follow in his father's footsteps as an administrator. Monash thought that his friend had been rather worried about his financial affairs lately, but not to the extent of doing anything desperate about them.

"He didn't give you any indication of something unusual being up on Friday?" asked the detective.

"Nothing. Don't think I saw him, except at 'Rollers.' We didn't as a rule see much of each other before tea—taking different schools, and in the afternoon I row, and he doesn't do anything serious—squash occasionally. I haven't the faintest idea what he's up to."

"Tell me quite frankly, sir: do you think this is either a practical joke or suicide?"

Monash gave the question careful consideration.

"No, I don't," he said. "I don't believe he'd carry a joke so far. As to suicide, he's the last chap—well, not the last, perhaps, but he's not that sort. I don't know what to think!"

"What about friends—is he liked?"

"Oh, yes; popular sort of chap. Willan—running blue—Collerack, and Vace are his particular friends, I should say—and myself. They'll tell you much what I have."

"Enemies?"

"Don't think so. Of course, some men didn't care for him—he used to rise the saps rather—but nothing serious."

"And the dons?"

"There again, the younger ones liked him—he amused them; but the older ones—the dean, and so on—were rather bored by him—though he went a bit too far, I suppose."

"One of the older ones seems to have liked him," said Poole. "Professor Cayzer was inquiring about him just now, when I was with the dean—he seemed upset about him."

"Old Cat-Gut?" Monash looked surprised. "I should have thought Gerry bored him more than any of 'em! The old chap's got a private museum in his rooms, and Gerry used to rag him about it—pretend he was fearfully keen on some dry subject—Cayzer always fell for it—he's a bit potty, I think—and then Gerry'd gradually pull his leg harder and harder, till at last the old chap couldn't help tumbling to it. I should have thought he rather barred him."

"Apparently not, sir. One does find that; old people rather like being teased by young ones, if it's not done maliciously. Now I must see some of his other friends. Can you get hold of them for me?"

For the next hour Poole listened to the views of Messrs. Willan, Collerack, and Vace, but apart from a statement by the first that he believed Gerry Catling had gone on a tour with a company that had been at the theatre last week, and with two of whose members he had struck up an enthusiastic friendship, nothing significant emerged. It was evidently time to substitute looking for listening. In response to the detective's request, Mr. Luddingham sent for Gerald Catling's scout, Pelfett, and instructed him to show Inspector Poole Mr. Catling's rooms and give him any information he required.

The two minutes' walk from the dean's rooms to those of Mr. Catling, in New Quad, were sufficient to reveal Pelfett's opinion of his charge. The elderly scout exactly represented the type that Poole had sketched to Monash—he snarled about the young gentleman's habit of teasing him, but evidently had a genuine fondness for him. He thought it quite obvious that Mr. Catling had absented himself with the sole object of irritating the dean—had he not already succeeded by bringing a Scotland Yard 'tec into the sacred precincts of St. Peter's? The degradation implied by this remark tickled Poole immensely.

Pelfett would clearly have liked to dispose of the intruder after a cursory glance at Mr. Catling's rooms, but Poole firmly reversed the process, and, having closed the heavy outer door to ensure freedom from interruption, set about a systematic survey of the missing man's environment—for here, he felt, must he look for the clue to the mystery.

It was in the bedroom, Poole thought, that young Catling's identity most clearly revealed itself. On the mantelpiece was a large photograph of a charming middle-aged lady, obviously "Mother"; on either side of it a vase of daffodils, now dead—Poole felt an unreasoning desire to kick the idle scout. On the chest of drawers was a small snapshot of a man in hunting kit—probably "Father"; Poole felt from this, and from what he had heard from the dean, that there was no close bond of affection between father and son. Above the boy's bed was a reproduction of "Lux Mundi," and on a chair beside it, a well-worn Bible and a copy of Stevenson's "Virginibus Puerisque."

A locked dispatch-box in a drawer of the writing-table was the first item to attract Poole's interest. It was a simple affair and soon yielded to the insinuations of a skeleton-key. Inside was a bundle of letters—a quick glance revealed them as entirely harmless love-letters of the calf variety; a cheque-book, pass-book, and a file of receipts and bills; in a separate pocket was a single letter, in a strong angular hand, which dealt fluently and unsympathetically with the subject of debt; it was dated a month back and was signed: "Your affect. Father." This might be important.

A drawer of the bedroom chest of drawers revealed a box of make-up, crêpe hair, grease paint, coconut-butter, spirit gum, and soiled towels, all complete—the tools of Mr. Catling's hobby. The clothes were good in quality but modest in quantity, and they were well cared for. On the dressing-table, among brushes and stud-boxes, lay a small heap of papers—a letter from "Your ever loving Mother," a theatre programme, one sheet of an essay, and a torn fragment of typewritten notepaper.

The scrap was so small that Poole nearly overlooked it, but a second glance showed that it might be important. It appeared to be part of a "dunning" letter and ran as follows:

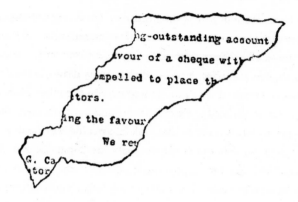

g-outstanding account
vour of a cheque wit
mpelled to place th
tors.
ing the favour
We re
G. Ca
tor

A straightforward demand, and probably not a very deadly one, but, to an inexperienced youth, who had lately been in trouble with his father on the subject of debt, it might represent a very real calamity.

In any case, it should not be too difficult to trace it to its source, and, armed with this and a list of Mr. Catling's tradesmen, culled from the files of receipts and bills, the detective made his way out of college.

His first action was to report to the headquarters of the city police and endeavour to make his peace with them and enlist their help. Fortunately, the superintendent in charge was a broadminded man, and Poole's line of conciliation and respect soon caused him to forget the slight he and his force had suffered at the hands of the college authorities—Poole explained that it was really Sir John Catling's doing.

The superintendent accepted the photograph of Gerald Catling which Monash had given to Poole, and promised to have discreet inquiries made at the railway stations. He could not identify the authorship of the dunning letter, but was able to advise the Scotland Yard man which of the tradesmen figuring on his list was most likely to have resorted to it. Curiously enough, he did not point to the large creditors—tailors and photographers, as the dean had shrewdly guessed—but to some of the smaller fry who might be in need of cash.

"The big firms like to let their accounts run on right to the end of an undergraduate's time here," said the superintendent. "They can afford to wait for their money, and long credit means large interest—if nothing more. I wonder the college authorities allow it, I must say."

Poole's round of visits to Catling's tradesmen, however—even though it was extended to include the greatest and the least of them—produced no result. A bright idea took him to a leading stationer who, after a close examination of the scrap of paper, opined that it did not emanate from any firm in Oxford. It was superfine paper, distinctly costly, and not at all such as was likely to be wasted upon unobservant undergraduates—pearls before swine, in fact. It was much more likely to belong to some very high-class and select London firm—something a cut above tailors at that.

This was more interesting, and as it was really the only clue he had to work on, Poole decided to return to London and follow it up at once. Having ascertained from the dean that a thorough search of the college premises and cross-examination of the gate porters had already been made, without result, he caught the 5 p.m. train back to town and before seven was closeted with the stationery expert at Scotland Yard.

Detective-Inspector Bodley, having always evinced a marked capacity in that direction, was now employed on little but the examination and classification of stationery, printing, and ink. His work was of extraordinary value to his colleagues, as his almost uncanny powers enabled him to reduce their fields of search in this subject to very conscribed limits. One glance at the scrap of paper enabled him to tell Poole what firm—fortunately a Thames-side one—had made it.

It was too late to do any more that evening, except to have dinner and, over a cup of coffee and a pipe, to think out the problem upon which, as yet, so little light had been shed. The detective felt instinctively opposed to the idea of suicide—a high-spirited boy of the type of Gerald Catling surely could not take life so seriously as to quail before a simple money trouble. Practical joke was more possible, but plain disappearance, such as this, was so senseless—and so cruel. Accident seemed much more probable, but it was difficult to believe that such a thing could remain undiscovered in a crowded hive of busy life like Oxford. Foul play was surely out of the question in such an environment.

Ten o'clock on the following morning found Poole in the office of the Blackfriars Paper Manufacturing Company. The manager recognised the specimen shown to him as being one of the highest grade papers produced by his firm—Imperial Bond. Only three stationers in London stocked it; one in the City, one in Holborn, and one in Kingsway. To each in turn went Poole, gathering a list of firms supplied, which, select though it might be, was still long enough to make him dislike the prospect of interviewing them all. Poole decided first of all to see whether Inspector Bodley could not in some way whittle down the list; he had identified the paper, perhaps he could do the same for the typewriter that had performed on it.

This was exactly what Inspector Bodley, on inquiry, could do. The typewriter used was a No. 3 Chanticleer—an expensive model which was not too common. This further known factor reduced the problem to workable proportions; it was an easy matter for three men at Scotland Yard, on three separate telephone lines, to run through the list of firms and inquire whether a No. 3 Chanticleer typewriter was used by them. The result exceeded Poole's highest hopes—only two firms used both Imperial Bond paper and a No. 3 Chanticleer typewriter: the Archaeological Supply Association and the Connoisseur Book Company. Both were in the neighbourhood of Kingsway, and Poole, taking a taxi, drove to the nearest.

The manager of the Archaeological Supply Association received Poole in his office with dignified restraint. The atmosphere of the place—sombre, dark, redolent somehow of the dead past—had impressed itself upon the detective's spirits as he made his way through the cases of fossils, scarabs, mummified cats, and other treasures so dear to the expert, so dispiriting to the layman. He unconsciously lowered his voice as he spoke.

"Can you tell me whether the letter of which this scrap is a part came from your office, sir?"

"If it did, it is clearly a confidential matter. May I ask why you are inquiring about it?"

"I am investigating the disappearance of an undergraduate—at Oxford. I have reason to believe that this letter to him may be connected with his disappearance."

"To an undergraduate?" The manager allowed the shadow of a smile to cross his face. "I can give you my assurance that this letter is not in any way connected with an undergraduate. It does, as you have surmised, emanate from this office—though how you discovered that I fail to understand—but—. It clearly has reached your hand in error."

"But it's got his name on it! Look—'G....'—obviously the beginning of 'G. Catling'—a 'Gerald Catling'—'St. Peter's College' too—his address."

The manager looked keenly at Poole.

"I see I shall have to divulge a confidential matter," he said; "it will, of course, go no further?"

"Not unless it is necessary in the interest of justice."

"Then I will tell you. This letter was addressed to Professor Grantham Cayzer, holder of the Assington Chair of Egyptology at Oxford University. He also resides, by what appears to be an astonishing coincidence at St. Peter's College."

Poole was flabbergasted. "Old Cat-Gut"—as Monash had disrespectfully called him—being dunned for a bill like any young rake! The manager evidently read what was passing in his mind and hastened to justify his firm's action.

"The course we have taken in the matter has been most distasteful to us," he said, "but when I tell you that we have received no payment over five years for an account that has risen into four figures, I think you will see that there had to be some limit—this letter, of course, is the last of a series. When I add that there is talk of the professor—but that is going beyond my brief."

Poole left the establishment with a feeling of deep depression; he had been chasing a red herring and must now begin all over again. It had been a particularly neat chase, too—thanks to Inspector Bodley. He took a midday train back to Oxford, and went straight to police headquarters; not a scrap of news, of any but a completely negative character, awaited him; neither did it at St. Peter's. Young Catling had disappeared completely, without leaving the smallest trace of his line of departure.

It was just worth while, Poole thought, to interview Professor Cayzer and ascertain from him how the scrap of paper had come into Catling's possession. Tea-time seemed a likely time to find the professor in his rooms, and alone. Directed by the head porter, Poole made his way to the end staircase of the Old Quad, and, scanning the list of names on the board, mounted to the top floor. A deep voice responded to his knock; he opened the door and walked in.

The professor, an old Norfolk jacket substituted for the regulation sub-fusc coat, was standing beside a table before the fire. A spirit lamp was cooking some white concoction in a saucepan, the professor stirring it from time to time, adding a few drops of liquid from a bottle. The process appeared to absorb him, as he did not look up at Poole's entry, but continued to stir; a sound like a solemn chuckle suggested that he found his pastime as amusing as it was absorbing.

"I'm sorry to disturb you, sir," said Poole.

The professor looked up.

"Eh? Oh! Who are you?"

"I am Detective-Inspector Poole, of Scotland Yard, sir. I was with the dean yesterday morning when you came to inquire about Mr. Catling; it was on that subject that I wanted to consult you."

As Poole spoke, it seemed to him that a sudden look of concentrated attention came into the professor's eyes. It was quickly succeeded, however, by a rather meaningless smile.

"You'll forgive me if I go on with my preparations? A rather special meal for my cats. Poor Catling; yes. Poor boy—high-spirited, full of innocent fun—he will be greatly missed, inspector. I myself shall miss him, perhaps, as much as anybody."

He broke off abruptly.

"You are employed to find him?" he asked.

"Yes, sir; I just came to ask you—"

"And you have some news of him?"

"None, sir, I'm sorry to say—there's not a trace of him anywhere. I just wanted to ask if you—"

Again the professor interrupted. He appeared to ignore the detective's attempt to question him. Blowing out the spirit-lamp, he lifted the saucepan to his nose and sniffed it.

"Delicious!" he exclaimed. "Come, inspector, I will show you my cats."

Turning abruptly, he flung open a door beyond the fireplace.

"My bedroom, really, but I have transformed it into a treasure-house."

Poole, following behind his host, found himself on the threshold of a large room fitted out as a museum. Glass cupboards lined the walls, wooden cases with glass tops stood upon the floor. The light was poor, but the detective could make out vessels of earthenware and metal, head-dresses, fragments of stone and plaster covered with Egyptian figures—all the familiar treasures of the Egyptologist. The professor whisked a piece of American-cloth from a glass case.

"My cats," he said.

Under the glass lay a number of mummified cats—most of them black and withered, but a few covered with fur and looking like ordinary dead cats. One form, wrapped completely in bandages, looked terribly human—like the victim of some ghastly accident. Poole felt a shudder of horror pass through him. What had the professor meant about that concoction—"for his cats"? Could it possibly be—he turned to ask a question, but found that Cayzer had left him and was standing by a sarcophagus under the window.

"My great treasure!" The professor bent over and stroked the surface of the wooden lid. "A masterpiece of the great Rameses II.—his own process—a unique process—a usurer! The king used him to complete his experiment. The process lasted a hundred days—a hundred days—it is not complete!"

The detective had joined his host while the latter spoke. As he listened, a cold sweat broke out over his body and he felt himself tremble from head to foot. He looked at the man beside him and saw a light in his eyes—fierce, cruel, insane—that completed the terror that he felt.

With a violent effort, Poole bent down and wrenched off the lid of the sarcophagus, flinging it to the floor at one side. Inside lay what appeared to be a mummy—a human form—wrapped from head to foot, as the cat had been, in bandages, even the face being covered. Throwing a look over his shoulder, he saw the gaunt figure of the professor towering above him, one arm flung back, madness blazing from his eyes. Quick as thought, Poole flung himself downwards and sideways, against the professor's legs; something crashed against the wooden coffin and the two men rolled over in a heap upon the floor.

Fortunately for Poole, the professor's head struck against the corner of one of the cases and he lay still—the detective knew well enough that he would have stood little chance against the superhuman strength of the maniac that this man must be. Rising to his feet, he bent over the sarcophagus, and with a penknife ripped away the bandages from the face of the "mummy." As the fabric came away, there was exposed to view the white, shrunken face of a young man; the eyes were open, but the light in them was dim—they seemed barely conscious, except of unfathomable terror.

Poole rushed out on to the landing and shouted for help at the top of his voice. Two undergraduates came running up from a room below.

"Get a doctor quickly, one of you, and the police!" exclaimed the detective. "Young Catling's here—barely alive. You other come and help me!"

He dashed back into the museum—only just in time—the professor was struggling to his knees. Poole flung him back upon the floor, knelt on his shoulders, and clung to a wrist with each hand.

"Find some string or bandages and tie his ankles," he cried. "Good chap! Now his wrists—that's it—that'll do for the moment. Now help me lift this poor chap out."

Together the two men carefully lifted the bound figure from its coffin—Poole was almost glad to see that the boy had fainted—and carried it to a sofa in the sitting-room. Carefully they unwound the bandages and chafed the bare, cold limbs. The boy opened his eyes and gazed wildly, uncomprehendingly about him.

"It's all right!" said Poole cheerfully. "It's quite all right now—you're with friends!"

The eyes came to rest on his face, but instead of the relief that Poole had hoped to see in them, there came terror, dawning and growing terror. The lips moved, and Poole, putting his ear close to them, caught faintly the words: "Milk! Cement—liquid cement!"

Again the boy fainted, and at the same moment there was a clatter of feet on the stairs and a uniformed police-sergeant and two constables appeared in the doorway.

"Your man's next door. Take care, he's a madman. I advise you to get an ambulance and strap him to a stretcher. Cover it with a blanket.

You don't want the whole college to see what you've got. Ah, that you, doctor? Thank heaven you've come. This poor chap's nearly out."

Poole explained what he knew of the extraordinary circumstances of the case, and it was decided that, until the professor's concoction had been analysed and, perhaps, an X-ray photograph taken, it was wiser not to move Catling from his present position.

Before long the boy came to his senses, and, as his colour was distinctly better, he was allowed to tell his story. It was told haltingly, with many pauses, and some unintelligible passages, but the gist of it was as follows:

Having accidentally come across the letter sent by the Archaeological Supply Association to Professor Cayzer, Catling had thought it would be a rag to make up as a detective and "arrest" the professor for debt. He had got himself up in his rooms on Friday afternoon after lunch, and, choosing the middle of the afternoon, when everybody would be out playing games, rowing, or working, had slipped round to Old Quad, knowing well from experience that the professor always spent Friday afternoon in his rooms.

The professor had at first "risen" magnificently; he stormed and swore in the most satisfactory manner. Then he had suddenly quietened down, apparently accepting the inevitable, and offered to show the "detective" the treasures for which he was being dunned. Catling did not know whether this change implied that the professor had recognised him or not; he had followed the professor into the museum and, while looking at the mummified cats, had suddenly received a violent blow on the back of the head, and had not recovered consciousness till he found himself, bound as Poole had found him, except for his face, lying in the sarcophagus, and the professor bending over him and explaining with ghastly glee the experiment he proposed to carry out on him.

Apparently Rameses II.'s "process" of mummification, perfected, according to legend, at any rate, by experiment upon an unfortunate usurer who had angered him, consisted of the very gradual instillation into the system of the victim, while he yet lived, of some compound which gradually solidified within him; the compound contained, apparently, a preservative as well as a solidifying property, so that the mummy retained not only its shape but also its flesh. The bandages, used by the professor successfully in his experiments on cats, kept the body in its proper shape—prevented "bulging"—as the madman had gleefully explained to his unfortunate victim.

In all probability, the cruelty of the process had gradually affected the professor's brain and turned him from a scientific experimenter into an insane monster. In any case, he never recovered his reason and was never brought to trial.

Analysis of the compound in the saucepan revealed the presence of an unknown element with some of the properties of cement, but it was in such minute percentage to the whole that there was good hope of its not having completely solidified the organs to which it adhered. This proved to be the case, and young Catling, after months of practically experimental treatment, recovered his full health. In all probability, the madman's cruel desire to spin out the experiment as long as possible had saved his life.

When it was known that he was out of danger, Poole received an invitation from the dean to dine with him in Hall. With some trepidation he journeyed down to Oxford and found himself received, especially over the "nuts and wine" in Senior Common Room after dinner, as a distinguished fellow-graduate of the University of Oxford.

"I knew you would prefer to be treated purely in your official capacity while the case was in hand," said Mr. Luddingham, "but I had great difficulty in not remonstrating with you when you asked me 'to approximately estimate' the amount of young Catling's debts. You must be a changed man indeed, my dear Poole—and probably a bigger one—calmly to split an infinitive in the presence of the Dean of St. Peter's."

THE GILDED PUPIL

Ethel Lina White

Ethel Lina White (1876–1944) came from Abergavenny and was one of nine children. Her father was a builder and inventor and the family became increasingly prosperous, moving to Fairlea Grange, an imposing house in the Gothic style which her father built in the 1880s. Today it is a listed building and a holiday let, with a website which highlights the connection with Ethel and states: "Fairlea is an old quirky house with idiosyncratic features, and that's much of its charm... The tall, bay windows illuminate the house whilst the staircase is imposing and grand and would make a great photograph!... there are wonderful views up to the Welsh mountains above the town."

In 1890, Ethel passed the Government Examination (Second Class) in freehand drawing at Newport School of Art, which was later absorbed into what is now known as the University of Wales, Newport. She seems to have remained in Wales until she was in her mid-thirties before moving to London and trying her hand at short stories. At the time of the 1921 census she was living in Wandsworth with two of her sisters and describing herself as an author, although her first novel was not published for another six years. Subsequent moves took her to Hounslow and then Chiswick. This story was included by Raymond Postgate (two of whose own novels have been published as British Library Crime Classics) in *Detective Stories of Today* (1940). Roy Glashan's online bibliography indicates that it appeared in the

United States four years earlier, but although I presume she also sold it to a British magazine, I haven't been able to trace where it was published.

THE ESSENTIAL PART OF THIS TALE IS THAT ANN SHELLEY WAS an Oxford M.A.

Unfortunately, so many other young women had the same idea of going to college and getting a degree that she found it difficult to harness her qualifications with a job. Therefore, she considered herself lucky, when she was engaged as resident governess to Stella Williams, aged 15—the only child of a millionaire manufacturer.

It was not until her final interview with Stella's mother, in a sun room which was a smother of luxury, that she understood the exact nature of her duties. Lady Williams—a beautiful porcelain person, with the brains of a butterfly—looked at her with appealing violet eyes.

"It's so difficult to explain, Miss Shelley. Of course, my husband considers education comes first, but what I want is some one to exercise a moral Influence on Stella. She—she's not normal."

"Thymus gland?" hinted Ann.

"O far worse. She won't wash."

Ann thought of the times she had been sent upstairs to remove a water mark, because she had overslept, or wanted to finish a thriller, and she began to laugh.

"That's normal, at her age," she explained. "School girls often scamp washing."

Lady Williams looked sceptical, but relieved.

"The trouble began," she said, "when she was too old for a nurse. Nannie used to wash and dress her, like a baby. But she refuses to let her maid do anything but impersonal things, like clothes. It's her idea of independence. She's terribly clever and socialistic. She'll try to catch you out."

"That sounds stimulating," smiled Ann.

All the same, she was not impressed pleasantly by her new pupil. Stella was unattractive, aggressive, and superior. Her sole recommendation to Ann's favour was her intelligence, which was far above the average.

On her first Saturday half holiday, Ann walked out to the grounds of Arlington Manor—the residence of the earl of Blankshire—to visit her old governess, Miss West. It was a May day of exciting weather, with concealed lightning bursting through a white windy sky. She thrilled with a sense of liberation, when she turned in to the road through the woods, where the opening beeches were an emerald filigree against the blue shadows of the undergrowth.

Miss West's cottage suggested a fairy tale, with its thatched roof and diamond-paned windows. It stood in a clearing, and was surrounded by a small garden, then purple with clumps of irises.

Ann's knock was answered by the maid, Maggie—a strapping country girl. She showed the visitor into the bed-sitting-room, where her mistress, who was crippled with rheumatism, was sitting up in bed. Miss West was an old woman, for she had also been a governess to Ann's mother. Her mouth and chin had assumed the nutcracker of age, so that she looked rather like an old witch, with her black blazing eyes and snowy hair.

Her dominant quality was her vitality. Ann could still feel it playing on her, like a battery, as they exchanged greetings.

"I love your little house," she remarked later, when Maggie had brought in tea. "But it's very lonely. Are you ever nervous?"

"Nervous of what?" asked Miss West. "There's nothing here to steal, and no money. Everyone knows that the earl is my banker."

This was her way of explaining that she was a penniless pensioner of the earl, whom she had taught in his nursery days.

"Every morning, some one comes down from the manor with the day's supplies," she said. "At night, a responsible person visits me for my orders and complaints... O you needn't look down your nose. The earl is in my debt. He is prolonging my life at a thrilling expense to himself, but I saved his life, when he was a child, at the risk of my own."

Her deep voice throbbed as she added, "I still feel there is nothing so precious as life."

Later, in that small, bewitched room, Ann was to remember her words.

"Life's big things appeal most to me," she confessed. "Oxford was wonderful—every minute of it. And I'm just living for my marriage with Kenneth. I told you I was engaged. He's a doctor on a ship, and we'll have to wait. In between, I'm just marking time."

"You have the important job of moulding character," Miss West reminded her. "How does your gilded pupil progress?"

"She's a gilded pill," Ann grimaced.

"Is Oxford responsible for your idea of humour?" asked Miss West, who had a grudge against a university education.

"No, it's the result of living in a millionaire's family. Please, may I come to see you, every Saturday afternoon? You make me feel recharged."

Although Miss West had acted like a mental tonic, Ann was conscious of a period of stagnation, when she walked back through the wood. She taught, in order to live, and went to see an old woman, as recreation. Life was dull. It might not have appeared so flat had she known that she was marked down already for a leading part in a sinister drama, and that she had been followed all the way to the cottage.

For the next few weeks life continued to be monotonous for Ann, but it grew exciting for Stella, as, gradually, she felt the pull of her governess' attraction. Ann had a charming appearance, and definite personality.

She made no attempt to rouse her pupil's personal pride by shock tactics, but relied on the contrast between her own manicured hands and the girl's neglected nails.

Presently she was able to report progress to the young ship's doctor.

"My three years at Oxford have not been wasted," she wrote. "The gilded pupil has begun to wash."

In her turn, she became fonder of Stella, especially when she discovered that the girl's aggressive manner was a screen for an inferiority complex.

"I always feel people hate me," she confided to her governess, one day. "I'm ashamed of having a millionaire father. He didn't make his money. Others make it for him. He ought to pay them a real spending income, and, automatically, increase the demand, and create fresh employment."

Ann found these socialistic debates rather a trial of tact, but she enjoyed the hours of study. Stella was a genuine student, and always read up her subject beforehand, so that lessons took somewhat the form of discussions and explanations. Ann was spared the drudgery of correcting French exercises and problems in algebra.

But her gain was some one else's loss. She had no idea how seriously she was restricting the activities of another in the plot.

Doris—the schoolroom maid—hunted daily amid the fragments in the wastepaper basket for something which she had been ordered to procure. And she searched in vain.

When Stella's devotion to the bathroom was deepening to passion, she began to grow jealous of her governess' private hours.

"Do you go to the pictures on Saturday?" she asked.

"No. I visit an old witch, in a cottage in the wood."

"Take me with you."

"You'd be bored. It's my old governess."

"Your governess? I'd love to see her. Please."

Ann had to promise a vague "some day." Although she was sorry to disappoint Stella, she could not allow her to encroach on her precious liberty.

By this time, however, her timetable was an established fact to the brains of the plot. Therefore, the next Saturday she visited Miss West she was followed by a new trailer.

She noticed him when she came out of the great gates of the millionaire's mansion, because he aroused a momentary sense or repugnance. He was fair and rather womanish in appearance, but his good looks were marred by a cruel red triangular mouth.

He kept pace with her on the opposite side of the street when she was going through the town, but she shook him off later on. Therefore, it gave her quite a shock when she turned into the beech avenue—now a green tunnel—to hear his footsteps a little distance in the rear.

Although she was furious with herself, she hurried to reach the cottage, which was quite close. The door was opened before she could knock, because her arrival was the signal for Maggie's release. It was Ann herself, who had suggested the extra leisure for the maid while she kept the old lady company.

Miss West, whose bed faced the window, greeted her with a question.

"When did you lose your admirer?"

"Who?" asked Ann, in surprise.

"I refer to the weedy boy who always slouches past the minute after your knock."

"I've never noticed him... But I thought I was followed here today by a specially unpleasant-looking man."

"Hum. We'd better assume that you were... How much money have you in your bag?"

"More than I care to lose."

"Then leave all the notes with me. I'll get the manor folk to return them to you by registered post... And, remember, if the man attacks you on your way home, don't resist. Give him your bag—and run."

"You're arranging a cheerful programme for me," laughed Ann.

When nine struck, Miss West told her to go.

"Maggie is due now any minute," she told her, "and so is the housekeeper from the manor. Goodbye—and don't forget it means 'God be with you.'"

Ann was not nervous, but when she walked down the garden path she could not help contrasting the dark green twilight of the woods with the sun-splashed beech avenue of the afternoon. Clumps of fox-gloves glimmered whitely through the gloom, and in the distance an owl hooted to his mate.

She passed close by the bushes where a man was hiding. He could have touched her, had he put out his hand. She was his quarry, whom he had followed to the cottage, so he looked at her intently.

Her expensive bag promised a rich haul. Yet he let her go by and waited, instead, for someone who was of only incidental interest to the plot.

A few minutes later Maggie charged down the avenue like a young elephant, for she was late. She had not a nerve in her body, and only three pence in her purse. As she passed the rhododendron thicket a shadow slipped out of it like an adder—a black object whirled round in the air—and Maggie fell down on the ground like a log.

The mystery attack was a nine days' wonder, for bag-snatching was unknown in the district. But while Maggie was recovering from slight concussion, in the hospital, Ann had the unpleasant task of mentally bludgeoning her pupil out of a "rave." After the weekly visit of the hairdresser, Stella appeared in the schoolroom with her hair cut and waved in the same fashion as Ann's.

"Like it?" she asked self-consciously.

"It's charming." Ann had to be tender with the inferiority complex. "But I liked your old style better. That was you. Don't copy me, Stella. I should never forgive myself if I robbed you of your individuality."

Stella wilted, like a pimpernel in wet weather.

"I'm not going to have a crush on you," she declared. "Too definitely feeble. But we're friends aren't we? Let's have a sort of friend's charter, with a secret signature, when we write to each other. Like this." She scrawled a five-fingered star on a piece of paper and explained it eagerly. "My name."

Ann was aware that Doris, the schoolroom maid, was listening with a half grin, and she decided to nip the nonsense in the bud.

"You'll want a secret society next, you baby," she said, as she crumpled up the paper. "Now, suppose we call it a day and go to the pictures."

Stella especially enjoyed that afternoon's entertainment, because the film was about a kidnapped girl, and she was excited by the personal implication.

"If a kidnapper ever got me, I'd say 'Good luck' to him. He'd deserve it," she boasted, as they drove home. "They wouldn't decoy me into a taxi with a fake message."

Ann's private feeling was that Stella's intelligence was not likely to be tested, since she ran no possible risk. Lady Williams was nervous on the score of her valuable jewellery, so the house was burglar proof, with flood-lit grounds and every kind of electric alarms.

Besides this, Stella either went out in the car, driven by a trusted chauffeur, or took her walks with a pack of large dogs.

So it was rather a shock to Ann when the girl lowered her voice.

"I'll tell you a secret. They've had a shot for me. They sent one of our own cars to the dancing class, but I noticed Hereford wasn't driving so I wouldn't get in. I wouldn't tell them at home because of mother."

Ann, who was still under the influence of the picture, was horrified.

"Stella," she cried, "I want you to promise me something. If ever you get a note signed by me take no notice of it."

"I promise. But if you signed it with our star, I'd know it was genuine. And if you were in danger nothing and no one would stop me from coming to your rescue."

"Single-handed, like the screen heroines who blunder into every trap?"

"Not me. I'll bring the police with me... Isn't that our schoolroom maid coming down the drive? Isn't she gorgeous?"

Doris, transformed by a marine cap and generous lipstick, minced past the car. She had to be smart, because she was meeting a fashionable gentleman with a cruel red mouth.

When she saw him in the distance she anticipated his question by shaking her head.

"No good swearing at me," she told him. "I can't get what isn't there. But I've brought you something else."

She gave him a sheet of crumpled paper on which was the rough drawing of a star.

The next time Ann went to the cottage in the wood the door was opened by the new maid—an ice-cold competent brunette, in immaculate livery. There was no doubt she was a domestic treasure, and a great improvement on Maggie, but Ann was repelled by the expression of her thin-lipped mouth.

"I don't like your new maid's face," she said to her old governess when Coles had carried out the tea table.

"Neither do I," remarked Miss West calmly. "She's far too good for my situation—yet she's no fool. My opinion is she's wanted by the police and has come here to hide. It's an ideal spot."

"But you won't keep her?"

"Why not? She's an excellent maid. There's no reason why I should not benefit by the special circumstances, if any. After all, it's only my suspicion."

"What about her references?"

"Superlative. Probably forged. The housekeeper hadn't time to inquire too closely. The place isn't popular, after the attack on Maggie."

"But I don't like to think of you alone, at her mercy."

"Don't worry about me. She's been to the cupboard and found out it's bare. I've nothing to lose."

Ann realised the sense of Miss West's argument, especially as she was in constant touch with the manor. Not long afterwards she wondered whether she had misjudged the woman, for she received a letter, by the next morning's post, which indicated that she was not altogether callous.

Its address was the cottage in the wood.

Dear Madam, (it ran,)

Pardon the liberty of my writing to you, but I feel responsible for Miss West in case anything happens to her and there's an inquest. I would be obliged if you would tell me is her heart bad and what to do in case of a sudden attack. I don't like to trouble her ladyship as I am a stranger to her and Miss West bites my head off if I ask her. I could not ask you today because she is suspicious of whispering. Will you kindly drop me a line in return and oblige.

Yours respectfully,
Marion Coles.

Ann hastily wrote the maid a brief note, saying that Miss West had good health—apart from the crippling rheumatism—but recommending a bottle of brandy, in case of emergency. She posted it and forgot the matter.

Meanwhile, Miss West was finding Coles' competency a pleasant change. On the following Saturday, when she carried in her mistress' lunch, Miss West looked, with approval, at her spotless apron and muslin collar.

After she had finished her well-cooked cutlet and custard, she lay back and closed her eyes, in order to be fresh for Ann's visit.

She had begun to doze when she heard the opening of the front door. Her visitor was before her usual time.

"Ann," she called.

Instead of her old pupil, a strange woman entered the bedroom. Her fashionably thin figure was defined by a tight black suit and a halo hat revealed a sharp rouged face.

As Miss West stared at her she gave a cry of recognition.

"Coles!"

The woman sneered at her.

"Here's two gentlemen come to see you," she announced.

As she spoke, two men, dressed with flashy smartness, sauntered into the room. One was blond and handsome, except for a red triangular mouth; the other had the small cunning eyes and low-set ears of an elementary criminal type.

"Go out of my room," ordered Miss West. "Coles, you are discharged."

The men only laughed as they advanced to the bed.

"We're only going to make you safer, old lady," said the fair man. "You might fall out of bed and hurt yourself. See?"

Miss West did not condescend to struggle while her feet and hands were secured with cords. Her wits told her that she would need to conserve every ounce of strength.

"Aren't you taking an unnecessary precaution with a bedridden woman?" she asked scornfully.

"Nothing too good for you, sweetheart," the fair man told her.

"Why have you come here? My former maid has told you that there is nothing of value in my cottage."

"Nothing but you, beautiful."

"How dare you be insolent to me? Take off your hats in a lady's presence."

The men only laughed. They sat and smoked cigarettes in silence, until a knock on the front door made them spring to their feet.

"Let her in," ordered the ringleader.

Miss West strained at her cords as Coles went out of the room. Her black eyes glared with helpless fury when Ann entered, and stood— horror stricken—in the doorway.

"Don't dare touch her," she cried.

The men merely laughed again, as they seized the struggling girl, forced her down on a bedroom chair and began to bind her ankles.

"Ann," commended the old governess. "Keep still. They're three to one. An elementary knowledge of arithmetic should tell you resistance is useless."

The pedantic old voice steadied Ann's nerves.

"Are you all right, Miss West?" she asked coolly.

"Quite comfortable, thanks."

"Good." Ann turned to the men. "What do you want?"

They did not answer, but nodded to Coles, who placed a small table before Ann. With the deft movements of a well-trained maid she arranged stationery—stamped with Miss West's address and writing materials.

Then the fair man explained the situation.

"The Williams' kid wot you teach is always pestering you to come here and see the old lady. Now, you're going to write her a nice little note, inviting her to tea this afternoon."

Ann's heart hammered as she realised she had walked into a trap. The very simplicity of the scheme was its safeguard. She was the decoy bird. The kidnappers had only to install a spy in the Williams' household, to study the habits of the governess.

Unfortunately she had led them to an ideal rendezvous—the cottage in the wood.

"No," she said.

The next second she shivered as something cold was pressed to her temple.

"We'll give you five minutes to make up your mind," said the fair man, glancing at the grandfather clock. "Then we shoot."

Ann gritted her teeth. In that moment her reason told her that she was probably acting from false sentiment and a confused sense of values. But logic was of no avail. She could not betray her trust.

"No," she said again.

The second man crossed to the bed and pressed his revolver to Miss West's head.

"Her, too," he said.

Ann looked at her old governess in an agony, imploring her forgiveness.

"She's only fifteen," she said piteously, as though in excuse.

"And I'm an old woman," grunted Miss West. "Your reasoning is sound. But you forget someone younger than your pupil. Your unborn son."

Ann's face quivered, but she shook her head. Then the old governess spoke with the rasp of authority in her voice.

"Ann, I'm ashamed of you. What is money, compared with two valuable lives, not to mention those still to come? I understand these—gentlemen do not wish to injure your pupil. They only want to collect a ransom."

"That's right, lady," agreed the fair man. "We won't do her no harm. This will tell the old man all hell want to know."

He laid down a typewritten demand note on the table and added a direction to Ann.

"When we've gone off with the kid, nip off to the old man as fast as you can go and give him this."

"With her legs tied to a chair?" asked the deep sarcastic voice of the old woman.

"She's got her hands free, ain't she? Them knots will take some undoing, but it's up to her, ain't it?"

"True. No doubt she will manage to free herself... But suppose she writes this note and the young lady does not accept the invitation? What then?"

The fair man winked at his companion.

"Then you'll both be unlucky," he replied.

Ann listened in dull misery. She could not understand the drift of Miss West's questions. They only prolonged the agony. Both of them knew they could place no reliance on the promise of the kidnappers. The men looked a pair of merciless beasts.

If she wrote that note she would lure her poor little gilded pupil to her death.

She started as her governess spoke sharply to her.

"Ann, you've heard what these gentlemen have said." She added in bitter mockery of their speech. "They wouldn't never break their word. Write that note."

Ann could not believe her ears. Yet she could feel the whole force of her vitality playing on her like an electric battery. It reminded her of a former experience, when she was a child. Her uncle, who paid for her education, was an Oxford don and he raised an objection against Miss West because she was unqualified.

In the end he consented to give his niece a viva-voce examination, on the result of which depended the governess' fate.

Ann passed the test triumphantly, but she always felt, privately, that Miss West supplied the right answers, as she sat staring at her pupil with hypnotic black eyes.

Now she knew that the old magic was at work again. Miss West was trying to tell her something without the aid of words.

Suddenly the knowledge came. Her old governess was playing for time. Probably she was expecting some male visitors from the manor, as the earl and his sons often came to the cottage. What she, herself, had to do was to stave off the five-minute sentence of death by writing a note to Stella, which was hallmarked as a forgery so that the girl would not come.

As she hesitated she remembered that she had extracted a promise from her pupil to disregard any message. The question was, whether it would be obeyed, for she knew the strength of her fatal attraction, and that Stella was eager to visit the cottage.

Hoping for the best, she began to write, disguising her handwriting by a backward slant.

"Dear Stella—"

With an oath the man snatched up the paper and threw it on the floor in a crumpled ball.

"None of them monkey tricks," he snarled. "We know your proper writing. And sign it with this."

Ann's hope died as the man produced the letter which she had written to Coles about Miss West's health and also Stella's rough drawing of a star.

She was defeated by the evidence—a specimen of her handwriting—for which Doris, the schoolroom maid had searched in vain—and the secret signature.

"I—can't," she said, feebly pushing away the paper.

Again the pistol was pressed to her head.

"Don't waste no time," growled the fair man.

"Don't waste no time," echoed Miss West. "Ann, write."

There was a spark in the old woman's eyes and the flash of wireless. Impelled to take up the pen, Ann wrote quickly, in a firm hand, and signed her note with a faithful copy of the star.

The men hung over her, watching every stroke and comparing the writing with Coles' letter.

"Don't put no dots," snarled the fair man, who plainly suspected a cypher, when Ann inserted a period.

He read the note again when it was finished and then passed it to his companion, who pointed to a word suspiciously. The old woman and the girl looked at each other in an agony of suspense as they waited for the blow to fall.

Then the fair man turned sharply to Miss West.

"Spell 'genwin'," he commanded.

As she reeled off the correct spelling he glanced doubtfully at his companion, who nodded.

"O.K.," he said.

Miss West's grim face did not relax and Ann guessed the reason. She was nerving herself for the second ordeal of Coles' inspection.

Fortunately, however, the men did not want their female confederate's opinion. The job was done and they wanted to rush it forward to its next stage. The fair man sealed the note and whistled on his fingers.

Instantly the weedy youth who had followed Ann to the cottage appeared from behind a clump of laurels in the drive, wheeling a bicycle. He snatched the letter from Coles and scorched away round the bend of the road.

Ann slumped back in her chair, feeling unstrung in every fibre. Nothing remained but to wait—wait—and pray Stella would not come.

The time seemed to pass very slowly inside the room. The men smoked in silence until the carpet was littered with cigarette-stubs and the air veiled with smoke. Miss West watched the clock as though she would galvanise the minute hand.

"Don't come," agonised Ann. "Stella, don't come."

But absent treatment proved a failure for Coles, who was hiding behind a curtain, gave a sudden hoot of triumph.

"The car's come."

"Push the girl to the front," commanded the fair man.

He helped to lift Ann's chair to the window so that she saw the Williams' Lanchester waiting in front of the cottage. Stella stood on the drive and the chauffeur, Hereford, was in the act of shutting the door. He sprang back to his seat, backed, saluted, and drove swiftly away.

Ann watched the car disappear with despairing eyes. She could not scream because fingers were gripping her windpipe, nearly choking her. But Stella could distinguish the pale blue of her frock behind the diamond-paned window and she waved her hand as she ran eagerly up the garden path.

Had Ann been normal she might have guessed the truth from Stella's reaction to the scene when she burst into the room. Instead of appearing surprised, she dashed to Ann and threw her arms around her.

"They didn't fool me," she whispered.

Then she began to fight like a boxing kangaroo, in order to create the necessary distraction, while the police car came round the bend of the drive.

The prelude to a successful raid was Mr. Williams' call for prompt action, when his daughter brought him Ann's note.

"It's her writing and our private star," she told him. "But—read it."

He glanced at the few lines and laughed.

"An impudent forgery," he said.

"No, it's an S.O.S. It looks like a second try for me."

After she had told her father about the first unsuccessful attempt to kidnap her, he realised the importance of nipping the gang's activities in the bud.

This seems the place to print the note, which was the alleged composition of an Oxford M.A.

Dear Stella,

Miss West will be pleased if you will come to tea this afternoon. Don't waste no time and don't run no risks. Let Hereford drive you in the car. To prove this is genuine I'm signing it with our star, same as you done, one day in the schoolroom.

Yours,
Ann Shelley.

1933

MURDER AT PENTECOST

Dorothy L. Sayers

Dorothy Leigh Sayers (1893–1957) was born in Oxford, where her father was chaplain of Christ Church and headmaster of Christ Church Cathedral School; he later became a rector in East Anglia and after years of home tuition she went to Godolphin School in Salisbury, where another future crime writer Josephine Bell, four years her junior, was also a pupil. In 1912, she gained a scholarship to Somerville College, Oxford, where she studied modern languages. Her time at Oxford made a great impression on her and her love of the place and its academic traditions is especially apparent in *Gaudy Night* (1935), in which the detective novelist Harriet Vane—to some extent a self-portrait of Sayers—returns to Shrewsbury College, a thinly disguised version of Somerville.

In that novel, Harriet finally accepts a proposal of marriage from Lord Peter Wimsey. Sayers' account of the evolution of their relationship over the course of several books was a hugely influential innovation which changed the way crime writers wrote about their series characters. Wimsey, a Balliol man, appears in eleven of Sayers' twelve novels, whereas Sayers' second-string detective, the jaunty wine salesman Montague Egg, only featured in short stories, including this one from her collection *Hangman's Holiday* (1933).

"BUZZ OFF, FLATHERS," SAID THE YOUNG MAN IN FLANNELS. "We're thrilled by your news, but we don't want your religious opinions. And, for the Lord's sake, stop talking about 'undergrads', like a ruddy commercial traveller. Hop it!"

The person addressed, a pimply youth in a commoner's gown, bleated a little, but withdrew from the table, intimidated.

"Appalling little tick," commented the young man in flannels to his companion. "He's on my staircase, too. Thank Heaven, I move out next term. I suppose it's true about the Master? Poor old blighter—I'm quite sorry I cut his lecture. Have some more coffee?"

"No, thanks, Radcott. I must be pushing off in a minute. It's getting too near lunchtime."

Mr. Montague Egg, seated at the next small table, had pricked up his ears. He now turned, with an apologetic cough, to the young man called Radcott.

"Excuse me, sir," he said, with some diffidence. "I didn't intend to overhear what you gentlemen were saying, but might I ask a question?" Emboldened by Radcott's expression, which, though surprised, was frank and friendly, he went on: "I happen to be a commercial traveller—Egg is my name, Montague Egg, representing Plummet & Rose, wines and spirits, Piccadilly. Might I ask what is wrong with saying 'undergrads'? Is the expression offensive in any way?"

Mr. Radcott blushed a fiery red to the roots of his flaxen hair.

"I'm frightfully sorry," he said ingenuously, and suddenly looking extremely young. "Damn stupid thing of me to say. Beastly brick."

"Don't mention it, I'm sure," said Monty.

"Didn't mean anything personal. Only, that chap Flathers gets my goat. He ought to know that nobody says 'undergrads' except townees and journalists and people outside the university."

"What ought we to say? 'Undergraduates'?"

"'Undergraduates' is correct."

"I'm very much obliged," said Monty. "Always willing to learn. It's easy to make a mistake in a thing like that, and, of course, it prejudices the customer against one. The Salesman's Handbook doesn't give any guidance about it; I shall have to make a memo for myself. Let me see. How would this do? 'To call an Oxford gent an—'"

"I think I should say 'Oxford man'—it's the more technical form of expression."

"Oh, yes. 'To call an Oxford man an undergrad proclaims you an outsider and a cad.' That's very easy to remember."

"You seem to have a turn for this kind of thing," said Radcott, amused.

"Well, I think perhaps I have," admitted Monty, with a touch of pride. "Would the same thing apply at Cambridge?"

"Certainly," replied Radcott's companion. "And you might add that 'To call the university the 'varsity is out of date, if not precisely narsity.' I apologise for the rhyme. 'Varsity has somehow a flavour of the nineties."

"So has the port I'm recommending," said Mr. Egg brightly. "Still, one's sales-talk must be up to date, naturally; and smart, though not vulgar. In the wine and spirit trade we make refinement our aim. I am really much obliged to you, gentlemen, for your help. This is my first visit to Oxford. Could you tell me where to find Pentecost College? I have a letter of introduction to a gentleman there."

"Pentecost?" said Radcott. "I don't think I'd start there, if I were you."

"No?" said Mr. Egg, suspecting some obscure point of university etiquette. "Why not?"

"Because," replied Radcott surprisingly, "I understand from the regrettable Flathers that some public benefactor has just murdered the Master, and in the circumstances I doubt whether the Bursar will be able to give proper attention to the merits of rival vintages."

"Murdered the Master?" echoed Mr. Egg.

"Socked him one—literally, I am told, with a brickbat enclosed in a Woolworth sock—as he was returning to his house from delivering his too-well-known lecture on Plato's use of the Enclitics. The whole school of Literae Humaniores will naturally be under suspicion, but, personally, I believe Flathers did it himself. You may have heard him informing us that judgement overtakes the evil-doer, and inviting us to a meeting for prayer and repentance in the South Lecture-Room. Such men are dangerous."

"Was the Master of Pentecost an evil-doer?"

"He has written several learned works disproving the existence of Providence, and I must say that I, in common with the whole Pentecostal community, have always looked on him as one of Nature's worst mistakes. Still, to slay him more or less on his own doorstep seems to me to be in poor taste. It will upset the examination candidates, who face their ordeal next week. And it will mean cancelling the Commem. Ball. Besides, the police have been called in, and are certain to annoy the Senior Common Room by walking on the grass in the quad. However, what's done cannot be undone. Let us pass to a pleasanter subject. I understand that you have some port to dispose of. I, on the other hand, have recently suffered bereavement at the hands of a bunch of rowing hearties, who invaded my rooms the other night and poured my last dozen of Cockburn '04 down their leathery and undiscriminating throttles. If you care to stroll round with me to Pentecost, Mr. Egg, bringing your literature with you, we might be able to do business."

Mr. Egg expressed himself as delighted to accept Radcott's invitation, and was soon trotting along the Cornmarket at his conductor's athletic heels. At the corner of Broad Street the second undergraduate left them, while they turned on, past Balliol and Trinity, asleep in the June sunshine, and presently reached the main entrance of Pentecost.

Just as they did so, a small, elderly man, wearing a light overcoat and carrying an M.A. gown over his arm, came ambling short-sightedly across the street from the direction of the Bodleian Library. A passing car just missed whirling him into eternity, as Radcott stretched out a long arm and raked him into safety on the pavement.

"Look out, Mr. Temple," said Radcott. "We shall be having you murdered next."

"Murdered?" queried Mr. Temple, blinking. "Oh, you refer to the motor-car. But I saw it coming. I saw it quite distinctly. Yes, yes. But why 'next'? Has anybody else been murdered?"

"Only the Master of Pentecost," said Radcott, pinching Mr. Egg's arm.

"The Master? Dr. Greeby? You don't say so! Murdered? Dear me! Poor Greeby! This will upset my whole day's work." His pale-blue eyes shifted, and a curious, wavering look came into them. "Justice is slow but sure. Yes, yes. The sword of the Lord and of Gideon. But the blood—that is always so disconcerting, is it not? And yet, I washed my hands, you know." He stretched out both hands and looked at them in a puzzled way. "Ah, yes—Greeby has paid the price of his sins. Excuse my running away from you—I have urgent business at the police-station."

"If," said Mr. Radcott, again pinching Monty's arm, "you want to give yourself up for the murder, Mr. Temple, you had better come along with us. The police are bound to be about the place somewhere."

"Oh, yes, of course so they are. Yes. Very thoughtful of you. That will save me a great deal of time, and I have an important chapter to finish. A beautiful day, is it not, Mr.—I fear I do not know your name. Or do I? I am growing sadly forgetful."

Radcott mentioned his name, and the oddly assorted trio turned together towards the main entrance to the college. The great gate was shut; at the postern stood the porter, and at his side a massive figure in blue, who demanded their names.

Radcott, having been duly identified by the porter, produced Monty and his credentials.

"And this," he went on, "is, of course, Mr. Temple. You know him. He is looking for your Superintendent."

"Right you are, sir," replied the policeman. "You'll find him in the cloisters... At his old game, I suppose?" he added, as the small figure of Mr. Temple shuffled away across the sun-baked expanse of the quad.

"Oh, yes," said Radcott. "He was on to it like a shot. Must be quite exciting for the old bird to have a murder so near home. Where was his last?"

"Lincoln, sir; last Tuesday. Young fellow shot his young woman in the Cathedral. Mr. Temple was down at the station the next day, just before lunch, explaining that he'd done it because the poor girl was the Scarlet Woman."

"Mr. Temple," said Radcott, "has a mission in life. He is the sword of the Lord and of Gideon. Every time a murder is committed in this country, Mr. Temple lays claim to it. It is true that his body can always be shown to have been quietly in bed or at the Bodleian while the dirty work was afoot, but to an idealistic philosopher that need present no difficulty. But what is all this about the Master, actually?"

"Well, sir, you know that little entry between the cloisters and the Master's residence? At twenty minutes past ten this morning, Dr. Greeby was found lying dead there, with his lecture-notes scattered all round him and a brickbat in a woollen sock lying beside his head. He'd been lecturing in a room in the Main Quadrangle at nine o'clock, and was, as far as we can tell, the last to leave the lecture-room. A party of American ladies and gentlemen passed through the cloisters a little after 10 o'clock, and they have been found, and say there was nobody about there then, so far as they could see—but, of course, sir, the murderer might have been hanging about the entry, because, naturally, they wouldn't go that way but through Boniface Passage to the Inner Quad and the chapel. One of the young gentlemen says he saw the Master cross the Main Quad on his way to the cloisters at 10.5, so he'd reach the entry in about two minutes after that. The Regius Professor of Morphology came along at 10.20, and found the body, and when the doctor arrived, five minutes later, he said Dr. Greeby must have been dead about a quarter of an hour. So that puts it somewhere round about 10.10, you see, sir."

"When did these Americans leave the chapel?"

"Ah, there you are, sir!" replied the constable. He seemed very ready to talk, thought Mr. Egg, and deduced, rightly, that Mr. Radcott was well and favourably known to the Oxford branch of the Force. "If that there party had come back through the cloisters, they might have been able to tell us something. But they didn't. They went on through the Inner Quad into the garden, and the verger didn't leave the chapel, on account of a lady who had just arrived and wanted to look at the carving on the reredos."

"And did the lady also come through the cloisters?"

"She did, sir, and she's the person we want to find, because it seems as though she must have passed through the cloisters very close to the time of the murder. She came into the chapel just on 10.15, because the verger recollected of the clock chiming a few minutes after she came in and her mentioning how sweet the notes was. You see the lady come in, didn't you, Mr. Dabbs?"

"I saw a lady," replied the porter, "but then I see a lot of ladies one way and another. This one came across from the Bodleian round about 10 o'clock. Elderly lady, she was, dressed kind of old-fashioned, with her skirts round her heels and one of them hats like a rook's nest and a bit of elastic round the back. Looked like she might be a female don—leastways, the way female dons used to look. And she had the twitches—you know—jerked her head a bit. You get hundreds like 'em. They goes to sit in the cloisters and listen to the fountain and the little birds. But as to noticing a corpse or a murderer, it's my belief they wouldn't know such a thing if they saw it. I didn't see the lady again, so she must have gone out through the garden."

"Very likely," said Radcott. "May Mr. Egg and I go in through the cloisters, officer? Because it's the only way to my rooms, unless we go round by St. Scholastica's Gate."

"All the other gates are locked, sir. You go on and speak to the Super; he'll let you through. You'll find him in the cloisters with Professor Staines and Dr. Moyle."

"Bodley's Librarian? What's he got to do with it?"

"They think he may know the lady, sir, if she's a Bodley reader."

"Oh, I see. Come along, Mr. Egg."

Radcott led the way across the Main Quadrangle and through a dark little passage at one corner, into the cool shade of the cloisters. Framed by the arcades of ancient stone, the green lawn drowsed tranquilly in the noonday heat. There was no sound but the echo of their own footsteps, the plash and tinkle of the little fountain and the subdued chirping of chaffinches, as they paced the alternate sunshine and shadow of the pavement. About midway along the north side of the cloisters they came upon another dim little covered passageway, at the entrance to which a police-sergeant was kneeling, examining the ground with the aid of an electric torch.

"Hullo, sergeant!" said Radcott. "Doing the Sherlock Holmes stunt? Show us the bloodstained footprints."

"No blood, sir, unfortunately. Might make our job easier if there were. And no footprints neither. The poor gentleman was sandbagged, and we think the murderer must have climbed up here to do it, for the deceased was a tall gentleman and he was hit right on the top of the head, sir." The sergeant indicated a little niche, like a blocked-up window, about four feet from the ground, "Looks as if he'd waited up here, sir, for Dr. Greeby to go by."

"He must have been well acquainted with his victim's habits," suggested Mr. Egg.

"Not a bit of it," retorted Radcott. "He'd only to look at the lecture-list to know the time and place. This passage leads to the Master's House and the Fellows' Garden and nowhere else, and it's the way Dr. Greeby would naturally go after his lecture, unless he was lecturing elsewhere, which he wasn't. Fairly able-bodied, your murderer, sergeant, to get up here. At least—I don't know."

Before the policeman could stop him, he had placed one hand on the side of the niche and a foot on a projecting band of masonry below it, and swung himself up.

"Hi, sir! Come down, please. The Super won't like that."

"Why? Oh, gosh! Fingerprints, I suppose. I forgot. Never mind; you can take mine if you want them, for comparison. Give you practice. Anyhow, a baby in arms could get up here. Come on, Mr. Egg; we'd better beat it before I'm arrested for obstruction."

But at this moment Radcott was hailed by a worried-looking don, who came through the passage from the far side, accompanied by three or four other people.

"Oh, Mr. Radcott! One moment, Superintendent; this gentleman will be able to tell you about what you want to know; he was at Dr. Greeby's lecture. That is so, is it not, Mr. Radcott?"

"Well, no, not exactly, sir," replied Radcott, with some embarrassment. "I should have been, but, by a regrettable accident, I cut—that is to say, I was on the river, sir, and didn't get back in time."

"Very vexatious," said Professor Staines, while the Superintendent merely observed:

"Any witness to your being on the river, sir?"

"None," replied Radcott. "I was alone in a canoe, up a backwater—earnestly studying Aristotle. But I really didn't murder the Master. His lectures were—if I may say so—dull, but not to that point exasperating."

"That is a very impudent observation, Mr. Radcott," said the Professor severely, "and in execrable taste."

The Superintendent, murmuring something about routine, took down in a notebook the alleged times of Mr. Radcott's departure and return, and then said:

"I don't think I need detain any of you gentlemen further. If we want to see you again, Mr. Temple, we will let you know."

"Certainly, certainly. I shall just have a sandwich at the cafe and return to the Bodleian. As for the lady, I can only repeat that she sat at my table from about half-past nine till just before ten, and returned again at ten-thirty. Very restless and disturbing. I do wish, Dr. Moyle, that some arrangement could be made to give me that table to myself, or that I could be given a place apart in the library. Ladies are always restless and disturbing. She was still there when I left, but I very much hope she has now gone for good. You are sure you don't want to lock me up now? I am quite at your service."

"Not just yet, sir. You will hear from us presently."

"Thank you, thank you. I should like to finish my chapter. For the present, then, I will wish you good-day."

The little bent figure wandered away, and the Superintendent touched his head significantly.

"Poor gentleman! Quite harmless, of course. I needn't ask you, Dr. Moyle, where he was at the time?"

"Oh, he was in his usual corner of Duke Humphrey's Library. He admits it, you see, when he is asked. In any case, I know definitely that he was there this morning, because he took out a Phi book, and of course had to apply personally to me for it. He asked for it at 9.30 and returned it at 12.15. As regards the lady, I think I have seen her before. One of the older school of learned ladies, I fancy. If she is an outside reader, I must have her name and address somewhere, but she may, of course, be a member of the University. I fear I could not undertake to know them all by sight. But I will inquire. It is, in fact, quite possible that she is still in the library, and, if not, Franklin may know when she went and who she is. I will look into the matter immediately. I need not say, professor, how deeply I deplore this lamentable affair. Poor dear Greeby! Such a loss to classical scholarship!"

At this point, Radcott gently drew Mr. Egg away. A few yards farther down the cloisters, they turned into another and rather wider passage, which brought them out into the Inner Quadrangle, one side of which was occupied by the chapel. Mounting three dark flights of stone steps on the opposite side, they reached Radcott's rooms, where the undergraduate thrust his new acquaintance into an arm-chair, and, producing some bottles of beer from beneath the window-seat, besought him to make himself at home.

"Well," he observed presently, "you've had a fairly lively introduction to Oxford life—one murder and one madman. Poor old Temple. Quite one of our prize exhibits. Used to be a Fellow here, donkey's years ago. There was some fuss, and he disappeared for a time. Then he turned up again, ten years since, perfectly potty; took lodging in Holywell, and has haunted the Bodder and the police-station alternately ever since. Fine Greek scholar he is, too. Quite reasonable, except on the one point. I hope old Moyle finds his mysterious lady, though it's nonsense to pretend that they keep tabs on all the people who use the library. You've only got to walk in firmly, as if the place belonged to you, and, if you're challenged, say in a loud, injured tone that you've been a reader for years. If you borrow a gown, they won't even challenge you."

"Is that so, really?" said Mr. Egg.

"Prove it, if you like. Take my gown, toddle across to the Bodder, march straight in past the showcases and through the little wicket marked 'Readers Only', into Duke Humphrey's Library; do what you like, short of stealing the books or setting fire to the place—and if anybody says anything to you, I'll order six dozen of anything you like. That's fair, isn't it?"

Mr. Egg accepted this offer with alacrity, and in a few moments, arrayed in a scholar's gown, was climbing the stair that leads to England's most famous library. With a slight tremor, he pushed open the swinging glass door and plunged into the hallowed atmosphere of mouldering leather that distinguishes such temples of learning.

Just inside, he came upon Dr. Moyle in conversation with the doorkeeper. Mr. Egg, bending nonchalantly to examine an illegible manuscript in a showcase, had little difficulty in hearing what they said, since like all official attendants upon reading-rooms, they took no trouble to lower their voices.

"I know the lady, Dr. Moyle. That is to say, she has been here several times lately. She usually wears an M.A. gown. I saw her here this morning, but I didn't notice when she left. I don't think I ever heard her name, but seeing that she was a senior member of the University—"

Mr. Egg waited to hear no more. An idea was burgeoning in his mind. He walked away, courageously pushed open the Readers' Wicket, and stalked down the solemn medieval length of Duke Humphrey's Library. In the remotest and darkest bay, he observed Mr. Temple, who, having apparently had his sandwich and forgotten about the murder, sat alone, writing busily, amid a pile of repellent volumes, with a large attache-case full of papers open before him.

Leaning over the table, Mr. Egg addressed him in an urgent whisper:

"Excuse me, sir. The police Superintendent asked me to say that they think they have found the lady, and would be glad if you would kindly step down at once and identify her."

"The lady?" Mr. Temple looked up vaguely. "Oh, yes—the lady. To be sure. Immediately? That is not very convenient. Is it so very urgent?"

"They said particularly to lose no time, sir," said Mr. Egg.

Mr. Temple muttered something, rose, seemed to hesitate whether to clear up his papers or not, and finally shovelled them all into the bulging attache-case, which he locked upon them.

"Let me carry this for you, sir," said Monty, seizing it promptly and shepherding Mr. Temple briskly out. "They're still in the cloisters, I think, but the Super said, would you kindly wait a few moments for him in the porter's lodge. Here we are."

He handed Mr. Temple and his attache-case over to the care of the porter, who looked a little surprised at seeing Mr. Egg in academic dress, but, on hearing the Superintendent's name, said nothing. Mr. Egg hastened through quad and cloisters and mounted Mr. Radcott's staircase at a run.

"Excuse me, sir," he demanded breathlessly of that young gentleman, "but what is a Phi book?"

"A Phi book," replied Radcott, in some surprise, "is a book deemed by Bodley's Librarian to be of an indelicate nature, and catalogued accordingly, by some dead-and-gone humorist, under the Greek letter phi. Why the question?"

"Well," said Mr. Egg, "it just occurred to me how simple it would be for anybody to walk into the Bodleian, disguise himself in a retired corner—say in Duke Humphrey's Library—walk out, commit a murder, return, change back to his own clothes and walk out. Nobody would stop a person from coming in again, if he—or she—had previously been seen to go out—especially if the disguise had been used in the library before. Just a change of clothes and an M.A. gown would be enough."

"What in the world are you getting at?"

"This lady, who was in the cloisters at the time of the murder. Mr. Temple says she was sitting at his table. But isn't it funny that Mr.

Temple should have drawn special attention to himself by asking for a Phi book, today of all days? If he was once a Fellow of the college, he'd know which way Dr. Greeby would go after his lecture; and he may have had a grudge against him on account of that old trouble, whatever it was. He'd know about the niche in the wall, too. And he's got an attache-case with him that might easily hold a lady's hat and a skirt long enough to hide his trousers. And why is he wearing a top-coat on such a hot day, if not to conceal the upper portion of his garments? Not that it's any business of mine—but—well, I just took the liberty of asking myself. And I've got him out there, with his case, and the porter keeping an eye on him."

Thus Mr. Egg, rather breathlessly. Radcott gaped at him.

"Temple? My dear man, you're as potty as he is. Why, he's always confessing—he confessed to this—you can't possibly suppose—"

"I daresay I'm wrong," said Mr. Egg. "But isn't there a fable about the man who cried 'Wolf!' so often that nobody would believe him when the wolf really came? There's a motto in the Salesman's Handbook that I always admire very much. It says: 'Discretion plays a major part in making up the salesman's art, for truths that no one can believe are calculated to deceive.' I think that's rather subtle, don't you?"

RANULPH HALL

Michael Gilbert

Michael Gilbert, CBE, TD (1912–2006) was born at Billinghay in Lincolnshire and went to St. Peter's School in Seaford, East Sussex, and Blundell's School in Devon. He began to study law at London University, but was unable to continue due to financial pressures. He then taught for some time at Salisbury Cathedral School before return-ing to university to complete his studies. He qualified as a solicitor and enjoyed a highly successful career in the legal profession while estab-lishing himself as one of the leading British crime writers of his day.

His crime fiction was highly diverse, but he was first and foremost an entertainer with a smoothly readable prose style. *Smallbone Deceased*, *Death in Captivity*, and *Death Has Deep Roots*, all published in the 1950s, have been reissued as British Library Crime Classics. One of his later books, *The Night of the Twelfth*, is darker in tone than his other work (but equally successful) and has a well-realised "closed community" setting—in a prep school. The story which follows, written towards the end of his career, was included in *The Mathematics of Murder* (2000), a collection of stories connected with the law firm of Fearne and Bracknell.

T HE REVEREND SEBASTIAN STODDART, HEADMASTER OF RANULPH Hall Preparatory School for Boys, stirred uneasily in his bed.

In normal times he would have attributed the sound that had woken him to the efforts of the wind that irrupted from across the North Sea and made the shutters on the east side of the house rattle on their ancient hinges.

But the times were not normal.

Two weeks before, shortly after the start of the Easter term, Troop-Sergeant-Major Bailey ("Trooper" to the boys) had reported what he called an attempted break-in. The shutter that covered one of the ground-floor windows had been, he said, lifted from its hinges and laid against the wall.

"Next thing they were planning to do, sir, or so I'd guess, was attend to the window. Simple little catch. Slip it with a knife. No trouble. Only luckily they didn't have time."

At that moment a particularly violent gust had lifted the shutter from where it had been propped and sent it crashing across the courtyard and smack into the wall of the newly erected squash court. In its headlong career it had picked up a rubbish bin and carried that along with it.

The noise had roused the school more effectively than any getting-up bell. It had taken Stoddart, helped by his second-in-command Simon Truefortt, and the sergeant-major half an hour to round up the excited boys and get them back into their dormitories. After which they had managed to lift the heavy shutter back onto its hinges, had replaced the bar and returned, thankfully, to their beds.

It was on the following morning, after breakfast, that Bailey had first offered the headmaster his considered opinion that it was human hands, not the wind, that had lifted the shutter.

"No wind could have done it, sir, however strong," he said. "And look here." He pointed to two freshly made indentations in the bottom of the shutter. "Could only have been made by, say, a couple of jemmies. Push the points in here, see, then press down on the ends. Both together—and up she comes."

"Yes," said Stoddart, "I can see the marks. Mightn't they have been made when the shutters were being installed?"

"Look quite fresh to me, sir," said Bailey. "The blessing was they didn't have time to get the window open. You can see the scratches where they were trying to slip the catch. That was when the wind did us a good turn. Sent the shutter bowling across the courtyard, yanking up the dustbin, and making enough noise to wake the dead. So they didn't get anything for their trouble."

"End of story," said Stoddart thankfully. He didn't want to believe in burglars. Unfortunately Bailey must have talked and the exciting theory that he was propounding had become common knowledge. It also formed a welcome topic to enliven the traditionally dull Easter term. Stoddart couldn't ban discussion, but he censored their letters home. The last thing he wanted was visits from anxious parents.

After a short time, interest had died down and had been replaced by other more immediate and important topics, such as the romance that was believed to be blooming between Simon Truefortt and the matron, Miss Hellaby, who was young and unusually attractive as matrons went, a considerable improvement on her predecessor who had had a hooked nose and prominent teeth and had earned, and justified, her nickname, of "the Hag".

"The Hellaby's all right," said Colin Smedley, a precocious thirteen year old to his two particular friends. Ivo Fisher and Drew Bastable.

"Not exactly my idea of a glamour girl, but she sticks out in the right places."

"You're swanking," said Ivo. "You don't know a damn thing about girls."

Drew said, "Can't blame Mr. Truefortt. Just suppose he'd had to make love to the Hag."

The idea made all three of them laugh consumedly.

"All the same," said Colin, "since no one seems to be taking these burglars seriously, it's up to the CID to do something about them."

He was not, as his listeners understood, referring to the Criminal Investigation Department at New Scotland Yard, but to their own, more modest, organisation made up of the initials of Colin, Ivo and Drew. They had already notched up a number of minor successes, such as enforcing the departure of one of the temporary maids who had been stealing and selling part of their meagre sugar ration and they were primed for further exciting action.

"So what are we going to do?" said Ivo.

Colin said, "I had a word with Trooper. He's seen a man hanging about in the market place. He thought he recognised him as a criminal called Dandy Davis. And, sure enough, Dad had a picture of him in his album."

Colin's father was Captain Smedley who headed a private detective agency in the City. When Colin was home on weekend leave his father had allowed him to look through what he called his Black Bible and it was there that Colin had located a character who closely resembled the man the sergeant-major had described.

He must have acquired his name "Dandy", Colin thought, in the same way that someone six foot high and broad in proportion would be nick-named "Tiny", for he was an ugly-looking hunk, with a nose that had been broken more than once. His record included assault, housebreaking and theft.

"Shouldn't care to tangle with him," his father had said. "You'd better warn that headmaster of yours that this man has been seen hanging round."

"Violent, I suppose," said Drew, when Colin reported all this to his lieutenants.

They seemed more interested than alarmed.

"Very," said Colin. "So are the pair he works with Dad told me, Ikey Barnstow and a man called Celly James on account of him being able to force locks with a strip of celluloid."

"Three of them," said Ivo thoughtfully. "Rather a handful for the three of us to tackle."

"I've been thinking about one way we might level the odds," said Colin.

He talked for some time. His two assistants listened, doubtfully at first, but in the end they agreed with him. It was clear who was boss of the CID in that district.

As may be supposed the boy's warning, duly delivered, did nothing to calm the headmaster's fears. He had fifty boys to look after, he and a houseful of women. The sergeant-major slept out—he had a cottage in the garden. The only man on the premises was Simon Truefortt—an enthusiastic member of the local Territorial Army, and a useful ally, but could the two of them tackle three professional criminals?

It was this thought that had kept him from falling asleep. Lying uncomfortably in bed, he had heard midnight strike from Westbury parish church. As the sound of the chimes died away, he heard something else. Difficult to say what it was, but there was definitely movement somewhere in the house.

Though a sixty-year-old academic, Sebastian Stoddart was no sort of coward, and he had all of the Englishman's dislike of people who invaded his privacy. He got out of bed, pulled on a sweater, armed himself with a steel fire-rake, and started out to investigate.

Dandy Davis and his two accomplices had, on this occasion, made a more discreet entry leaving the window shutters alone and opening a basement door with their own set of keys before proceeding upstairs towards their goal, which seemed to be the headmaster's study.

Here they encountered a militant group, consisting of Colin, Ivo and Drew. Unarmed they would have had small chance of opposing the intruders, but they were not unarmed and the night's proceedings opened to the sound of a rattling volley of small arms' fire. It stopped Dandy Davis and his party dead, but it didn't check Mr. Stoddart, who continued to advance, with considerable courage but extreme caution.

What he saw brought him finally to a startled halt.

The boys had apparently visited the miniature rifle range, and each had armed himself with a .22 rifle.

"What's all this?" Shock had sent his voice up several octaves. "What in the world are you playing at?"

"Defending the premises," said Colin. He seemed unperturbed.

"Did you hit anyone?"

"Don't think so," said Drew. "But they didn't stop to find out. We heard them crunching off down the drive." He, too, seemed quite satisfied with what they had achieved.

"If you had hit them, you'd be in very serious trouble."

"Why?" said Colin. "Isn't a householder entitled to defend his house?"

This brought a temporary halt to the headmaster's indignation. Might there be something in what the boy said? He appealed to Simon, who had arrived in dressing-gown and slippers.

"Tell the young idiots that they can't go round shooting people."

"I'm not sure," said Simon. "I'm not really a lawyer. Not yet. Only a student. I've started on Contract and Tort. I haven't got onto Crime yet. But I understand that you are entitled to use reasonable force in the protection of your property."

"Are guns reasonable?"

"Bearing in mind that they are boys, who could scarcely be expected to tackle grown men without the help of some sort of weapon, it might be argued that what they did was reasonable. However, I do remember one case where a man waited inside an open window with a shot-gun, and potted a burglar who tried to climb through. That was held to be unreasonable. Clearly what we need here is professional advice."

"Right," said Stoddart. He seemed to get comfort from the word "professional", which he repeated. "So how do we get professional advice?"

"There's a young friend of mine, Hugo Bracknell. He's a junior partner in the firm of Fearne & Bracknell, City solicitors. Perhaps you could ask him down here for the night? He might want to bring his clerk, Mr. Piggin, with him. An excellent man, I'm told, who has advised him in a number of tricky situations."

"I can think of no one better. They acted for me when I bought this place. And I remember Mr. Piggin, who did much of the work. Invite them both. Touch wood, no invalids yet, so we've plenty of spare beds in the sick-room. We can explain the whole situation to your friend and he'll let us know what we can do. And"—he turned to the boys who had reluctantly grounded their arms—"*what we can't do.*"

Some days later, when the rifles had been securely locked up, as they should have been before, and a sequence of peaceful nights had some-what calmed Mr. Stoddart's immediate fears, he and Simon were in conference with the two newcomers. He was glad that Hugo Bracknell should have brought his clerk, a Mr. Piggin, with him. Hugo was young, and likely to be rash; Mr. Piggin, on the other hand, was of a sensible age, in fact, almost exactly the same that he was himself. And he seemed to be eminently sound in his views.

It was he who finally said, "I'm sorry that neither of us has been able to give you a definite answer. Self-defence is certainly allowed to all citizens. The only question is whether it is reasonable. The dicta on this point are many, and largely contradictory. It is clear that the age and physical condition of the victim are both to be taken into account, but on the whole I should advise you against the use of knives or fire-arms. It would be preferable that the defenders should be armed with sticks or clubs and, more important, that they should be in telephonic communication with the police. However," he continued, "there is one line of enquiry that we ought to be pursuing and which might go a long way to answering the important question of what lies behind these visitations. Ought we not to be asking ourselves *what are these criminals looking for?*"

Mr. Stoddart said, with evident approval, "I have been thinking on the same lines. When I purchased this place from the squire, Roger Ranulph, I made some enquiries about his past and his background. I was surprised to find that he was by no means an estimable character. In fact, if he had not been killed in the gun battle which immediately preceded the sale, he might well have ended up in prison himself."

He indicated the pile of books on the table, each one flagged with a number of markers.

"These are reminiscences and memorials of Ranulph's contemporaries. They were, for the most part, written before his decease and are, understandably, circumspect. The more recent ones less so. There is really no doubt that Ranulph was a bad man."

"Morally bad," said Hugo, "or criminally?"

"The records tell us very little about his morals, but a criminal, certainly. He seems to have been a notable fence, a receiver of stolen goods of all sorts. And one man speaks of hidden paths which lead down from the eastern end of what is now one of the playing fields—it was then under plough—to a secluded beach under the cliff where a small boat could be hidden. This could be rowed out, at night, to the mouth of the Yare, where the water was deep enough for a sea-going craft to lie at anchor. You see the idea?"

"An excellent arrangement," said Mr. Piggin. He appreciated neatness, even in his adversaries. "The stolen goods, destined no doubt for the Low Countries, would have been stored in Ranulph Hall, in perfect safety, since Ranulph was a magistrate. You mentioned a gun battle—?"

"Indeed. It must have taken place shortly before I purchased the property. I can only surmise that there had been a falling-out of thieves over the cargo they were running. It must have been an exceptionally valuable one, which gave rise to a difference of opinion about the sharing of the proceeds between the parties concerned. These were, on the one side, Ranulph and his steward, Hopcraft—who seems to have been as black a villain as his master. On the other side the three smugglers, a dangerous trio. Dandy Davis, Tom Cotton and Micky Marden, all known—only too well known—to the police. The gun fight ended in a draw—though a far from bloodless one."

Through the open window they could hear what seemed to be a rehearsal of the "Hallelujah Chorus", the boys' clear voices forming an incongruous background to the dark tale that was being unrolled.

"Ranulph and his steward were both killed, as were two of the robbers, Cotton and Marden. Davis was wounded, but survived. Subsequently he was charged with taking part in an armed affray by night—a very serious offence, for which he received a sentence of fifteen years' penal servitude."

Mr. Piggin had been making careful notes as the headmaster spoke. He said, "One point, Headmaster, if you please. Do you happen to know how Davis behaved himself in prison?"

"When I spoke to Superintendent Holbeach, of the Norfolk Police, he told me that Davis was a violent and implacable prisoner. He was guilty of more than one assault on the warders who were guarding him, as a result of which he forfeited all remission of his sentence."

"And so served his full term of fifteen years?"

"Certainly. He might even have been charged on account of his conduct in prison and received an additional sentence, but this is not often done. He must, in fact, have been released in the early months of this year."

"Precisely," said Mr. Piggin, whose eyes had been glued to the calendar, "and does that not constitute a possible answer to your question? An answer that may appear even clearer when I add certain facts that have recently come my way."

Although he spoke as though he sat still while facts came flocking round him like homing pigeons, Hugo knew that they were usually the result of enquiries made by Mr. Piggin among his wide circle of friends and acquaintances.

"Who have you been talking to now, Piggy?" he said.

"I have been discussing some aspects of the matter with a man who should be better known than he is. I will refer to him, if I may, as Mr. X. But for his modesty, understandable in the circumstances, his would be a household name. He has made a lifelong study of the origins and subsequent movement of crystalline carbon in tetrahedral and in octahedral or dodecahedral form."

Noting the blank looks on the faces of his audience, he kindly explained, "I mean, of course, stones which are commonly referred to, by a species of incorrect shorthand, as diamonds."

Diamonds.

Whilst the word was still echoing round the room the voices outside reached the climax of their singing with a triumphant shout of Hallelujah!

In the silence which ensued, Mr. Piggin continued with his report. He said, "There was one other piece of information he gave me that interested me greatly. It seems that when the Low Countries were invaded by the Germans, machinery and skilled craftsmen in the diamond field were hurriedly extracted and transferred to the comparative safety of this country."

"Comparative," murmured Mr. Stoddart, himself a survivor of the London blitz.

"Sufficient was brought across to set up a diamond cutting and polishing industry here. Many famous stones came to rest here. Not, of course, the most famous of all, the Cullinan diamond. That has been part of the British regalia for some years, but a number of lesser stones, smaller, but extremely valuable. The Cape Blue, the Mortimer and the Brazilian Vargas. All such stones are well documented, and their ultimate destination is known, with one major exception. A hundred-carat stone, known as the October diamond after the date of its arrival in Belgium. It was in the State Museum in Brussels and was extracted ahead of the arrival of the Germans—wisely, in view of Goering's known weakness for precious stones—and it was planned to bring it to England. The courier who was carrying it would appear to have been inefficiently guarded—though one must bear in mind the confusion and disorganisation of the times—and his body was subsequently discovered in a thicket in the New Forest. His throat had been cut. Since then the October diamond has vanished."

"Surely that is unusual," said Mr. Stoddart. "Such stones do not usually hide their light under a bushel."

Hugo could contain himself no longer.

"What you're suggesting, Piggy, is that this stone, the October diamond was brought across here and entrusted to Ranulph to dispose of."

"I am suggesting nothing," said Mr. Piggin coldly. "I am simply exploring possibilities. A man who laid hands dishonestly, on such a prize, would be concerned, first of all, to hide it. As soon as the war was over, and the European market opened again, one of the people he could certainly have approached would have been Ranulph. His experience and expertise in disposing of stolen goods was widely known. And, to take the matter one step further, yes, it is possible that it was in a quarrel over this extremely valuable prize that the four deaths we have heard about took place. If that is the truth, it does explain a number of points which have been, so far, in doubt."

"But surely," said Hugo, who was finding Mr. Piggin's step-by-step approach infuriating, "surely it explains everything. Davis and his friends come here with the stone. They commission Ranulph to arrange for its disposal. There is a dispute over the division of the profits—a dispute which ended in violence. Four of the five men concerned are killed. Davis is wounded, and arrested. *And he alone knows for certain that Ranulph was entrusted with the stone.*"

"But not where he concealed it," said Simon, who had been following Mr. Piggin's exposition with equally close attention.

"Right. So the stone is back where Ranulph hid it. Davis bides his time. Fifteen years later—if he had been able to control his temper it would have been ten years—he comes out of prison and takes on two new assistants."

"Probably men encountered in prison," Simon suggested.

"Very likely. And comes to Ranulph Hall with them to get his hands on the stone."

"To find," said Mr. Stoddart with a smile, "that it is no longer a private residence, but a flourishing preparatory school. Tell me, how can he have been sure that the stone had not come to light and been disposed of long since?"

"His allies in the diamond disposal field would have told him. My friend Mr. X would certainly have known of it at once."

"Then the possibility you have been exploring," Mr. Stoddart chose his words carefully, "is that the October diamond could still be somewhere here." The idea seemed to interest more than alarm him.

"And all we have to do," said Simon, "is to find it. We return it, openly, to the museum, and our troubles are at an end."

"That is all," agreed Mr. Piggin.

"It would help," said Mr. Stoddart, "if we knew more precisely what we were looking for."

"According to the records it is a stone of one hundred carats. It is octahedral and its overall measurements are between twenty-five and thirty millimetres in diameter and ten to fifteen millimetres in depth. I suggest that you make a model, in soft wood and paint it white. That will give us a target to set our sights on."

"I'm not much of a hand at carving. But Captain Smedley's son, Colin, is, as I know an accomplished practitioner. No doubt his father has kept him fully informed of what we've been up to. I'll set him to work at once."

"Believe it or not," said Colin, to the other members of the CID, "this is what they're looking for."

He indicated the neat little eight-sided model.

"Have they got any idea where to start?"

"Not the slightest," said Colin.

"Then it'll take them months and months," said Drew.

"Years," said Ivo.

But fortunately Mr. Piggin was able to narrow the field.

In conference with Simon and Mr. Stoddart he said, "What we have to bear in mind is that the school was not in existence when the stone was hidden. We can, therefore, ignore all scholastic additions: the squash court, the gymnasium and the two pavilions. What we must concentrate on are the original pieces of Ranulph Hall that now form part of the school. And such of its contents as have come down here with it."

Mr. Stoddart said, "I can give you a reasonably accurate account of the contents. I have looked up the schedules that were prepared at the time of the sale to me. I agreed to purchase the furniture, pictures and books—Ranulph had inherited an excellent library, though I doubt if he ever opened a book. The contents were listed individually along with the more important items of furniture."

"Excellent," said Mr. Piggin. "Then you have a record of everything that was in the building at that time."

"Everything except a few items that were disposed of earlier. A week or so before the main sale the executors—short of cash I imagine—organised a local sale. Not of any of the major items. Small objects which it had not been worth the trouble to add to the schedules."

"Yes," said Mr. Piggin. "I see." He did not sound happy about this. "But let us concentrate, for the moment, on what you call the major items. You would have purchased them, I take it, to furnish the private part of your school."

"Quite so. My study and library, and my private dining-room and drawing-room."

"Then we've only really got four rooms to examine," said Simon.

Mr. Piggin still seemed to be worried. He said, "I suppose you haven't by any chance got a list of the small items that were disposed of locally."

"I'll see if I can find one, but I doubt it."

"There must be people living round here who were at the local sale. They will remember who was there. They may even remember what they and other people bought."

"They might," said Mr. Stoddart. "But bear in mind that it was more than fifteen years ago."

*

The Junior CID had ideas of their own.

Ivo said to Colin, "What we ought to do is have a word with your great-aunt."

"Great-aunt Beatrice? She's supposed to be a witch."

"Tells fortunes, doesn't she?" said Drew. "Why couldn't she look into that magic globe of hers and tell us where this diamond is?"

Colin thought about it. Beatrice Smedley, nearly ninety, was not a reputable member of the family. People avoided mentioning her, as much as they could. Also they avoided offending her.

"You ask her," said Ivo. "We all know she's potty about you."

"Marry you if you gave her half a chance," said Drew.

Colin disregarded this persiflage, all of which he had heard many times before. All the same, there was a substratum of truth in it.

"She might help us," he said. "It's true she seems to like me a lot, for some reason, but if I get the wrong side of her, she might turn me into a toad."

"We'll look after you," said Ivo.

"Feed you slugs," said Drew.

"Your kindness overwhelms me," said Colin. "Very well. I'll have a shot at it."

Meanwhile the senior researchers had done a great deal of work with, so far, disappointing results. But that morning a ray of light appeared. The headmaster, making a final examination of his records, unearthed, from under a pile of printed papers, two photographs that had been taken at the time of his purchase. One of them showed the drawing-room of Ranulph Hall, the other the study, both in fair detail.

The study was unhelpful, being furnished with one large table and half-a-dozen steel filing cabinets.

"When I took it over," said Stoddart, "I emptied the papers out.

They were mostly catalogues, and a few bills and accounts. I made a bonfire of the lot."

"Oh dear," said Mr. Piggin.

"The table had two drawers in it. You can see them in the photograph. I emptied them too."

"And burned the contents," said Mr. Piggin sadly.

"It's all very well being wise after the event. How were we to know that we'd be hunting round for clues to the whereabouts of a priceless diamond?"

"You weren't, of course," said Mr. Piggin. "But I agree that we can disregard the office; the drawing-room looks much more promising."

"A typical Victorian set-up," said Hugo, voicing the massive intolerance of youth. "How could people ever be happy with ghastly stuff like that all round them?"

There was a lot of Benares brass; there were vases of dried grass and palm leaves; there were anti-macassars on the chairs and knitted pictures on the walls in frames of brightly coloured beads.

"I can't see anyone giving twopence for the lot," said Simon. He cast an eye down the list of people known, or thought to have attended the private sale. Some were dead, others had left the neighbourhood. There seemed to be a lot of hard work ahead of them, without much chance of success at the end of it.

Great-aunt Beatrice welcomed Colin to her den, a dark and crowded pair of attic rooms overlooking the river. She listened fondly to Colin's explanations, interrupting them only by cackling from time to time.

When he had finished, she said, "I'm not a magician, and I can't tell you anything about the diamond. I didn't even know it existed. But I do remember the sale." She studied the list of names. "Mostly they bought vases and pictures. And my goodness, those pictures!" She seemed to be overcome by the remembrance of them. "*Knitted* pictures. Yes, actually knitted in different coloured wools. Can you imagine it?"

Colin could imagine it, and he shuddered sympathetically.

"I only bought one thing myself, and I've still got it, though I've sometimes been tempted to throw it away. It's a girandole. You wouldn't understand what that means."

Colin shook his head. The warm and crowded room was beginning to overpower him.

"They come in different shapes and forms. Mine, as you can see, is a plain mirror, with two candle-holders in front of it. Not everyone's taste, I agree, but there must have been something about it that appealed to me at the time."

Colin had got up to look at it. What interested him was not the mirror or the candlesticks: it was the thick border of beads round the mirror. As he examined them he put his thin, strong fingers through them.

Then he said, "I think it's lovely. Would you sell it to me?"

"For God's sake," said Ivo. "What do you want a thing like that for?"

"Just an idea I had."

"How much was she asking for it?"

"It cost her two pounds. I had to offer the same."

"Had you got two pounds?"

"Actually all I had was sixty pence. I promised to raise the balance as quickly as I could. I thought you might help."

Drew said, "I've got one pound." Ivo said, "And I can make up the other forty pence. I hope you know what you're doing."

"I hope so," said Colin.

He had placed the mirror of the girandole on the table, under the light.

"All right," said Ivo. "What happens next?"

"I didn't want to mess about with it until Dad and Mr. Piggin were here. I think that's them now. I told them what I'd been up to and they seemed to think I might be on the right track."

Drew said, "For God's sake, let's get going. The suspense is killing me."

When they had made room at the table for the two newcomers, Colin took out a pair of nail scissors, and began, very carefully, to cut the threads which held the beads. As these came away the layer behind them was revealed: a dozen small, but perfectly cut octahedrons, which fitted neatly into a slot in the woodwork.

Mr. Piggin lifted one of them out. Under the electric light it seemed to be self-luminous, with an adamantine lustre of its own.

"You see," said Colin modestly. "It occurred to me that you might perhaps have been looking for the wrong thing. With a famous stone on his hands, I thought, surely the first thing Ranulph would do, would be to have it cut up."

"So what we should have been looking for," said Mr. Piggin, "was not one diamond about the size of a billiard ball, but ten or twelve diamonds each the size of a large bead." He laid the one he had picked up back on the table.

"How much did you pay for them?" said Mr. Piggin.

When Colin had told him how much he had paid, Mr. Piggin said to Captain Smedley, "I'd advise you to retain, at all cost, the services of your son. I feel sure that he'll be worth his keep."

THE FIELD OF PHILIPPI

E. W. Hornung

Ernest William Hornung (1866–1921) was born in Middlesbrough and his main place of education was Uppingham School in Uppingham, a historic market town in Rutland. Uppingham School dates back to 1583 and, like Stonyhurst College, thrives to this day. Hornung shared with Arthur Conan Doyle, whose sister he later married, a love of cricket and was thrilled that his coach at the school was H. H. Stephenson, one of the finest players of his era and the first to be awarded a hat for taking three wickets in consecutive balls, giving rise to the term "hat-trick". Hornung's passion for the summer game was shared by his most famous character, the amateur cracksman A. J. Raffles. Hornung's biographer, Peter Rowland, has described the author's admiration for the school, but his time at Uppingham was limited to just three years because his asthma deteriorated to such an extent that he felt he had to abandon any thought of further education.

His poor health prompted a move to Australia, in the hope that he would benefit from living in a warmer climate. Whilst he was there, he started to write and over the years his time on the other side of the world furnished a good deal of material for his fiction. Although not as celebrated as Raffles, Stingaree the bushranger, who first appeared in *Irralie's Bushranger*, anticipates him in some respects as a Jekyll and Hyde figure who is charming and sophisticated but also, as Rowland says, "not a man to meet on a dark night (especially when he has those Quandong diamonds in his valise and needs to make a quick getaway)". This Raffles story first appeared in *Collier's Weekly* in the US in April 1905 and thereafter in the collection *A Thief in the Night*.

NIPPER NASMYTH HAD BEEN HEAD OF OUR SCHOOL WHEN Raffles was captain of cricket. I believe he owed his nickname entirely to the popular prejudice against a day-boy; and in view of the special reproach which the term carried in my time, as also of the fact that his father was one of the school trustees, partner in a banking firm of four resounding surnames, and manager of the local branch, there can be little doubt that the stigma was undeserved. But we did not think so then, for Nasmyth was unpopular with high and low, and appeared to glory in the fact. A swollen conscience caused him to see and hear even more than was warranted by his position, and his uncompromising nature compelled him to act on whatsoever he heard or saw: a savage custodian of public morals, he had in addition a perverse enthusiasm for lost causes, loved a minority for its own sake, and untenable tenets for theirs. Such, at all events, was my impression of Nipper Nasmyth, after my first term, which was also his last. I had never spoken to him, but I had heard him speak with extraordinary force and fervour in the school debates. I carried a clear picture of his unkempt hair, his unbrushed coat, his dominant spectacles, his dogmatic jaw. And it was I who knew the combination at a glance, after years and years, when the fateful whim seized Raffles to play once more in the Old Boys' Match, and his will took me down with him to participate in the milder festivities of Founder's Day.

It was, however, no ordinary occasion. The bicentenary loomed but a year ahead, and a movement was on foot to mark the epoch with an adequate statue of our pious founder. A special meeting was to be held at the school-house, and Raffles had been specially invited by the new head master, a man of his own standing, who had been in the eleven with him up at Cambridge. Raffles had not been near the old place for years; but I had never gone down since the day I left; and I will not dwell on the emotions which the once familiar journey awakened in my unworthy bosom. Paddington was alive with Old Boys of all ages—but very few of ours—if not as lively as we used to make it when we all landed back for the holidays. More of us had moustaches and cigarettes and "loud" ties. That was all. Yet of the throng, though two or three looked twice and thrice at Raffles, neither he nor I knew a soul until we had to change at the junction near our journey's end, when, as I say, it was I who recognised Nipper Nasmyth at sight.

The man was own son of the boy we both remembered. He had grown a ragged beard and a moustache that hung about his face like a neglected creeper. He was stout and bent and older than his years. But he spurned the platform with a stamping stride which even I remembered in an instant, and which was enough for Raffles before he saw the man's face.

"The Nipper it is!" he cried. "I could swear to that walk in a pantomime procession! See the independence in every step: that's his heel on the neck of the oppressor: it's the nonconformist conscience in baggy breeches. I must speak to him, Bunny. There was a lot of good in the old Nipper, though he and I did bar each other."

And in a moment he had accosted the man by the boy's nickname, obviously without thinking of an affront which few would have read in that hearty open face and hand.

"My name's Nasmyth," snapped the other, standing upright to glare.

"Forgive me," said Raffles undeterred. "One remembers a nickname and forgets all it never used to mean. Shake hands, my dear fellow! I'm Raffles. It must be fifteen years since we met."

"At least," replied Nasmyth coldly; but he could no longer refuse Raffles his hand. "So you are going down," he sneered, "to this great gathering?" And I stood listening at my distance, as though still in the middle fourth.

"Rather!" cried Raffles. "I'm afraid I have let myself lose touch, but I mean to turn over a new leaf. I suppose that isn't necessary in your case, Nasmyth?"

He spoke with an enthusiasm rare indeed in him: it had grown upon Raffles in the train; the spirit of his boyhood had come rushing back at fifty miles an hour. He might have been following some honourable calling in town; he might have snatched this brief respite from a distinguished but exacting career. I am convinced that it was I alone who remembered at that moment the life we were really leading at that time. With me there walked this skeleton through every waking hour that was to follow. I shall endeavour not to refer to it again. Yet it should not be forgotten that my skeleton was always there.

"It certainly is not necessary in my case," replied Nasmyth, still as stiff as any poker. "I happen to be a trustee."

"Of the school?"

"Like my father before me."

"I congratulate you, my dear fellow!" cried the hearty Raffles—a younger Raffles than I had ever known in town.

"I don't know that you need," said Nasmyth sourly.

"But it must be a tremendous interest. And the proof is that you're going down to this show, like all the rest of us."

"No, I'm not. I live there, you see."

And I think the Nipper recalled that name as he ground his heel upon an unresponsive flagstone.

"But you're going to this meeting at the school-house, surely?"

"I don't know. If I do there may be squalls. I don't know what you think about this precious scheme Raffles, but I..."

The ragged beard stuck out, set teeth showed through the wild moustache, and in a sudden outpouring we had his views. They were narrow and intemperate and perverse as any I had heard him advocate as the firebrand of the Debating Society in my first term. But they were stated with all the old vim and venom. The mind of Nasmyth had not broadened with the years, but neither had its natural force abated, nor that of his character either. He spoke with great vigour at the top of his voice; soon we had a little crowd about us; but the tall collars and the broad smiles of the younger Old Boys did not deter our dowdy demagogue. Why spend money on a man who had been dead two hundred years? What good could it do him or the school? Besides, he was only technically our founder. He had not founded a great public school. He had founded a little country grammar school which had pottered along for a century and a half. The great public school was the growth of the last fifty years, and no credit to the pillar of piety. Besides, he was only nominally pious. Nasmyth had made researches, and he knew. And why throw good money after a bad man?

"Are there many of your opinion?" inquired Raffles, when the agitator paused for breath. And Nasmyth beamed on us with flashing eyes.

"Not one to my knowledge as yet," said he. "But we shall see after tomorrow night. I hear it's to be quite an exceptional gathering this year; let us hope it may contain a few sane men. There are none on the present staff, and I only know of one among the trustees!"

Raffles refrained from smiling as his dancing eye met mine.

"I can understand your view," he said. "I am not sure that I don't share it to some extent. But it seems to me a duty to support a general movement like this even if it doesn't take the direction or the shape of our own dreams. I suppose you yourself will give something, Nasmyth?"

"Give something? I? Not a brass farthing!" cried the implacable banker. "To do so would be to stultify my whole position. I cordially and conscientiously disapprove of the whole thing, and shall use all my influence against it. No, my good sir, I not only don't subscribe myself, but I hope to be the means of nipping a good many subscriptions in the bud."

I was probably the only one who saw the sudden and yet subtle change in Raffles—the hard mouth, the harder eye. I, at least, might have foreseen the sequel then and there. But his quiet voice betrayed nothing, as he inquired whether Nasmyth was going to speak at next night's meeting. Nasmyth said he might, and certainly warned us what to expect. He was still fulminating when our train came in.

"Then we meet again at Philippi," cried Raffles in gay adieu. "For you have been very frank with us all, Nasmyth, and I'll be frank enough in my turn to tell you that I've every intention of speaking on the other side!"

It happened that Raffles had been asked to speak by his old college friend, the new head master. Yet it was not at the school-house that he and I were to stay, but at the house that we had both been in as boys. It also had changed hands: a wing had been added, and the double tier of tiny studies made brilliant with electric light. But the quad and the fives-courts did not look a day older; the ivy was no thicker round the study windows; and in one boy's castle we found the traditional print of Charing Cross Bridge which had knocked about our studies ever since a son of the contractor first sold it when he left. Nay, more, there was the bald remnant of a stuffed bird which had been my own daily care when it and I belonged to Raffles. And when we all filed in to prayers, through the green baize door which still separated the master's part of the house from that of the boys, there was a small boy posted in the passage to give the sign of silence to the rest assembled in the hall, quite identically as in the dim old days; the picture was absolutely unchanged; it was only we who were out of it in body and soul.

On our side of the baize door a fine hospitality and a finer flow of spirits were the order of the night. There was a sound representative assortment of quite young Old Boys, to whom ours was a prehistoric time, and in the trough of their modern chaff and chat we old stagers might well have been left far astern of the fun. Yet it was Raffles who was the life and soul of the party, and that not by meretricious virtue of his cricket. There happened not to be another cricketer among us, and it was on their own subjects that Raffles laughed with the lot in turn and in the lump. I never knew him in quite such form. I will not say he was a boy among them, but he was that rarer being, the man of the world who can enter absolutely into the fun and fervour of the salad age. My cares and my regrets had never been more acute, but Raffles seemed a man without either in his life.

He was not, however, the hero of the Old Boys' Match, and that was expected of him by all the school. There was a hush when he went in, a groan when he came out. I had no reason to suppose he was not trying; these things happen to the cricketer who plays out of his class; but when the great Raffles went on to bowl, and was hit all over the field, I was not so sure. It certainly failed to affect his spirits; he was more brilliant than ever at our hospitable board; and after dinner came the meeting at which he and Nasmyth were to speak.

It was a somewhat frigid gathering until Nasmyth rose. We had all dined with our respective hosts, and then repaired to this business in cold blood. Many were lukewarm about it in their hearts; there was a certain amount of mild prejudice, and a greater amount of animal indifference, to be overcome in the opening speech. It is not for me to say whether this was successfully accomplished. I only know how the temperature of that meeting rose with Nipper Nasmyth.

And I dare say, in all the circumstances of the case, his really was a rather vulgar speech. But it was certainly impassioned, and probably as purely instinctive as his denunciation of all the causes which appeal to the gullible many without imposing upon the cantankerous few. His arguments, it is true, were merely an elaboration of those with which he had favoured some of us already; but they were pointed by a concise exposition of the several definite principles they represented, and barbed with a caustic rhetoric quite admirable in itself. In a word, the manner was worthy of the very foundation it sought to shake, or we had never swallowed such matter without a murmur. As it was, there was a demonstration in the wilderness when the voice ceased crying. But we sat in the deeper silence when Raffles rose to reply.

I leaned forward not to lose a word. I knew my Raffles so well that I felt almost capable of reporting his speech before I heard it. Never was I more mistaken, even in him! So far from a gibe for a gibe and a taunt for a taunt, there never was softer answer than that which A. J. Raffles returned to Nipper Nasmyth before the staring eyes and startled ears of all assembled. He courteously but firmly refused to believe a word his old friend Nasmyth had said—about himself. He had known Nasmyth for twenty years, and never had he met a dog who barked so loud and bit so little. The fact was that he had far too kind a heart to bite at all. Nasmyth might get up and protest as loud as he liked: the speaker declared he knew him better than Nasmyth knew himself. He had the necessary defects of his great qualities. He was only too good a sportsman. He had a perfect passion for the weaker side. That alone led Nasmyth into such excesses of language as we had all heard from his lips that night. As for Raffles, he concluded his far too genial remarks by predicting that, whatever Nasmyth might say or think of the new fund, he would subscribe to it as handsomely as any of us, like "the generous good chap" that we all knew him to be.

Even so did Raffles disappoint the Old Boys in the evening as he had disappointed the school by day. We had looked to him for a noble raillery, a lofty and loyal disdain, and he had fobbed us off with friendly personalities not even in impeccable taste. Nevertheless, this light treatment of a grave offence went far to restore the natural amenities of the occasion. It was impossible even for Nasmyth to reply to it as he might to a more earnest onslaught. He could but smile sardonically, and audibly undertake to prove Raffles a false prophet; and though subsequent speakers were less merciful the note was struck, and there was no more bad blood in the debate. There was plenty, however, in the veins of Nasmyth, as I was to discover for myself before the night was out.

You might think that in the circumstances he would not have attended the head master's ball with which the evening ended; but that would be sadly to misjudge so perverse a creature as the notorious Nipper. He was probably one of those who protest that there is "nothing personal" in their most personal attacks. Not that Nasmyth took this tone about Raffles when he and I found ourselves cheek by jowl against the ballroom wall; he could forgive his franker critics, but not the friendly enemy who had treated him so much more gently than he deserved.

"I seem to have seen you with this great man Raffles," began Nasmyth, as he overhauled me with his fighting eye. "Do you know him well?"

"Intimately."

"I remember now. You were with him when he forced himself upon me on the way down yesterday. He had to tell me who he was. Yet he talks as though we were old friends."

"You were in the upper sixth together," I rejoined, nettled by his tone.

"What does that matter? I am glad to say I had too much self-respect, and too little respect for Raffles, ever to be a friend of his then. I knew too many of the things he did," said Nipper Nasmyth.

His fluent insults had taken my breath. But in a lucky flash I saw my retort.

"You must have had special opportunities of observation, living in the town," said I; and drew first blood between the long hair and the ragged beard; but that was all.

"So he really did get out at nights?" remarked my adversary. "You certainly give your friend away. What's he doing now?"

I let my eyes follow Raffles round the room before replying. He was waltzing with a master's wife—waltzing as he did everything else. Other couples seemed to melt before them. And the woman on his arm looked a radiant girl.

"I meant in town, or wherever he lives his mysterious life," explained Nasmyth, when I told him that he could see for himself. But his clever tone did not trouble me; it was his epithet that caused me to prick my ears. And I found some difficulty in following Raffles right round the room.

"I thought everybody knew what he was doing; he's playing cricket most of his time," was my measured reply; and if it bore an extra touch of insolence, I can honestly ascribe that to my nerves.

"And is that all he does for a living?" pursued my inquisitor keenly.

"You had better ask Raffles himself," said I to that. "It's a pity you didn't ask him in public, at the meeting!"

But I was beginning to show temper in my embarrassment, and of course that made Nasmyth the more imperturbable.

"Really, he might be following some disgraceful calling, by the mystery you make of it!" he exclaimed. "And for that matter I call first-class cricket a disgraceful calling, when it's followed by men who ought to be gentlemen, but are really professionals in gentlemanly clothing. The present craze for gladiatorial athleticism I regard as one of the great evils of the age; but the thinly veiled professionalism of the so-called amateur is the greatest evil of that craze. Men play for the gentlemen and are paid more than the players who walk out of another gate. In my time there was none of that. Amateurs were amateurs and sport was sport; there were no Raffleses in first-class cricket then. I had forgotten Raffles was a modern first-class cricketer:

that explains him. Rather than see my son such another, do you know what I'd prefer to see him?"

I neither knew nor cared: yet a wretched premonitory fascination held me breathless till I was told.

"I'd prefer to see him a thief!" said Nasmyth savagely; and when his eyes were done with me, he turned upon his heel. So that ended that stage of my discomfiture.

It was only to give place to a worse. Was all this accident or fell design? Conscience had made a coward of me, and yet what reason had I to disbelieve the worst? We were pirouetting on the edge of an abyss; sooner or later the false step must come and the pit swallow us. I began to wish myself back in London, and I did get back to my room in our old house. My dancing days were already over; there I had taken the one resolution to which I remained as true as better men to better vows; there the painful association was no mere sense of personal unworthiness. I fell to thinking in my room of other dances... and was still smoking the cigarette which Raffles had taught me to appreciate when I looked up to find him regarding me from the door. He had opened it as noiselessly as only Raffles could open doors, and now he closed it in the same professional fashion.

"I missed Achilles hours ago," said he. "And still he's sulking in his tent!"

"I have been," I answered, laughing as he could always make me, "but I'll chuck it if you'll stop and smoke. Our host doesn't mind; there's an ash-tray provided for the purpose. I ought to be sulking between the sheets, but I'm ready to sit up with you till morning."

"We might do worse; but, on the other hand, we might do still better," rejoined Raffles, and for once he resisted the seductive Sullivan. "As a matter of fact, it's morning now; in another hour it will be dawn; and where could day dawn better than in Warfield Woods, or along the Stockley road, or even on the Upper or the Middle? I don't want to turn in, any more than you do. I may as well confess that the whole show down here has exalted me more than anything for years. But if we can't sleep, Bunny, let's have some fresh air instead."

"Has everybody gone to bed?" I asked.

"Long ago. I was the last in. Why?"

"Only it might sound a little odd, our turning out again, if they were to hear us."

Raffles stood over me with a smile made of mischief and cunning; but it was the purest mischief imaginable, the most innocent and comic cunning.

"They shan't hear us at all, Bunny," said he. "I mean to get out as I did in the good old nights. I've been spoiling for the chance ever since I came down. There's not the smallest harm in it now; and if you'll come with me I'll show you how it used to be done."

"But I know," said I. "Who used to haul up the rope after you, and let it down again to the minute?"

Raffles looked down on me from lowered lids, over a smile too humorous to offend.

"My dear good Bunny! And do you suppose that even then I had only one way of doing a thing? I've had a spare loophole all my life, and when you're ready I'll show you what it was when I was here. Take off those boots, and carry your tennis-shoes; slip on another coat; put out your light; and I'll meet you on the landing in two minutes."

He met me with uplifted finger, and not a syllable; and downstairs he led me, stocking soles close against the skirting, two feet to each particular step. It must have seemed child's play to Raffles; the old precautions were obviously assumed for my entertainment; but I confess that to me it was all refreshingly exciting—for once without a risk of durance if we came to grief! With scarcely a creak we reached the hall, and could have walked out of the street door without danger or difficulty. But that would not do for Raffles. He must needs lead

me into the boys' part, through the green baize door. It took a deal
of opening and shutting, but Raffles seemed to enjoy nothing better
than these mock obstacles, and in a few minutes we were resting with
sharp ears in the boys' hall.

"Through these windows?" I whispered, when the clock over the
piano had had matters its own way long enough to make our minds
quite easy.

"How else?" whispered Raffles, as he opened the one on whose
ledge our letters used to await us of a morning.

"And then through the quad—"

"And over the gates at the end. No talking, Bunny; there's a dormi-
tory just overhead; but ours was in front, you remember, and if they
had ever seen me I should have nipped back this way while they were
watching the other."

His finger was on his lips as we got out softly into the starlight. I
remember how the gravel hurt as we left the smooth flagged margin
of the house for the open quad; but the nearer of two long green
seats (whereon you prepared your construe for the second-school
in the summer term) was mercifully handy; and once in our rubber
soles we had no difficulty in scaling the gates beyond the fives-courts.
Moreover, we dropped into a very desert of a country road, nor saw
a soul when we doubled back beneath the outer study windows, nor
heard a footfall in the main street of the slumbering town. Our own
fell like the night-dews and the petals of the poet; but Raffles ran his
arm through mine, and would chatter in whispers as we went.

"So you and Nipper had a word—or was it words? I saw you out
of the tail of my eye when I was dancing, and I heard you out of the
tail of my ear. It sounded like words, Bunny, and I thought I caught
my name. He's the most consistent man I know, and the least altered
from a boy. But he'll subscribe all right, you'll see, and be very glad I
made him."

I whispered back that I did not believe it for a moment. Raffles had not heard all Nasmyth had said of him. And neither would he listen to the little I meant to repeat to him; he would but reiterate a conviction so chimerical to my mind that I interrupted in my turn to ask him what ground he had for it.

"I've told you already," said Raffles. "I mean to make him."

"But how?" I asked. "And when, and where?"

"At Philippi, Bunny, where I said I'd see him. What a rabbit you are at a quotation!

> "'And I think that the field of Philippi
> Was where Caesar came to an end;
> But who gave old Brutus the tip, I
> Can't comprehend!'

"You may have forgotten your Shakespeare, Bunny, but you ought to remember that."

And I did, vaguely, but had no idea what it or Raffles meant, as I plainly told him.

"The theatre of war," he answered—"and here we are at the stage door!"

Raffles had stopped suddenly in his walk. It was the last dark hour of the summer night, but the light from a neighbouring lamppost showed me the look on his face as he turned.

"I think you also inquired when," he continued. "Well, then, this minute—if you will give me a leg up!"

And behind him, scarcely higher than his head, and not even barred, was a wide window with a wire blind, and the name of Nasmyth among others lettered in gold upon the wire.

"You're never going to break in?"

"This instant, if you'll help me; in five or ten minutes, if you won't."

"Surely you didn't bring the—the tools?"

He jingled them gently in his pocket.

"Not the whole outfit, Bunny. But you never know when you mayn't want one or two. I'm only thankful I didn't leave the lot behind this time. I very nearly did."

"I must say I thought you would, coming down here," I said reproachfully.

"But you ought to be glad I didn't," he rejoined with a smile. "It's going to mean old Nasmyth's subscription to the Founder's Fund, and that's to be a big one, I promise you! The lucky thing is that I went so far as to bring my bunch of safekeys. Now, are you going to help me use them, or are you not? If so, now's your minute; if not, clear out and be—"

"Not so fast, Raffles," said I testily. "You must have planned this before you came down, or you would never have brought all those things with you."

"My dear Bunny, they're a part of my kit! I take them wherever I take my evening-clothes. As to this potty bank, I never even thought of it, much less that it would become a public duty to draw a hundred or so without signing for it. That's all I shall touch, Bunny—I'm not on the make tonight. There's no risk in it either. If I am caught I shall simply sham champagne and stand the racket; it would be an obvious frolic after what happened at that meeting. And they will catch me, if I stand talking here: you run away back to bed—unless you're quite determined to 'give old Brutus the tip!'"

Now we had barely been a minute whispering where we stood, and the whole street was still as silent as the tomb. To me there seemed least danger in discussing the matter quietly on the spot. But even as he gave me my dismissal Raffles turned and caught the sill above him, first with one hand and then with the other. His legs swung like a pendulum as he drew himself up with one arm, then shifted the position of the other hand, and very gradually worked himself waist-high with the sill. But the sill was too narrow for him; that was as far as he could get unaided; and it was as much as I could bear to see of a feat which in itself might have hardened my conscience and softened my heart. But I had identified his doggerel verse at last. I am ashamed to say that it was part of a set of my very own writing in the school magazine of my time. So Raffles knew the stuff better than I did myself, and yet scorned to press his flattery to win me over! He had won me: in a second my rounded shoulders were a pedestal for those dangling feet. And before many more I heard the old metallic snap, followed by the raising of a sash so slowly and gently as to be almost inaudible to me listening just below.

Raffles went through hands first, disappeared for an instant, then leaned out, lowering his hands for me.

"Come on, Bunny! You're safer in than out. Hang on to the sill and let me get you under the arms. Now all together—quietly does it—and over you come!"

No need to dwell on our proceedings in the bank. I myself had small part in the scene, being posted rather in the wings, at the foot of the stairs leading to the private premises in which the manager had his domestic being. But I made my mind easy about him, for in the silence of my watch I soon detected a nasal note overhead, and it was resonant and aggressive as the man himself. Of Raffles, on the contrary, I heard nothing, for he had shut the door between us, and I was to warn him if a single sound came through. I need scarcely add that no warning was necessary during the twenty minutes we remained in the bank. Raffles afterward assured me that nineteen of them had been spent in filing one key; but one of his latest inventions was a little thick velvet bag in which he carried the keys; and this bag had two elastic mouths, which closed so tightly about either wrist that he could file away, inside, and scarcely hear it himself. As for these keys, they were clever counterfeits of typical patterns by two great safe-making firms. And Raffles had come by them in a manner all his own, which the criminal world may discover for itself.

When he opened the door and beckoned to me, I knew by his face that he had succeeded to his satisfaction, and by experience better than to question him on the point. Indeed, the first thing was to get out of the bank; for the stars were drowning in a sky of ink and water, and it was a comfort to feel that we could fly straight to our beds. I said so in whispers as Raffles cautiously opened our window and peeped out. In an instant his head was in, and for another I feared the worst.

"What was that, Bunny? No, you don't, my son! There's not a soul in sight that I can see, but you never know, and we may as well lay a scent while we're about it. Ready? Then follow me, and never mind the window."

With that he dropped softly into the street, and I after him, turning to the right instead of the left, and that at a brisk trot instead of the innocent walk which had brought us to the bank. Like mice we scampered past the great schoolroom, with its gable snipping a paler sky than ever, and the shadows melting even in the colonnade underneath. Masters' houses flitted by on the left, lesser landmarks on either side, and presently we were running our heads into the dawn, one under either hedge of the Stockley road.

"Did you see that light in Nab's just now?" cried Raffles as he led.

"No; why?" I panted, nearly spent.

"It was in Nab's dressing-room."

"Yes?"

"I've seen it there before," continued Raffles. "He never was a good sleeper, and his ears reach to the street. I wouldn't like to say how often I was chased by him in the small hours! I believe he knew who it was toward the end, but Nab was not the man to accuse you of what he couldn't prove."

I had no breath for comment. And on sped Raffles like a yacht before the wind, and on I blundered like a wherry at sea, making heavy weather all the way, and nearer foundering at every stride. Suddenly, to my deep relief, Raffles halted, but only to tell me to stop my pipes while he listened.

"It's all right, Bunny," he resumed, showing me a glowing face in the dawn. "History's on its own tracks once more, and I'll bet you it's dear old Nab on ours! Come on, Bunny; run to the last gasp, and leave the rest to me."

I was past arguing, and away he went. There was no help for it but to follow as best I could. Yet I had vastly preferred to collapse on the spot, and trust to Raffles's resource, as before very long I must. I had never enjoyed long wind and the hours that we kept in town may well have aggravated the deficiency. Raffles, however, was in first-class training from first-class cricket, and he had no mercy on Nab or me. But the master himself was an old Oxford miler, who could still bear it better than I; nay, as I flagged and stumbled, I heard him pounding steadily behind.

"Come on, come on, or he'll do us!" cried Raffles shrilly over his shoulder; and a gruff sardonic laugh came back over mine. It was pearly morning now, but we had run into a shallow mist that took me by the throat and stabbed me to the lungs. I coughed and coughed, and stumbled in my stride, until down I went, less by accident than to get it over, and so lay headlong in my tracks. And old Nab dealt me a verbal kick as he passed.

"You beast!" he growled, as I have known him growl it in form.

But Raffles himself had abandoned the flight on hearing my downfall, and I was on hands and knees just in time to see the meeting between him and old Nab. And there stood Raffles in the silvery mist, laughing with his whole light heart, leaning back to get the full flavour of his mirth; and, nearer me, sturdy old Nab, dour and grim, with beads of dew on the hoary beard that had been lamp-black in our time.

"So I've caught you at last!" said he. "After more years than I mean to count!"

"Then you're luckier than we are, sir," answered Raffles, "for I fear our man has given us the slip."

"Your man!" echoed Nab. His bushy eyebrows had shot up: it was as much as I could do to keep my own in their place.

"We were indulging in the chase ourselves," explained Raffles, "and one of us has suffered for his zeal, as you can see. It is even possible that we, too, have been chasing a perfectly innocent man."

"Not to say a reformed character," said our pursuer dryly. "I suppose you don't mean a member of the school?" he added, pinking his man suddenly as of yore, with all the old barbed acumen. But Raffles was now his match.

"That would be carrying reformation rather far, sir. No, as I say, I may have been mistaken in the first instance; but I had put out my light and was looking out of the window when I saw a fellow behaving quite suspiciously. He was carrying his boots and creeping along in his socks—which must be why you never heard him, sir. They make less noise than rubber soles even—that is, they must, you know! Well, Bunny had just left me, so I hauled him out and we both crept down to play detective. No sign of the fellow! We had a look in the colonnade—I thought I heard him—and that gave us no end of a hunt for nothing. But just as we were leaving he came padding past under our noses, and that's where we took up the chase. Where he'd been in the meantime I have no idea; very likely he'd done no harm; but it seemed worth while finding out. He had too good a start, though, and poor Bunny had too bad a wind."

"You should have gone on and let me rip," said I, climbing to my feet at last.

"As it is, however, we will all let the other fellow do so," said old Nab in a genial growl. "And you two had better turn into my house and have something to keep the morning cold out."

You may imagine with what alacrity we complied; and yet I am bound to confess that I had never liked Nab at school. I still remember my term in his form. He had a caustic tongue and fine assortment of damaging epithets, most of which were levelled at my devoted skull during those three months. I now discovered that he also kept a particularly mellow Scotch whiskey, an excellent cigar, and a fund of anecdote of which a mordant wit was the worthy bursar. Enough to add that he kept us laughing in his study until the chapel bells rang him out.

As for Raffles, he appeared to me to feel far more compunction for the fable which he had been compelled to foist upon one of the old masters than for the immeasurably graver offence against society and another Old Boy. This, indeed, did not worry him at all; and the story was received next day with absolute credulity on all sides. Nasmyth himself was the first to thank us both for our spirited effort on his behalf; and the incident had the ironic effect of establishing an immediate *entente cordiale* between Raffles and his very latest victim. I must confess, however, that for my own part I was thoroughly uneasy during the Old Boys' second innings, when Raffles made a selfish score, instead of standing by me to tell his own story in his own way. There was never any knowing with what new detail he was about to embellish it: and I have still to receive full credit for the tact that it required to follow his erratic lead convincingly. Seldom have I been more thankful than when our train started next morning, and the poor, unsuspecting Nasmyth himself waved us a last farewell from the platform.

"Lucky we weren't staying at Nab's," said Raffles, as he lit a Sullivan and opened his Daily Mail at its report of the robbery. "There was one thing Nab would have spotted like the downy old bird he always was and will be."

"What was that?"

"The front door must have been found duly barred and bolted in the morning, and yet we let them assume that we came out that way. Nab would have pounced on the point, and by this time we might have been nabbed ourselves."

It was but a little over a hundred sovereigns that Raffles had taken, and, of course, he had resolutely eschewed any and every form of paper money. He posted his own first contribution of twenty-five pounds to the Founder's Fund immediately on our return to town, before rushing off to more first-class cricket, and I gathered that the rest would follow piecemeal as he deemed it safe. By an odd coincidence, however, a mysterious but magnificent donation of a hundred guineas was almost simultaneously received in notes by the treasurer of the Founder's Fund, from one who simply signed himself "Old Boy." The treasurer happened to be our late host, the new man at our old house, and he wrote to congratulate Raffles on what he was pleased to consider a direct result of the latter's speech. I did not see the letter that Raffles wrote in reply, but in due course I heard the name of the mysterious contributor. He was said to be no other than Nipper Nasmyth himself. I asked Raffles if it was true. He replied that he would ask old Nipper point-blank if he came up as usual to the Varsity match, and if they had the luck to meet. And not only did this happen, but I had the greater luck to be walking round the ground with Raffles when we encountered our shabby friend in front of the pavilion.

"My dear fellow," cried Raffles, "I hear it was you who gave that hundred guineas by stealth to the very movement you denounced. Don't deny it, and don't blush to find it fame. Listen to me. There was a great lot in what you said; but it's the kind of thing we ought all to back, whether we strictly approve of it in our hearts or not."

"Exactly, Raffles, but the fact is—"

"I know what you're going to say. Don't say it. There's not one in a thousand who would do as you've done, and not one in a million who would do it anonymously."

"But what makes you think I did it, Raffles?"

"Everybody is saying so. You will find it all over the place when you get back. You will find yourself the most popular man down there, Nasmyth!"

I never saw a nobler embarrassment than that of this awkward, ungainly, cantankerous man: all his angles seemed to have been smoothed away: there was something quite human in the flushed, undecided, wistful face.

"I never was popular in my life," he said. "I don't want to buy my popularity now. To be perfectly candid with you, Raffles—"

"Don't! I can't stop to hear. They're ringing the bell. But you shouldn't have been angry with me for saying you were a generous good chap, Nasmyth, when you were one all the time. Goodbye, old fellow!"

But Nasmyth detained us a second more. His hesitation was at an end. There was a sudden new light in his face.

"Was I?" he cried. "Then I'll make it *two* hundred, and damn the odds!"

Raffles was a thoughtful man as we went to our seats. He saw nobody, would acknowledge no remark. Neither did he attend to the cricket for the first half-hour after lunch; instead, he eventually invited me to come for a stroll on the practice ground, where, however, we found two chairs aloof from the fascinating throng.

"I am not often sorry, Bunny, as you know," he began. "But I have been sorry since the interval. I've been sorry for poor old Nipper Nasmyth. Did you see the idea of being popular dawn upon him for the first time in his life?"

"I did; but you had nothing to do with that, my dear man."

Raffles shook his head over me as our eyes met. "I had everything to do with it. I tried to make him tell the meanest lie. I made sure he would, and for that matter he nearly did. Then, at the last moment, he saw how to hedge things with his conscience. And his second hundred will be a real gift."

"You mean under his own name—"

"And with his own free-will. My good Bunny, is it possible you don't know what I did with the hundred we drew from that bank!"

"I knew what you were going to do with it," said I. "I didn't know you had actually got further than the twenty-five you told me you were sending as your own contribution."

Raffles rose abruptly from his chair.

"And you actually thought that came out of his money?"

"Naturally."

"In my name?"

"I thought so."

Raffles stared at me inscrutably for some moments, and for some more at the great white numbers over the grand-stand.

"We may as well have another look at the cricket," said he. "It's difficult to see the board from here, but I believe there's another man out."

LESSON IN ANATOMY

Michael Innes

Michael Innes was the pen-name of John Innes Mackintosh Stewart (1906–94), who went to school at Edinburgh Academy. In his memoir *Myself and Michael Innes*, he said that at the time, "the Academy was still something of a citadel of Edinburgh's haute bourgeoisie" and he didn't find his time there entirely enjoyable, but he obtained a place at Oriel College, Oxford, and life amid the dreaming spires suited him so well that he spent much of the rest of his life there, becoming a Student of Christ Church (in that college's curious terminology a Student is equivalent to a Fellow in other colleges) in 1949 and remaining there until his retirement in 1973, by which time he was a professor.

His Oriel contemporary, the eminent historian A. J. P. Taylor, claimed that Stewart laughed at Taylor's "excessive reading of detective novels", but the author was already enthusiastic about mysteries and discussed them "with luminaries of the magnitude of Ronald Knox and… T. S. Eliot". His first novel, *Death at the President's Lodging*, set in a fictitious university clearly modelled on Oxford, appeared in 1936; his last, *Appleby and the Ospreys*, was published half a century later. This story first appeared in *Ellery Queen's Mystery Magazine* in November 1946.

A LREADY THE ANATOMY THEATRE WAS CROWDED WITH STUDENTS: tier upon tier of faces pallid beneath the clear shadowless light cast by the one elaborate lamp, large as a giant cart-wheel, near the ceiling. The place gleamed with an aggressive cleanliness; the smell of formalin pervaded it; its centre was a faintly sinister vacancy—the spot to which would presently be wheeled the focal object of the occasion.

At Nessfield University Professor Finlay's final lecture was one of the events of the year. He was always an excellent teacher. For three terms he discoursed lucidly from his dais or tirelessly prowled his dissecting-rooms, encouraging young men and women who had hitherto dismembered only dogfish and frogs to address themselves with resolution to human legs, arms, and torsos. The Department of Anatomy was large; these objects lay about it in a dispersed profusion; Finlay moved among them now with gravity and now with a whimsical charm which did a good deal to humanise his macabre environment. It was only once a year that he yielded to his taste for the dramatic.

The result was the final lecture. And the final lecture was among the few academic activities of Nessfield sufficiently abounding in human appeal to be regularly featured in the local Press. Perhaps the account had become a little stereotyped with the years, and always there was virtually the same photograph showing the popular professor (as Finlay was dubbed for the occasion) surrounded by wreaths, crosses, and other floral tributes. Innumerable citizens of Nessfield who had never been inside the doors of their local university looked forward to this annual report, and laid it down with the comfortable conviction that all was well with the pursuit of learning in the district.

Their professors were still professors—eccentric, erudite, and amiable. Their students were still, as students should be, giving much of their thought to the perpetration of elaborate, tasteless, and sometimes dangerous practical jokes.

For the lecture was at once a festival, a rag, and a genuine display of virtuosity. It took place in this large anatomy theatre. Instead of disjointed limbs and isolated organs there was a whole new cadaver for the occasion. And upon this privileged corpse Finlay rapidly demonstrated certain historical developments of his science to an audience in part attentive and in part concerned with lowering skeletons from the rafters, releasing various improbable living creatures—lemurs and echidnas and opossums—to roam the benches, or contriving what quainter japes they could think up. On one famous occasion the corpse itself had been got at, and at the first touch of the professor's scalpel had awakened to an inferno of noise presently accounted for by the discovery that its inside consisted chiefly of alarm clocks. Nor were these diversions and surprises all one-sided, since Finlay himself, entering into the spirit of the occasion, had more than once been known to forestall his students with some extravagance of his own. It was true that this had happened more rarely of recent years, and by some it was suspected that this complacent scholar had grown a little out of taste with the role in which he had been cast. But the affair remained entirely good-humoured; tradition restrained the excesses into which it might have fallen; it was, in its own queer way, an approved social occasion. High University authorities sometimes took distinguished visitors along—those, that is to say, who felt they had a stomach for post-mortem curiosity. There was quite a number of strangers on the present occasion.

The popular professor had entered through the glass-panelled double doors which gave directly upon the dissecting-table. Finlay was florid and very fat; his white gown was spotlessly laundered; a high cap of the same material would have given him the appearance of a generously self-dieted chef. He advanced to the low rail that separated him from the first tier of spectators and started to make some preliminary remarks. What these actually were, or how they were designed to conclude, he had probably forgotten years ago, for this was the point at which the first interruption traditionally occurred. And, sure enough, no sooner had Finlay opened his mouth than three young men near the back of the theatre stood up and delivered themselves of a fanfare of trumpets. Finlay appeared altogether surprised—he possessed, as has been stated, a dramatic sense—and this was the signal for the greater part of those present to rise in their seats and sing *For he's a jolly good fellow*. Flowers—single blooms, for the present—began to float through the air and fall about the feet of the professor. The strangers, distinguished and otherwise, smiled at each other benevolently, thereby indicating their pleased acquiescence in these time-honoured academic junketings. A bell began to toll.

"*Never ask for whom the bell tolls*," said a deep voice from somewhere near the professor's left hand. And the whole student body responded in a deep chant: "*It tolls for THEE.*"

And now there was a more urgent bell—one that clattered up and down some adjacent corridor to the accompaniment of tramping feet and the sound as of a passing tumbrel. "*Bring out your dead*," cried the deep voice. And the chant was taken up all round the theatre. "*Bring out your dead*," everybody shouted with gusto. "*Bring out your DEAD!*"

This was the signal for the entrance of Albert, Professor Finlay's dissecting-room attendant. Albert was perhaps the only person in Nessfield who uncompromisingly disapproved of the last lecture and all that went with it—this perhaps because, as an ex-policeman, he felt bound to hold all disorder in discountenance. The severely aloof expression on the face of Albert as he wheeled in the cadaver was one of the highlights of the affair—nor on this occasion did it by any means fail

of its effect. Indeed, Albert appeared to be more than commonly upset.
A severe frown lay across his ample and unintelligent countenance.
He held his six-foot-three sternly erect; behind his vast leather apron
his bosom discernibly heaved with manly emotion. Albert wheeled in
the body—distinguishable as a wisp of ill-nourished humanity beneath
the tarpaulin that covered it—and Finlay raised his right hand as if to
bespeak attention. The result was a sudden squawk and flap of heavy
wings near the ceiling. Somebody had released a vulture. The ominous
bird blundered twice round the theatre, and then settled composedly on
a rafter. It craned its scrawny neck and fixed a beady eye on the body.

Professor Finlay benevolently smiled; at the same time he produced
a handkerchief and rapidly mopped his forehead. To several people,
old stagers, it came that the eminent anatomist was uneasy this year.
The vulture was a bit steep, after all.

There was a great deal of noise. One group of students was doggedly and pointlessly singing a sea shanty; others were perpetrating
or preparing to perpetrate sundry jokes of a varying degree of effec-
tiveness. Albert, standing immobile beside the cadaver, let his eyes
roam resentfully over the scene. Then Finlay raised not one hand but
two—only for a moment, but there was instant silence. He took a step
backwards amid the flowers which lay around him; carefully removed a
couple of forget-me-nots from his hair; gave a quick nod to Albert; and
began to explain—in earnest this time—what he was proposing to do.

Albert stepped to the body and pulled back the tarpaulin.

"And ever," said a voice from the audience, "at my back I hear the
rattle of dry bones and chuckle spread from ear to ear."

It was an apt enough sally. The cadaver seemed to be mostly bones
already—the bones of an elderly, withered man—and its most prominent feature was a ghastly *rictus* or fixed grin which exposed two long
rows of gleamingly white and utterly incongruous-seeming teeth. From
somewhere high up in the theatre there was a little sigh followed by a

slumping sound. A robust and football-playing youth had fainted. Quite a number of people, as if moved by a mysterious or chameleon-like sympathy, were rapidly approximating to the complexion of the grisly object displayed before them. But there was nothing unexpected in all this. Finlay, knowing that custom allowed him perhaps another five minutes of sober attention at this point, continued his remarks. The cadaver before the class was exactly as it would be had it come before a similar class four hundred years ago. The present anatomy lesson was essentially a piece of historical reconstruction. His hearers would recall that on one of Rembrandt's paintings depicting such a subject—

For perhaps a couple of minutes the practised talk flowed on. The audience was quite silent. Finlay for a moment paused to recall a date. In the resulting complete hush there was a sharp click, rather like the lifting of a latch. A girl screamed. Every eye in the theatre was on the cadaver. For its lower jaw had sagged abruptly open, and the teeth, which were plainly dentures, had half-extruded themselves from the gaping mouth, rather as if pushed outwards by some spasm within.

Such things do happen. There is a celebrated story of just such startling behaviour on the part of the body of the philosopher Schopenhauer. And Finlay, perceiving that his audience was mark-edly upset, perhaps debated endeavouring to rally them with just this learned and curious anecdote. But even as he paused, the cadaver acted again. Abruptly the jaws closed like a powerful vice, the lips and cheeks sagged; it was to be concluded that this wretched remnant of humanity had swallowed its last meal.

For a moment something like panic hovered over the anatomy theatre. Another footballer fainted; a girl laughed hysterically; two men in the back row, having all the appearance of case-hardened physicians, looked at each other in consternation and bolted from the building. Finlay, with a puzzled look on his face, again glanced backwards at the cadaver. Then he nodded abruptly to Albert, who replaced the tarpaulin. Presumably, after this queer upset, he judged it best to interpose a little more composing historical talk before getting down to business.

He was saying something about the anatomical sketches of Leonardo da Vinci. Again he glanced back at the cadaver. Suddenly the lights went out. The anatomy theatre was in darkness.

For some moments nobody thought of an accident. Finlay often had recourse to an epidiascope or lantern, and the trend of his talk now led people to suppose that something of the sort was in train now. Presently, however, it became plain that there was a hitch—and at this the audience broke into every kind of vociferation. Above the uproar the vulture could be heard overhead, vastly agitated. Matches were struck, but cast no certain illumination. Various objects were being pitched about the theatre. There was a strong scent of lilies.

Albert's voice made itself heard, cursing medical students, cursing the University of Nessfield, cursing Professor Finlay's final lecture. From the progress of this commination it was possible to infer that he was groping his way towards the switches. There was a click, and once more the white shadowless light flooded the theatre.

Everything was as it had been—save in two particulars. Most of the wreaths and crosses which had been designed for the end of the lecture had proved missiles too tempting to ignore in that interval of darkness; they had been lobbed into the centre of the theatre and lay there about the floor, except for two which had actually landed on the shrouded cadaver.

And Finlay had disappeared.

The audience was bewildered and a little apprehensive. Had the failure of the lighting really been an accident? Or was the popular professor obligingly coming forward with one of his increasingly rare and prized pranks? The audience sat tight, awaiting developments. Albert, returning from the switchboard, impatiently kicked a wreath of lilies from his path. The audience, resenting this display of nervous irritation, cat-called and booed. Then a voice from one of the higher benches called out boisterously: "The corpse has caught the dropsy!"

"It's a-swelling," cried another voice—that of a devotee of Dickens—"It's a-swelling wisibly before my eyes."

And something had certainly happened to the meagre body beneath its covering; it was as if during the darkness it had been inflated by a gigantic pump.

With a final curse Albert sprang forward and pulled back the tarpaulin. What lay beneath was the body of Professor Finlay, quite dead. The original cadaver was gone.

The vulture swooped hopefully from its rafter.

"Publicity?" said Detective-Inspector John Appleby. "I'm afraid you can scarcely expect anything else. Or perhaps it would be better to say notoriety. Nothing remotely like it has happened in England for years."

Sir David Evans, Nessfield's very Welsh Vice-Chancellor, passed a hand dejectedly through his flowing white hair and softly groaned. "A scandal!" he said. "A scandal—look you, Mr. Appleby—that peggars description. There must be infestigations. There must be arrests. Already there are reporters from the pig papers. This morning I have been photographed." Sir David paused and glanced across the room at the handsome portrait of himself which hung above the fireplace. "This morning," he repeated, momentarily comforted, "I have been photographed, look you, five or six times."

Appleby smiled. "The last case I remember as at all approaching it was the shooting of Viscount Auldearn, the Lord Chancellor, during a private performance of *Hamlet* at the Duke of Horton's seat, Scamnum Court."

For a second Sir David looked almost cheerful. It was plain that he gained considerable solace from this august comparison. But then he shook his head. "In the anatomy theatre!" he said. "And on the one day of the year when there is these unseembly pehaviours. And a pody vanishes. And there is fultures—fultures, Mr. Appleby!"

"One vulture." Dr. Holroyd, Nessfield's professor of human physiology, spoke as if this comparative paucity of birds of prey represented one of the bright spots of the affair. "Only one vulture, and apparently abstracted by a group of students from the Zoo. The Director rang up as soon as he saw the first report. He might be described as an angry man."

Appleby brought out a notebook. "What we are looking for," he said, "is angry men. Perhaps you know of someone whose feelings of anger towards the late Professor Finlay at times approached the murderous?"

Sir David Evans looked at Dr. Holroyd, and Dr. Holroyd looked at Sir David Evans. And it appeared to Appleby that the demeanour of each was embarrassed. "Of course," he added, "I don't mean mere passing irritations between colleagues."

"There is frictions," said Sir David carefully. "Always in a university there is frictions. And frictions produce heat. There was pad frictions between Finlay and Dr. Holroyd here. There was personalities, I am sorry to say. For years there has been most fexatious personalities." Sir David, who at all times preserved an appearance of the most massive benevolence, glanced at his colleague with an eye in which there was a nasty glint. "Dr. Holroyd is Dean of the Faculty of Medicine, look you. It is why I have asked him to meet you now. And last week at a meeting there was a most disgraceful scene. It was a meeting about lavatories. It was a meeting of the Committee for Lavatories."

"Dear me!" said Appleby. Universities, he was thinking, must have changed considerably since his day.

"Were there to be more lavatories in Physiology Puilding? Finlay said he would rather put in a path."

"A path?" said Appleby, perplexed.

"A path, with hot and cold laid on, and an efficient shower. Finlay said that in his opinion Dr. Holroyd here padly needed a path."

"And did Dr. Holroyd retaliate?"

"I am sorry to say that he did, Mr. Appleby. He said that if he had his way in the matter Finlay's own path would be a formalin one. Which is what they keep the cadavers in, Mr. Appleby."

Dr. Holroyd shifted uneasily on his chair. "It was unfortunate," he admitted. "I must freely admit that unfortunate nature of the dispute."

"It was unacademic," said Sir David severely. "There is no other word for it, Dr. Holroyd."

"I am afraid it was. And most deplorably public. Whereas your own quarrel with Finlay, Sir David, had been a discreetly unobtrusive matter." Dr. Holroyd smiled with sudden frank malice. "And over private, not University, affairs. In fact, over a woman. Or was it several women?"

"These," said Appleby rather hastily, "are matters which it may be unnecessary to take up." Detectives are commonly supposed to expend all their energy in dragging information out of people; actually, much of it goes in preventing irrelevant and embarrassing disclosure. "May I ask, Sir David, your own whereabouts at the time of the fatality?"

"I was in this room, Mr. Appleby, reading Plato. Even Vice-chancellors are entitled to read Plato at times, and I had given orders not to be disturbed."

"I see. And I take it that nobody interrupted you, and that you might have left the room for a time without being observed?"

Sir David gloomily nodded.

"And you, Dr. Holroyd?"

"I went to poor Finlay's final lecture and sat near the back. But the whole stupid affair disgusted me, and I came away—only a few minutes, it seems, before the lights went out. I composed myself by taking a quiet walk along the canal. It was quite deserted."

"I see. And now about the manner of Finlay's death. I understand that you have inspected the body and realise that he was killed by the thrust of a fine dagger from behind? The deed was accomplished in what must have been almost complete darkness. Would you say that it required—or at least that it suggests—something like the professional knowledge of another anatomist or medical man?"

Holroyd was pale. "It certainly didn't strike me as the blind thrust of an amateur made in a panic. But perhaps there is a species of particularly desperate criminal who is skilled in such things."

"Possibly so." Appleby glanced from Holroyd to Sir David. "But is either of you aware of Finlay's having any connections or interests which might bring upon him the violence of such people? No? Then I think we must be very sceptical about anything of the sort. To kill a man in extremely risky circumstances simply for the pleasure of laying the body on his own dissecting-table before his own students is something quite outside my experience of professional crime. It is much more like some eccentric act of private vengeance. And one conceived by a theatrical mind."

Once more Sir David Evans looked at Dr. Holroyd, and Dr. Holroyd looked at Sir David Evans. "Finlay himself," said Sir David, "had something theatrical about him. Otherwise, look you, he would not have let himself pecome the central figure in this pig yearly joke." He paused. "Now, Dr. Holroyd here is not theatrical. He is pad-tempered. He is morose. He is under-pred. But theatrical he is not."

"And no more is Sir David." Holroyd seemed positively touched by the character sketch of himself just offered. "He is a bit of a humbug, of course—all philosophers are. And he is not a good man, since it is impossible for a Vice-Chancellor to be that. Perhaps he is even something of a *poseur*. If compelled to characterise him freely"—and

Holroyd got comfortably to his feet—"I should describe him as Goethe described Milton's *Paradise Lost*." Holroyd moved towards the door, and as he did so paused to view Sir David's portrait. "Fair outside but rotten inwardly," he quoted thoughtfully. "But of positive theatrical instinct I would be inclined to say that Sir David is tolerably free. Good afternoon."

There was a moment's silence. Sir David Evans's fixed expression of benevolence had never wavered. "Pad passions," he said. "Look you, Mr. Appleby, there is pad passions in that man."

Albert was pottering gloomily among his cadaver-racks. His massive frame gave a jump as Appleby entered; it was clear that he was not in full possession of that placid repose which ex-policemen should enjoy.

Appleby looked round with brisk interest. "Nice place you have here," he said. "Everything convenient and nicely thought out."

The first expression on Albert's face had been strongly disapproving. But at this he perceptibly relaxed. "Ball-bearing," he said huskily. "Handle them like lambs." He pushed back a steel shutter and proudly drew out a rack and its contents. "Nicely developed gal," he said appreciatively. "Capital pelvis for childbearing, she was going to have. Now, if you'll just step over here I can show you one or two uncommonly interesting lower limbs."

"Thank you—another time." Appleby, though not unaccustomed to such places, had no aspirations towards connoisseurship. "I want your own story of what happened this morning."

"Yes, sir." From old professional habit Albert straightened up and stood at attention. "As you'll know, there's always been this bad be'aviour at the final lecture, so there was nothing out of the way in that. But then the lights went out, and they started throwing things, and something 'it me 'ard on the shins."

"Hard?" said Appleby. "I doubt if that could have been anything thrown from the theatre."

"No more do I." Albert was emphatic. "It was someone came in through the doors the moment the lights went out and got me down with a regular Rugby tackle. Fair winded I was, and lost my bearings as well."

"So it was some little time before you managed to get to the switch, which is just outside the swing doors. And in that time, Professor Finlay was killed and substituted for the cadaver, and the cadaver was got clean away. Would you say that was a one-man job?"

"No, sir, I would not. Though—mind you—that body 'ad only to be carried across a corridor and out into the courtyard. Anyone can 'ave a car waiting there, so the rest would be easy enough."

Appleby nodded. "The killing of Finlay, and the laying him out like that, may have been a sheer piece of macabre drama, possibly conceived and executed by a lunatic—or even by an apparently sane man with some specific obsession regarding corpses. But can you see any reason why such a person should actually carry off the original corpse? It meant saddling himself with an uncommonly awkward piece of evidence."

"You can't ever tell what madmen will do. And as for corpses, there are more people than you would reckon what 'as uncommon queer interests in them at times." And Albert shook his head. "I seen things," he added.

"No doubt you have. But have you seen anything just lately? Was there anything that might be considered as leading up to this shocking affair?"

Albert hesitated. "Well, sir, in this line wot I come down to since they retired me it's not always possible to up'old the law. In fact, it's sometimes necessary to circumvent it, like. For, as the late professor was given to remarking, science must be served." Albert paused and tapped his cadaver-racks. "Served with these 'ere. And of late we've been uncommon short. And there's no doubt that now and then him and me was stretching a point."

"Good heavens!" Appleby was genuinely startled. "This affair is bad enough already. You don't mean to say that it's going to lead to some further scandal about body-snatching?"

"Nothing like that, sir." But as he said this Albert looked doubtful. "Nothing *quite* like that. They comes from institutions, you know. And nowadays they 'as to be got to sign papers. It's a matter of tact. Sometimes relatives come along afterwards and says there been too much tact by a long way. It's not always easy to know just how much tact you can turn on. There's no denying but we've 'ad one or two awkwardnesses this year. And it's my belief as 'ow this sad affair is just another awkwardness—but more violent like than the others."

"It was violent, all right." Appleby had turned and led the way into the deserted theatre. Flowers still strewed it. There was a mingled smell of lilies and formalin. Overhead, the single great lamp was like a vast all-seeing eye. But that morning the eye had blinked. And what deed of darkness had followed?

"The professor was killed and laid out like that, sir, as an act of revenge by some barmy and outraged relation. And the cadaver was carried off by that same relation as what you might call an act of piety."

"Well, it's an idea." Appleby was strolling about, measuring distances with his eye. "But what about this particular body upon which Finlay was going to demonstrate? *Had* it outraged any pious relations?"

"It only come in yesterday. Quite unprepared it was to be, you see—the same as hanatomists 'ad them in the sixteenth century. Very interesting the late professor was on all that. And why all them young varmints of students should take this particular occasion to fool around—"

"Quite so. It was all in extremely bad taste, I agree. And I don't doubt that the Coroner will say so. And an Assize Judge too, if we have any luck. But you were going to tell me about this particular corpse."

"I was saying it only come in yesterday. And it was after that that somebody tried to break into the cadaver-racks. Last night, they did—and not a doubt of it. Quite professional, too. If this whole part of the building, sir, weren't well-nigh like a strong-room they'd have done it, without a doubt. And when the late professor 'eard of it 'e was as worried as I was. Awkwardnesses we've 'ad. But body-snatching in reverse, as you might say, was a new one on us both."

"So you think that the outraged and pious relation had an earlier shot, in the programme for which murder was not included? I think it's about time we hunted him up."

Albert looked sorely perplexed. "And so it would be—if we knew where to find him. But it almost seems as if there never was a cadaver with less in the way of relations than this one wot 'as caused all the trouble. A fair ideal cadaver it seemed to be. You don't think now"— Albert was frankly inconsequent—"that it might 'ave been an accident? You don't think it might 'ave been one of them young varmint's jokes gone a bit wrong?"

"I do not."

"But listen, sir." Albert was suddenly urgent. "Suppose there was a plan like this. The lights was to be put out and a great horrid dagger thrust into the cadaver. That would be quite like one of their jokes, believe me. For on would go the lights again and folk would get a pretty nasty shock. But now suppose—just suppose, sir—that when the lights were put out for that there purpose there came into the professor's head the notion of a joke of his own. He would change places with the cadaver—"

"But the man wasn't mad!" Appleby was staring at the late Professor Finlay's assistant in astonishment. "Anything so grotesque—"

"He done queer things before now." Albert was suddenly stubborn. "It would come on him sometimes to do something crazier than all them young fools could cudgel their silly brains after. And then the joke would come first and decency second. I seen some queer things at final lectures before this. And that would mean that the varmint thinking to stick the dagger in the cadaver would stick it in the late professor instead."

"I see." Appleby was looking at Albert with serious admiration; the fellow didn't look very bright—nevertheless his days in the Force should have been spent in the detective branch. "It's a better theory than we've had yet, I'm bound to say. But it leaves out two things: the disappearance of the original body, and the fact that Finlay was stabbed from behind. For if he did substitute himself for the body it would have been in the same position—a supine position, and not a prone position. So I don't think your notion will do. And, anyway, we must have all the information about the cadaver that we can get."

"It isn't much." Albert bore the discountenance of his hypothesis well. "We don't know much more about 'im than this—that 'e was a seafaring man."

The cadaver, it appeared, had at least possessed a name: James Cass. He had also possessed a nationality, for his seaman's papers declared him to be a citizen of the United States, and that his next-of-kin was a certain Martha Cass, with an indecipherable address in Seattle, Washington. For some years he had been sailing pretty constantly in freighters between England and America. Anything less likely to bring down upon the Anatomy Department of Nessfield University the vengeance of outraged and pious relations it would have been difficult to conceive. And the story of Cass's death and relegation to the service of science was an equally bare one. He had come off his ship and was making his way to an unknown lodging when he had been knocked down by a tram and taken to the casualty ward of Nessfield Infirmary.

There he had been visited by the watchful Albert, who had surreptitiously presented him with a flask of gin, receiving in exchange Cass's signature to a document bequeathing his remains for the purposes of medical science. Cass had then died, and his body had been delivered to the Anatomy School.

And, after that, somebody had ruthlessly killed Professor Finlay and then carried James Cass's body away again. Stripped of the bewildering nonsense of the final lecture, thought Appleby, the terms of the problem were fairly simple. And yet that nonsense, too, was relevant. For it had surely been counted upon in the plans of the murderer.

For a few minutes Appleby worked with a stop-watch. Then he turned once more to Albert. "At the moment," he said, "Cass himself appears to be something of a dead end. So now, let us take the lecture—or the small part of it that Finlay had got through before the lights went out. You were a witness of it—and a trained police witness, which is an uncommonly fortunate thing. I want you to give me every detail you can—down to the least squawk or flutter by that damned vulture."

Albert was gratified, and did as he was bid. Appleby listened, absorbed. Only once a flicker passed over his features. But when Albert was finished he had some questions to ask.

"There was an audience," he said, "—if audience is the right name for it. Apparently all sorts of people were accustomed to turn up?"

"All manner of unlikely and unsuitable folk." Albert looked disgusted. "Though most of them would be medical, one way or another. As you can imagine, sir, a demonstration of a sixteenth century dissecting technique isn't every layman's fancy."

"It certainly wouldn't be mine."

"I couldn't put a name to a good many of them. But there was Dr. Holroyd, whom you'll have met, sir; he's our professor of Human Physiology. Went away early, he did, and looking mighty disgusted, too. Then there was Dr. Wesselmann, the lecturer in Prosthetics—an alien, he is, and not been in Nessfield many years. He brought a friend I never had sight of before. And out they went too."

"Well, that's very interesting. And can you recall anyone else?"

"I don't know that I can, sir. Except of course our Vice-Chancellor, Sir David Evans."

Appleby jumped. "Evans! But he swore to me that—"

Albert smiled indulgently. "Bless you, that's his regular way. Did you ever know a Welshman who could let a day pass without a bit of 'armless deceit like?"

"There may be something in that."

"'E don't think it dignified, as you might say, to attend the final lecture openly. But more often that not he's up there at the far doorway, peering in at the fun. Well, this time 'e 'ad more than 'e bargained for."

"No doubt he had. And the same prescription might be good for some of the rest of us." Appleby paused and glanced quickly round the empty theatre. "Just step to a telephone, will you, and ask Dr. Holroyd to come over here."

Albert did as he was asked, and presently the physiologist came nervously in. "Is another interview really necessary?" he demanded. "I have a most important—"

"We shall hope not to detain you long." Appleby's voice was dry rather than reassuring. "It is merely that I want you to assist me in a reconstruction of the crime."

Holroyd flushed. "And may I ask by what right you ask me to take part in such a foolery?"

Appleby suddenly smiled. "None, sir—none at all. I merely wanted a trained mind—and one with a pronounced instinct to get at the truth of a problem when it arises. I was sure you would be glad to help."

"Perhaps I am. Anyway, go ahead."

"Then I should be obliged if you would be the murderer. Perhaps I should say the first murderer, for it seems likely enough that there were at least two—accomplices. You have no objection to so disagreeable a part?"

Holroyd shrugged his shoulders. "Naturally, I have none whatever. But I fear I must be coached in it and given my cue. For I assure you it is a role entirely foreign to me. And I have no theatrical flair, as Sir David pointed out."

Once more Appleby brought out his stop-watch. "Albert," he said briskly, "shall be the cadaver, and I shall be Finlay standing in front of it. Your business is to enter by the back, switch off the light, step into the theatre and there affect to stab me. I shall fall to the floor. You must then dislodge Albert, hoist me into his place and cover me with the tarpaulin. Then you must get hold of Albert by the legs or shoulders and haul him from the theatre."

"And all this in the dark? It seems a bit of a programme."

Appleby nodded. "I agree with you. But we shall at least discover if it is at all possible of accomplishment by one man in the time available. So are you ready?"

"One moment, sir." Albert, about to assume the passive part of the late James Cass, sat up abruptly. "You seem to have missed me out. Me as I was, that is to say."

"Quite true." Appleby looked at him thoughtfully. "We are short of a stand-in for you as you were this morning. But I shall stop off being Finlay's body and turn on the lights again myself. So go ahead."

Albert lay down and drew the tarpaulin over his head. Holroyd slipped out. Appleby advanced as if to address an audience. "Now," he said,

And Appleby talked. Being thorough, he made such anatomical observations as his ignorance allowed. Once he glanced round at the corpse, and out of the corner of his eye glimpsed Holroyd beyond the glass-panelled door, his hand already going up to flick at the switch. A moment later the theatre was in darkness and seconds after that

Appleby felt a sharp tap beneath the shoulder-blade. He pitched to the floor, pressing his stop-watch as he did so. Various heaving sounds followed as Holroyd got the portly Albert off the table; then Appleby felt himself seized in surprisingly strong arms and hoisted up in Albert's place. Next came a shuffle and a scrape as Holroyd, panting heavily now, dragged the inert Albert from the theatre. Appleby waited for a couple of seconds, threw back the tarpaulin and lowered himself to the floor. Then he groped his way through the door, flicked on the light and looked at his watch. "And the audience," he said, "is now sitting back and waiting—until presently somebody points out that the cadaver is the wrong size. Thank you very much. The reconstruction has been more instructive than I hoped." He turned to Holroyd. "I am still inclined to think that it has the appearance of being the work of two men. And yet you managed it pretty well on schedule when single-handed. Never a fumble and just the right lift. You might almost have been practising it."

Holroyd frowned. "Yachting," he said briefly, "—and particularly at night. It makes one handy."

And Albert looked with sudden suspicion at Nessfield's professor of Human Physiology. "Yachting?" he asked. "Now, would that have put you in the way of acquaintance of many seafaring men?"

Of James Cass, that luckless waif who would be a seafarer no longer, Appleby learned little more that afternoon. The cargo-vessel from which he had disembarked was already at sea again, and a couple of days must elapse before any line could be tapped there. But one elderly seaman who had recently made several voyages with him a little research did produce, and from this witness two facts emerged. There was nothing out of the way about Cass—except that he was a man distinctly on the simple side. Cass had been suggestible, Appleby gathered; so much so as to have been slightly a butt among his fellows.

And Appleby asked a question: had the dead man appeared to have any regular engagement or preoccupation when he came into port? The answer to this was definitive. Within a couple of hours, Appleby felt, the file dealing with this queer mystery of the anatomy theatre would virtually be closed for good.

Another fifteen minutes found him mounting the staircase of one of Nessfield's most superior blocks of professional chambers. But the building, if imposing, was gloomy as well, and when Appleby was overtaken and jostled by a hurrying form it was a second before he recognised that he was again in the presence of Dr. Holroyd.

"Just a moment," Appleby laid a hand on the other's arm. "May I ask if this coincidence extends to our both aiming at the third floor."

Holroyd was startled, but made no reply. They mounted the final flight side by side and in silence. Appleby rang a bell before a door with a handsome brass plate. After a perceptible delay the door was opened by a decidedly flurried nurse, who showed the two men into a sombre waiting-room. "I don't think," she said, "that you have an appointment? As an emergency has just arisen I am afraid there is no chance of seeing Dr—"

She stopped at an exclamation from Appleby. Hunched in a corner of the waiting-room was a figure whose face was almost entirely swathed in a voluminous silk muffler. But there was no mistaking that flowing silver hair. "Sir David!" exclaimed Appleby. "This is really a most remarkable rendezvous."

Sir David Evans groaned. "My chaw," he said. "It is one pig ache, look you."

Holroyd laughed nervously. "Shakespeare was demonstrably right. There was never yet philosopher could bear the toothache patiently— nor Vice-Chancellor either."

But Appleby paid no attention; he was listening keenly to something else. From beyond a door on the right came sound of hurried, heavy movement. Appleby strode across the room and turned the handle. He flung back the door and found himself looking into the dentist's surgery. "Dr. Wesselmann?" he said.

The answer was an angry shout from a bullet-headed man in a white coat. "How dare you intrude in this way!" he cried. "My colleague and myself are confronted with a serious emergency. Be so good as to withdraw at once."

Appleby stood his ground and surveyed the room; Holroyd stepped close behind him. The dentist's chair was empty, but on a surgical couch nearby lay a patient covered with a light rug. Over this figure another white-coated man was bending, and appeared to be holding an oxygen mask over its face.

And Nessfield's lecturer in Prosthetics seemed to find further explanations necessary. "A patient," he said rapidly, "with an unsuspected idiosyncrasy to intravenous barbiturates. Oxygen has to be administered, and the position is critical. So be so good—"

Appleby leaped forward and sent the white-coated holder of the oxygen-mask spinning; he flung back the rug. There could be no doubt that what was revealed was James Cass's body. And since lying on Professor Finlay's dissecting-table it had sustained a great gash in the throat. It had never been very pleasant to look at. It was ghastly enough now.

Wesselmann's hand darted to his pocket; Holroyd leaped on him with his yachtsman's litheness, and the alien dentist went down heavily on the floor. The second man showed no fight as he was handcuffed. Appleby looked curiously at Holroyd. "So you saw," he asked, "how the land lay?"

"In my purely amateur fashion I suppose I did. And I think I finished on schedule once again."

Appleby laughed. "Your intervention saved me from something decidedly nasty at the hands of Nessfield's authority on false teeth. By the way, would you look round for the teeth in question. And then we can have in Sir David—seeing he is so conveniently in attendance—and say an explanatory word."

"I got the hang of it," said Appleby, "when we did a very rough-and-ready reconstruction of the crime. For when, while playing Finlay's part, I glanced round at the cadaver, I found myself catching a glimpse of Dr. Holroyd here when he was obligingly playing First Murderer and turning off the lights. There was a glass panel in the door, and through this he was perfectly visible. I saw at once why Finlay had been killed. It was merely because he had seen, and *recognised*, somebody who was about to plunge the theatre in darkness for some nefarious, but not necessarily murderous, end. What did this person want? There could be only one answer: the body of James Cass. Already he had tried to get it in the night, but the housebreaking involved had proved too difficult."

The benevolent features of Sir David Evans were shadowed by perplexity. "But why, Mr. Appleby, should this man want such a pody?"

"I shall come to that in a moment. But first keep simply to this: that the body had to be stolen even at great hazard; that when glimpsed and recognised by Finlay the potential thief was sufficiently ruthless to silence him with a dagger secreted for such an emergency—and was also sufficiently quick-witted to exploit this extemporaneous murder to his own advantage. If he had simply bolted with Cass's body and left that of Finlay the hunt would, of course, have been up the moment somebody turned the lights on. By rapidly substituting one body for the other—Finlay's for that of Cass—on the dissecting-table, he contrived the appearance first of some more or less natural momentary absence of Finlay from the theatre, and secondly the suggestion of some possible joke which kept the audience wary and quiet for some seconds longer. All this gave additional time for his getaway. And—yet again—the sheer grotesque consequence of the substitution had great potential value as a disguise. By suggesting some maniacal act of private vengeance it masked the purely practical—and the professionally criminal—nature of the crime.

"And now, what did we know of Cass? We knew that he was a seaman; that he travelled more or less regularly between England and America; that he was knocked down and presently died shortly after landing; and that he was a simple-minded fellow, easily open to persuasion. And we also knew this: that he had a set of rather incongruously magnificent false teeth; that in the anatomy theatre these first protruded themselves and then by some muscular spasm appeared to lodge themselves in the throat, the jaw closing like a vice. And we also knew that, hard upon this, a certain Dr. Wesselmann, an alien comparatively little known in Nessfield and actually a specialist in false teeth, hurried from the theatre accompanied by a companion. When I also learned from a seaman who had sailed with Cass that he was often concerned about his teeth and would hurry off to a dentist as soon as he reached shore, I saw that the case was virtually complete."

"And would be wholly so when you recovered Cass's body and got hold of these." Holroyd came forward as he spoke, carrying two dental places on an enamel tray. "Sir David, what would you say about Cass's teeth?"

Nessfield's Vice-Chancellor had removed the muffler from about his jaw; the excitement of the hunt for the moment banished the pain which had driven him to Wesselmann's rooms. He inspected the dentures carefully—and then spoke the inevitable word. "They are pig," he said decisively.

"Exactly so. And now, look." Holroyd gave a deft twist to a molar; the denture which he was holding fell apart; in the hollow of each gleaming tooth there could be discerned a minute oil-silk package.

"What they contain," said Appleby, "is probably papers covered with a microscopic writing. I had thought perhaps of uncut diamonds. But now I am pretty sure that what we have run to earth is espionage. What one might call the Unwitting Intermediary represents one of the first principles of that perpetually fantastic game at its higher levels. Have a messenger who has no notion that he *is* a messenger, and you at once supply yourself with the sort of insulating device between cell and cell that gives spies a comforting feeling of security. Cass has been such a device. And it was one perfectly easy to operate. He had merely to be persuaded that his false teeth were always likely to give him trouble, and that he must regularly consult (at an obligingly low fee) this dentist at one end and that dentist at the other—and the thing was practically foolproof. Only Wesselmann and his friends failed to reckon on sudden death, and much less on Cass's signing away his body—dentures and all—to an anatomy school." Appleby paused. "And now, gentlemen, that concludes the affair. So what shall we call it?"

Holroyd smiled. "Call it the Cass Case. You couldn't get anything more compendious than that."

But Sir David Evans shook his beautiful silver locks "No!" he said authoritatively. "It shall be called *Lesson in Anatomy*. The investigation has been most interesting, Mr. Appleby. And now let us go. For the photographers, look you, are waiting."

DOVER GOES TO SCHOOL

Joyce Porter

Joyce Porter (1924–90) was born in Marple, Cheshire—the village whose name Agatha Christie, whose sister lived not far away at Abney Hall, borrowed for her famous detective. Her brother, who wrote a short essay about her for a collection of her short stories about Inspector Dover, said that she lived in the village for the first eighteen years of her life and that the local community inspired settings and characters that cropped up in her fiction. She attended the local church elementary school and then got a scholarship to the High School for Girls at Macclesfield, a few miles away. After that she studied at King's College, London, taking a degree in English. Her time at university coincided with the Second World War, towards the end of which she had a brief spell in the ATS, the women's section of the army. After various secretarial jobs, she joined the Women's Royal Air Force, where she was involved with confidential intelligence work and training for twelve years before being shifted to a recruitment role, which she enjoyed less. In 1963 she resigned to become a full-time author, having been offered a contract for the first three novels featuring Dover. She gave up writing detective fiction in 1980 and settled contentedly into village life in Wiltshire, but died on an aeroplane while travelling home from a holiday in China.

Dover One was televised in the BBC anthology series *Detective* in 1968 and the series enjoyed considerable success; more recently, Kenneth Cranham has starred as Dover in radio adaptations of the stories. This story first appeared in *Ellery Queen's Mystery Magazine* in February 1978.

D ETECTIVE CHIEF INSPECTOR DOVER WAS A CREATURE OF HABIT. Whenever he entered a room he made a point of selecting the most comfortable-looking seat and heading straight for it. On this occasion, as he waddled across the threshold of the large old-fashioned bathroom at Skelmers Hall College, he was not embarrassed by choice. The rim of the bath was definitely out and he didn't fancy the three-legged stool. That left only one place where 241 pounds of flab could be safely deposited, and the Chief Inspector sank gratefully onto the oval of polished mahogany. That flight of stairs up from the ground floor had taken it out of him.

Two other men entered the bathroom. One was the young and handsome Detective Sergeant MacGregor, Chief Inspector Dover's long-suffering assistant; the other was an older man in uniform, Inspector Howard. He was the representative of the local police force whose unenviable job it was to put these two clever devils from Scotland Yard in the picture.

It was Inspector Howard's first encounter with members of the prestigious Murder Squad and he was understandably somewhat diffident. Still, a man had to do what a man had to do. He cleared his throat. "Er—excuse me, sir."

Dover's mean little eyes opened slowly and balefully. "What?"

"Your—er—feet, sir."

"What about 'em?"

"They're resting on the—er—body, sir."

Dover glanced down and with ill grace shifted his boots back a couple of inches from the corpse that lay sprawled, in pyjamas and dressing gown, over the bathroom floor. "Thought you were supposed to be telling us what's happened," he observed nastily.

Inspector Howard swallowed. "Oh, yes, I am, sir."

"Well, get on with it, then! I don't want to sit here all morning gawping at a stiff!" Dover's pasty face twisted in a grimace.

Not surprisingly, Inspector Howard's account of the murder which had taken place in the bathroom at Skelmers Hall College was somewhat incoherent. Shorn of his stammerings and splutterings, and expurgated of Dover's increasingly obscene interjections, the story ran something like this:

Skelmers Hall College was an Adult Education Centre where members of the general public could attend courses on subjects of interest to them. The course which had been planned for that weekend was on icons and half a dozen enthusiasts had assembled just before supper on the previous evening, Friday. After supper they had been treated to an introductory lecture by the visiting expert, Professor Ross, and had then dispersed to their various bedrooms for the night. It was in the early hours of Saturday morning that one of the students, a young woman named Wenda Birkinshaw, had discovered the body.

"What's his name?" asked Dover, giving the corpse a poke with his boot.

"Er—Rupert Andrews, sir. Quite a well-known building contractor, I understand, and a County Councillor too."

"How was he croaked?"

"Ah, now that's rather interesting, sir." Inspector Howard's boyish enthusiasm didn't find much echo in his audience. "He was knocked unconscious, then strangled with the cord of his own dressing gown. This was probably one of the weapons, sir."

"This" proved to be a sausage-shaped object, about two feet long, still lying where it had been found on the floor by the washbasin.

Dover inspected it from a safe distance. "What the hell is it?"

"It's a draught excluder, sir. Mrs. Crocker, the Warden's wife, made it herself. It's just a tube of cloth some three inches in diameter filled with sand. You stretch it out along the windowsill to keep the draught out. There are several more of them about the Hall. These old houses generally seem to have badly fitting windows, don't they? This particular draught excluder weighs several pounds, sir, and would make a highly efficient cosh. It belongs here in the bathroom."

Dover had slumped back until his spine rested comfortably against the wall. "You always this bloody long-winded?" he asked unpleasantly. "Or is it just for my benefit? And don't," he added as poor Inspector Howard produced yet another prize exhibit, "bother telling me what that is because I know. It's a bath brush."

"It's another murder weapon, sir," explained Inspector Howard. He glanced for sympathy at Sergeant MacGregor, but that young gentleman was prudently keeping his head well down over his notebook. "The handle of the bath brush, sir, was inserted into the dressing-gown cord and used like a tourniquet to tighten it round the neck of the unconscious victim. The victim was a middle-aged man, sir, but quite strong. In the doctor's opinion quite a frail person could have killed him using this method."

"When I want the bloody doctor's opinion," grunted Dover who really worked at being ungracious, "I'll ask for it. Anything else?"

"I don't think so, sir," replied Inspector Howard miserably.

"What about bloody suspects?"

"Oh, yes, well, virtually everybody in the house last night is a suspect, sir." Inspector Howard shifted uneasily from one foot to the other. Things weren't going at all as he'd expected. Where was that friendly cooperation between one copper and another? That professional camaraderie— That happy exchange of— He caught Dover's jaundiced eye and hurriedly took up the thread of his story. "The Hall is securely locked up at night, sir, and there's no sign of a break-in. Of course we can't definitely exclude—"

"Let's have a few names," growled Dover.

"Of the suspects, sir?"

Dover rolled his eyes toward the ceiling.

"Well, there's Brigadier and Mrs. Crocker, sir, the resident Wardens of the College, and—"

"Here," said Dover as the thought suddenly struck him, "do you have to pay to come to this dump?"

"Oh, yes, sir. Not very much, though. The students' fees, I understand, only cover part of the cost of running the place. The rest comes from the government."

"Bully for some!" grumbled Dover. "Well, get on with it!"

There were, it turned out, no less than eight possible murderers currently at the Skelmers Hall College for Adult Education—and Chief Inspector Dover's face fell at the news. Apart from the Crockers, they were in alphabetical order: Miss Wenda Birkinshaw (who had discovered the body), Miss Betsy Gallop, Mr. and Mrs. Mappin, Professor Ross (the lecturer), and Peter Thorrowgood.

Somewhat to everyone's surprise, Dover had actually been listening. "No Mrs. Anfield?" he demanded indignantly.

"Anfield, sir?"

Sergeant MacGregor was more accustomed to the great man's idiosyncrasies. "I think you mean Andrews, sir," he said, looking up from his notebook. "The dead man was named Andrews."

"What I said!" snarled Dover before turning again on the shrinking Inspector Howard. "So where's his wife?"

Inspector Howard gave up trying to understand. "I gather he was divorced, sir."

"Pity," said Dover, sinking back into lethargy.

"Sir?"

In an untypical flush of generosity Dover tossed one pearl of his investigatory wisdom to this poor provincial bluebottle. "If Mrs. Ashford had been on the scene, laddie, we could just have arrested her and all gone home." He sensed that Inspector Howard needed something more. "Husbands, laddie," he added, disgruntled at having thus to gild the lily, "are always murdered by their wives. And vice versa."

Inspector Howard, to his eternal credit, took his courage in both hands. "Always, sir?"

"Near as damn it!" grunted Dover, hauling himself to his feet and stepping clumsily over the dead body. "It's a law of nature." He headed for the door. "If anybody wants me I'll be downstairs." As he passed MacGregor he fired off a valedictory behest in a voice that carried just far enough to do the most damage. "And get rid of *him!*"

Whether it was Dover's sensitive ears that had caught the clink of bottles or his delicate nostrils that had picked up the aroma of good malt whiskey at 150 paces, the world will never know. Suffice it to say that he made his way unerringly downstairs and straight into the small parlour that served Skelmers Hall College as a bar just as Brigadier Crocker raised his tumbler to his lips.

Caught red-handed, there was nothing a retired officer-and-gentleman could do but reach for another glass. The Brigadier introduced himself. "You look," he said, erroneously attributing Dover's habitual pallor to shock, "as though you could do with this."

"It wasn't a pretty sight," agreed Dover, reaching out an eager paw.

The Brigadier proposed a toast. "Absent friends!"

Dover emptied his glass and prudently got a refill before putting the boot in. "Pal of yours, was he?"

The Brigadier's indignation nearly sobered him. "Good lord, no! I never set eyes on the bounder before last night."

"Bounder?" queried Dover, who liked seeing people squirm.

"Well, what would you call a chappie of fifty who attends a weekend study course on icons accompanied by his teenage popsie?"

Dover mulled it over. "You sure?"

"Of course I'm sure. Him and Miss Birkinshaw—well, you only had to see them together to realise precisely what was going on."

Dover slowly examined his surroundings. "Bloody funny set-up for a romantic weekend," he commented.

"It's a jolly sight cheaper than a hotel," the Brigadier pointed out, replenishing the drinks with an unsteady hand. "And he'd be less likely to run into any of his business chums. County Councillor, indeed!" He stared sullenly into the depths of his glass. "I should have a good look at Miss Birkinshaw, if I were you, Chief Inspector. She found Andrews, you know, and in my opinion—"

There might have been further revelations if it hadn't been for the arrival of a very tall, very thin man who moved with the preternatural leisureliness of a giraffe.

"Ah, Professor Ross!" Brigadier Crocker accompanied his greeting with legerdemain which had the bottle of whiskey out of sight before you could say "usquebaugh."

"I simply want to know how much longer I'm supposed to keep on," bleated Professor Ross. "I've just finished my lecture on Iconography, Part One, but it's hard going. They're hardly a very receptive audience."

"Business-as-usual was my idea," the Brigadier told Dover proudly. "Takes their minds off the tragedy, keeps 'em out of your hair, *and* stops 'em asking for their money back." He addressed Professor Ross again. "What are they doing now?"

"Having their coffee break," whined the Professor. "That's what's on the timetable."

The Brigadier emerged reluctantly from behind his bar. "I'd better go and give the lady wife a hand before she starts feeling put upon, what? I'll bring you your coffee back here."

Left alone, Dover and the Professor eyed each other moodily. In the end it was Dover, his tongue no doubt loosened by the strong drink, who cracked first.

"You don't look like a professor to me," he said, just to be rude.

Professor Ross's face turned scarlet. "Well, actually," he admitted hoarsely, "I'm not, really."

Dover leered in evil encouragement.

"No," confessed the unfortunate academic with an agonised grimace. "It's just that people have got into the habit of calling me one."

Dover removed his bowler hat the better to scratch at his head. "And you didn't stop 'em?"

Professor Ross (as we may as well continue to call him) murmured, "Well…"

"Here," yelped Dover, almost overwhelmed by the audacity of his imagination, "did Ainsworth know about this?"

"Ainsworth?"

"The dead man!" screamed Dover. "Did he know you were sailing under borrowed plumes?"

"Good heavens, no!" wailed the Professor. "The loud-mouthed bully was unpleasant enough to me without that! Oh, *dear!*" Too late—far, far too late—Professor Ross clamped a restraining hand over his mouth.

The only thing left in life that gave Dover real pleasure was bullying the weak and helpless. Naturally he preferred pushing widows and orphans around but, failing them, Professor Ross would do. It wasn't long before the whole story poured out.

It had happened during Professor Ross's introductory lecture, given on the previous evening immediately after supper. Professor Ross had been guilty of a couple of slips of the tongue and Councillor Andrews had pounced on them with unconcealed relish. Professor Ross realised with dismay that he'd encountered every lecturer's nightmare—an expert in the audience. And there were eight more sessions to get through!

"I *knew*," whimpered Professor Ross, "that I was showing them a Hodegetria Mother of God, and I can't think *why* I called it Glykophilusa. It was just a momentary mental aberration."

Dover grunted. It was all Greek to him.

"And then, when I was talking about the metal covers, he pulled me up again. I was simply trying to keep things simple. I know there's a *technical* difference between a riza and an oklad, but really the terms are—"

Dover's threshold of boredom could be measured in microns, so it was fortunate that the Brigadier chose this moment to return with coffee and biscuits. Mrs. Crocker came bustling in behind him. She was one of those women who are always busy.

"You forgot the sugar, Tom." The empty whiskey glasses on the bar counter caught her eye and her routine wifely exasperation turned to real fury. "Oh, for God's sake, you've not been at the booze already, have you?"

Her husband grinned sheepishly at his male companions. "Just a quick snifter to speed poor old Andrews on his way, m'dear."

If this reference to the dear departed was an attempt to inhibit Mrs. Crocker's wrath, it failed. "Poor old Andrews?" she repeated incredulously. "That's not what you called him last night, my lad. Last night you couldn't find words bad enough for him. I don't know when I've seen you in such a blind temper."

She was so absorbed in rinsing out glasses and wiping the bar top down that she failed to notice her husband's frantic signals, and went blithely on, "I'm surprised you need reminding, Tom, that 'poor old Andrews' is the same bloody interfering swine who was going to get us both turned out into the streets without a penny to our name."

Brigadier Crocker glanced at Dover to see if he was paying any attention to this tirade. Strangely enough, he was. "Nonsense, old girl," said the Brigadier desperately. "Andrews hadn't that much influence. He wasn't God Almighty, y'know."

"He was chairman of that special committee the Council set up for slashing local government expenditures," snapped Mrs. Crocker, draping her towel over the beer pump. "And he's not the only one who thinks Skelmers Hall College is a waste of public funds. He just happens to be the most influential and dangerous one we've come across to date."

The arrival of MacGregor to announce that the body had been removed interrupted this heated exchange of views.

Dover hoisted himself to his feet. "About bloody time!"

"They'll let us have the post-mortem report as soon as possible, sir," said MacGregor as he followed Dover upstairs. "And then I was wondering if you'd like to examine Andrews's room now, sir. He only brought one small suitcase, of course, but—"

Dover marched straight into the bathroom and locked the door firmly behind him.

When he emerged five minutes later, he was not pleased to find Professor Ross waiting for him on the landing. The Professor jerked into life and caught Dover by the sleeve. "Remember the old adage," he advised hoarsely. "*Cherchez la femme!*"

Dover tried to brush him off but the Professor was tenacious.

"It's the fair sex you ought to be looking at, Chief Inspector. That Mappin woman for a start."

Dover progressed, carrying Professor Ross with him as he went. "And who's she when she's at home?"

Having twined himself right round Dover, Professor Ross was now able to whisper confidentially in his ear. "She's a student of the course. With her husband. Not that that's cramping her style. They arrived early last night, like Councillor Andrews. You should have seen the pair of them in the bar—Mrs. Mappin and Andrews. Getting on like a house on fire! Flirting. Making suggestive remarks. Saying things with double meanings."

"What was her husband doing?" asked Dover, trying without success to break Professor Ross's wrist.

"Oh, he was maintaining a very low profile. Most of the time he wasn't even there. No doubt he's used to it, but if it had been my wife carrying on like—"

"I'll bear it in mind," promised Dover. "Jealous husband."

"No, no," moaned Professor Ross frantically. "The *wife*, not the husband."

Dover was trying to use his feet. "Eh?"

"*Mrs.* Mappin!" said the Professor. "Don't you understand? She thought she'd made a conquest. But she hadn't. He was just passing the time until Miss Birkinshaw turned up."

Something stirred in Dover's subconscious. "The girl who found the body?"

"That's right. She arrived just before supper and the minute she arrived on the scene Andrews dropped La Mappin like a hot potato."

"Hmm," said Dover.

Professor Ross was an experienced teacher and he knew that you couldn't repeat a thing too often for some people. "Hell," he announced, "hath no fury like a woman scorned."

MacGregor looked round as Dover burst into the bedroom and slammed the door shut behind him.

"Find anything, laddie?"

"Nothing of any significance, I'm afraid, sir."

"No cigarettes?"

"Andrews was a nonsmoker, sir."

"Trust him!" Dover's bottom lip protruded. "You sure you haven't got any, laddie?"

"You smoked all mine on the way down, sir."

Dover crossed over to the bed and flopped down on it sulkily. "You could have brought some more," he pointed out. "And what's that you're holding?"

"It's a tie, sir."

"I can see that!" snarled Dover before sinking back and closing his eyes.

MacGregor gazed nostalgically at the dazzling blue-and-silver stripes. "Councillor Andrews must have been a Butcher's Boy, sir."

"Eh?" Unlike his sergeant, Dover had not had the advantage of a Public School education, and further elucidation was required.

"Oh, that's what we used to call the chaps who went to Bullock's College, sir," said MacGregor. "Bullock, you see, sir—and the blue-and-white stripes. Like a butcher's apron."

"So what?"

"Well, so nothing, actually, sir." MacGregor draped the tie back over the mirror. "Just that we used to play them at cricket and rugger. Annual events, you know." MacGregor chuckled softly to himself. "We usually beat 'em too!"

Dover wallowed luxuriously among the pillows. "Are you claiming you knew this Ambrose, laddie?"

"Andrews, sir." MacGregor made the correction without much hope. "No, he'd be years before my time."

"Pity," grunted Dover. "I was hoping we'd be able to chuck our hands in, seeing as how you were personally involved with the deceased."

MacGregor had given up counting to ten years ago. Nowadays he found it took 30 or even 40 to get his passions under control. "Shouldn't we start interviewing the suspects, sir?" he asked eventually.

Dover really fancied a preprandial nap but his superiors at the Yard had been hounding him a bit recently. "Oh, all right," he grumbled. "Wheel 'em in."

"We've got the use of a room downstairs, sir."

But Dover had reached the end of his concessions. "Here, laddie, here."

Miss Wenda Birkinshaw, as befitted her status as finder of the body, was the first victim and MacGregor fought to keep his eyes fixed on her face as she undulated, in a miasma of cheap scent, over to the chair which had been placed ready for her. She even got Dover sitting bolt upright and taking notice, but this was only because her first action, after provocatively crossing her legs, was to produce her cigarettes and ask if anyone minded. MacGregor broke the world record with his lighter, and Dover was only fractionally behind with the begging bowl.

"Keep the packet," said Miss Birkinshaw grandly, and thereby insured that, whoever stood before the bar of British Justice to answer for the murder of Rupert Andrews, it wouldn't be she.

She rattled off her story with admirable economy. "I work in the typing pool at County Hall and me and Randy—that's what he told me to call him—have been friends for a couple of months. This awful weekend was his idea. Well, you didn't think I was interested in holy pictures, did you?" Miss Birkinshaw uncrossed her legs.

"Mr. Andrews booked separate rooms for you?" said MacGregor from a tight throat.

"There's elections coming up and he didn't want any filthy talk till they were over. Last night he was supposed to wait till everybody'd got settled down and then nip along to my room. Well, I got cheesed off with waiting, didn't I? Mind you, I was in two minds. The way he'd been chatting with that old Mappin woman, the silly cow! I soon put a stop to that, I can tell you. 'If you're going in for geriatrics nowadays, Randy,' I told him, 'just let me know because I can easily fix myself up elsewhere.' What, dear? Oh, last night? Well, like I said, I went looking for him, didn't I? I saw the bathroom door was half open and the light on, so I popped my head round and—ugh. It was terrible!"

"What did you do then, Miss Birkinshaw?" asked MacGregor apologetically.

"Screamed the bleeding place down, dearie, and why don't you call me Wenda?"

"Er—were you and Mr. Andrews intending to get married?"

Miss Birkinshaw blinked her enormous baby-blue eyes. "What for?"

"Do you know anybody who'd want to murder Councillor Andrews?"

"Only just about everybody he ever met, dearie! Let's face it, he could be a right pig. He was on the outs with half the people here before I even arrived on the scene. And the other half after I got here."

Dover lit another of Miss Birkinshaw's cigarettes. "Anybody in particular?"

"Well"—Miss Birkinshaw didn't lose much sleep over the ethics of the situation—"there was that young lad, Peter Thorrowgood, for a start. Wet behind the ears? You wouldn't believe! Randy went over him like a bloomin' steamroller."

"Why?"

"Because of me, dearie! Randy thought he was trying to make time with me, though anybody could see the kid didn't know how many beans make five. Here"—Miss Birkinshaw changed the subject abruptly—"do I have to keep going to these damn old lectures? It's worse than school. I mean, *icons*—who cares?"

Dover graciously excused Miss Birkinshaw and said she could watch the telly instead. MacGregor barely managed to clear up a couple of minor points before the nubile young woman went on her way rejoicing. No, she'd never been to Skelmers Hall College before. No, she hadn't heard anything suspicious before she went out to look for Councillor Andrews, and finally she thought that Councillor Andrews had booked their places on the course about a month ago.

"What was that all about?" asked Dover after Miss Birkinshaw had departed. His mood had been much improved by the intake of nicotine.

"If the murder was premeditated, sir, the murderer would have had to apply for the course *after* Andrews did."

"Garn," said Dover, his mood not being as rosy as all that, "this murder wasn't premeditated! Stands out a mile—the joker just grabbed whatever was to hand and used it. How could he know in advance there'd be a bath brush and that sausage thing all ready and waiting?"

"He could if he'd attended a course here before, sir. That's why I asked Miss Birkinshaw if this was her first visit."

"'Strewth," said Dover, gazing fondly at his packet of cigarettes, "you're not suspecting that poor little girl of anything, are you?"

"The doctor did say no great strength would be required, sir. And who better than Miss Birkinshaw to catch him unawares?"

Dover had no intention of wasting his time on theoretical and unpalatable discussions. "Fetch that lad in she mentioned!" he commanded and playfully punched his fist into the palm of his other hand. "Let's see if we can't bash a nice free and voluntary confession out of him!"

Peter Thorrowgood, being immature, weedy, and extremely nervous, might have been tailor-made for Dover. He was so eager to cooperate that it wasn't necessary to lay a finger on him. He admitted that he was a frequent student on these weekend courses but insisted that this was his first visit to Skelmers Hall. He wasn't particularly interested in icons—nor in medieval monasticism or pottery for beginners, if it came to that. No, he attended these courses in order to make friends and meet people. Like young ladies of the opposite sex.

Dover sniffed.

Mr. Thorrowgood went pale and launched himself hurriedly into the rest of his *curriculum vitae*. Although currently training to be a shoe-shop manager, he didn't really consider he had as yet found his true vocation. He felt he would prefer a job which brought him more into contact with people. Like young ladies of the opposite sex. Young ladies of the opposite sex were, Mr. Thorrowgood confided, a bit thin at the moment. "Sometimes," he added, "I wonder if it's me."

Had he ever met Councillor Andrews before?

"No, never." Mr. Thorrowgood squared his shoulders. "And if you're going to ask me about that scene at the supper table, I'm quite prepared to admit that I did feel like murdering him—for a moment. He deliberately set out to humiliate me in front of everyone, you know. How was I to know that Miss Birkinshaw was some kind of special friend? In any case, all I did was indulge in some polite conversation. From the way Mr. Andrews went on, you'd have thought I'd tried to— Well, it was all very unpleasant and embarrassing. I'd be a hypocrite if I said I was sorry Mr. Andrews is dead, but that doesn't mean I killed him. Because I didn't."

And from this position young Mr. Thorrowgood refused to budge. Even Dover couldn't shake him. MacGregor took over the questioning as Dover sank back, sullen and exhausted, on the bed.

Mr. Thorrowgood was willing but unhelpful. He'd neither seen nor heard anything out of the ordinary last night. He'd never met any of his fellow suspects before and his application for the course had been sent in at least six months ago because you never knew if these things booked up and, no, he couldn't think of anybody who would have wanted to murder Mr. Andrews except—well—

Young Mr. Thorrowgood paused and licked his lips.

MacGregor exuded encouragement.

Sneaking seemed to be endemic at Skelmers Hall.

"Miss Gallop was getting pretty uptight."

"She's a fellow student?"

Mr. Thorrowgood nodded. "I thought she was going to scratch Councillor Andrews's eyes out at one point."

"Why?"

Mr. Thorrowgood didn't know. "She sort of railed against him as soon as she realised who he was. Something to do with donkeys. And goats. I couldn't make head nor tail of it. Anyhow, whatever it was, Miss Gallop claimed it was all Andrews's fault."

"When did this happen?"

"After the first lecture last night. Andrews had drawn a fair amount of attention to himself by having quite a heated argument with Professor Ross." Mr. Thorrowgood took time off to seize another straw. "That's somebody else you might have a word with—Professor Ross. He was looking pretty sick by the time Councillor Andrews had finished with him."

"Let's just stick to Miss Gallop," said MacGregor, who didn't want Dover getting all muddled up. "What was Mr. Andrews's reaction to her attack?"

"Oh, he gave back as good as he got." Mr. Thorrowgood was plainly envious. "Told her he hadn't got where he had in life by letting silly old maids like her push him around. Miss Gallop looked as though she was going to have a fit."

Dover and MacGregor were given lunch in a small room by themselves. As Mrs. Crocker explained, even before she'd seen Dover's table manners, it would be less embarrassing for all concerned.

"I don't suppose," she said as she put the soup on the table, "that they want to hobnob with you any more than you do with them. Not," she added as she watched Dover stuffing handfuls of bread down his gullet, "that one has much to complain about as far as this course is concerned. They're a fairly civilised lot. We've just had the one gentleman turning up for supper in an open-necked shirt, but then we've had nobody going around all day in bedroom slippers or parking their chewing gum under the chairs in the lecture room."

It was no good looking to Dover for polite conversation at feeding time, so MacGregor, raising his voice to be audible over the splashing and sloshing, did the honours. "I would imagine you get a pretty decent type here on the whole," he said politely.

"Yes, we do, really," agreed Mrs. Crocker, finding it hard to tear her eyes away from the spectacle of Dover eating. "We try to preserve the old country-house atmosphere, you know, and most people are very cooperative. Well, we're all starved for gracious living these days, aren't we? That's what makes it so depressing when somebody like Mr. Mappin lets the side down. It isn't"—she watched Dover mop up the last of his soup with the last of his bread—"as though he hadn't got a tie because he was wearing one when he arrived. Well, I'll fetch the next course, shall I? It's a beef casserole."

It would be absurd to pretend that Dover's drive, acumen, and general get-up-and-go weren't a little impaired after lunch. Two helpings of everything is hardly the formula for a dynamic afternoon.

The remaining interviews were held in the room in which the two detectives had had their lunch, and there is every reason to believe that Dover slept through the first one. This was no mean feat because Miss Betsy Gallop was a woman of strong character, loud voice, and a distinct aroma of goat.

"Never heard of Gallop Goats?" she said in disbelief. "You do surprise me. Thought everybody'd heard of Gallop Goats. S'why I got so enraged with the late unlamented. I mean, Gallop Goats are practically a national institution. Not," she added in a sour afterthought, "that they would have been much longer if Andrews had had his foul way."

MacGregor's pencil flew over the pages of his notebook as Miss Betsy Gallop let it all come gushing out.

"My small holding is on the edge of Donkey Bridge Wood," she confided. "That rotter, Andrews, bought up a chunk of land about a quarter of a mile away on which he proposed to build a housing tract. Planning permission? A mere formality, dear boy! He was on the

Council, wasn't he? That bunch of pusillanimous sycophants would have given him the moon if he'd asked for it. You can see where that left yours truly, can't you? Right up the creek and without a paddle!"

MacGregor raised the shapeliest eyebrows in Scotland Yard, police-women not excepted.

"Approach roads, dear boy!" explained Miss Gallop. "Scheduled to go right through the middle of my herd of pedigreed beauties! It would have put the kibosh on my whole way of life. Don't just breed goats, you know. See this trouser suit I'm sporting?"

MacGregor nodded. He'd been wondering about that trouser suit.

"Hair from my own goats!" claimed Miss Gallop proudly. "Woven by a chum of mine. That"—her brown eyes filled with tears—"was what Andrews was going to destroy, the philistine. Well, somebody's cooked his goose for him!"

The elegant MacGregor eyebrows rose again.

Miss Gallop's scowl wouldn't have looked out of place on Dover's face. "Certainly not me!"

"What happens to the housing scheme now?"

Miss Gallop turned a grubby thumb downward. "No other builder's got the pull Andrews had with the Council. I'll be able to disband my little action committee."

MacGregor turned to other aspects of the case. Was Miss Gallop interested in icons?

"No jolly fear! Just happens this is the only weekend I could get a goat-sitter. It's not everybody who can stand it, you know. When did I book? Oh, a couple of months ago. I generally give myself a little break at this time of year." She started fishing in her hip pocket. "Can give you the exact date, if you—"

MacGregor said it didn't matter.

Miss Gallop was equally forthright when it came to the events of Friday night. "Didn't hear a thing, dear boy! Dead to the world as soon as my head touches the pillow. Even the screams didn't wake me," she added. "Had to be wakened specially."

And that was that. The closing of the door must have roused Dover and there was a great deal of snorting and puffing.

MacGregor tried to put his superior in the picture as tactfully as possible. "Well, at least Miss Gallop didn't try to pin the murder on somebody else."

"Gerrumphahugh!" said Dover. He smacked his lips "'Strewth, I could do with a cup of tea."

"Tea's ordered for four o'clock, sir, and we've only got Mr. and Mrs. Mappin left to see. Just enough time. We've got on quite well, all things considered."

"People don't realise what a strain it all is," said Dover through a yawn. He extracted another of Miss Birkinshaw's cigarettes and waited for MacGregor to give him a light. "Well, fetch 'em in," he growled. "The sooner we start, the sooner we finish."

"Shall we take the lady first, sir?" asked MacGregor, sensibly striking while the iron was lukewarm.

He'd reckoned without Dover's cunning. "We'll see 'em both together, laddie! It'll be quicker."

Harold and Cynthia Mappin approached their ordeal with understandable apprehension. MacGregor ran an experienced eye over them as he invited them to sit down. Mrs. Mappin was well into her middle forties in spite of fighting every day of the way. From the way she was dressed MacGregor surmised that a hefty proportion of the family income finished up on her back. Mr. Mappin was older, greyer, and shabbier. He was in a sober, badly cut suit which he had tried to enliven by permitting a tantalising glimpse of his hairy chest to peep through the open neck of his shirt.

Dover opened the proceedings. "You can smoke if you want to."

He was out of luck. The Mappins didn't.

Dover washed his hands of the pair of 'em.

MacGregor soon found out that it was Mrs. Mappin who did the talking, answering not only her own questions but her husband's. She had a quick and decisive mind and the preliminaries were soon dispensed with. Her husband was an assistant bank manager, this was their first visit to Skelmers Hall College, and Mrs. Mappin was the one who was passionately "into" icons. Neither of them had ever heard of Councillor Andrews before.

MacGregor cautiously broached the question of the alleged flirtation between Mrs. Mappin and the deceased and was not surprised to be presented with a version which differed considerably from the one supplied by Professor Ross. Mrs. Mappin modestly pictured herself as the innocent target of a lascivious brute's unbridled lust. "I simply couldn't get rid of him," she complained. "Could I, Harold? He just wouldn't leave me alone. And his hands, Sergeant, were *everywhere!*"

MacGregor avoided catching anyone's eye.

"You've no idea what a relief it was when that girl finally turned up," Mrs. Mappin went on, twisting her lips in a sneer. "Such a cheap-looking little thing! Still, she no doubt would provide *exactly* what Councillor Andrews was looking for."

MacGregor tried to draw Mr. Mappin into the conversation but, once again, it was Mrs. Mappin who was quicker on the draw.

"Jealous?" she echoed with an unpleasant laugh. "Harold? You must be joking, Sergeant! My precious husband wouldn't so much as bat an eyelid if he saw me being attacked on the hearthrug at his feet. Councillor Andrews wasn't the first man to make a pass at me, and I doubt if he'll be the last. I've learned to protect myself and not rely on Harold's strong right arm—if any."

An uncomfortable silence followed, during which Harold Mappin grinned vaguely at nothing in particular.

MacGregor addressed the voluptuous Cynthia again. "Did you hear anything suspicious last night?"

Mrs. Mappin shook her head in a drumroll of oversize earrings. "I was so upset I took a sleeping pill."

"Because of Councillor Andrews's unwelcome attentions?"

"That," said Mrs. Mappin with a spiteful glance at her husband, "and other things."

"How about you, Mr. Mappin?"

Harold Mappin jumped. "Oh, no, nothing! I—er—sleep very soundly."

"Like a log," agreed his wife.

"Er—twin beds?" asked MacGregor, never very happy when having to deal with such intimate matters.

"What else?" queried Mrs. Mappin.

MacGregor let them go.

"Well, that's that, sir," he said as he resumed his seat. "We've seen all the people who were in the Hall last night."

"Mouldy lot," grumbled Dover. "Could have been any one of 'em."

"I'm afraid it could, sir. Anybody could have guessed that Andrews would be creeping along to Miss Birkinshaw's room as soon as things were quiet. It'd be easy enough to lie in wait for him, strike him down with the draught excluder, drag him into the bathroom, and strangle him. No,"—MacGregor tucked his pencil away in his pocket—"we're going to have our work cut out to crack this one. It'll probably take weeks."

Work? Weeks? "I fancy that last joker," Dover said desperately.

"Harold Mappin, sir? To avenge his wife? Oh, I hardly think so. From the looks he kept giving her, I think he'd more likely murder *her*."

Dover didn't care for being crossed. "He had the opportunity!" he snarled.

"They'd *all* had the opportunity, sir."

Dover scowled. It was rapidly becoming a point of honour to drop a noose round Harold Mappin's scrawny neck. Neck? Dover was reduced to clutching at any straw. "That's why he's not wearing a tie!"

One day, MacGregor promised himself, he really would pick up the nearest blunt instrument and—"Andrews was strangled with the cord of his own dressing gown, sir, not by a necktie."

But Dover was nothing if not a whole-hogger. "Says who? Look, What's-his-name ambushes Who's-your-father and garrottes him with his tie. See? But, since he's not a complete idiot, he doesn't leave the corpse lying there with his tie round its neck. No, he removes the tie and substitutes the dead man's own dressing-gown cord. What's wrong with that?"

"Mr. Mappin simply has no motive, sir."

"He's jealous of his wife." Dover looked his sergeant up and down before forestalling his objection. "I mean, you're no flaming expert on married life, are you?" MacGregor's carefree bachelor status never ceased to irritate.

MacGregor retreated to his notebook. "Practically everybody in Skelmers Hall has a better motive than Mappin, sir. The Crockers were in danger of losing their jobs here, and Professor Ross was in much the same boat. Miss Gallop might have been turned out of her goat farm and—"

"What about Wenda Birkinshaw?" demanded Dover, who could remember names perfectly well when he wanted to. "Or that reedy young man?"

"Miss Birkinshaw could have had a hundred reasons for killing Andrews," retorted MacGregor. "As for Mr. Thorrowgood—well, he admitted he could cheerfully have murdered him, given half a chance."

Dover wasn't listening. "Fetch him back!"

"Mappin, sir?"

Dover grinned. "We'll have a confrontation!" Raising his arm he managed to get a couple of wiggles out of the fat over his biceps. "I'll soon clout the whole story out of him. And if you don't like it, laddie," he added contemptuously, "try looking the other bloody way!"

MacGregor knew that he should have put up more of a fight, but there was nothing like years of close association with Dover to knock the heroics out of Dover's assistant.

Mr. Mappin returned to the interview room alone, looking even more henpecked without his wife than he did with her.

Dover acknowledged that the burden of this particular examination rested solely on his own shoulders. He opened the proceedings with typical finesse. "Where's your bloody tie?"

Mr. Mappin clutched at his throat. "My—my tie?"

Dover grew bored with all this fencing about. "You killed What's-his-name!" he roared.

To MacGregor's eternal disgust these tactics worked.

"I knew I'd never get away with it," said Mr. Mappin bitterly. "Not with my luck." He looked up and appealed to Dover. "I'm not unintelligent. I work hard. I'm honest. I've got my fair share of imagination. So why am I always a failure? Why me? Why am I the one who's passed over for promotion, left out of the first team? Damn it"—he banged his fist down on the arm of his chair—"I've only got her word for it that the boy's my son!"

It was no good expecting sympathy from Dover. "What did you do it for?"

"I knew Andrews would recognise me sooner or later. Bound to. After all, I knew him right away."

Dover blinked. "You knew Andrews?"

"Of course. We were at school together. He was the school bully and I was the school butt—a poor bespectacled little runt, no good at games, a coward... For three years he made my life hell on earth."

"'Strewth!" said Dover. "And you've been nursing a grudge ever since?"

"Not a grudge exactly," said Harold Mappin wearily. "More of a promise, I suppose. Or the inability to keep a promise."

"And that's as clear as mud!" snapped Dover.

"I'm sorry." Harold Mappin sighed and tried again. "It's just that when I was a kid I always promised myself that one day I'd be a tremendous success at *something*. I didn't know what. I just knew I'd finish up a field marshal or a multimillionaire or... something. It was the only thing that kept me going. Without a dream like that to hang on to, I'd have cut my throat. Well"—Harold Mappin shrugged helplessly—"I never made it. I'm an assistant bank manager and that's my limit. I've a wife who flaunts her unfaithfulness and a son who despises me. And I'm up to my ears in debt. I've no money, no friends, and no bloody hopes for the future. Andrews would have had a field day with me. He'd have put the clock back thirty years! Well, I couldn't face it. I kept out of his way as much as I could last night, but I couldn't hope to dodge him for the rest of the weekend."

Dover relaxed with a triumphant smirk at MacGregor. "So you strangled him with your tie."

Mr. Mappin seemed mildly irritated. "No, I used the cord of his dressing gown. Why should I use my tie? I may be unlucky but I'm not stupid."

Dover frowned. Damn it, even murderers started giving you cheek these days. "Look, mate," he snarled, "you arrived here last night wearing a tie. Right? And before supper you took it off and you haven't worn it since. Well, why—if it isn't the bloody murder weapon?"

"But I've explained all that!" protested Mr. Mappin. "I didn't want Andrews to recognise me. Damn it all, that's why I killed him."

Dover leaned across and caught Mr. Mappin by the lapels. "So?"

"So the tie I was wearing was my old school tie, wasn't it? My wife nagged me into putting the damned thing on. She thinks it impresses people. Well, Andrews may not have recognised my face right away, but he would have recognised that tie because it was exactly the same as the one he was wearing!"

MacGregor saw Harold Mappin in a new light. "So you're a Butcher's Boy too!" he cried with evident delight and held out his hand. "I was at St. Spyridon's, myself."

Dover, whose formative years had been spent at the Peony Street Mixed Infants, slumped back in his chair.

WHEN THE DEAF CAN HEAR

Malcolm Gair

Malcolm Gair produced half a dozen thrillers in as many years, starting with *Sapphires on Wednesday* (1957). He was published by Collins Crime Club in hardback and Pan in paperback, two imprints associated with many highly successful crime writers, but the brevity of his career meant that his name soon disappeared from the shelves of bookshops and libraries and he was duly forgotten. His work in the genre was drawn to my attention by book dealer Jamie Sturgeon, who pointed out that Gair was a pseudonym of John Dick Scott (1917–1980). Born in Lanarkshire, Scott was educated at Edinburgh University, where he studied History.

His working life was varied and evidently successful. During the Second World War, he became Assistant Principal at the Ministry of Aircraft Production in London. Later, he joined the Cabinet Office as an official war historian. He was literary editor of *The Spectator* from 1953 until 1956 and in 1963 he moved to the United States in order to take up the editorship of the World Bank's periodical *Finance and Development*. His first mainstream novel, *The Cellar*, appeared under his own name in 1947 and he continued to write general fiction; his final novel, *The Pretty Penny*, appeared in 1963; he also published a book called *Life in Britain: A Guide to British Institutions, Traditions and Contemporary Life*. He adopted the Gair name for his crime novels. Mark Raeburn, his series character, also appeared in short stories including this one, which was published in the *Nottingham Evening Post* on 19 September 1959.

"HOW DO YOU DO, MR. RAEBURN." THE HEADMASTER SHOOK hands and indicated a chair. He was an elderly man with a fine head of silver hair, but stooped and drawn-looking about the face. "I'm afraid that this may seem a trivial affair to you," he went on. "And the money is trivial.

"I have views about cricket, Mr. Raeburn, and about 'playing cricket.' I daresay they're old-fashioned views.

"But the idea that this money was stolen by a member of the XI is—well, it's been a terribly painful shock, Mr. Raeburn. It has made me feel an old man."

"Your letter told me very little," said Mark. "Perhaps you would give me further details."

"Of course. I am retiring at the end of this term, Mr. Raeburn, and several presentations are to be made. Now in addition to whatever else was being done the XI decided to subscribe for a small cup to be presented annually in my name to the batsman with the highest average. The members of the XI kept the whole thing secret."

"No one outside the XI knew of this fund?"

"No one whatsoever. The money itself was kept in a room called the Turf Room, which is a kind of club room for members of the XI only. Each of them has a key. No one else."

"Excuse me," said Raeburn, "but this may be important. Surely someone else has a key—Who cleans the room, for instance?"

"I have a key myself," the headmaster replied, "but no one else has. The room is officially spring-cleaned every Easter holidays, and for the rest its a fagging divver, as we call it. The fags always work under supervision, however, and the fund was never mentioned in their presence."

"This Turf Room is in the cricket pavilion, I suppose?"

"No. It's in a cottage called Founders Arms, which is on the edge of Turf, as we call the cricket field.

"Part of it is occupied by an old man called Treddle, a retired school professional. The other part is the Turf Room."

"Treddle might have overheard the boys."

"I have thought about Treddle, Mr. Raeburn. He might well have taken the money, because he has something of a grudge over his pension.

"But he has no key, and, besides, he's stone deaf."

"Very well," said Raeburn. "I'd like your key of the Turf Room and I'd like to see each member of the XI there separately."

Twenty minutes later, Raeburn walked out of the cloisters and bumped into a small stout man who was walking in the opposite direction. Both apologised, and Raeburn realised that the stout man was looking at him closely.

"Good lord," he said, "you must be the dick from London."

Raeburn smiled.

"And you are the school doctor," he said.

"How do you know? Is my stethoscope showing?"

"No. Your thermometer." The doctor put his hand to his waistcoat pocket and grinned.

"I confess," he said. "I'm Dr. Bartlett. But I didn't pinch the presentation money. Who did?"

"I don't know yet," said Raeburn, "but I wonder whether the old man, Treddle, is really as deaf as he pretends."

"Well," said Dr. Bartlett. "I can tell you. He is. I used to try to get him to apply for an Army disability pension but he wouldn't. He's a cross-grained independent old cuss."

"Do his duties take him into the Turf Room?"

"He has no duties. He's retired. He sits studying the racing news."

"If Treddle didn't do it, Doctor, who did?" The Doctor looked at Raeburn for a long moment.

"Most of the boys in the XI," he said, "are a decent, ordinary lot. Anyway this is a school for the rich, you know. The parents have money running out of their ears."

Raeburn's interrogation of the members of the XI followed a routine. Yes, each boy had a key of the Turf Room. No, he had neither lost it nor lent it to anyone. No, he had not mentioned the fund to anyone. Then the same question to everyone.

"Suppose you were in a jam for money, what would you do?"

"If I was really in a jam, sir, my mother would help out." Or "my brother in the City would come across."

Only Maine was different. He was a big dark boy, looking older than his 18 years.

"Of course, I never mentioned the fund to anyone. Why should I? The whole business bored me silly."

"I see. Now I'm asking everyone this question, so I hope you won't mind answering it. If you were in a real difficulty about money, what would you do?"

"Grin and bear it," said Maine. "But I wasn't in a jam about money. And I can prove it."

Slowly, looking at Raeburn, the boy produced his wallet and took out six five pound notes. "Three weeks ago," he said, "before the theft of this money, mark you, I won nearly £40 on the Derby."

"I imagine that betting is against the school rules," said Raeburn. Maine shrugged.

"Of course. Almost everything but cricket is."

"Let's agree then, Maine, that you didn't need the money and didn't steal it. Someone did. No other member of the XI had any more motive than you. Treddle, on the other hand, is a poor man. And he has a grudge."

"Treddle is as honest as the day," said Maine warmly. "In any case—" Maine broke off.

"In any case, you were going to say, Treddle doesn't need the money." Maine's head snapped up.

"How do you know that?"

"You've told me the whole story." Maine's eyes opened.

"But I don't know who stole the money, I swear I don't. And it's true that Treddle doesn't need it, although I don't know how you know it."

"It isn't very difficult," said Raeburn. "When I said I suspected Treddle you replied that Treddle was honest. How did you know that? What financial dealings could you have had with Treddle? I'd been told the old man was interested in racing, so I deduced he placed your bets.

"Now if you won as much as £40 on the Derby it's possible that Treddle made a big killing, too. And of course, you gave Treddle the information about the fund."

Raeburn's voice rose a little, and Maine's brown cheeks paled.

"You were in it with him and you'll be lucky to get off with expulsion." Maine began to speak but at the same moment the door opened and an elderly man in a cloth cap and long hair curling out from under it burst into the room.

"You best leave Mr. Maine alone," he said. "He never told me."

"No," said Raeburn equably. "I know he didn't, Treddle. I just thought it was time you stopped listening at the door and joined us. How much did you win?"

"About £400."

"And how much did the hearing aid cost?"

"It's a special German thing. Cost sixty quid."

"How did you know about it?" Maine asked.

"It had to be Treddle," said Raeburn. "He had the opportunity. I was always sure he had an extra key of the room in his own cottage. He has a grudge against the headmaster. He knows that the headmaster makes a fetish of cricket, and that a theft by a member of the XI would be a terrible blow to him. Yet no one told him about the fund. If that's true, and I believed it was true, then there is only one way he could know. He must have overheard.

"How can a deaf man hear? Only by a hearing aid. The doctor told me Treddle was cross-grained. A cross-grained man might buy a hearing aid and keep quiet about it purely to find some way of working off a grudge. And that's what Treddle did. But he came across when I told you you'd be expelled.

"I think—" Raeburn's smile was faintly sardonic, "that may be called playing cricket. I fancy the headmaster won't prosecute."

LOW MARKS FOR MURDER

Herbert Harris

Herbert Harris (1911–95) had an impressive literary heritage: his great-grandfather was the Poet Laureate, Robert Southey. As a boy, he once said, he "feasted greedily on The Masterpiece Library of Short Stories, edited by J. A. Hammerton, which ran to twenty volumes" and clearly influenced his own writing career. He won a scholarship to Clapham College and worked in Fleet Street before becoming a full-time author, specialising in short stories and articles for newspapers and magazines such as the *Evening Standard, Tit-Bits, Reveille, Argosy, Mike Shayne's Mystery Magazine, The Saint Detective Magazine, Parade, London Mystery Magazine,* and *Weekend.* Because he was so productive, much of his work appeared under pseudonyms such as Frank Bury, Michael Moore, Peter Friday, Harris de Vere, Tom Claygate, H. H. Given, and Jerry Regan; he featured in the *Guinness Book of Records* as the most prolific author of short stories in the country. His first full-length novel was *Who Kill to Live* (1962) and he also published two novels linked to the *Hawaii Five-O* television series, *Serpents in Paradise* and *The Angry Battalion.*

Herbert Harris joined the Crime Writers' Association shortly after its inception in 1953 and his involvement with its early publications for members led in 1964 to his being awarded a Red Herring by the CWA for services to the Association. In 1966, he became editor of the CWA's annual anthology—then called *John Creasey's Mystery Bedside Book*—in succession to Roy Vickers. In all, he edited twenty-four CWA anthologies, the last one being *John Creasey's Crime Collection 1990*; six years later I took over as editor of the annual CWA anthology, so although our paths never crossed in person, I feel a kinship with him. This story appeared in *John Creasey's Crime Collection 1973*.

GEORGE FARADAY, THE LANGUAGES MASTER, RAISED THE SASH window of his bedroom on the top floor of Cullingford School, then carefully and furtively leaned part of his body out to watch the approach of the man he intended to murder—Dr. Theodore Whittington, M.A., D.Phil., L.R.A.M., the Headmaster.

Cullingford is a medium-sized public school between the Cotswolds and the Chilterns. It is not ranked particularly highly, and exists largely for the nouveaux-riches who have not quite enough money to send their sons to Winchester or Haileybury but are anxious that they should carry public school colours when they are entered in the rat race.

The building itself had been an architectural folly perpetrated by an eccentric mid-Victorian brewer. It is built unattractively of drab, porous grey stone, prone to disintegrate, and parts of the structure, suggestive of a medieval battlemented castle, are crumbling into decay.

The teaching staff is, academically, reasonably good, but a long way below the top echelon. George Faraday belonged to this sad, slightly pathetic fraternity who are destined to do nothing superlatively. He was a middle-aged man, somewhere between the early forties and early fifties, with rather heavy lines on his face and a fair amount of silver inlaid in the thick crop of ebony hair, but handsome in a seedy kind of way, particularly to vulnerable women.

Dr. Theodore Whittington, quite unmindful of his imminent demise, emerged from the east wing, or classroom-block, and made his way in the deepening dusk across the long terrace, of weed-strewn York paving, which bordered the rear of the school's central building.

He was a tall, stooping man, with a celery-stalk neck, and as he walked, the upper part of his body seemed to be thrust forward like a long-necked animal. George Faraday saw this elongated construction of the Headmaster as an aid to his homicidal intentions, since the very extent of Dr. Whittington's upper corporal area afforded a better target than might normally be the case.

The man at the top floor window looked at his wristwatch and noted with satisfaction that it was exactly 7.32 p.m. Dr. Whittington, for all his many shortcomings, was at least a stickler for punctuality, as any Headmaster ought to be.

Every day, sharp on 7.30 p.m., Dr. Whittington brought the boys' choir practice to a close. Then, striding along with his head and shoulders thrust forward, his black gown flowing behind him, and a collection of Bach's choral works gripped under one arm, it took him approximately four minutes to walk from the classroom-block to his private cottage, formerly a steward's lodge, on the other side of the school grounds.

It took him only two minutes to reach the halfway mark, immediately beneath Faraday's window, where the ornate Victorian drinking-fountain, embellished with bronze dolphins, was situated.

George Faraday knew exactly what the Headmaster, a man of fixed habits, would do next. The ritual never varied. Dr. Whittington would halt at this point. He would bend his giraffe-like form, with its rather small, greying, mostly bald head, down low over the drinking-fountain's basin. His throat being dry after leading the choral practice, he would noisily gulp in several mouthfuls of the fountain-water.

This was, perhaps, a curious habit, since he would arrive at his private cottage in only two minutes more, and could drink all the water he needed from a tumbler. Dr. Whittington would often explain, however, that the water in the fountain came from a chalybeate spring, and to pause here and drink a while each day was of benefit to his health.

Faraday was planning to prove just the opposite.

The languages master had realised for some time that it would be the easiest thing in the world to drop a heavy lump of stone on the Headmaster's head as he stood bent low over the fountain's basin.

Just above the top of Faraday's window, and within easy reach of his hand when he stood on a chair, were the fake crenellated battlements forming an indented parapet. The copes or merlons sticking up from the embrasures or crenelles were like a row of rotten teeth grinning out over the English countryside.

Now and again one of the loose, weatherbeaten stone blocks of which they had been constructed ("by a fly-by-night Victorian builder," one of the masters had once joked in the Common Room) would come hurtling down. Nobody had yet been killed by one. This was another fundamental of Cullingford life which Faraday was about to reverse.

A loose lump of stone had fallen not too long ago from a point just above Faraday's window (the stonework was in pretty bad shape just about there) and had crushed a new hybrid tea rose that the school Matron, Miss Prudence Turvey, had only just planted with loving care outside the window of her room on the ground floor.

Miss Turvey had complained bitterly to the Headmaster.

"Oh, dear, oh dear, oh dear," Dr. Whittington had muttered petulantly, obviously irritated by yet a further complaint from the Cullingford staff, "I suppose we shall have to try and find some money to get that confounded parapet repaired!" He had then proceeded, as usual, to forget the whole thing, and nothing whatever was done. By this inaction he had signed his own death warrant.

The Headmaster was a stupid and ineffectual man, Faraday often told himself, a man who might almost be said to be suffering from premature senility.

This was a very sad thing for Rhona Whittington. How on earth had she ever come to marry a man like Theodore Whittington? Pushed into a safe and prestigious match by her social-climbing widowed mother, no doubt. Rhona was so much younger than her husband, so much more vital, so much more *earthy*...

"Whatever would the poor frustrated little darling do without *me*?" Faraday sometimes asked himself.

If Dr. Whittington should ever find out how much time his young wife spent in the loving arms of the languages master, George Faraday... If he but knew how desperately she needed Faraday... how desperately he needed *her*...!

Rhona was just right for him. He liked a woman to be a sexual athlete, one who left you sweaty and unhygienic and entwined by her limbs like a kitten entangled in a skein of wool. A complete contrast to the cold academic world of Cullingford. They both needed relief—he and Rhona—and without the restricting influence of old Whittington, or The Twit, as the boys called him.

This situation alone would have been enough to justify the Headmaster's swift removal from our mortal coil. But there was, in fact, another motive, equally strong.

Faraday had always seen himself as the natural choice for Assistant Headmaster as soon as the doddering old Henderson retired, which was any moment now. Everybody had expected Faraday to replace him, even Henderson himself.

But Dr. Whittington had already intimated that Faraday would not be nominated for the job. Whittington simply disliked him. It was not that he had any suspicion of the languages master's illicit affair with his wife. It was just that he disliked Faraday instinctively—he always had.

This was a most unfortunate decision for the Headmaster to make. It merely reinforced the already pressing need for George Faraday to remove his odious presence.

The choir practice for a school performance of a Bach oratorio would be continuing for several weeks yet. There was, therefore, enough time for Faraday to practise his aim at the vital spot—the spot where the nape of Dr. Whittington's long neck would be, and the fragile cerebellum, as he lowered his head and shoulders over the shallow basin of the drinking-fountain to swallow his tonic spring water for the last time.

George Faraday, known as a first-class bowler in school cricket matches, had always possessed a good aim. And now, after regular practising in front of his window, he could deposit a stone chipping right inside the fountain's basin with unerring accuracy every time.

As soon as he felt ready, the small chipping would become one of the blocks from the decomposing roof parapet a few feet above him, a piece larger than a brick and considerably heavier, quite ample to shatter the back of Whittington's skull when thrown from an upper window.

After that, Rhona's soft, yielding, enveloping warmth would be all his. And the Headmastership too, no doubt, for the school's board of governors would have no reason to oppose him without Whittington's adverse influence.

When it came to the actual moment for Faraday to carry his plan into action, he found himself quite ready, almost indecently eager. He had given so much thought to his programme that his whole mind was now directed towards its efficient prosecution.

First the clock business. This should establish a really acceptable alibi.

The room right next to Faraday's was Seagrave's, and none of them ever locked a bedroom door. He waited for Seagrave to go out, then slipped in without being seen. He looked at the electric clock on Seagrave's bedside table, then turned the minute-hand back ten minutes. Seagrave would not know that his clock was ten minutes slow because he had nothing with which to compare it. Faraday knew that he had taken his watch to a jeweller's in the town to have the spring seen to.

Now to get hold of the stone…

The dusk was getting a little deeper every day, and the gathering darkness—not dark enough to hinder him, but sufficient to make his activity less obvious—helped him. He wore gloves to handle the stone, to protect his skin as much as to avoid leaving any prints.

Standing on a chair and leaning slightly out of the window of his room, he loosened the most dislodgeable stone within reach. Slowly and with extreme caution he transferred it from the section of parapet above his window to the floor inside his room. So far so good.

And now the waiting period. This was the worst part of all. He was sweating slightly and acutely conscious of the thumping of his heart against his ribcage. But this was not so much tension, he thought, as exultation, the thrill of turning theory into reality. The minutes crawled by like paralytic tortoises...

Then, at 7.32 p.m. precisely, dead on cue, Dr. Whittington's tall, stooping outline loomed out of the twilight. It was not until he arrived close to the fountain, however, that he could be absolutely certain it was the Headmaster.

Dr. Whittington, according to his wont, slowed down and then halted. The grey-tufted and partly bald head lowered itself over the basin of the fountain...

The stone had been carefully manoeuvred into position, and was held poised only momentarily in the steady and confident hand. Then Faraday pitched...

The languages master scarcely winced as the lump of stone thudded, with a deadly precision, on the Headmaster's brittle skull. He asked himself if he were a sadist. He *should* have felt *some* emotion. But it hardly mattered now. One thud of stone on flesh, then stone on stone, and it was over, all over.

Faraday had recoiled back into his room after lobbing the stone. Now he peered out cautiously, just long enough to establish that Dr.

Whittington was sprawled out on the weed-flecked paving stones, arms and legs forming an ungainly swastika.

He withdrew quickly again, shut the sash window quietly, removed the gloves and put them away, and then went straight into Seagrave's room next door. Seagrave, who taught science, was in there now and looked up as his neighbour walked in.

"Sorry to barge in, old chap," Faraday said, maintaining deceptive calm, "but have you got the right time? It would seem that my *own* wristwatch has packed up now!"

Seagrave glanced towards the electric-clock which Faraday had retarded. "It's 7.24," he said.

"Thanks, old boy," Faraday smiled pleasantly. "What's the book you're reading? Looks like another new thriller."

"It's a Hitchcock anthology, and you can't have it till I've finished with it!"

Faraday grinned. "But you wouldn't mind if I borrowed one from your collection? I'm very short of entertaining reading matter at the moment."

"Well, there's the bookcase right behind you—help yourself, old man," Seagrave invited.

Faraday sat in the small easy chair beside the bookcase. He deliberately took his time, browsing over the books, putting them back, chatting with Seagrave.

Finally, making his choice, he looked at Seagrave's electric clock and exclaimed, "Holy cow! It's ten to eight. I didn't realise I'd wasted so much of your time, old chap. I've really got to dash. I've got some test-papers to mark and I don't want to be at it all night. Well, cheerio, old boy, and many thanks for the loan of the book."

And then he was back again in his own room. With the utmost stealth he looked out of the window again. Although it was getting dark he could see that a small group had gathered by the drinking-fountain.

He could hear the low murmur of voices above the whispering night sounds and last birdcalls. So far, so good.

They would know the time that Whittington had died... about 7.33... and at that very moment he had been sitting talking idly with Seagrave in the latter's room. Well, according to Seagrave's clock, anyway.

And now, of course, there would be the inevitable interrogations. The probing, questioning, arguing, speculating. Those crumbling old stones were dangerously loose, admittedly—had not some fallen, and one only recently?—but, then again, somebody over-perceptive might think that the stone had dropped at a curiously oblique angle...

(*"If, my dear Watson, you will look at the position of this stone,"* Holmes remarked, *"and compare it with that of the stone which I allowed to fall naturally..."*)

Yes... well, let them think what they damned well liked. Let them try to *prove* what had really happened. Let them try to make it stick.

It was the Chairman of the school's Board of Governors who had turned up first. A certain Lt. Col. Bulstrode, with whisky-purpled complexion and belligerent moustache.

He had wanted to avoid any kind of publicity, even to the extent of "hushing the blasted business up". But Miss Prudence Turvey, the Matron, outside whose bedroom window the unfortunate Headmaster had been struck down and who considered that she might well be the next victim, said that you could not possibly hush up a thing like that.

"Who," demanded the Chairman of the Governors, "wants to send his son to a place where blasted boulders are showering down like blasted hailstones all over the blasted place?"

He knew, of course, that the news could never be suppressed but it was not until quite late that the "accident", as Colonel Bulstrode insisted on calling it, was reported to the local constabulary. And it was not until next morning that a certain Detective-Inspector Ellison, from the Divisional HQ of the Criminal Investigation Department, arrived at Cullingford School to begin his "routine" enquiries.

Seeing the police actually there, in the flesh, Faraday could not altogether suppress a feeling of nervous tension. And this tension increased when Lt. Col. Bulstrode summoned him to the room that had been the study of the dead Headmaster.

Inspector Ellison was there, as Faraday had anticipated. He was a rather stocky man with a pink skin, thinning sandy-coloured hair and bright, restless eyes of a quite vivid blue. His polite and disarming manner obviously camouflaged a calculating mind and ruthless determination.

Ellison began, "Ah, Mr. Faraday… good morning, sir. I've been busy checking up on the late Dr. Whittington's regular habits. He was a man of unswerving habits, I'm told."

"Yes, he was," Faraday answered.

"I understand that he always walked across from the classroom block to his private cottage on the other side of the grounds at the same time each evening… a minute or two after 7.30?"

Faraday pretended to think. "Yes, I believe that's true, Inspector."

"And his route took him across the terrace immediately below your own window?"

Faraday hesitated a moment before answering. "Er—yes, it would do. And Mr. Seagrave's window also."

"Ah, yes. I understand it was the Headmaster's unfailing habit to stop on the terrace on his way across?"—the bright blue eyes of the C.I.D. man never left Faraday's face.

Faraday paused again. He knew that the Inspector had spoken to the others. It might seem deliberately evasive to show ignorance of Dr. Whittington's movements. He said: "You mean that the

Headmaster would stop to drink at the fountain? Yes, I think he usually did that. He said that drinking the spring water did him good."

"Not, I fear, on this occasion," put in Col. Bulstrode, but with no intention to be witty.

The Inspector ignored him and concentrated on the languages master. "Miss Turvey, the Matron, says she heard this accident happen. Right outside her room. I daresay you were in your own room, then—at 7.32, the Matron says."

Faraday thought a moment. "No, I wasn't, Inspector. I was with Seagrave in his room next door to mine. We were sitting in there chatting about books."

"Ah, yes, of course!" exclaimed Inspector Ellison. "Mr. Seagrave has already told me that." He looked at a notebook on the corner of the desk. "Seagrave says he remembers looking at his electric-clock when you went in and telling you that it was 7.24."

Faraday allowed himself a gentle and respectful smile. "I rather fancy that lets me out, Inspector, doesn't it?"

The blue eyes under the thick sandy eyebrows were fastened immovably on his face again. "For the moment, yes, Mr. Faraday. I note that your wristwatch has righted itself again?"

"My wristwatch?"

"You told Mr. Seagrave it had packed up?"

There was the faintest ripple of unease in Faraday's throat. "Oh, yes. It did seem to be playing tricks last night. I think it's all right now." He looked at the watch again. "Actually, Inspector, I have a class waiting. If there's nothing else…"

"Not right at this moment, sir," the Inspector said.

Once outside the late Headmaster's study, Faraday frowned anxiously. His reaction to the question about the wristwatch had been clumsy in the extreme. If he were ever caught out, it would be through his forgetfulness, the absent-mindedness of the proverbial professor. No murderer could ever gain high marks *that* way...

He made his way thoughtfully across to the classroom block. The Upper Fifth would be waiting for their French lesson. But it would be all right. Harrison Major would keep the class in order; he was an excellent Prefect.

Even so, the boys were surprisingly quiet as he arrived. No doubt the conversation would have been all about the sudden demise of The Twit. The callous little beasts might already have made up disrespectful couplets.

"A stone came tumbling down and hit
The cranium of the poor old Twit."

Une pierre?—un rocher?—une brique...? His head felt muzzy and he shook it. He put down his books, and looked at his wristwatch again.

Oh, Christ... The clock. He had put Seagrave's clock back ten minutes, but he had not returned, as he had planned, to put it right again...

Quite suddenly there was sweat on his face. He got up. "Excuse me a few moments, boys..."

"Are you all right, sir?" Harrison Major asked.

"Yes, of course. There's a book I forgot to bring. I'm going back to get it." God. What book? He would have to bring back the Racine... start them on the Racine sooner than he expected to...

If Seagrave had not noticed the clock was wrong, there was still time to correct it. He knew that Seagrave was not in his room. At this time he should be in the School Laboratory with the Upper Fourth.

He hurried up to the top floor of the central block and to Seagrave's room. It was all right, he was not there. Swiftly he put the science master's clock right, checking with his own watch, and, after collecting the copy of Racine from his bookcase—God, he'd remembered it!—he returned to take the Upper Fifth through their languages period.

He knew he was sweating and out of breath—not the calm, collected front he had hoped to maintain—but he felt more at ease now that he had attended to that clock.

Later on he was sent for again by the Chairman of the School Governors, and went once more to the late Headmaster's study with the same slight feeling of trepidation that he had once experienced as a boy when he was summoned to the presence of the Head.

He looked at the faces of Col. Bulstrode and Inspector Ellison and felt the first real and painful stirrings of disquiet. No polite and sympathetic smiles, no nods of greeting. Just cold granite faces. Both the men had blue eyes, he noticed—steel blue. Granite and steel.

"Mr. Faraday," Inspector Ellison began brutally, "I understand that you have been having a clandestine affair with Mrs. Rhona Whittington, the late Headmaster's wife."

Faraday faltered, then asked, "Did she tell you that herself?"

"Not voluntarily," Ellison answered. "But she confirmed it when we pressed her."

"You mean you bullied her," Faraday said.

The Colonel put in gruffly, "No need for that kind of talk, Faraday."

"Her husband was a great deal older than she is," Faraday said by way of defence.

"Yes, quite." The detective's mouth tightened into a thin line, then loosened up again. "Mrs. Whittington also confirmed that her husband was against nominating you for the post of Assistant Headmaster."

"Yes, that's true," Faraday replied. He palmed back his hair, an excuse to wipe away the perspiration at his hairline. His hand was shaking. "Dr. Whittington disliked me, I'm afraid. And *I* disliked *him*. It was always like that."

"Did you dislike him enough to kill him?" the Inspector demanded frankly.

"Are you accusing me of killing him, Inspector?"

"Yes, Mr. Faraday."

"On what sort of evidence?" Faraday asked. He was blinking quickly, an old nervous habit. Presently, if this went on, he would feel slightly sick, and the throbbing would start up in his head.

"I am now quite convinced, Mr. Faraday, that the piece of stone which crushed Dr. Whittington's head didn't just fall of its own accord."

"Some have fallen before, Inspector."

"I know. But this one was carefully lobbed with great accuracy. You're Cullingford's best bowler, I'm told."

"Now we're getting really fanciful, Inspector."

"You knew that the Headmaster stopped at the fountain to drink. You mentioned this fact to me of your own free will—you were the only one who did mention it, in fact." Ellison's gaze was constant. "You practised, didn't you?"

"Practised?"

"Practised by throwing small stones?"

"What a vivid imagination you have, Inspector."

"Not really, Mr. Faraday. Miss Turvey, the Matron, actually heard some of those stones coming down. She actually thought that some of the boys were throwing them."

"Perhaps the boys were. Boys do throw stones, you know," Faraday answered. The irony misfired. His voice was too tremulous.

The Inspector ignored this comment. He glanced briefly at his notebook on the desk.

"Mr. Seagrave told me that his clock was showing 7.24 when you went into his room to ask the time—and said your wristwatch wasn't working, although I believe it was. This doesn't tally with what Miss Turvey tells me."

Faraday frowned. "And where does Matron come into this?"

"Well, you see, when you entered Mr. Seagrave's room, he had only just that minute put his telephone down. Miss Turvey had rung him to give him a message from one of the boys in the sick bay."

"I can't see what you are driving at, Inspector."

"Miss Turvey said that she rang Mr. Seagrave at 7.31. She said that she never did ring Mr. Seagrave until just after 7.30, on Mr. Seagrave's own instructions. So, you see, Mr. Faraday, when you went into his room, his clock must have been about ten minutes slow. You get my drift, I hope?"

"I... I must say I find this all very theoretical," Faraday said. He was not sure what to do with his hands; he was using them like parcels he wanted to put down somewhere.

"It's not really theoretical at all," Inspector Ellison went on, watching his hands, watching the sweat on his face, watching his inner agony with his bright X-ray eyes. "You see, I did check Mr. Seagrave's clock earlier on and found it was ten minutes slow.

"This was a bit odd really, Mr. Faraday, because electric clocks don't usually go wrong unless there is a power-cut, in which case all the electric-clocks go wrong, don't they? So I worked on the theory that somebody might have tampered with the clock."

"It was certainly not me!" Faraday shouted. Oh, damn... It was a mistake to shout. He really mustn't shout.

"You're lying, Mr. Faraday, and you're a terribly bad liar. You see, I know you changed the clock."

"How, for God's sake, how?"

The faintest of smiles, a chilly smile, twitched the corners of Ellison's mouth.

"I polished Mr. Seagrave's clock, you see. Then I waited for somebody to have a staggering afterthought and rush up there and put the clock right before anybody noticed. You will have realised, Mr. Faraday, that whoever did that would also leave a set of fingerprints on the clock at the same time."

The languages master stared unbelievingly at the C.I.D. man. His throat throbbed convulsively as he tried to swallow saliva, but there was no saliva to swallow.

"You walked neatly into that trap, Mr. Faraday. Not very high marks for that, I'm afraid."

"Well?" barked Colonel Bulstrode.

Faraday's face was now utterly without colour. For a moment he went on staring at the two men behind the deceased Headmaster's desk.

Then, like that wilting schoolboy faced with the Head's penal bamboo, he started to weep with small blubbering cries.

THE HARROWING OF HENRY PYGOLE

Colin Watson

Colin Watson (1920–83) was born in Surrey and educated in Croydon at the Whitgift Grammar School; originally founded in 1596 by John Whitgift, the Archbishop of Canterbury, it became fully independent in 1946 and is now an independent day school with limited boarding and known as the Whitgift School. Watson worked as a journalist and lived for many years in Folkingham, Lincolnshire. His witty first novel, *Coffin, Scarcely Used* (1958), was the first of the dozen novels that formed "The Flaxborough Chronicles", his major contribution to mystery fiction. *Hopjoy was Here* (1962), won the CWA Silver Dagger and is arguably the best book in the series.

Four of the Flaxborough novels were televised as *Murder Most English*, with Anton Rodgers playing Watson's likeable Inspector Purbright, The scripts were written by Richard Harris, a high-calibre screenwriter, but the series didn't win large enough audiences to survive beyond seven episodes. As well as an obscure non-series novel *The Puritan* (1966), Watson published an entertaining, if highly judgmental and sometimes erratic, study of crime and thriller fiction, *Snobbery with Violence*; he enjoyed poking fun at Golden Age fiction and what he would have made of the success of British Library's Crime Classics is anyone's guess. This is one of Watson's few short stories; it first appeared in 1974 in *Winter's Crimes 6*, edited by George Hardinge.

B Y THE TIME ONE REACHES THE SIXTH FORM OF AN ENGLISH
public school, one's judgement of character is pretty dependable.
That, after all, is one of the main objects of the exercise. It would be an
awful waste of effort if one were to end up with one's head crammed
with maths and history and physics but without an idea of how to
sum a fellow up and how to deal with him accordingly. Dealing with
people—that's what is really important. Any education which leaves
that out of account isn't worth a damn.

Goltho School may not have been too hot on the academic side,
but it certainly developed what used to be called "character" and the
ability to assess it in others.

"Know your man" was the favourite saying of Doc Gittins. He was
the headmaster at the time. In most respects the Doc was a seedy old
bore, but the fact that one still remembers his "Know your man" does
show how well the principle was rammed home.

So you can see that when I decided Henry Pygole to be a prig of
the first water I wasn't just giving in to annoyance or prejudice or anything like that. I mean, I'd been at Goltho nearly six years and I really
did know what to think about people. There was no question about
it: Pygole was the bloody end.

I wasn't the only one to think so, actually. Another man in the Sixth,
Bernard Sweet, came out with the very same opinion. If anything,
he was even more worked up. One could understand why. Sweet was
due to leave Goltho that term and he most definitely was not trailing
any clouds of glory. Not that it mattered—his people had no end
of money. But flopping so badly in the exams had not predisposed

him to feel friendly towards Pygole, who was an obvious cert for
Cambridge.

Henry Pygole was one of those people who make cleverness offensive by wrapping it up in humility. There was always a sort of dubious
smile on his face, as if he knew he was going to make a balls-up of
whatever happened to be on hand at the moment. He didn't, of course.
He came tops. Time after time. In everything. But he forever had that
droopy, self-deprecating air.

One remembers particularly how diffident dear Henry looked on
the afternoon of the inter-house tennis finals. That was the day when
Sweet and I decided that something would have to be done about him.

We were sitting together on a bench when Pygole arrived at the
courts. He came along the path from Upper School looking like an
unemployed ball-boy: eyes down, shoulders hunched. We could just
catch that shy, sickly little smile of his when he raised his head now and
then to see where he was going. He didn't swing his racquet or carry
it under one arm like the other fellows, but nursed it in both hands as
if it were some fearfully lethal weapon. Somebody shouted: "You on
form, Pie?" He just smiled meekly and shook his head. I heard Sweet
make a vomiting noise.

Both Bernard and I had rotten luck and were out of the contest
early, so we had plenty of opportunity to watch Pygole's technique—if
that's the word for it. He would stand on the court looking embarrassed
and sort of penitent; then he'd clumsily brace himself and toss up a
ball, slow and high. Again and again we watched up to that point, but
not once did we spot what happened next. There was just a sort of
propeller-like blur and that ball simply disappeared like a burst soap
bubble. Then somebody on the far side of the court was picking it up
and Pygole was listening to the umpire calling out his score—listening
as if he couldn't understand it.

He won, naturally. Every bloody game.

That night Sweet and I went into serious conference. By lights out, the whole scheme of Pygole's fully deserved punishment had been worked out in detail.

The plan was not entirely altruistic from Bernard's point of view. As one has said, he was on the point of leaving Goltho and he had toyed for some time with the idea of taking a week or two off for what he called "private enjoyment". The way he said this made it sound fearfully immoral but, quite frankly, one doubts if old Sweet could have told an orgy from a hand of canasta. All the same, he was game for breaking out for a while and this provided the basis for our dealing with the odious Pygole.

Next morning, I stuck close to Sweet during prayers and when we came out of Hall the two of us peeled off and went across to the kitchen.

Mrs. Judd was there on her own, as we'd known she would be; the other women didn't arrive until half past nine. I left Sweet outside the door while I jollied the old girl along a bit and pretended that I wanted half a lemon to make a drink during Inters. She made a show of refusing, but one's always been able to get round her and after a while she went clattering along to the storeroom. I went with her and kept her talking long enough for Sweet to be able to dodge into the kitchen and reach the fridge.

He was waiting in the corridor when I came out with my half lemon. There was a soft grin over his face and he held something behind his back. He showed me what it was—a whopping great lump of mutton wrapped in paper.

One must have stared pretty hard at the stuff because he laughed and said I wasn't to worry, there was tons more of it in the fridge. I told him to get it hidden quickly in his room and I'd wait for him coming down. The only other things we needed I would get myself from the woodwork shop during the first afternoon period.

Sweet and I had a private smile over lunch when we heard other men at our table complaining that the mutton broth was even thinner than usual. Nothing was said officially, though, so one supposes Mrs. Judd hadn't noticed.

In woodwork I managed to swipe a screwdriver and a gimlet and a handful of two-inch screws. These I was to pass over to Sweet later.

Men in the Sixth were expected to take tea in their own rooms and we generally got together in twos and threes, sharing the meal until five when we were supposed to split up again for an hour's private study. Sweet came to my room and I made some tea and toast.

All the rooms on our wing were identical. Each had a fireplace, but of course this was never used because the central heating, such as it was, was considered adequate. There was a little hotplate thing in the hearth, though—electric—for boiling water and toasting. The bed stood against one wall and in the corner was a combined locker and wardrobe. The rest of the space was taken up by a small table and a couple of chairs.

The only other thing worth mentioning was a rather queer door, about a foot high and two feet wide, set very low in the wall opposite the fireplace: at floor level, in fact.

This door led to a recess that was not only deeper than one might have expected but surprisingly long as well. One still called it the "trunk hole" and no doubt it had been intended originally as a store for luggage. In more recent years it became usual for rugger boots and some of the other sports gear to be kept there. But then the Old Man got one of his hygiene fits. All the cupboards were cleared out, and Heddon, the porter, was told to start nailing them up.

Sweet's trunk hole, further down the corridor, had been done already. Mine was still open, though, and so was Pygole's, in the next room but one.

It was about the trunk holes that Sweet and I had something to say during tea. He was not quite so confident as he had been the night before.

"So long as you tuck your great feet up, you'll be all right," I told him.

He munched toast and stared at the cupboard door. "Are you positive they're all the same size?" A fragment of toast flew out of his mouth when he said "positive". Sweet's table manners weren't exactly endearing.

"Of course they are. Mine and Pygole's are, anyway. I've checked."

He got up and went over to the cupboard and squatted beside it. Several times he pulled open and shut the door. "Is the catch on his the same as this?"

"Just the same." I wasn't absolutely certain, actually but he was ready enough to cry off without one's giving him an excuse. It was a hundred to one that the catches were standard fittings, anyway.

He opened the door fully, turned on his side, and began to wriggle into the trunk hole, feet first. It took him only a few seconds to get the whole of his body inside.

He grumbled a bit at the squeeze, but looked rather pleased with himself all the same. Again he tested the door. It seemed perfectly easy to push open from the inside.

He came out and ate all the rest of the toast.

We arranged to meet again at half past six. I gave him the tools and screws.

During the next hour and a half I devised at least a dozen ways of provoking a normal fellow to homicidal assault. The trouble was, I could not think of one that was likely to have that effect on Pygole. Placidity was one of the most infuriating things about him. The chap really was a creep. I was just wondering if some positively frightful remark about his mother might do the trick when Sweet barged in again.

"Come on," he said. "I want to be away by eight."

I asked him if he'd decided how he was going to get Pygole to hit him.

He said he hadn't, actually, but he was sure something would occur to him on the spur of the moment. One said one hoped so, and tried not to look too doubtful.

We marched into Pygole's room like a couple of customs men looking for a still.

Pygole was sitting at the table, doing some prep. One thought how bloody typical. And he didn't jump or anything—just looked up and gave us a wet grin.

Sweet stood over him and flicked shut the book he'd been working from.

"Come on, Pie-eye," Sweet said. "What have you done with it?"

I closed the door behind us.

Pygole goggled at Sweet, then at me. "Done with what?"

"You know damn well," Sweet said. He moved in closer and nudged Pygole with his knee.

The Pie nearly fell off his chair, but he didn't get ruffled. He just made some wet remark. "I've eaten it"—something crashingly sarcastic.

"We want it," Sweet said, "and we've come to get it."

"Right-o," Pygole said, cool as ever.

One could see that Sweet didn't quite know what to do next. "We'll have to look for it, then," I said.

"That's the idea," Sweet said. He pushed some books on to the floor. One saw Pygole's face stiffen up a bit, but he didn't move.

Bernard glanced round the room, then went across to the bed. He pulled everything off it and pretended to look under the mattress.

At that, Pygole stood up. "Look, if only you'll tell me what you're supposed to have lost…"

"Shut up," Sweet said. He tugged the locker door open. Pygole turned to me, and I gave him a helpless, sympathetic sort of look. Well, it was important that he shouldn't think of me as hostile.

Bernard had taken a tin down from one of the locker shelves and he was trying to get it open.

Pygole walked across and held out his hand, as if to take the tin, but the lid was off by then. Pygole said: "Why don't you run along and play storm troopers somewhere else, fat boy?"

That was really asking for trouble, and one thought that Sweet would land him one there and then, but one was wrong. What he did was to hold that tin up high and turn it upside down.

There was a cake in it, a whole cake, with icing and everything. When it hit the floor, it broke into three raggy chunks.

That did it. Pygole made a sudden grab at Sweet's coat and pulled, swinging him away from the locker. Bernard let himself go, then pretended to trip. He managed to come down with a terrific crash against the fireplace. And in that instant, one saw him wink. Now it was my turn.

I rushed across in front of Pygole and knelt by Bernard. I made out to be feeling his head. The Pie just stood and stared. His face was absolutely white.

After a while, I let go of Sweet's head and took his wrist. I looked up at Pygole with my mouth hanging open a little. He was obviously scared as hell. Then I pulled Bernard's coat open and stuck my ear against his shirt. I was praying he wouldn't giggle.

Fortunately, Pygole was too shocked to come looking for Sweet's hefty great pulse himself. He stood where he was, hanging on to the locker door.

I let another couple of minutes go by. Then I sat back on my heels and gave a fair imitation of a shattered friend. Pygole watched me shake my head. He whispered: "What are we going to do?"

One stared all round the room, pretending to be thinking desperately of a solution.

At last, Pygole let go of the locker door. "I'd better go and fetch somebody."

I shook my head again quickly. "No. You can't do that."

"But we've got to," he kept saying. He was a pretty thick case, was the Pie.

"Look," I said, "*you* know you didn't mean to kill the poor bloke, and *I* know you didn't, but who will believe that we aren't lying just to shield each other? There's only one way to deal with this. Get him back into his own room. Then they'll just have to make what they can of it. At least *you* won't be involved. All you need say is that you heard a bump somewhere but thought no more about it."

Poor old Pygole was in no state to argue. He started lurching off there and then. I grabbed him before he could open the door. "No, not now, for God's sake!"

He turned round slowly to face me, but carefully avoided looking at Sweet.

I said: "Heddon's working somewhere along the corridor. We shall have to wait a bit."

"But suppose somebody comes in?"

I waited a few moments for that to worry him thoroughly. Then I walked straight to the trunk hole and pulled the door wide open. One hoped one was looking awfully determined and competent.

"In there," I said. "Just until lights out. Then I'll slip back and we'll get everything cleared up. Keep your nerve, that's all; it's only for a couple of hours."

Sweet weighed a ton. Stuffing him into that cupboard was about the toughest job I've ever had to tackle. The Pie wasn't much help, of course. I didn't dare let him be, in case he discovered the truth. I'll say this for Bernard, though: once his head and shoulders were safely out of sight, he did his best to ease himself in without giving the game away.

When we had finished, we sat on the bed for a breather and then I helped Pygole to tidy the room. The next item on the programme was to leave Sweet with a free hand for half an hour or so. I didn't anticipate any difficulty. Pygole, one knew perfectly well, would be glad to keep clear of the scene of his "crime" as long as possible.

It was just too bad that old Carson, my housemaster, should have chosen that particular moment to come looking for me. I'd forgotten to do some fixture lists for him and nothing would satisfy the old goat but that one should come down straight away and make them out in his study. I hinted as broadly as I could to Pygole that he should wait for me in my room, then off I had to go.

Carson kept me for ages. First, the fixtures. After that, a lot of rot about some bicycle race or other—he was one of those fiendish "wheeler" veterans. And for a finale he had the neck to make me drink a mug of the most filthy cocoa you could imagine. It was lumpy, practically milkless, and absolutely scalding. By the time I did get away, my mouth was one big blister and the "rooms" bell was being rung, which meant one was supposed to be getting ready for bed.

There were still one or two fellows popping in and out of our corridor. I went straight into my own room and changed into pyjamas. Then I waited until things quietened down. There was one more piece of high-grade acting to be done that night and one didn't want anybody butting in to spoil it.

When one looked into the corridor again, it was empty. I nipped along to Pygole's room and went in. The light was still on. The first thing I looked at was the door of the trunk hole. I nearly made the mistake of heaving a sigh of relief. Standing out from the wood were four or five shiny new screw heads.

I gaped at them, looking as horrified as I could, and said "Christ!" in a kind of throaty gasp. One thinks it was quite impressive, actually.

Then I looked at Pygole.

He didn't seem to realise I was there. He was in his pyjamas, sitting bolt upright in bed and staring in front of him. His face was still nearly as white as when old Bernard had done his dying act.

"It must have been Heddon," I said. "He was doing some of the others earlier on. I told you, didn't I?"

As far as Pie was concerned, one might as well not have been there. He sat stiff as a post, gawping at nothing.

One tried again.

"There's one thing about it—it does sort of solve things, doesn't it? In a way."

He took not the slightest notice. I felt a bit annoyed with him. After all, one doesn't like being cut dead—even by a chap who thinks he's got a corpse in his room. One had even been prepared to feel a little sorry for him. But Pygole wasn't the sort you could sympathise with for very long. I didn't say any more, just quietly pushed off.

One had to have a little laugh to oneself when one got into bed. Well, it really was one of Goltho's best jokes for years. And it would get better as time went on. One pictured the fuss there would be the next morning: the stern inquisition at school—the fearfully tactful enquiries at the railway station—probably at the local pub, too—the embarrassed telephone call to Sweet's old man—the pained face of Doc Gittins when he spoke "in absolute confidence you understand, dear fellow" to his police inspector friend at Harrowby. It was going to be marvellous.

And all the time poor old Pygole would be padding around like a fugitive from the gallows! That ought to take some of the priggishness out of him.

Sweet would miss the fun, of course, and yet I couldn't help feeling slightly envious of him at that moment. He hadn't actually said where he was going, but I had an idea that he would hole up for a while at the Anglers' Arms in Tatford, a couple of miles up the river. Perhaps what he'd said about the barmaid there was just randy rot, but the Anglers' certainly was a smashing little pub and Bernard didn't have to worry about money, one knew that.

The following day was exactly as I had imagined it would be. During the morning, all the men on Sweet's corridor were called one by one into the Doc's study. The rumours flying about were absolutely gorgeous. The best I heard was that Sweet had eloped with the wife of a junior housemaster called Richardson. Another tale had it that he'd burgled the bursar's safe and was being hunted by Scotland Yard.

When it was my turn to be questioned, I met Pygole coming out of the Doc's study. He looked as if he hadn't slept for weeks. I was a bit worried, in case he'd given something away, and I asked him how he'd got on. He just walked past me as if he hadn't heard.

Gittins put all the expected questions. When had I last seen Sweet? Had he said anything to me? Did I know if he'd been in trouble of any kind? I was politely unhelpful, of course, and he let me go after a few minutes. It looked as if the Pie had kept his trap shut after all.

Nothing much happened in the next few days, apart from the spreading of some more wild tales. On the Thursday, somebody said the police were dragging the river. I went down during Inters but there was nothing to see.

Then there came a rumour that poor old Bernard had been arrested in Ireland. It was all rather enjoyable. The trouble was that there was no one with whom one dared share the joke. If one had had the nerve, one could have slipped off to the Anglers' for an hour some night after lights out. The risks were pretty terrific, though.

Anyway, there was always the sight of Pygole's face to make life worth while. One had never seen a fellow so changed. From morning to night, he looked absolutely grim. I could swear he'd begun to twitch. His work went right off and for the first time ever he got really thrashed at tennis—and by a fourth former, at that.

It was more than a week before the joke went into what we'd called "phase two". I had been expecting it, of course, but the weather had been fairly cool and neither Bernard nor I had known how long the thing would take to work.

I was coming out of my room to go down to supper when I noticed a man called Henderson standing outside Pygole's door and sniffing away like a bloodhound.

"What's this bloody awful pong?" he asked me.

"Awful" was just about right. For a second or two, it didn't connect. Then it dawned on me that the chunk of mutton Sweet had stuffed into the trunk hole before screwing down the door must be absolutely heaving. One damn nearly laughed out loud, but managed to turn it into a cough. Henderson looked pewky and pushed off.

As soon as he'd gone, I opened Pygole's door. I wanted to see how he was taking it.

Pie was already in bed, lying flat and staring up at the ceiling. One thought how thin he looked, really gaunt and scraggy, and with yellowish eyes. A pretty revolting specimen, actually.

The window was wide open. Even so, there was no getting away from that smell. How he was going to stick it all night, one just couldn't think.

He turned his head and looked at me and said, "Not very nice, is it?" in a queer, far-away sort of voice. It was the first time he had spoken to me since Sweet had hopped it.

I pretended horrified sympathy.

Pygole just raised and flopped a thin wrist. Talk about the death of Little Nell! Anyway, one didn't want to lose all appetite for supper, so one made one's farewells and departed.

That call on Pygole must have taken longer than I thought, because by the time I reached the Upper School dining-room practically all the food had gone. Not that it distressed me very much: old Ma Judd could always be persuaded to produce something extra in a needy cause.

I found her in the larder, messing about amongst her jars and things. I was just about to turn on the charm when I realised she was staring at me as if I was a cockroach or something.

"You needn't come wheedling round here," she said. "Not after that trick you played last week."

I told the silly old cow I didn't know what she was talking about and all I wanted was a couple of sandwiches.

"I'll sandwich you," she said. "You and that young blackguard Sweet. It comes to something when lads of your education sneak in here to steal food. I suppose you thought you were being clever. Of course, it never occurred to you that there was enough meat there for twenty or thirty dinners and that other boys would have to go short."

She went nadging on and on. I did the only thing possible, which was to give her a flat denial. After all, she was only guessing. If she'd known for certain that Bernard and I were responsible, she would have reported us.

The old cow goggled at me and said: "Do you mean to stand there and tell me you know nothing about that piece of meat?"

"What piece of meat?" I asked her.

"Why, that great piece of mutton that Sweet took out of the fridge and up to his room while you were making sure my back was turned."

Up to his room? One was beginning to get a pretty queer feeling. Still, one brazens these things out.

"If all this is true, Mrs. Judd," I said, "which I dispute, I should just like you to tell me what evidence you have. *I* certainly haven't seen any meat, in Bernard Sweet's room or anywhere else."

"In his room," she said again, nodding her thick old head. "And you can dispute all you like. That's where it was found, all right. The same night as he ran away. And you needn't ask me the name of the boy who found it and was decent enough to bring it down to me, because I wouldn't put it past you to bully him, instead of being thankful to him as you ought to be, because it was him who made me promise not to say anything to Doctor Gittins about it."

I don't know how much longer she would have waffled on. I got out. I was trying to think. I wasn't frightened, exactly. Not then. But something was building up in my head. I couldn't hear properly. I knew I had to talk to Pygole, though.

Twice on the stairs I fell over. I remember limping along the corridor and somebody asking if I'd hurt a leg. I got to Pygole's door. There were questions I had to ask him and I tried to think what they were before I went in, but I couldn't think at all, not of anything. All I knew was that I did not dare draw breath. I just stood there, slowly suffocating, as if I was under water. I think I would have died rather than take a breath. In the end, I turned and ran along the corridor, back towards my own door, still with mouth and nose tight shut. It was like drowning. I couldn't see and there was a huge whoomph-whoomph noise in my head.

Somehow I got into my room. I was on the floor. And at last I took a great gulp of air.

I think that I screamed then.

The smell. It had escaped. It had come after me. With me. It was in my clothes. I opened the door. It was there, too. I slammed the door and got the window open. That made no difference.

God knows how many times I was sick during the night. I threw up again and again. When I wasn't being sick, I lay fully dressed on the bed, with my eyes open, shivering.

I've no idea what I must have looked like when I dragged myself into prayers the next morning. Half the chaps were looking at me and nudging one another. I didn't care, actually. I was so cold and numb and sick that I hardly knew what I was doing or what anybody was saying. What I did notice a bit later on, though, was that some policemen had arrived at the school and that there was a lot of activity over by the residence block.

It was nearly lunchtime when I was sent for by the headmaster. Old Carson came into the physics lab and took me across personally. He seemed worried in case I should fall over, and kept taking my arm. He didn't say a word, just knocked on the study door and ushered me in like some kind of hospital patient. Then he left.

Gittins was standing by the window. At the desk where the Doc usually sat was a man I'd never seen before. He was a solemn-looking cove with a big chin and a moustache and cold little blue eyes. He told me to sit down and said he was Inspector something-or-other. Gittins just stood and kept quiet.

I'll say this for the man at the desk—he came straight to the point.

"We have found the body of a boy named Bernard Allistair Sweet in a cupboard in one of the sixth form bedrooms, and I have reason to believe that you may be able to tell me something about it."

It's funny, but although I'd made up my mind to give him the whole story there and then, I simply couldn't get a word out. I opened and shut my mouth like an idiot but I couldn't manage a sound.

The inspector waited a bit, then he said: "It appears from a preliminary examination that Sweet died of suffocation. That is scarcely surprising. The cupboard door fits very closely and it has a strong catch—apart from the screws that had been driven in. Perhaps for a start"—he drew a sheet of paper towards him—"you might tell me how Sweet came to be in that cupboard in the first place."

The bloke didn't seem all that bothered. One felt much steadier now, less frightened. "He got in himself," I said. "As a sort of joke, actually." I thought it would be safer to leave the Pie out of it, for the time being anyway.

The inspector nodded and wrote something. "We can talk some more about that later on," he said. "Now tell me why you put those screws in. Was that supposed to be part of the joke?"

I gave him an indulgent sort of smile. "Oh, but I didn't put them in. Bernard did. That was what we'd arranged before we…"

Too late I saw the absurdity of what I had said. Oddly enough, this was the very first moment of my realisation that somebody other than Sweet must have sealed that cupboard. I'd assumed from the start that the screwing down had been Sweet's doing. It had become so fixed in my mind that not even learning of his death had dislodged it.

The inspector looked at me pityingly. "You say, do you, that Sweet drove the screws into that door while he was behind it?"

"No, of course not. I wasn't thinking. It must have been Pygole, naturally."

He glanced down at something on the desk. "Henry Pygole, of the sixth form?"

"Yes."

He did some rearranging of papers. Then his eyes were on me again and the scared feeling came back worse than ever.

"I think," he said, "that you ought to hear the substance of a statement which has been made already by the boy Pygole." He looked down.

"Pygole says that he was away from his room between six-thirty and approximately seven-thirty on the evening of the fourteenth of July—that was when Sweet was last seen alive. He says he came back to find you there on your own. You were, in his words, 'rather agitated' but before he could say much to you a Mr. Carson arrived and took you off to write out some sporting fixtures. Pygole says it was then that he noticed the cupboard door had been screwed shut. He knew that the school porter, Heddon, had been doing work of a similar kind elsewhere on that floor and he assumed that it was Heddon who was responsible. Pygole thought nothing more about the matter until yesterday, when he noticed a peculiar smell in the room. He reported it this morning and the cupboard was opened on the orders of the headmaster."

I could hardly wait for him to finish before I was screaming the true facts. That was silly, I know, but I just couldn't help it. I simply yelled at the man, yelled out the whole truth, from beginning to end.

Of course he didn't believe it. One knew he wouldn't. He had one of those impenetrably stupid official faces.

When I'd done, he took the lid off a shallow cardboard box near his elbow. He showed me what was inside. A screwdriver, a gimlet, and three or four new screws.

"An officer found these tucked away behind some books in your locker," he said. "They have been identified as belonging to the school carpentry shop. And they are similar to tools which"—he picked up another of his damned papers and glanced at it—"which a boy called George Mason saw you slip into your pocket during a woodwork period on the afternoon of the fourteenth."

"It was Pygole!" I shouted. "I got those for Sweet but he left them in his room and Pygole found them. As he did the meat. And it was Pygole who used them, I tell you! He planted them in my room afterwards. He must have done! God, can't you bloody understand?"

He looked at me for a long while with those cold little eyes of his. He didn't like me one little bit. At last he cleared his stupid throat and began to preach his stupid policeman's sermon.

"Your best course now is to make a clean breast of it, lad," the fool said. "Believe me, you're not going to do yourself any good by trying to put the blame on another boy. Apart altogether from the evidence—with which I might say I am perfectly satisfied—anyone with half an eye can see that poor Pygole just isn't in your class when it comes to practical jokes."

DOG IN THE NIGHT-TIME

Edmund Crispin

Edmund Crispin was the name under which Bruce Montgomery (1921–78) wrote detective fiction. He entered Merchant Taylors' School, having won a scholarship, at the age of twelve in 1934; his love of music developed during his teens and he began to try his hand at composition. Next stop was St. John's College, Oxford, where he studied modern languages and was the organ scholar. His Oxford contemporaries included Kingsley Amis and Philip Larkin, and at this stage in their lives Montgomery seemed to possess more dazzling gifts than either of his friends. His first detective novel, *The Case of the Gilded Fly*, was written while he was still an undergraduate and published in 1942.

Crispin's series detective was the affable don Gervase Fen of St. Christopher's College, an invented seat of learning which Crispin placed next door to St. John's. Fen's breezy style of sleuthing is seen at its most exuberant in *The Moving Toyshop* (1946), an Oxford mystery which Crispin dedicated to Larkin, who is also name-checked in the story. He combined crime writing with music—including the composition of many film scores—but ill-health and alcoholism probably contributed to the writer's block that meant he only wrote one novel after the age of thirty. "Dog in the Night-Time" (which has also been published under the inferior title "Looking for a Diamond") was first published in the *Evening Standard* on 4 August 1954.

GERVASE FEN, PROFESSOR OF ENGLISH LANGUAGE AND LITERATURE in the University of Oxford, found Ann Cargill waiting for him in his rooms in college when he returned there from dinner at the George on a certain bitter February evening.

She was a quiet, good-looking girl, the most pleasant, if not the brightest, of the few undergraduates to whom he gave private tuition.

"Nice to see you back," he said. For he knew that Ann's father had recently died, and that she had been given leave of absence for the first few weeks of term in order to cope with the situation and its aftermath.

"It's not about work, I'm afraid," she confessed. "Not altogether, I mean. I—I was wondering if you could help me over something—something personal."

"Surely your moral tutor—" Fen began, and then suddenly remembered who Ann's moral tutor was. "No," he said. "No, of course not... Wait while I get us some drinks, and then you can tell me all about it."

"I'm probably being several sorts of a fool," said Ann, as soon as they were settled with glasses in their hands. "But here goes, anyway... I don't know if you know anything about my family, but my mother died years ago. I'm an only child, and my father—well, the important thing about him, for the moment, is that he had a passion for jewels.

"Jewels weren't his business. They were his hobby. And two or three months ago he sank an enormous amount of money—about three-quarters of his capital, I should think—into buying a single diamond that he'd set his heart on, a huge thing, quite flawless.

"Well, now, at the beginning of this year Daddy shut up our house at Abingdon—I live on my own in the vacs, you see, in a flat in Town;

he liked me to do that—and flew out to Australia on business. He didn't take the diamond with him. It was left in the house—"

Fen lifted his eyebrows.

"Ah, yes, but the point is, it was really quite as safe there as it would have been in the bank. At the time he started collecting jewels Daddy had his study made as near burglar-proof as money could buy; and there was only one set of keys to the door and the safe; and when he went to Australia he left those with Mr. Spottiswoode, his solicitor."

Ann took a deep breath. "And then he—he was killed. In a street accident in Sydney... I—I went down to Abingdon after the wire came, and wandered about there a bit. Remembering. That was when I saw Mr. Spottiswoode, the solicitor, driving away from the house.

"I don't think he saw me. I called after him, but he didn't stop. And, of course, being Daddy's executor, he had a perfect right to be there. But I always hated Mr. Spottiswoode..."

Ann wriggled in her chair. "And I'm pretty sure," she added, "that he was a crook."

After a brief pause: "I've no proof of that," she went on. "And you don't have to believe it if you don't want to. I only mentioned it because it's one of the reasons why I've come to you. Mr. Spottiswoode—"

"You say he 'was' a crook."

"Yes, that's the next thing. Mr. Spottiswoode's dead, you see. He died three weeks ago, very soon after I saw him at Abingdon; quite suddenly of a heart attack. And at that stage he hadn't yet got what they call a grant of probate of Daddy's will.

"So that what's happened since, is that my Uncle Harry, who's now my legal guardian, has been made administrator of the estate on my behalf. In other words, Mr. Spottiswoode *did* have the keys to Daddy's study, and Uncle Harry has them *now*."

"And is Uncle Harry a crook too?"

Ann wriggled still more. "I know it must sound as if I've got some hellish great neurosis, persecution mania or something, but—well, yes, frankly, I think he is. Only not the same kind as Mr. Spottiswoode. Uncle Harry's the rather nice, inefficient, sentimental sort of crook who always gets caught sooner or later."

"In which case we must hope that it's he who has stolen your father's diamond, and not Mr. Spottiswoode," said Fen briskly. "I take it that theft is what you have in mind?"

"It's crazy, I know, and we shall probably find the diamond in the safe where Daddy put it. But—look, Professor Fen: Uncle Harry's meeting me at the house tomorrow morning to unlock the study and—and go through its contents. He's been in America up to five days ago, so there hasn't been a chance before. If I could just have someone with me…"

And Fen nodded. "I'll come," he said. For he had known Ann Cargill long enough to be aware that, however erratic her views on *Beowulf* or Dryden, she was nobody's fool.

Uncle Harry proved to be a big, florid, amiable man dressed in checks with a black arm-band. And like his niece, he appeared at the Abingdon house next morning with a companion.

"Humbleby!" said Fen, pleased; and: "Well, well," said Detective Inspector Humbleby of Scotland Yard as he shook Fen's hand: "And what are you doing here?"

"Looking for a diamond," said Fen. "Miss Cargill is a pupil of mine… Ann, meet the inspector."

"We're all looking for a diamond," said Uncle Harry. "And from what the inspector told me yesterday, there's a damn good chance we shan't find one."

"Twenty thousand pounds," said Humbleby, "is somewhere about what the average high-class fence would give for a diamond like your father's, Miss Cargill. And £20,000 is what Mr. Spottiswoode's executors found hidden in his house after his death. Being honest men, they came and had a word with us about it at the Yard. We've been working on the case for a fortnight now, and we still don't know where that money came from. Nothing legitimate, you can be sure...

"But there was never any secret about your father's buying that jewel; and his death was reported in the papers; and his name was on the list of Mr. Spottiswoode's clients. So of course we started putting two and two together, and yesterday I had a word with your uncle about it, and he very kindly invited me down here, subject to your having no objection—"

"Of course not," said Ann.

"So that now," Humbleby concluded, "we shall see what we shall see."

A woman, Ann explained, had been coming in once or twice a week to keep the house dusted, but her ministrations had not, of course, included the study, which would undoubtedly be in a mess. And so it turned out.

When Uncle Harry had manipulated the elaborate locks, thrown the study door open and switched on the lights (for the room was in darkness, thanks to the solid steel shutters on the windows), they saw that dust—five weeks' dust—lay undisturbed on the furniture, the bare polished boards of the floor, everything.

Also it was cold in there: while Uncle Harry fumbled with the safe, Ann turned on the big electric fire and stood warming her hands at it. Presently, Fen, who had been peering at the marks left by their feet on the dusty floor, lifted his head and sniffed.

"Is there something burning?" he asked suspiciously.

They all sniffed. "I can't smell anything," said Ann. "Nor me," said Humbleby. "Nor me," said Uncle Harry, pausing in his labour: and added ruefully, "But then, it's years since I was able to smell anything."

Fen shrugged. "My mistake," he said. Though as a matter of fact it had not been a mistake, since he himself had not been able to smell anything burning, either. His eye caught Humbleby's. "Dog," he confided solemnly, "in the night-time."

Humbleby scowled. "Dog in the—"

"Eureka!" said Uncle Harry inaccurately: actually, all he had contrived to do so far was to get the safe door open. But a moment later he emerged from it holding a handsome jewel-box. "Would this be—"

"Yes, that's it," said Ann. "Open it, please."

And Uncle Harry opened it. And it was empty.

"It couldn't," Humbleby suggested, "be somewhere else?"

"No." Ann shook her head decisively. "I was with my father just before he left, and that was where he put it."

Uncle Harry grunted. "Anyway, there's your explanation of Spottiswoode's £20,000."

But Fen apparently did not agree. "No," he said. "Insufflator."

"Beg pardon?"

"Insufflator. For example, one of those rubber-bulb things barbers use for blowing powder on to your chin. And dust, as such, isn't really very hard to come by. It would take a little time, and a little care, but I'm willing to bet that given 24 hours you could re-dust the entire room."

An ugly gleam had appeared in Uncle Harry's eye. "Just what," he enunciated slowly, "are you suggesting?"

"I was suggesting a likely means for you to have used to cover up your traces after stealing the diamond. You stole it last night, I suppose, after Humbleby's account of Spottiswoode's hoard—which I should guess is probably blackmail money accumulated over a good many years—had suggested to you how you could disperse the blame. As to why Spottiswoode didn't forestall you—well, it may simply be that he didn't know of any means of disposing of such a distinctive stone."

"The man's mad," said Uncle Harry, with conviction. "Now look, sir: granted I *could* have stolen the diamond and then covered my traces with all this—this insufflator rubbish, what the devil makes you think I actually *did?* Where's your evidence, man, your proof?"

"The dog in the Sherlock Holmes story," said Fen, "did nothing in the night-time. And that was the curious incident."

"*Dog?*"

"Like this electric fire, here," Fen explained. "No smell of burning, you recall, when it was first switched on. But there *ought* to have been a smell of burning if the fire had been accumulating dust since (at the latest) Spottiswoode's death three weeks ago. Ask any housewife. Ergo, the fire had been very recently used...

"And I'm afraid, Mr. Cargill, that that means you."

BATTLE OF WITS

Miriam Sharman

Miriam Sharman (1914–1994) had a lengthy and successful writing career, yet her work is largely forgotten today. Born Maisie Sharman in Glasgow, she studied at Glasgow University before leaving Scotland "to find fame and fortune in the south". Working as a secretary for a film producer, she began to try her hand at writing and while still in her early twenties she worked on the screenplay for the film *Night Journey* (1938). She wrote or co-wrote several other films as well as television dramas, including *Headline* (1943), a thriller based on a novel by Ken Attiwill. *Death Goes to School* (1953) is an entertaining mystery which starred Barbara Murray as a teacher whose scarf is used to strangle a colleague; detective duties were undertaken by Gordon Jackson and Sam Kydd. The story was based on *Death in Seven Hours*, a novel Sharman published under the name Stratford Davis. There's a pleasing joke when Barbara Murray gives as her alibi the fact that she was reading a thriller called *Death in Seven Hours*; I bet Sharman enjoyed writing that. Five Stratford Davis novels were published (by three different publishers) between 1952 and 1963.

She joined the Crime Writers' Association and began to write as Miriam Sharman. *Death Pays All Debts* was published in 1965 by Gollancz, who described it as "a 'first' suspense thriller by the author of the BBC TV play *Late Harvest*". Gollancz claimed on the front cover of her next book, *Seeds of Violence*, that "Miriam Sharman is developing a new genre: the thriller that thrills—and thrills superbly—by reason of its very quiet". By this time she'd married Ken Bolton who, she told the CWA members' newsletter *Red Herrings*, farmed 450 acres of arable land in Buckinghamshire. She produced a few more novels and a handful of short stories, but her writing career quietly faded away. However, this story, first published in *Ellery Queen's Mystery Magazine* in June 1967, was adapted by the accomplished television writer Roger Marshall for an episode in *Orson Welles' Great Mysteries* in 1973, starring Ian Bannen and Brewster Mason.

A S THE LINGERING DUSK OF A SUMMER'S EVENING TOOK ITS reluctant departure, the headmaster drew the curtains across the tall french windows and switched on the lamp, angling the shaft of light on to his desk. The room, now framed in deepening shadows, suited his mood of quiet contemplation, which was almost immediately shattered by the unexpected, unremitting ringing of the doorbell.

The visitor was a tall, lean man in his late 40s, wearing a loose, light-weight coat. He was hatless, an informality that brought a frown to the headmaster's brow.

"You are Richard Lumsden?"

At least, the headmaster thought, the voice was that of an educated man. He nodded. "You wish to see me?"

The beam of light from the study signalled the way. The visitor entered, followed by the headmaster, silently disapproving. They seated themselves at the desk, facing each other.

"You're a parent of one of the boys here?" Lumsden asked, politely. His eyes flickered with annoyance at the other's silence. The man's pale, narrow face was expressionless, his body taut. His air of remoteness was disturbing. "School business had better be left until my successor moves in," the headmaster said. "My authority here is at an end."

"My name is Dean—"

"Dean." Lumsden echoed the name, suddenly wary.

"Gregory Dean."

"Ah—the actor!" Lumsden smiled. There was no answering smile, only the cold, steady stare. Lumsden glanced towards the fireplace, then immediately regretted his instinctive reaction. Dean was across the room in a moment, studying the framed photographs on the wall, one of which finally held his attention. He eased it free with his gloved hands, brought it back to the desk, and thrust it at the headmaster.

"The school dramatic society," Lumsden murmured.

Dean jabbed at the peaked face of a fourteen-year-old boy.

"A most distressing business," the headmaster said, quietly. His relief at placing his visitor in context was modified by the latter's odd behaviour. Lumsden felt impelled to elaborate. "Among younger children, of course, it is not uncommon, this petty pilfering. They grow out of it. But with a boy of fourteen…" He shook his head, regretfully. "And he had been warned several times."

Dean maintained his unnerving silence. Lumsden felt the stirrings of anger. "If you have nothing to say, Mr. Dean, I must ask you to leave. I still have some odds and ends to clear up." In his determination to sound natural, he explained rather too carefully: "I'm taking a leisurely tour abroad. No doubt to you the prospect of travel is not so attractive. But I am looking forward to it. Yes, indeed, I have a carefully planned itinerary—"

"I'm sure you have," Dean interrupted, curtly. "Everything according to plan. And at what stage did you plan to get rid of my boy?"

The headmaster was taken aback at the unexpected frontal attack. "What are you talking about? Your boy was an incorrigible thief. It was unfair to the others to keep him here." He added, with a note of reproof: "I wrote and told you of my decision."

"Your letter was forwarded to me in Belgrade. They put in my understudy and I flew back immediately."

Lumsden was relieved at the more rational turn to the conversation. "Well," he said, mildly, "that was scarcely my responsibility."

"Your responsibility was of a very different order. Why did you not ask me to come and take the boy away quietly, without fuss?" Dean's voice trembled on the question. "Why did you expel him before the whole school?"

Dean's eyes, glittering now with hostility, made the headmaster choose his next words carefully. "The boy had been given several chances, some of the masters had intervened on his behalf on previous occasions. And all to no avail." He felt his confidence returning. "This final act of defiance had to be dealt with firmly—for the boy's own sake. I have run this school in my own way. If you disapproved of my methods, you had a simple remedy—to remove your boy."

"I wish to God I had." The bitter passion in the words startled Lumsden. Dean continued, more quietly: "But my mistakes as a parent do not exonerate you."

"Come, come," Lumsden said, patronisingly. "I stand by my judgement. I am in no need of exoneration."

"In that last interview you had with my son," Dean continued, "you had him at your mercy."

The headmaster shrugged. "A somewhat theatrical conception."

Dean's face set doggedly. "How many boys have you expelled from this school?"

"Not many," Lumsden replied, a little smugly. "Only three—in twelve years."

"And how many publicly?"

"What do you mean—publicly?" the headmaster countered. "To the assembled school? With the boy present? One."

"And because I am a public figure, it got into the press." Dean's face was bleak. "You abused your power."

The highly unsatisfactory interview had gone far enough for Lumsden. He spoke briskly, authoritatively. "If you are merely going to be offensive…" He stood up. "You must leave—now. I have one or two things to attend to before I leave for the airport."

"You're not going to the airport." The gun in the gloved hand pointed unwaveringly at Lumsden's head. "Sit down."

Slowly, incredulously, the headmaster lowered himself into his seat.

"What did you say to my son in that final interview?"

In spite of the gun, Lumsden's indignation spilled over. "Why don't you ask him?"

There was a tiny pause. The headmaster sensed the tremor that passed through the other man's body. At the highest point of expectancy, with the timing of a good actor, Dean said: "I can't ask him. He's dead."

Lumsden stared, shocked, at the gaunt, white face. Dean's bald statement seemed to have effected some kind of release. His words flowed in a harsh monotone. "I have a small flat in London. I called there with my luggage just before coming here. And there was my son—hanging from the ceiling—quite dead."

There was, then, reason to fear the gun, Lumsden thought. "Dreadful," he murmured. "Poor boy, he felt his disgrace keenly."

"You broke his spirit—you broke his spirit." Dean's misery was almost tangible. "Useless at games—scholastic work not up to much—too sensitive, too interested in the dramatic society. You could have helped him. You preferred to crucify him!"

The headmaster suddenly perceived the flaw. "Why haven't the police been in touch with me?" he demanded.

"Because I haven't told them," Dean replied, simply. "First things first. Why did you choose that moment and that manner of humiliating my son?"

Lumsden hesitated. "You think a gun will produce the answers you want to hear?"

"A trick question. The gun is for killing. You are going to kill yourself with it."

Fear was at last threading its way into the headmaster's consciousness. "I can't be forced to kill myself."

"Obviously I shall have to do the actual shooting but the verdict
will be suicide."

"If you murder me, you will be caught."

Dean shook his head. "Mistakes come from taking too many precautions. I have concentrated on only the basic ones. Nobody saw me
arrive and nobody will see me leave. It is very quiet round here. I came
in a very ordinary car and parked it among several other ordinary cars,
about half a mile away."

"But you will be an obvious suspect because you have motive."

"You admit that!" Dean's reply was like an explosion.

Lumsden frowned at his slip. "The motive is irrational," he
explained. "But it would make you their first suspect."

"Suspicion is one thing, proof another. I've been over all that in
my mind." He sounded a warning note. "You haven't a monopoly of
reason or logic."

"Believe me," the headmaster spoke feelingly. "I do not underes-
timate you for one moment, but I must draw your attention to the
weaknesses of your position. If all you have to do is shoot me and put
the gun in my hand—" He broke off. The beginnings of an idea stirred
in his agile mind. "Why sit here and discuss it?"

Dean's reply came almost eagerly. "Because I respect your mind,
with its trained thinking capacity. You only have to convince me that
I cannot succeed—and you will be safe."

"I don't possess a gun," Lumsden pointed out, quickly.

"It's an old service revolver, untraceable. You came across it in your
final clearing up."

Fear was ebbing a little as confidence returned. "And how do you
propose to establish that?" the headmaster queried.

"No need to try. That's the sort of perfectionism that leads to

mistakes." The faint smile actually held a touch of genuine amuse-
ment. "You and I won't be present to hear it, but I'll wager somebody
will remember having glimpsed the gun, somewhere, so strong is the
power of suggestion."

"The inference of suicide may come readily to the police," Lumsden
said, "but it will be challenged by all who know me. Using a gun would
simply not occur to me."

"If you had a choice, perhaps not. But there was the weapon to
hand—quick, clean, a man's way." Dean paused and his next words
came harshly. "Not like hanging. A quick death for you." His voice
rose. "Not like my son's—my desperate, distracted son."

That anguish was suspect, Lumsden thought, as if Dean had
remembered a line from a play. The conversation must be restored
to its rational basis.

"I am the last person in the world to take my own life," the
headmaster said, quietly, "especially today, my last day as head of
this school. You are a man of imagination. Can't you hear my colleagues—and friends—? 'He had planned a long tour abroad to which
he was looking forward with great enthusiasm. He had the respect
of his pupils—and his staff. It is inconceivable that he would, at the
close of a distinguished career, kill himself'." Lumsden had warmed
up thoroughly to this picture of himself. Dean's smile of disdain failed
to halt him. "'He was enjoying the knowledge of a job well done. He
had been dedicated to his work, seeing it, not as a job, but as a fulfilment. He left the school with its prestige higher than at any time in
its history.'"

Dean's expression was thoughtful but the gun was unwavering.
He took his time before replying. "Take those same points—and turn
them upside down."

"Ah." Lumsden leaned forward as if in eager enjoyment of the cut
and thrust of the argument. Dean's response was to tighten his finger

on the trigger and aim the gun a little closer. The headmaster withdrew to his former distance across the table.

"The boys and the staff left here before noon today," Dean said. "That's common practice on the last day of term. Yet you arranged to spend the rest of your last day on your own—"

"I had a great deal of clearing up to do," Lumsden interrupted, sharply.

Dean shook his head, commiseratingly. "Surrendering yourself to memories, deeply moved by the good wishes and gifts of your colleagues and your pupils—a somewhat sentimental indulgence for a man like you. And so, as the dusk of evening approached, a sense of desolation swept over you. Years of loneliness lay ahead. You are a widower, without family, with few friends. It was a mistake to devote yourself so exclusively to your work, to have had so few outside interests." Dean's voice throbbed a little. "As these last minutes, amid the surroundings you had loved, closed in, the realisation swept over you that the future was without savour—that life had lost its meaning—and the gun was temptingly to hand—"

Lumsden broke the spell. "It's weak. How can anyone guess what goes on in the mind of a suicide? Your boy, for instance…" His provocation was deliberate. "You are very quick to assume that it was his expulsion—"

Dean stood up, suddenly, quickly but the gun remained steady. "He left a note," he said, softly. "Like all reliable suicides, he left a note, expressing his sorrow for having let me down. He referred to your big scene—and how you had made him feel there was no place for him—anywhere. I destroyed the note because I wanted to play down his expulsion." He paused. "You, too, are going to leave a note."

"You intend to forge my handwriting?" the headmaster asked, warily.

"You must know I wouldn't be as stupid as that. You will write the note yourself."

"You cannot force me to do that," Lumsden said, firmly. "Even at the point of a gun." It was as if his prayer had been answered. Now that he felt on the verge of victory, he experienced an inner thrill of exhilaration.

Dean walked cautiously round the desk, taking up his position alongside the headmaster. He gave his orders in a firm voice. "Pull that pad towards you. Pick up that pen."

If his scheme failed, Lumsden warned himself, he was a dead man. He made no move to touch pen or pad. Dean seemed not surprised. He placed the pad in front of the headmaster and, with his gloved hand, picked up the pen which he used to punctuate his words. "Even in your despair, your language must be somewhat literary." Dean pondered for a few moments. "I thought to welcome the quiet years ahead. I thought to savour a sense of fulfilment. Instead, I find the prospect bleak and empty. I prefer to cut it short." Dean paused. "Pretty good, eh?"

Lumsden shook his head. "Not my style—much too purple."

"You are not yourself. There must be an indication of deep disturbance."

"They won't—believe it," Lumsden said, with deliberate hesitation.

"The police can only go on the evidence and all the evidence will confirm suicide. Why should they look for any other explanation?"

The headmaster slumped dejectedly into his chair. Dean looked down on him with grim satisfaction. He thrust the pen forward. "Write as I dictate. Write!"

Lumsden let his words come angrily. "Why should I! If I write this note, you will kill me. So why should I write it?"

Dean looked at his watch. "There's not much time left. The scene has gone on too long." He pressed the gun closer to Lumsden's right temple. At the touch of the cold metal on his flesh, the headmaster shuddered.

"It's a psychological impossibility," Dean pursued, relentlessly, "to reject another few minutes of life. You will write because you feel the touch of death, because the time taken to write that note could be vital to you. Something could happen to save you—a ring at the door—"

He paused with theatrical timing and it was if both men were suspended, expecting just such a thing to happen. But there was utter silence.

With apparent hopelessness, as Dean's finger curled round the trigger, the headmaster slowly accepted the pen which was thrust into his right hand. Dean sighed, softly, as Lumsden wrote the dictated farewell.

"That's good," Dean murmured, "that unsteady handwriting— indicates a man in an emotional state."

The headmaster, keyed up to the testing moment, replaced the pen.

"There," said Dean, pleasantly. "That wasn't so difficult, was it?" He tore off the sheet bearing the farewell message and laid it alongside the pad.

Now, thought Lumsden. With a quick, controlled movement, he picked up the pen with his left hand and re-wrote on the fresh top sheet the same farewell words. Dean, perplexed, tense, stood watching. His eyes flickered warily. "So," he said. "Something I didn't think of—you're left-handed." But he sounded doubtful.

With his right hand, Lumsden tore off the top sheet and placed the two suicide notes side by side in front of him. Dean looked carefully first at one, then the other.

"That's the one," he pointed. "The left-handed one."

It had started to work, the headmaster thought, his scheme had started to work. "How can you tell?" he asked, keeping all triumph out of his voice. "Both notes are legible."

"You're bluffing," Dean said, quickly. "You're right-handed. If you'd been left-handed, I'd have noticed."

"There was nothing for you to notice. I haven't used either hand since I planned this piece of mystification. Are you trusting your memory before that?"

Dean peered into the shadowy corners of the study.

"You'll get no help from this room," Lumsden said. "All my personal papers are already in store. Only the clothes I need for my trip and some of my books are here. Even the labels on those suitcases in the corner were typed by my secretary. There is not a single specimen of my handwriting in this room." He had difficulty in controlling his exultation at taking over the initiative.

"This trick hasn't saved you." Dean sounded reasonably confident. "When I've killed you, I'll have time to search the room. I'll find something to—"

The headmaster interrupted. "You want to check these drawers?" He indicated the desk.

"You'd like me to give you the chance to make a grab at the gun."

"I've no use for weapons of violence," Lumsden said, firmly. "I'm fighting you with my intellect, that is what you wanted. I've pointed out the serious flaw in your juvenile scheme of vengeance."

There was a hint of desperation in Dean's voice. "The main thing is—I've got the note now. I'll use the one I think best when you're dead." His gloved finger curled round the trigger as he pressed the muzzle closer. Lumsden braced himself.

"Are you quite sure," he asked, calmly, "that you're in the right position for the kill?" He did not dare make any movement, any attempt to measure Dean's reaction. "If you don't know for certain," he went on, with deliberation, "whether I'm right- or left-handed, how can you know which side to shoot from?"

There was no reply from Dean. Then, after an eternity, the head-master knew the gun had been lowered. He waited a few seconds before cautiously turning his head, raising his eyes to glimpse Dean's face. It looked so different from the face of the man who had sat opposite that he almost exclaimed aloud. The face had become a mask of total weariness. Lumsden watched, fascinated, as Dean, the gun dangling from his hand, walked slowly round the desk, sat down, and leaned forward slightly as if needing support his body visibly crumpling.

The headmaster seasoned his relief with admonitions of caution. His superior intellectual power had triumphed but Dean's hand still hovered near the gun on the desk in front of him.

"Tomorrow," Lumsden murmured, "you will be grateful to me—that you did not commit the ultimate crime."

He had the impression that Dean had not even heard these sympathetic words, that, in some odd sort of way, Dean was beyond communication. Lumsden raised his voice as if to penetrate the barrier. "I am not a vindictive man, I shall make no charge. I don't want my travelling plans disrupted by police enquiries—nor unpleasant publicity for the school…" He glanced at his watch. He had less than twenty minutes in which to get rid of his unwelcome visitor; and the sooner the better, before he inadvertently revealed whether or not he was right-handed.

Dean's deep sigh seemed to come from another world.

"Please…" His voice was little more than a croak as he indicated the carafe of water. "A drink…?"

Lumsden just prevented himself from reaching forward with his right hand for the glass. "Help yourself," he said, shortly.

The water restored Dean a little but his eyes were puzzled as he peered round the room then blinked vacantly. Lumsden could even feel a twinge of pity for the man.

"You must go now, Mr. Dean. I promise you, you will hear no more of this." He eased himself effortlessly into his thinking habits. "Try to see your son's death whole. There's no saying what further sorrow he might have caused you. The seeds of delinquency were in him." Wrapped up in his own vindication, his voice was persuasive. "I knew all about him, you see—his unwholesome devotion to one of the masters and to Bowen, the head boy. We have to be on the alert for things of that sort in a boy's school. I let him know what I suspected. I brought a blush to his cheek. I could not tolerate a new headmaster inheriting a situation in the least doubtful, so I made an example…" He stopped suddenly. He had let himself be carried away. Had he said too much?

It was Dean who eventually broke the silence. "Forgive me," he said, apologetically, in a gentle voice. "I haven't really taken in all that. It made no sense to me but I hesitated to interrupt you."

Lumsden swallowed his astonishment as the other man again looked round the shadowy room.

"Before I try to explain, would you make a telephone call for me?" he asked.

Lumsden took a pull at himself. "That is asking rather much," he replied, sharply.

"It is important." The visitor was almost pleading. "May I make it myself?"

The headmaster nodded. The other man drew the telephone towards him, his lower arm resting on the gun. He seemed not to notice this, indeed he seemed not to notice anything—troubled, diffident, apparently drained of all emotion.

"St. Andrew's Hospital?" His voice was weary. "Dr. Boyce, please—George Denham." He kept his eyes lowered.

"St. Andrews, the private mental hospital?" Lumsden asked the question, already anticipating the answer.

His visitor nodded. He spoke into the receiver. "Dr. Boyce. Yes, it is. Please send quickly." He raised his eyes to Lumsden. "What is this place?"

"Michelson's School, Parkway."

The visitor repeated the address into the 'phone and hung up. "I'm a patient there," he said. "Have been for nearly two years."

"Schizophrenia?" Lumsden queried, cautiously.

The other shrugged. "That's the label. How long will it take a car to get here from St. Andrew's?"

"Ten to fifteen minutes."

Lumsden tried to tidy up his disordered thoughts. "I'll have a word with the doctor when he calls for you," he said, casually.

"They send a male nurse with the driver, the doctor doesn't come himself."

Lumsden raised an eyebrow. "It's happened to you before, this sort of thing?"

"Three times—no four." He sounded indifferent. "I can't remember." As he leaned back wearily in his chair, he noticed the gun on the desk. "I—I brought this—did I?" he stammered.

"You threatened me with it." Much as the headmaster would have liked to take possession of the gun, he felt he must not yet make any obvious movement with either hand.

"Non-violent," the visitor murmured, "up till now—this is the first time…" His voice trailed off in despair.

"Don't give up hope," Lumsden said. "Medical science is making remarkable strides these days. What did you do, for a living, Mr…?"

"Denham—George Denham." He stirred restlessly, looked at his watch, strained his ears for the sound of a car. "Why are you so interested in me?"

"You came here, impersonating the father of one of my boys, you were determined to kill me for some imaginary grievance. You must remember something of that?"

"No, nothing." His voice sounded hopeless. He gripped his head between his hands. "Let me try. I can remember having tea, in the dining-room—bread and butter and fruit-cake. Then, I was one of the first in the lounge so I got a comfortable chair." He slowed down with the intensified effort at concentration. "I picked up a newspaper, the *Chronicle* I think it was. I started to read it." With a sigh, he gave up. "Nothing after that, nothing."

Lumsden longed to believe him and thus restore young Dean to life. "When you found yourself sitting here," he asked, "at what moment did you cease to be the obsessed parent and become the wandering hospital patient?"

"It isn't like that—like a photographic shutter, one minute open, the next moment closed. There's a sort of no-man's land."

"Where would you have got a gun?"

"I don't know." The visitor took a wallet from his inside pocket, extracted some notes. "I could have bought it, I suppose, I should have more money than this."

Lumsden, nearly convinced that George Denham was genuine, asked the key question. "How did you know young Dean had been expelled?"

"Expelled? Poor kid."

Lumsden mustered all his quiet authority. "How did you know to come here? That's the crux of it. You're faking, you must be!"

The visitor blinked, anxiously. He seemed more confused than intimidated. "I—I—" He began to go through his coat pockets, bringing out a freshly laundered handkerchief and a newspaper. It took a tremendous effort of will on the headmaster's part not to reach out for the handkerchief. Instead, the visitor pushed it across the desk.

"Initials, GD. George Denham."

"Or Gregory Dean," Lumsden said, abruptly.

The visitor shrugged as if everything was now beyond him. He looked at his watch. "They should be here," he muttered.

"You must have some means of identification on you," Lumsden insisted.

"I expect so." The visitor gave this a moment's thought as he was about to stuff the newspaper back into his pocket. Something in it caught his eye. He read it, held the paper out to Lumsden who, still on his guard, took it with both hands. "The celebrated actor, Gregory Dean, flew in from Belgrade today. His son, Christopher, was recently expelled from Michelson's School."

Lumsden's suspicions flooded back. "There's nothing here about the boy's suicide," he said, sharply.

"Suicide?" The visitor's shocked expression was almost immediately replaced by compassion. "You mustn't blame yourself," he said, tentatively.

"How could you have invented the suicide and the note?" Lumsden desperately wanted the reassurance that young Dean was alive, that there would be no publicity, no inquest to upset his future plans.

The visitor licked his dry lips. His face twitched. "I—I did that? I caused you such pain?" He sighed. "I identify very, very intensively with the personalities I assume. Something starts me off—this time, the same initials, possibly…" Suddenly, he stood up. "There it is—the car." His movements were hurried now.

Lumsden decided on a final challenge. "I'll come with you and have a word with the doctor."

"Yes, yes, do that—if you wish."

The headmaster hesitated. If he went to the hospital now, he would have to reorganise all his travel arrangements, a difficult thing at this time of year. The man had surely established his identity.

"You're not coming?" The visitor was already in the hall. "You'll get in touch with the hospital yourself?"

"Yes. When I return." Through the open study door, the headmaster watched him leave. He thought he heard the faint sound of a car. What was it the visitor had said about the power of suggestion?

Suddenly Lumsden realised he was trembling and soaked in perspiration. He found some brandy in a cupboard. It restored him to near normality. Something glinting on the carpet near the desk caught his eye. He picked it up. It was a few seconds before he recognised it—a stick of greasepaint.

He found the telephone number in the directory. "St. Andrew's? Dr. Boyce. It's urgent."

The reply came crisply. "Are you sure you have the right number? No doctor of that name here."

"A patient, then," Lumsden almost shouted. "George Denham…" He kept the receiver to his ear. His glance fell on the ridiculous suicide notes. The newspaper still lay on the desk. The gun. Where was the gun? Under the newspaper…

"No patient of that name," the crisp voice announced.

Lumsden slammed down the receiver and reached over for the newspaper. At the same moment, his eyes were drawn to the curtains across the french windows. One gloved hand was parting them; the other was holding the gun.

It was clear to Lumsden that Dean, from that vantage point, had watched him pour a drink, pick up the greasepaint, make a 'phone call, reach for the newspaper—all with his right hand. And now Dean was moving purposefully round the desk, into the right position—for the kill.

THE BOY WHO COULDN'T READ

Jacqueline Wilson

Dame Jacqueline Wilson, DBE, FRSL is one of the very few authors to have her work published in the British Library's Crime Classics series while she is still alive—and still writing very successfully. She was educated at Coombe Girls' School in Surrey and Carshalton Technical College. In 2008, she told the *Guardian* that she left school at the age of sixteen out of "bolshiness" and a dislike of being told what to do; however, in 2017 she returned to open a school building that had been named after her. By her late teens she was working for the publisher D.C. Thomson. Today she is world famous as an author of thoughtful but highly entertaining fiction for young people, and it may come as a surprise to many readers to find a story of hers in this book.

However, in the late 1970s, when I was dreaming of becoming a crime writer, I began to study the novels of young authors whose writing struck a chord with me. Jacqueline Wilson was one of them. She published five snappy psychological crime novels that were readable but also thought-provoking. *Snap*, for instance, features a teenage girl with a crush on her schoolteacher; it's foreseeable that this relationship will end badly, but how, exactly? *Making Hate*, her fifth crime novel, is a highly ambitious if flawed attempt to explore the psychology of a rapist. I think it's entirely possible that, had she continued to work in the genre, she would have rivalled Ruth Rendell, but she has certainly made a huge success of her change of literary direction. This story first appeared in *Winter's Crimes 10*, edited by George Hardinge, in 1978.

M R. CROFT WORKED THE CHILDREN HARD FOR MOST OF THE day. He believed in getting straight down to it, first day of term or not. But he'd relented by the last lesson. He was a little worried by their sullen obedience. They gathered round the other teachers in the playground and laughed and chatted without any inhibitions but no one ever came and talked to him now. Perhaps he was too hard on them?

He decided to give them a little treat. He'd read to them for twenty minutes and then let them draw a picture. He fumbled in the back of the cupboard and found his old copy of *The Mountain of Adventure*. You couldn't beat a good Enid Blyton adventure story, no matter what all these trendy educationalists said. Let them read obscure fantasies or sordid kiddie kitchen sink. He knew what the children liked.

But one child didn't like *The Mountain of Adventure*. Mr. Croft looked up after a couple of pages and saw David Bates hunched up over his own book. He stopped reading aloud and the children held their breath. It took David a few seconds before he noticed the expectant silence.

"What are you doing, David Bates?"

"I'm sorry," said David, snapping his book shut.

"Let me see that."

David sighed and handed the book over. It was a book on astronomy. Mr. Croft thumbed through it and then gave it back.

"Why were you looking at that instead of listening to the story?"

"I—I'm interested in astronomy."

"Oh yes? And I take it you're not interested in *The Mountain of Adventure*?"

"Not really."

"Why, may I ask?"

"Well, I think it's a bit infantile, if you really want to know."

Someone tittered.

"Infantile. Oh, I see. The boy wonder prefers to read an adult book on astronomy, correct?"

"Yes."

"What tosh! You silly little boy. We all know you can't even read properly. Of course you can't manage to read that astronomy book, you're just showing off."

"I can read it," said David, his face getting red.

"I've heard you read, boy. You have to have your special coaching, don't you?"

"I *can* read."

"Very well. Demonstrate. Come out to the front of the class. You're always trying to tell me my job. Well, you take over altogether. Here's *The Mountain of Adventure*. Very infantile, right? Well, read it then. Read it out loud to the class."

David stood up, burning. He took the book and cleared his throat. He read, stumbling, hesitating, with little expression. Another child giggled nervously, but most were still and silent, their own faces red.

"That's enough, lad. A five-year-old could do better," said Mr. Croft. "You can hardly read at all. Sit down then."

Mr. Croft read on to the end of the chapter. David Bates sat motionless throughout. Then Mr. Croft handed round pieces of paper and told the children to do a drawing to illustrate the story. There were only ten minutes left of the lesson but they passed very slowly. The bell rang at last and the children stretched and sighed. One stood up, several disappeared behind their desk lids.

Mr. Croft rapped on his own desk with the blackboard eraser.

"What are you doing? I didn't say that the lesson is over," he said, although he had also sagged with relief. He decided he was too exhausted to make an issue of it. It was the first day of term after all. They always took a few days to simmer down, especially after Christmas.

"Very well. Off you go," he said, in a kindlier fashion. "Hand in your drawings as you go."

They handed in their efforts. Some were hastily scribbled and coloured with school wax crayon. Others were lovingly embellished with privately owned felt-tip pen. Gideon Symons handed in a masterpiece worthy of a gold star, his artistic ability enormously aided by his huge tin of forty Caran D'Ache.

David Bates passed Mr. Croft's desk without pausing.

"David?"

The child's face was still unusually red but he maintained his irritating composure.

"Yes, Mr. Croft?"

"Hand in your drawing, David."

"There's little point," said David, and he handed in a blank sheet of paper. He waited.

Mr. Croft looked at the blank paper, wanting to crumple it.

"I suppose you think you're being clever," he said eventually.

David chose not to reply. Mr. Croft looked at his peaky face and spiky hair and round spectacles. A sparrow of a child with owl eyes. There'd been other kids equally bright. Disturbing kids. Kids who wet themselves or couldn't sit still or had epileptic fits on the woodblock floor. Kids with nits, kids with knives. Kids like Gideon Symons with his Caran D'Ache crayons and his yellow Kickers boots. All sorts of kids, but he'd never hated one the way he hated David Bates.

It was hard keeping the hatred out of his voice.

"You're being very silly, David. Now take your paper, go back to your desk, and do me a drawing."

The few remaining children raised their eyebrows and nudged each other. Mr. Croft glared at them and they whisked out of the classroom. David looked at the door, swinging open. For a moment Mr. Croft thought he was going to ignore him and walk straight out after them. But David merely sighed elaborately and did as he was told. At least, he took the sheet of paper and sat down at his desk. He did not draw.

"Come along, lad. Get on with it," said Mr. Croft.

David did nothing.

Mr. Croft decided to ignore him for five minutes. He picked up his briefcase and took out the compositions 2A had written that morning.

"'What I did at Christmas'. Everyone must fill at least two sides of paper. Neat writing, don't forget punctuation and watch that spelling."

Well, what did they do over Christmas? He gave the first few a glance.

"Mum let me stay up to see Morecambe and Wise it was smashing."

"My mum and dad and my aunties and uncles all had a few and got ever so tiddly and my Auntie Vi did a can-can and we did have a laugh."

"I didn't get what I wanted. I really wanted a poodle nightdress case. I got lovely presents and Mum and Dad gave me a Bionic Woman but I really did want a poodle nightdress case."

Mr. Croft leafed through the compositions until he found David's. It was untidy and hopelessly misspelt. He tried to follow the general gist but it became impossible. He wanted to put a savage red line through the incomprehensible essay, but Maple, the headmaster, insisted that David had to be handled sensitively. Mr. Croft wondered what Maple would say if he got to hear about this afternoon's little contretemps and his armpits prickled with anxiety. Reluctantly he picked out a handful of misspelt words in David's composition and wrote out the correct spellings, leaving space for David to copy each word ten times. Dyslexia! Once upon a time if a kid couldn't read properly by the time it was nearly nine it was thick and that was that. Well, all right, David Bates was no fool, although he wasn't necessarily another Einstein. His Stanford Binet assessment might be up in the 160s, but that only meant he was good at puzzles. That was all these I.Q. tests really were when you got down to it. And what was the use of being able to do silly puzzles when you could barely write your own name?

He glanced at the child. David returned his stare calmly. The piece of paper was still blank.

"I've just about had enough of this behaviour, Bates. Now get drawing. Go on, do as you're told."

David remained motionless.

"Pick up that pencil and *draw!*"

Mr. Croft marched to the desk and wrapped the child's small cold hand round the pencil.

"Now draw," he said, giving him a hard prod in the back.

David leant on one elbow and let the pencil slide out of his hand back on to the desk.

"I'm warning you, Bates," said Mr. Croft. "Stop this silly act. You're not impressing me at all. Just get on with your drawing, do you hear?" He waited. *"Pick up that pencil!"*

David jumped but didn't obey. Mr. Croft wanted to hit the boy so badly that he went back to his own desk, scared of losing control altogether. David watched him, his small face impassive.

"All right," said Mr. Croft. "You want to play silly games, we'll play silly games. We shall sit it out. You are not leaving this classroom until you have done me a drawing. Do you understand? We shall sit here until breakfast if necessary."

"Then may I phone my mother?" David asked.

"No, you may not."

"But she will be worried about me. She always worries if I'm late. It isn't very fair on her," said David reasonably.

"I'm afraid I can't help that. It's you choosing to worry her, laddie, not me. Do me a drawing and you can be home in no time."

"Why do you want me to do a drawing so badly?" said David.

"Don't be so damn impertinent! Just remember who you are. You're not here to ask clever-dick questions. You're here to do as you're told. Now *do* as you're told."

Mr. Croft longed to loosen his tie. His shirt was sticking to him. The central heating was turned up ridiculously high. He went to open a few windows. He had to use the window pole, although his hands were shaking badly so that the pole nudged uselessly against the glass many times before connecting. But he persevered, determined not to be defeated.

And he wasn't going to let this supercilious little twerp defeat him either. There wouldn't have been any problem in the old days. One swish of the cane and there wouldn't be any further argument. Not that he was one of these sadistic perverts getting some kind of kick out of caning kiddies. The cane had grown dusty in the cupboard, its very presence serving enough purpose.

He was sure he'd been popular with children then. The boys looked up to him and the little girls had all giggled at his jokes. They'd called him Sir and opened the door for him and worked hard. But now that some of their own children were at the school things were very different. 2A were a lost cause anyway after Jeff Priestly's influence. They spent a whole year in his form without learning how to write a decent sentence or any of their times tables. All they seemed to do was mess around with egg-boxes and toilet rolls. It seemed modern education was literally a load of old rubbish.

But it was no use complaining any more. Jeff Priestly was well in with Maple, thought to be a fine teacher, for God's sake. What sort of influence was he on the kids, with his shoulder-length hair and his tattered jeans and his cock-eyed Marxist theories? He wasn't even clean: he'd obviously been wearing that ridiculous Cambridge

University sweatshirt for days. Cambridge University! Jeff Priestly was probably lucky to scrape five O-levels. Yet the way things were going he'd probably end up a headmaster. He wouldn't stay an underpaid and unappreciated junior school teacher.

But even Jeff Priestly had had a bit of bother with David Bates.

"He's the sort of kid who gets up my nose," he'd said once in the staff room, in his usual unprepossessing way. "He seems to have been born middle-aged. He's got this way of peering through his specs at you like a little professor."

David was peering through his glasses now, arms folded.

"You're obviously intending to spend the night here, my boy," said Mr. Croft. "Well, it's no skin off my nose. I've got a lot of work here to be getting on with. I'm in no hurry to get home."

He pretended to mark the children's compositions. He wasn't really bluffing. The Christmas holidays seemed to have gone on for ever, a horrible reminder that this was what it was going to be like all the time when he retired. Only another year and two terms to go.

He hadn't thought he'd mind when Elaine finally moved out. They'd never really got on well together. He thought it would be a relief to be free of her whining. But the house was unpleasantly silent nowadays and although he kept it reasonably clean there was a dead atmosphere to the place, as if it had been sealed up for years.

"What I did at Christmas." Mr. Croft had cooked his small oven-ready chicken and his mini Christmas pudding, but halfway through his meal he'd pushed his plate away, put his head down on the checked tablecloth, and wept.

He found his eyes were stinging now and he blinked quickly, horrified. Perhaps he was going to pieces, heading for a breakdown? No, he was just feeling a bit seedy, that was all. Perhaps he was starting 'flu, there was a bug going around at the moment. Maybe that was why he was so hot.

He loosened his tie after all and yawned several times. He was tired too, of course. He hadn't been sleeping well. He'd spent most of last night tossing about under his Marks and Spencer duvet, the double bed growing larger and more lonely by the minute. At least you could tuck yourself in tightly with good old-fashioned sheets and blankets. He'd tried wrapping the duvet round him until he felt like a giant Swiss roll but it still didn't help him to sleep. He'd grown so used to Elaine's warm brushed nylon bulk that he'd lost the knack of sleeping without her.

Funny how you could miss a woman you didn't even like. He hadn't thought much of her right from the start. A silly little shopgirl with painted lips, not his sort at all. She was all right for a bit of messing about, but that was all. Messing about was an accurate description too. Elaine might sport a blonde rinse and lipstick but she knew as little about sex as he did. It was a wonder their Betty ever managed to get herself conceived, her parents' coupling was so brief and inadequate.

Betty had been another disappointment. She'd appalled him as a red-faced shrieking baby, but she'd been an enchanting little girl, with her mother's fluffy good looks and a quick wit that took him by surprise. He had her whizzing through the Beacon Readers by the time she was four. She was top of the class all the way up her junior school and passed to the grammar without any bother. When she was twelve she was on Junior Criss Cross Quiz and did very well for herself too. But everything went wrong when she reached puberty. She wouldn't do her homework, went out dancing, sat around coffee bars. Her mother all over again. He tried pleading with her, slapping her, even locking her out of the house, but she wouldn't see reason.

She was three months pregnant when she took her O-levels. She only passed Domestic Science and Art and didn't seem to give a damn, because she had a wedding ring safe on her finger now. His Betty, swollen with the child of a greasy little garage mechanic who'd been in the lowest stream of a tough Secondary Modern.

The marriage had lasted, much to his surprise, and Betty's husband had his own garage now. Elaine had gone to live with them in their four-bedroomed neo-Georgian house on a posh new estate in Surrey. Betty had tried to keep in touch. She'd even invited him for Christmas too, not wanting to appear to take sides, but he wasn't having any.

"Can we come in and do you now?"

Mr. Croft looked round, startled. It was a couple of cleaning women, looking impatient.

"We've left you till last, you know. We really ought to be off now."

David sat up properly. Oh no, you little bugger, thought Mr. Croft, I'm not giving up yet.

"I'm afraid you'll have to give this classroom a miss this afternoon, ladies," he said, in his most authoritative tones.

They tutted a little but went off with their brushes and brooms. The school was very still. It began to get much colder. The heating had obviously gone off for the night. David started shivering. Mr. Croft was cold too now, but he decided to put up with his own discomfort.

"We seem to be the only ones left in the school," he said. "What a silly boy you are, Bates. Isn't it time you came to your senses?"

David said nothing.

Mr. Croft said nothing.

They stared at each other and then both started when they heard the door slam at the end of the corridor. Maple's door. Oh God, he'd forgotten Maple.

David's eyes glinted behind his glasses. There was going to be hell to pay with Maple. He was never keen on any kind of punishment. He hated the idea of children being kept after class. And it would be a hundred times worse because it was his precious David Bates.

There had been a bit of a barney last term. Mr. Croft had made a slip when he was chalking some arithmetic on the board and David Bates immediately pointed out the mistake. He did it in such an offensive

way, sighing heavily, eyebrows raised, that Mr. Croft couldn't let it go at
that. So he blustered, pretending that the mistake had been deliberate.
He thought he sounded reasonably convincing, but David Bates gave
a tight smile of contempt. Mr. Croft sent the boy out of the room for
insolence. Maple was indulging in one of his little tours of inspection
and found the kid stuck outside the classroom.

Maple was angry but he handled it tactfully enough, saying nothing in front of the children. He waited and had a little chat with Mr.
Croft after school was over.

"Please don't think I'm interfering, Arthur," he said, taking pains
to sound matey. "I know just how tiresome these gifted children can
be. Maybe I'd have done the same myself. But I don't feel it's quite the
right way of coping with the situation. Young David's a highly sensitive
child and he needs careful handling. He got off to a very bad start at
that other school. His mother assures me he could read fluently before
he went to school, but when they started messing him about, insisting
he start at the Look, Janet, Look stage, and in i.t.a. too, it confused and
frustrated him so much that he became mildly dyslexic. Thank heavens
we seem to be winning through. His reading age is only slightly below
par now, and when he gets a bit of confidence I'm sure he'll make even
greater progress. Can't you see why he badly needs to show off a bit in
the lessons he's good at? If I were you I'd praise him as much as possible,
Arthur. Thank God we've got rid of the poisonous gold star and form
prize competitive claptrap, but kids still need a pat on the back at times."

Mr. Croft shook his head and nodded at the appropriate moments
because he had no other choice, but inwardly he burned with resent-
ment. Maple thought he knew it all because he'd done a course in child
psychology but he knew nothing. The kids had liked getting their gold
stars for good work. When there weren't any more stars they stopped
working. It was as simple as that. And mollycoddling insolent little
sods like David Bates made them cockier than ever.

Mr. Croft remembered his own schooldays. Miss Jennings at his little village school had been a wonderful woman, but she was a stickler for discipline. The tinies had to sit with their hands on their heads if they were naughty, and the older children got a stinging slap on the back of their legs if they dared get up to mischief. No one would have dreamed of pointing out a mistake to Miss Jennings.

Mr. Croft had been a polite little boy, neat and well-scrubbed, his hair smarmed oilily into submission. He had been top of the school and Miss Jennings' favourite. He'd sat the scholarship and passed to the big boys' Grammar in the town.

"You're destined to go far, my boy," Miss Jennings said, but she had been wrong. Mr. Croft had expected to be top of the big boys' Grammar school too but to his shame and horror he was nearer the bottom of the form. He didn't give up. He worked even harder. He passed his school certificate and stayed on in the sixth form and spent every spare minute studying, but it wasn't enough. Boys like David Bates hardly worked at all but they got their scholarships to Oxford and Cambridge. Mr. Croft didn't manage university at all. He did well enough at his Teacher Training College and after a while he thought he'd got over his disappointment. He decided to make a go of things and end up a headmaster, but it hadn't worked out that way.

Now he was only hanging on to his job by the skin of his teeth. Maple had already made a few hints about an early retirement. Oh God, this was the very opportunity Maple was looking for.

Mr. Croft clenched his fists, waiting for the soft pad of Maple's Hush Puppies along the corridor, come to see why there was still a light in 2A long after everyone else had gone home.

But he didn't come. He couldn't have spotted the light. They heard him go outside, the slam of his car door, the splutter of his ignition key. They heard him drive away.

"Draw me a picture, David," said Mr. Croft.

"I'm not going to," said David, and for the first time he sounded childish and defiant. "I'm going home."

He stood up but Mr. Croft was by his side in an instant.

"Sit down again. At once!"

"You can't keep me here by force," said David, but he didn't sound sure. Mr. Croft wasn't a very big man but David was small and slight for his age.

"Draw, David." Mr. Croft put his face very close to the child's. Their breaths mingled. *"Draw!"*

David's face crumpled. He bit his lips, fighting for control, but tears spilled behind his glasses.

"Aah! Poor little diddums," said Mr. Croft.

"You shut up!" David sobbed furiously.

"Don't use that tone with me."

"You keep making these threats but you can't do anything," David said. "I'm going home now. My mother will be ever so worried."

"Poor little Mumsie's crybaby, eh?"

"You're mad. You're a real nutcase," David shouted, and he made a run for it.

Mr. Croft caught him at the classroom door. David struggled and kicked but Mr. Croft had his spindly arms in a pincer grip. David's feet barely touched the ground as Mr. Croft pulled him back to his desk. He pushed him down so hard that the child's head juddered with shock.

"There! Now draw, you little runt, draw!"

"I can't! I don't know what to draw," David wailed.

"Every other child in the class drew me a picture, David Bates. I told them to draw me a scene from *The Mountain of Adventure*. That's what you're going to do, boy. You're no different from the others. You're not getting preferential treatment from me. You're going to draw, do you understand?" He was shouting, spittle shining on his chin.

"But I wasn't—I didn't listen to it," David sobbed. "I don't know what it's about. You know I wasn't listening. I *can't* draw."

"Can't even draw, eh? Can't read. Can't write. Now it turns out the boy wonder can't even draw. Well, you'd better learn fast," said Mr. Croft. "I'm going to count to five, David Bates. One. Two. Three. Four."

David picked up the pencil. He drew one jagged uncontrolled line and the lead broke.

"You did that on purpose!" Mr. Croft shouted, and he slapped the boy hard across the face.

Mr. Croft had caned children in the past. He'd prodded them and pulled them, he'd thrown blackboard chalk at them and rapped their knuckles with his ruler. But he'd never once struck a child across the face. His hand was trembling, wanting to hit again and again. He clenched it, panting.

"Find another pencil," he said, his voice high-pitched.

David fumbled in his satchel, whimpering, his nose running into his mouth.

"I—I haven't got one."

Mr. Croft felt in his breast pocket for his own ballpoint pen.

"Use this then. Draw with it, draw, draw, *draw*."

Sudden pain flared in his chest. Mr. Croft stared at the child and then doubled up. Red-hot agony. Chest, arm, everywhere. He couldn't draw breath. Couldn't talk. Christ Almighty, the pain.

He swayed in front of David, still holding the ballpoint pen.

"Help! Get help! I'm ill! I'm having a heart attack!" he screamed, but he could only gurgle and drool in the grip of the pain. He clutched the pen and stabbed at the piece of drawing paper.

"P-h-o-n-e 999," he scrawled desperately. "*Heart*."

David Bates looked at the piece of paper and then he looked at Mr. Croft.

"I can't read, can I?" he said.

Mr. Croft slumped to his knees. David walked round him, crumpling the paper and stuffing it into his pocket. He switched off the light, walked along the corridor and out of the silent school.

He met his mother hurrying along the road.

"David, where on earth have you been? I've been so worried."

"Sorry, Mum. That hateful Croft man kept me in again."

"This is getting ridiculous. I think I'd better go and see him, David. Come on, we'll go back to the school and have it out with him."

"No, he'll have gone by now," David said quickly. "Don't fuss, Mum. Things will work out. You'll see."

David tucked his hand in her arm and they went straight home.

453

ALSO AVAILABLE
IN THE BRITISH LIBRARY
CRIME CLASSICS SERIES

Big Ben Strikes Eleven	DAVID MAGARSHACK
Death of an Author	E. C. R. LORAC
The Black Spectacles	JOHN DICKSON CARR
Death of a Bookseller	BERNARD J. FARMER
The Wheel Spins	ETHEL LINA WHITE
Someone from the Past	MARGOT BENNETT
Who Killed Father Christmas?	ED. MARTIN EDWARDS
Twice Round the Clock	BILLIE HOUSTON
The White Priory Murders	CARTER DICKSON
The Port of London Murders	JOSEPHINE BELL
Murder in the Basement	ANTHONY BERKELEY
Fear Stalks the Village	ETHEL LINA WHITE
The Cornish Coast Murder	JOHN BUDE
Suddenly at His Residence	CHRISTIANNA BRAND
The Edinburgh Mystery	ED. MARTIN EDWARDS
Checkmate to Murder	E. C. R. LORAC
The Spoilt Kill	MARY KELLY
Smallbone Deceased	MICHAEL GILBERT
The Story of Classic Crime in 100 Books	MARTIN EDWARDS
The Pocket Detective: 100+ Puzzles	KATE JACKSON
The Pocket Detective 2: 100+ More Puzzles	KATE JACKSON

Many of our titles are also available
in eBook, large print and audio editions